THE FABRIC OF SIN

THE FABRIC OF SIN

Phil Rickman

Quercus

First published in Great Britain in 2007 by

Quercus
21 Bloomsbury Square
London
WC1A 2NS

A CIP catalogue record for this book is available
from the British Library

ISBN (HB) 1 84724 084 4
ISBN-13 978 1 84724 084 2
ISBN (TPB) 1 84724 085 2
ISBN-13 978 1 84724 085 9

10 9 8 7 6 5 4 3 2 1

Typeset by e-type, Aintree, Liverpool
Printed and bound in Great Britain by Clays Ltd, St Ives plc.

Shapen of clay and kneaded with water
A bedrock of shame and a source of pollution
A cauldron of iniquity and a fabric of sin …
What can I say that hath not been foreknown
Or what disclose that hath not been foretold?

The Essenes: *Poems of Initiation*

PART ONE

Do I believe in ghosts …? I answer that
I am prepared to consider evidence and
accept it if it satisfies me.

M. R. James. Introduction to his
Complete Ghost Stories.

Third Hill

ALTHOUGH THE COUNTRYSIDE around the barn was open and level, three landmark hills were laid out along the horizon. Like ancient and venerated body parts, Merrily thought, the bones of the Border. Holy relics on display in the sunset glow.

Standing at the barn window with Adam Eastgate, she tracked them, right to left, from the southern end of the Black Mountains: the volcanic-looking Sugar Loaf and the ruined profile of The Skirrid which legend said had cracked open when Jesus Christ died on the cross.

Still somehow sacred, these hills. No towns crowded them, nobody messed with them.

At least, not the way someone had with the third and lowest hill, the only one this side of the Welsh border but still maybe a dozen miles away. The third hill had been stabbed under its summit, some kind of radio mast sticking out like a spear from the spine of a fallen warrior, a torn and bloody pennant of cloud flurrying horizontally from its shaft.

'Oh,' Merrily said, realizing. '*Right*. They say it's like another country up there.'

Garway.

The light through the window was this deep, fruity pink, the sun dying somewhere behind the hill with its radio mast, its famously enigmatic church and a farmhouse called the Master House that they were saying was haunted.

Adam Eastgate had been aiming a forefinger like he wanted to stab the hill himself, again and again. Sighing, he let his hand fall.

'We don't often make mistakes, Merrily.'

She'd never actually been to Garway Hill. Nor, before today, to this place either – a tidy cluster of converted farm buildings off a dead-end country lane, maybe three miles outside the city. Pieces of Herefordshire adding up to more than twelve thousand acres were administered from here, on behalf of perhaps the most prestigious landlord in the country, and she hadn't even heard of it.

All the stuff you ought to know about and didn't. Sometimes this county could be just a little *too* discreet. All a bit awkward. Merrily turned away from the window and the hills.

'Jane and I – my daughter – we keep planning to go over to Garway, check out the Knights Templar church. Somehow never seem to find the time.'

'Aye, we saw it with the Man, when he came to inspect the farm. Likes a quiet stroll when he can. And, of course, it's always so quiet there, nobody noticed us even when—' Adam Eastgate slipping her a cautious glance. 'Why are you smiling?'

'You might not have seen a soul, but it'd be all over the hill before he was back in his Land Rover.' Merrily looked down at the outline plans on the conference table. They were blurred. She rubbed her eyes. 'He inspects every property you take on? Personally?'

'Aw, hey, he's not just a figurehead.'

The brackeny accent digging in – Northumbria. In his dry, soldierly way, Adam Eastgate was affronted. Very protective of the Man, the people working here.

'Does *he* know about this particular problem then?'

Eastgate didn't reply, which could have meant *yes* or *no* or *not something you're supposed to ask.*

'OK, then.' Merrily sat down in one of the high-backed chairs, red brocade. 'What, specifically, are we looking at?'

'Oh hell, *I* can't tell you. Perhaps I wasn't listening hard enough, y'know?'

'Or you find it embarrassing?'

'Not a question of embarrassment, Merrily, I'm just not the man it happened to. If anything did.'

4

Always the get-out clause.

'How would you like me to play it, then?'

'How would you normally play it?'

'Well …' Dear God, how long was this going to take? 'To begin with, we usually try to find out if there's a back-story. Talk to local people, village historian – there's always a village historian. Or maybe—' She clocked his wince. 'That would be the wrong approach, would it?'

'Depends if you want it on American TV before the week's out.'

'Seriously?'

'Merrily …' Tight smile. 'I'm the land-steward. Deal with builders, architects … and tenants, right? Most of whom … good as gold. But we know if we're forced to evict somebody who hasn't parted with the rent for two years, next day's tabloids we're half-expecting *Prince Puts Family on the Street.*'

'Oh.'

'You see where we're going?'

'*Haunted Prince calls in Exorcist?*'

Eastgate shuddered. Nice chap, Adam, the Bishop had said. Knows what he wants and how to get it done. But raising this had taken the best part of half an hour and three false starts.

This had been two nights ago, one of those receptions where the Duchy was explaining its ambitious conservation plans to the great and the good of Hereford. The Bishop and the Archdeacon and their wives were having a drink afterwards with Adam Eastgate when the Garway investment had come up. And its complications. You could imagine the Bishop nodding helpfully. *We do have a person, you know, looks after this kind of thing.*

'I mean, you'll've read the stuff, same as I have,' Eastgate said. 'He only has to venture an off-the-cuff opinion on whatever it is – architecture, alternative medicine, GM foods …'

'The benefits of talking to plants?'

'*See*, there you go! That's exactly *it*. How many years ago was that? But do they ever forget?'

Well, no. This was the nation's last bit of official glitter, a face from commemorative investiture plaques, Royal Wedding mugs on your gran's dresser. Merrily feeling slightly ashamed that, although she'd known it was most unlikely that the Man would be here today, she *was* wearing her best coat. Her mother would have agonized, changing tops, changing shoes, inspecting her hair many times in the car mirror, just in case.

'Who is it safe to talk to, then? Who's actually living in the house?'

'Well … nobody. I'm trying to explain, this came from the builder. Canny fella, normally. Or so I thought till he's ringing us up – Adam, man, I think you're going to have to find somebody else for this one. I'm going, *What?*'

Eastgate walked to the darkening window, glanced out briefly, unseeing, turned and came back.

'We're good employers, Merrily. In some ways, the best. Never short of tenders and once they're allocated we don't get jobs chucked back at us. Doesn't happen.'

Merrily nodding. They'd be a fairly significant name on a builder's CV. But it worked both ways, Eastgate said. This builder had a rare feel for an old property. And the Master House itself …

'See, normally, we're not interested in anything less than about two hundred acres, and this is, what, ninety-five? But it's a forgotten bit of old England, right down there on the very edge of Wales. Not much you find these days completely unrestored, hardly touched in over a century. We get to *tease out* the past. Plus, I'm thinking craft workshops in the barns, the stables, the granary … a little working community, new economic life. And green. Very green. Woodburners, rainwater tanks, sheep's-wool insulation …'

'Oh, he loves all that, doesn't he?'

'The Man? It's his number one, and it influences us all, naturally.' Eastgate shook his head. 'I'm going, come on, Felix, what is this *really* about? You sick? Domestic problems? Adam, he says to us, maybe this is an old place that doesn't *want* to be restored. His words. *Hostile.* That was another. One of his team had a powerful feeling they were *not wanted.*'

'He pulled out of the whole project because one person thought he—?'

'It's a she, Merrily.'

'Oh.'

The sun had gone, leaving a raspberry hue on the room, but you could still make out the shapes of the fields and the fuzz of hedgerows on the side of Garway Hill.

'I'm going to leave it in your hands, all right?' Eastgate gathered up the plans into a black cardboard folder. 'You take these, they're only copies. See what he's putting in jeopardy.'

'The bottom line being you'd like him back on the job ASAP.'

'Only if he's normal. Look, if you want to ask a few questions locally, go ahead. We've nothing to hide. Bought in good faith, and what we have in mind is going to be good for the community. I'd just say exercise a bit more discretion than usual.'

Merrily nodded.

'My watchword, Adam.'

She had a headache.

They walked into the forecourt, deeply shadowed now. Not quite six, and everyone seemed to have gone home. Maybe Adam Eastgate had timed their meeting for the tail-end of the working day so he wouldn't have to explain any of this to the staff.

All the leaves were still on the trees and it was still warm – too warm. A long, flooded summer and the planet in the condemned cell. At least the nights were drawing in now, the tindery musk of autumn on the air as Eastgate walked with Merrily to the old Volvo. It had been nicked last summer – in the dark, obviously – and then swiftly abandoned, presumably after they'd heard the engine.

'So – just to get this right – what exactly will you do at the house, Merrily, to, ah …?'

'Depends what it is.'

'You work on your own?'

'I … like to think not.' She smiled wearily; he didn't get it. 'OK, there are a few advisers I can call on, if necessary. Usually when there are people involved who might have particular problems – psychological … psychiatric? When you're looking at an empty … that is, a house not lived in, as such …'

Oh, the way you shaped and trimmed your glossary of terms when addressing ingrained scepticism. Adam Eastgate cleared his throat.

'Only I didn't think you'd be so ...'

'Small? Female?'

'I was going to say, matter-of-fact about it.'

Meaning, *like it's real.*

'I don't do it all the time. There's also a parish – weddings, funerals, rows with the churchwardens.'

'I suppose *medieval* was the word I was groping for.'

'*I'm* medieval?' She looked up at him through the fast-thickening air. 'You're working for an institution dating back, if I've got this right, to thirteen—?'

'Thirty-seven. Duchy was created by Edward III, to provide an income for his son, the Prince of Wales. The king's father having been the first to hold the title.'

'Well ... the first Englishman.'

'And by that you mean ... what, exactly, Merrily?'

'Well, they ...' Flinching at the sharpness of Eastgate's glance. 'They had their own, didn't they? The Welsh. For a long time.'

And even after the princes of Wales had become English there was Owain Glyndwr, in the fifteenth century, still trying to get it back. But maybe mentioning this would not be very tactful.

'Not my subject, Welsh history. Thank God.' Eastgate straightened up. 'Anyway, you'll keep us up to speed, I hope.'

'Obviously tell you what I can. Without, you know ... breaking any confidences that might arise.'

Not that this was likely. It didn't seem to be any more than what Huw Owen would call a *volatile* or a *delinquent*: the wonky fuse box, the dripping tap – Deliverance-*lite*.

Merrily unlocked the car.

'It's an empty house. If anything's happening, nobody has to live with it day-to-day. So we're looking at ... probably, prayers, a room-by-room blessing. Or, if a particular and persistent personality is identified, maybe a Requiem Eucharist involving the people most closely involved, present and – where possible – past. Nine times out of ten, this is enough to restore a kind of calm. Adam, why's it called the Master House?'

'If anybody was able to explain that,' Eastgate said, 'they didn't want to. Maybe the main house when there were subsidiary farms. Or the local schoolmaster used to live there?'

'Mmm.'

She had a last look at the hill, where isolated white lights had appeared, its big sisters, the Skirrid and the Sugarloaf fading, uninhabited, into the dried-blood sky.

Adam Eastgate said, 'Ever get scared yourself, Merrily?'

'Me?'

Merrily laughed, an unconvincing hollow sound in the stillness. An early owl picked it up, or seemed to, and flew with it as she got into the car.

2

Lament

'THEN HE WAS back on the phone,' Merrily told Lol in the pub. 'Soon as I got in. Barely had time to put the kettle on.'

'The Duchy guy?'

'No, the *Bishop*. Must've rung several times already. I don't think I've ever known him this jumpy. I just … I don't get it.'

She took a drink. Serious decadence: a house-white spritzer in the Black Swan – oak beams, low lights – with one's paramour. How long had it been before she'd felt able to do this comfortably? Six months? A year?

Seemed stupid now; nobody glanced at them twice – although this was probably because almost nobody knew them. Thursday night, and most of the drinkers in the lounge bar were from outside the village, having drifted in for dinner. Some probably responding to the dispiriting *Daily Telegraph* travel feature identifying Ledwardine as the black-and-white, timber-ribbed heart of the New Cotswolds.

Like, when did *that* happen? Couple of years ago, the village was still on the rim of the wilderness. Now there was talk of the Black Swan chasing a Michelin star.

'The Cotswolds are coming.' Merrily listened to the brittle laughter at the bar. 'Ominous. Like a melting ice cap. Rural warming. Feels suddenly claustrophobic, or is that just me?'

Final confirmation of the county's new economic status: the major investment in Herefordshire by the old Cotswolds' most distinguished resident.

Charles Windsor, Highgrove.

'Does *he* know about this?' Lol said.

'Well, that's what *I* asked. Didn't get an answer.'

'He'd probably be fascinated. Has his other-worldly side.'

'Only, he keeps quieter about it these days.' Merrily looked around, making sure nobody could overhear them in their corner, well back from the bar. 'Since the tabloids labelled him as a loony who talks to plants. Maybe they've been advised not to tell him, just get it quietly disposed of. As for the Bishop ...'

'You can see his problem. This is the guy next in line for head of the Church of England.'

'That didn't escape me. I suppose it's as good a reason as any to play it by the book.'

No reason, however, for the Bishop to go adding extra, entirely gratuitous chapters. *Full attention, I think, Merrily. We'll need to get you a locum for at least a week. Move you over there.*

And she'd gone, 'What?'

Like ... *what*? Sounding like Jane, probably.

'Lol, I don't *want* to go and stay in Garway for a week. I just ... I don't see the point.'

'In which case ...' Orange sparks from the electric candles on the walls were agitating in Lol's glasses '... why not just tell the Bishop to, you know, piss off?'

'Because he's a friend. Because I owe him. Because ...'

Merrily shook her head, helpless. Lol leaned back. He was looking good, actually. Old denim jacket over a *Baker's Lament* T-shirt, which he wore like a medal but always keeping the motif at least partly covered up, as if he could still only half-believe what was finally happening to him. He put down his lager, thoughtful.

'Suppose I come with you.'

'You're touring.'

'It's only three gigs next week, just the one night away. I could reschedule ... or cancel.'

'That is not a word we use, Lol. You give anybody the slightest reason to think you're slipping back ...'

A year ago, the thought of three gigs – three *solo* gigs – would have given him palpitations, night sweats.

Lol looked into his glass, obviously knowing she was right, and Merrily watched him across the oak table, through this haze of love and pride blurred by fatigue. Very happy for him, if concerned that he might just be feeling he didn't deserve it. Ominously, when she'd gone over to the cottage to drag him out to the pub, she'd heard the voice of his long-dead muse, Nick Drake, from the stereo. Worst of all, it was 'Black-Eyed Dog', Nick's voice pitched high in bleak and terminal despair. Lol had turned it off before he opened the door, Merrily staring at him in alarm but finding no despair in his eyes, just this sense of puzzlement.

'Besides,' she said, 'I'm supposed to be staying with the local priest. They haven't got a vicar in the Garway cluster at present, so a retired guy's taking services meanwhile. He and his wife do B. & B. I turn up there with a boyfriend, how's that going to look?'

'What about Jane?'

'Jane stays here. Can't miss any school at this stage. Woman curate called Ruth Wisdom's lined up to mind the parish. Work experience. She's OK. And Jane's less likely to drive her to self-mutilation than at one time, and she—'

Merrily looked up. A woman was standing behind Lol's chair.

'Excuse me. You just have to be Lol Robinson?'

She was tall and very slender. She'd been with a group of women in their twenties, with fancy cocktails, their backs to the bar. All of them now looking at Lol, hands over smiles.

'Nobody *has* to be anybody,' Lol said.

Mr Enigmatic. The woman was leaning over him now, her glossy black dress like oil on a dipstick, one small breast almost touching his cheek.

'Lol, I just wanted to say, we all went to see *The Baker's Lament* at the Flicks in the Sticks special preview, and it was … absolutely enchanting. Especially the music, obviously. But, listen, when I went to buy the CD in Hereford they hadn't even *got* it? Nobody had?'

'Well, it … it all takes time,' Lol said.

'And I'm like, for Christ's sake, this guy's *local*? And the manager guy, he eventually admitted they'd had about fifteen orders just that day?

Fifteen orders in one morning? This tells me you need to get a better recording company, Mr Robinson. I couldn't even find a download?'

'Well, it's kind of caught them on the hop,' Lol said. 'All of us, really. We didn't actually—'

'Well, *I* have to say I just totally love it. Hope you don't mind me coming over?'

'Er, no,' Lol said. 'No, not at all. Thank you.'

The young woman straightened up. As did her conspicuous nipples. She looked across at Merrily and smiled at her.

Merrily felt small and dowdy and old.

'He's lovely, isn't he?' the woman said.

Walking back across the village square, Lol avoided the creamy light of the fake gaslamps; Merrily was a pace behind him.

'Fifteen orders? In one morning?'

'She was probably exaggerating.'

'Why would she?' Merrily pulled on her woollen beret, zipped up her fraying fleece. 'She doesn't know you. Although she'll probably be telling people she does, now.'

'One small song in one small film?'

'Not so small now. And you know what? People will remember the song when they've half-forgotten the film. Because it's somehow caught the mood. The *zeitgeist* ... whatever. You have become a cool person, Laurence.'

'It's not real.' Lol was shaking his head, as if to clear it after his two halves of lager. 'It's a freak accident.'

Sometimes you wanted to encircle his neck with your hands and ...

Over a year now since this young guy, Liam Brown, not long out of film school, had written to Lol, telling him about his self-financed rural love story. How badly, after hearing it on Lol's album, *Alien*, he wanted 'The Baker's Lament' on the soundtrack, only wasn't sure he could afford it. Just take it, Lol had told him, the way Lol would, sending him three versions of the song, including an unreleased instrumental track, and forgetting all about it. Not even mentioning it to Merrily until the middle of July, when the first DVD arrived.

The Baker's Lament. There on the label, with a bread knife stuck into a country cob. The guy had named the movie after the song.

Shooting the picture with unknown actors who'd formed some kind of workers' cooperative. Lol and Merrily had watched it together at the vicarage: the tragicomic story of a young couple setting up a village bakery on the Welsh border in the 1960s when the supermarkets were starting to starve small shopkeepers out of business. Following through to the new millennium when the couple were played – and not badly, either – by the actors' own parents and the village had turned into something like contemporary Ledwardine, the bakery now a twee delicatessen.

The movie was simple and charming and unpretentious, a rural elegy with Lol's music seeping through it like a bloodstream, carrying the sense of change and loss and a kind of resilience.

Liam Brown was even worse than Lol at self-promotion, and they hadn't known it had been released – in a limited way, on the art-house circuit – until it was in the papers that an obscure British independent film had picked up some debut-director award at Cannes. Then the *who is this guy?* calls had started coming in to Lol's producer, Prof Levin.

Change was coming. New Costwolds, new Lol.

They stopped on the edge of the cobbles, where they'd go their separate ways, Merrily to the vicarage, Lol to his terraced cottage in Church Street. When he took her hand, his felt cold.

'Apparently, the next question they ask is, Is he still alive? Thinking maybe it's a forgotten recording from the Sixties, by some contemporary of ...'

'Nick Drake?'

'It should be him, Merrily. Not me.'

'Lol, he's dead. He died in 1974, after a mere five, six years of not being successful. You get to double that ... *and* some.'

She pulled him under the oak-pillared village hall and – bugger it, if there were people watching, let them watch – clasped her hands in his hair and found his lips with her mouth and then unzipped her fleece and tucked one of his cold hands inside.

'All this,' she said, aware of the ambivalence, 'is something overdue. Remember that.'

Trying to banish the image of the girl in the pub, showing him her implants out of a dress that must have cost something close to two weeks' stipend.

Jane said, 'You're a soft touch, Mum. Always were. A doormat.'

'Thanks.'

It was getting late, but it was Friday night and Merrily had lit a small log fire in the vicarage sitting room. The whole place was colder since they'd said goodbye to the oil-gobbling Aga. Which, while it had to be done, meant she wasn't looking forward to winter.

'And I don't mean one of those rough, spiky doormats,' Jane said.

'You'll *like* Ruth. She rides a motorbike.'

'Jeez, if there's anything worse than a trendy lesbian cleric in leathers with a vintage Harley between her legs … Like, maybe I could arrange to stay at Eirion's …'

Jane's voice dried up, and her face went blank. Eirion was away at university now, and she still hadn't got used to that. OK, it was only Cardiff, and he came home to Abergavenny at weekends, but things, inevitably, had changed.

'Ruth's not a lesbian, Jane.'

'Not a problem, anyway.' Jane, on her knees on the hearthrug, stared into the desultory yellow flames. 'I was thinking of giving girls a try for a while, actually.'

Shock tactic. Cry for help. Merrily pulled up an armchair.

'He didn't phone, then.'

'Erm … no.'

'How long?'

'Ten days? No problem. I don't think he was even able to get home last weekend, didn't I mention that?'

'No, but I kind of assumed that was why you suddenly had to work on your project.'

'All that's gone quiet, too. They may not even start the dig until the spring.'

'Oh.'

Pity about that. Jane had been hyper for a while after her campaign to stall council plans for *executive homes* in Coleman's Meadow. Convinced that the field had once been crossed by an ancient trackway and, amazingly, she'd been right. They'd found prehistoric stones there, long buried by some superstitious farmer. Sensational archaeology, for a place like Ledwardine.

'He'll call,' Merrily said. 'He's Eirion.'

'I don't care if he calls or not.'

'Yes, you do.'

'Like, it's very demanding, university life.' Jane didn't look at her. 'Lots of guys you're obliged to get smashed with. Lots of girls to assist with their essays and stuff.'

'Eirion was never like that.'

'He was never at university before.'

University. Further education. This could be the time to talk about it again. Just over six months from her A levels, Jane needed to start applying to universities ... like now. But Jane wasn't interested, because that was what *everybody* did. She kept saying she could feel *The System* trying to *stereotype* her. And look at the cost. Tuition fees. Could they afford it? Was it really worth it? Especially as she hadn't yet decided on a career. Like, you didn't just do further education for the sake of having done it.

'*You* went to uni,' Jane said, looking down at the rug, 'and got pregnant before you were into your second year.'

'We were naïve in those days. Well ... comparatively immature. Although I suppose every generation gets to say that.'

'In which case I must be—' Jane turned to her, moist-eyed, or was it the light? 'I must be very seriously immature, then. Pushing eighteen and only the one real boyfriend? That's not normal, Mum. That wasn't even normal in your day. That's, like, almost perverted?'

'Well, actually, flower, I think it's really quite—' The phone rang then, offering her a timely get-out, which she felt compelled to ignore. 'I'll let the machine—'

'No, you get it. Go on. You'll only sit there worrying until you find an excuse to sneak off and play the message.'

Merrily nodded, got up.

'It's a doormat thing,' Jane said sweetly to her back.

'Thanks.'

She took the call in the scullery office, padding over the flags in the cold kitchen where no stove rumbled, scooping up the phone with one hand, switching on the desk lamp with the other.

'Ledwardine Vic—'

'Mrs Watkins, is it?'

'Yes, it is.'

'Adam Eastgate likely mentioned me.'

'Oh … right. Mr …'

'Barlow.' Low-level local accent. 'Felix.'

'Right. I was going to call you tomorrow, actually, see if we could arrange to meet.'

'Tomorrow would be all right for us, yes.'

'At the house?'

Owls whooping it up in the orchard. Silence in the old black bakelite phone, the kind of phone that could really carry a silence.

'The house at Garway?' Merrily said.

'No,' Mr Barlow said. 'I don't think so.'

'Any … particular reason?'

'Well, see … person you need to talk to, more than me, is my plasterer. It's my plasterer had the experience.'

'Your plasterer.'

'I call her that. We're converting this barn at Monkland, see. We're in a caravan on the site.'

'That's not far for me. It's just I thought you might find it easier to explain the problem in situ,' Merrily said.

'No,' he said. 'No, I don't think so.'

'You couldn't spare the time?'

Another silence; no owls even. She waited.

'I think you're gonner have to come here,' he said. 'We don't plan to go back, see.'

'To the Master House.'

This was what he was ringing to tell her? That they weren't, on any account, going back to the house?

'That's correct,' he said.

She had the feeling that he was working to a script and whoever had written it was standing at his shoulder. She felt another question coming and hung on for it.

'I was told you … you were the Hereford exorcist.'

'More or less.'

'And you'll have the, um, full regalia, is it?'

'Regalia?'

'We'd like it if you came with all the regalia,' Felix Barlow said. 'The full bell, book and candle, kind of thing.'

'Oh.'

'If that's all right with you,' Barlow said.

3

Fuchsia

SHE WAS BEAUTIFUL and shimmery in the mist. Like one of those exotic birds that weren't supposed to migrate here. Greens and blues in her dark, tangly hair, skin like milky coffee. She stood by the long green caravan, in her pink-splashed overalls and her turquoise wellingtons, calling out when Merrily was close enough for the dog collar to show.

'Will you bless me?'

'I'm sorry?'

'In the old-fashioned way, please,' she said. 'That is, with all due ceremony?'

From the field gate, through the lingering mist – a keen hint of first frost – she'd looked as young as Jane. Close up, you guessed she was nearly thirty. Still not Merrily's idea of a plasterer.

'I'm serious.'

'I can tell.'

Merrily looked into eyes which were startlingly big and round, like an owl's, and widely separated.

'It strengthens the aura,' the woman said. 'Isn't that right?'

'I'm sure it must be.' Merrily parted her woollen cloak to expose the cassock, hemmed with mud now. The full regalia could be a pain. 'But would it be all right if we talked first?'

'I just wanted to ask you while Felix wasn't here. He's not religious.' The woman turned away and moved back to the caravan. 'Fuchsia,' she said over her shoulder. 'Fuchsia Mary Linden.'

Which meant that her parents had been either gardeners or big fans of the *Gormenghast* trilogy. Following her into the caravan, Merrily's money was on *Gormenghast*.

She felt tired again, had a lingering headache. She'd awoken a good hour before dawn, her body all curled up, tense with resentment.

Never her favourite negative emotion, resentment. Most times it came hissing like poison gas out of inflated self-esteem – they can't treat *me* like this. Seldom objective, never exactly Christian and hardly (thank you, Jane) the Way of the Doormat.

At six a.m. she'd been hugging a pot of tea, Ethel the black cat on her knees, in the frigid kitchen. Watery sunlight eventually seeping into the windows before the mist had blotted it up.

The more she'd thought about the Duchy job, the more senseless it had seemed. She was expected to desert the parish – and Jane and Lol – for up to a week to address some *embarrassment* in an empty house?

An *empty* house. That was the other point. No family life disrupted there. Nobody's sanity at risk. Was there, in fact, anything more on the line than the reputation of the Bishop of Hereford as a faithful servant of the monarchy, and the professional judgement of the Duke of Cornwall's land-steward?

Merrily had put on her pectoral cross and knelt, in her bathrobe, on the cold stone flags and prayed. And listened.

The result had been inconclusive.

It was a substantial, professional caravan, with a living room and a good-sized kitchen area, copper pans on hooks conveying weight and a sense of permanence. Twin doors at the bottom of the living area suggesting a separate bedroom and bathroom.

The walls of the living room were lined with oriental rugs, and there was a wood-burning stove, lit, the sweet scent of apple logs mingling with the sweeter fumes of cannabis. Fuchsia kicked off her wellies, picked up a rubberized walkie-talkie.

'I'll call Felix. He's over at the barn. Have a seat, please, Merrily.'

Shrugging off the black woollen cloak, Merrily made a space for herself between tumbled books on one of the fitted sofas. She could see the barn, its bay agape, through the window opposite and the golden-brown mist. The window behind her framed the church tower across the rutted field and the lane where she'd left her car. Monkland was a main-road village on the way to Leominster; this was the first time she'd penetrated its hinterland.

'So the barn's going to be …?'

'Our home. It's supposed to be finished by now.' Fuchsia prodded at the walkie-talkie. 'But that's what it's like with builders, Merrily, they fit in their own projects between jobs. If a builder's home looks like some wretched hovel, that means he's doing very well.'

The ephemeral beauty didn't include her voice, which was quite slow. And loud, in an uncontrolled way, like a child's.

Merrily folded the cloak over her knees, less puzzled now about why it, or the cassock, had been necessary. Why Felix Barlow, though not religious himself, had thought traditional priestly attire would be appropriate.

The walkie-talkie cackled and Fuchsia said, 'She's here, babes,' and clicked it off. 'He'll come now, Merrily. He was getting a bit frazzled and he needed to work with his hands to calm himself down. Felix has problems talking about the non-physical. Which is very odd because he's really perceptive, and buildings speak to him.'

'How do they do that?

'They send him information, communicating what they were and what they can be again. It's like dowsing. He feels it in his muscles – the needs of the stone and the oak. Well, in some buildings, anyway.'

'What about the farmhouse at Garway?'

'The Master House had been left to rot.' Fuchsia was wrapping her thin arms around herself as if to crush a shudder. 'And it wasn't complaining. Houses know when they've gone bad.'

'And this is what it said to Felix?'

'This one didn't speak to Felix, Merrily,' Fuchsia said. 'It spoke to me.'

'I see.'

'And now my aura's permeated with darkness.' Fuchsia opened her arms. '*Can* you see?'

'I'm afraid not.'

'Some priests can. Not the man at Garway, he was no help at all, but there was a very good guy in the place I grew up. He'd packed it in, but it never goes away. It's a calling, like they say. I believe that, Merrily. If you answer the call, you may receive gifts.'

'It's as well to be careful about gifts,' Merrily said. 'You can never be too sure who they're from.'

Fuchsia crouched in front of the stove and opened up its vents, pale flames spurting in the glass square. On a shelf to the left of the stainless steel flue, Merrily read titles from a stack of paperbacks. *The Gap in the Curtain, The Secrets of Dr Taverner, The Flint Knife, Ghost Stories of an Antiquary.*

'Where *did* you grow up, Fuchsia?'

'West Wales. Cardiganshire.' Fuchsia watched the flames. 'I was born there.'

No Welsh accent, though. Through the caravan window, Merrily saw a man in a hat coming out of the mist.

'Felix was there, too,' Fuchsia said.

'In Cardiganshire?'

'In the place where I was born. He was there when I entered the world.' Fuchsia smiled, her face reflected, stretched and warped, in the shiny flue. 'Felix cut my cord, Merrily.'

Merrily blinked.

'Which makes for a lifelong connection,' Fuchsia said.

Something you learned as a deliverance minister: whatever ghosts were, there were people who saw them and people who *wanted* to see them, and they were seldom the same people.

Put it this way: if whatever had happened at Garway had happened to Felix Merrily would have been more inclined to believe it.

He was a big, untamed-looking man in a leather waistcoat. Long red-grey hair in a rubber-banded ponytail, a wide smile through a stubble like sharp sand. He'd left his wellies at the bottom of the caravan steps, and she saw that his woollen socks had been darned. How often nowadays did socks get darned?

'Didn't really want this, Mrs Watkins.' He lowered himself with a sigh into the sofa opposite her; he had to be a good twenty years older than

Fuchsia. 'I just wanted off the job, and that would be an end to it, but Adam … he's like a terrier, is Adam.'

'He likes you. Trusts you to get it right.'

'He should know better.' Felix pulled out a dented cigarette tin and Rizlas. 'All right if I …?'

'Please do. In fact …' Merrily reached gratefully down to her bag, bringing out the Silk Cut and the Zippo. 'And he doesn't want to see you lose the contract, if something can be … cleared up.'

'I never asked for this. I want you to know that. I said to Adam, leave it. It's just one of those things.'

'But then he told me,' Fuchsia said, 'and I realized you must be meant, Merrily.'

'Meant,' Merrily said.

'It's a matter of metaphysics.'

Merrily looked at Felix, who said nothing, and back at Fuchsia whose wide-eyed gaze met hers full-on.

'That house is diseased, you see. We need spiritual antibiotics.'

'You know a bit about these things, then.'

'I know that this is about good and evil, Merrily,' Fuchsia said, 'and I've experienced the evil.'

'OK.' Merrily lit a cigarette. 'Do you want to tell me?'

Nearest the Scissors

Dust sheets?

Mostly heavy-duty plastic, Felix explained. They'd laid them on the floor where the damp and sunken stone flags had been taken up. This was after the roof had been made safe. First things first. They'd spread the dust sheets on the floor, so they could make a start on the walls.

'Lime-plaster,' Fuchsia said. 'I love it.'

'You should see her,' Felix said. 'She moves like a dragonfly.'

'Not *that* day.' Fuchsia moved closer to the wood stove. 'There was no air that day. It was close and heavy outside, but still damp inside the house. My wings …' She giggled bleakly, a sound like pills rattling in a jar. 'My wings were drooping.'

'It was the first time she'd been there, see,' Felix said. 'I have three blokes in the regular team, they'd made a start on the roof.'

Fuchsia watched the flames.

'I was looking forward to it. It seemed a lovely area. It has two personalities, Merrily. Long, light views on the English side, and then deep green and full of drama as it swoops down to the Monnow Valley and Wales.' She gripped her knees. 'All spoiled now.'

Felix looked at her, worried, then he turned to Merrily.

'So … Ledwardine, eh? You know Gomer Parry?'

'Oh, yes.' She smiled. 'Very well.'

'Danny Thomas?'

'Not quite as well. I didn't meet him until he became Gomer's partner in the plant-hire.'

'I was in Danny's band in the Seventies,' Felix said. 'Bass. Fingers always too messed up for anything more delicate than a bass guitar, and a bit clumsy at that. I think we did one gig, and I wouldn't say folks was actually walking out the door—'

'It was full of death,' Fuchsia said. 'The cold, white, waxy stillness of death.'

Merrily saw Felix grit his teeth, turning away from Fuchsia, whose elongated reflection in the stainless-steel flue was starting to look like Munch's *Scream*.

'I didn't know whether it wanted me out or it wanted me dead, Merrily.'

'Stop it, girl.'

Felix's fingers gripping his knees. Merrily knelt down next to Fuchsia on the rug.

'What made you think that something wanted *you* dead?'

Fuchsia shrugged.

'I *tried* to work – I went out, I came back, I went out again. And then I went back. I *am* a professional.' She stared defiantly at Merrily. 'Felix went back on his own the next day, and when he came home it was like it was all over him. I made him shower and then I burned all the clothes he'd been wearing. Just out there, Merrily. I poured petrol on them.'

Merrily nodded. Very early in her deliverance career she'd been advised to do something similar, to draw a line under a particular situation. Some things it was easier not to question.

'You said you went back.'

'It was under the dust sheets.'

'What was?'

'I tried to ignore it, but all the time I could hear the dust sheets behind me, wriggling and rippling and whispering. The air was really thick and heavy and I wouldn't let myself turn round.'

'Felix wasn't there?'

'I was checking out the granary,' Felix said. 'Working out how many steps could be repaired. Heard her screaming, started running …'

Fuchsia was staring down at her hands, mumbling something. Merrily bent to her.

'I'm sorry …?'

'*A face of crumpled linen,*' Felix said. 'She's said that a few times.'

'That's what you saw?'

Fuchsia nodded her head violently and bent forward as if she had awful stomach-ache, and Felix looked depairingly at Merrily, and then Fuchsia said, 'Can we do it in the church?'

'The blessing. Don't see why not. But I'd need to clear it with the vicar.'

'No. There's no need, Merrily.'

'Well, it's what we usually do, but ...' At least she was on fairly good terms with the minister at Monkland; she could get away with it. 'If you'd rather not make a thing out of it ...'

'Not *this* church,' Fuchsia said.

She'd insisted on changing first, into something white.

The old-fashioned way. All due ceremony.

Merrily went back across the field, through the clearing mist, to the car and brought the blue case out of the boot. Inside it were the holy water and oil for anointing. Borrowed from Roman Catholicism but it was sometimes helpful. Partly theatre.

She waited in the field, with Felix.

'Those books on the shelf near the stove – are they yours or Fuchsia's?'

'I don't read much nowadays. Half a page and I fall asleep. If they en't technical books, they en't mine.'

'I meant the ghost stories.'

'Oh. Aye, she likes the old ghost stories. Sometime she'll read one aloud and it scares the pants off me, but she just giggles. Finds them comforting, mabbe. The old houses, the formality, the stiff way people talk. Stilted. Sometimes she says she was born out of time. Wrong place, wrong time.'

'Where *was* she born?'

'She didn't tell you?'

'She said Cardiganshire.'

'Well, that ...' Felix half smiled. 'That's more or *less* right. You heard of Tepee City?'

'Blimey, is it still there?'

'I reckon. Likely the longest-surviving alternative community in Britain by now. I was there about a year, as a young feller. Gap year, as you might say. Nice folks, in the main. Had to pull your weight, mind, or you wouldn't be welcome for too long.'

'So you were a tepee dweller.'

'Bender, in my case. You know – the ole bent-over sapling kind of thing?'

'Vaguely.'

'Only there a year, like I say, but I never regretted it. When you eventually graduate to building and rebuilding proper houses, if the first ones you ever put together was benders you've probably got your priorities right – make it warm, watertight and use natural insulation.'

'Fuchsia said you, erm …'

'Cut her cord? Aye, she likes to tell people that.'

'Is it true?'

'It is, actually.' Felix squeezed his prickly jaw. 'Childbirth in the valley, it could be like a communal event. I just happened to be nearest the scissors. Afterwards, Mary asked me to be her … godfather, kind of thing. Though we never went to church, just down the wood. Where we lit a fire, asked the gods to bless the child … bit pagan, sorry about that, but they did, kind of … you know, they included Jesus.'

Merrily smiled faintly.

'Then we played some music, smoked some weed, and I held the child for a bit and made some vows in the smoke.'

'So you and Fuchsia's mother – I'm sorry for asking personal questions but it helps to know a few basics …'

'No,' Felix said. 'Me and Mary, that never really happened. I wanted it to, at the time, I en't denying that. She was beautiful. Thin. Fragile. Didn't have much to say. Needed looking after. When she turned up at Tepee City, she was already pregnant. Said the father'd buggered off to America to go on the road in a pick-up truck. I suppose I got closer to her than anybody, but not as close as I'd've liked, you know? She stayed a few months, and then she … she just left.'

'With the baby?'

'No, she left the baby in the Valley. With another family.'

'Just like that?'

'More or less. Rachel, the woman who took Fuchsia, she was this earth-mother type, done it before. I mean, it was that kind of place. Fuchsia was a child of the tribe, kind of thing. We thought Mary was gonner come back – she said she'd been offered a job, good money and she'd be back for the kid. The social services tried to find her, got nowhere. So it ended up with Rachel adopting Fuchsia, or fostering her, whatever. And I kept in touch, kind of thing. Helped out. Sent money.'

'You left when it was clear that Fuchsia's mother wasn't going to come back?'

'No, no, what happened, my ole feller died suddenly, I had to sort things out. He had a builder's yard, my dad. I sold it after a bit, went to work for a firm of conservation builders. Learning the trade, kind of thing. Then went on my own, built up a business. Got married, got divorced. Then Fuchsia showed up.'

'What, just appeared?'

'We'd put her through art college, see.'

'*You* had?'

'Had the money by then, Mrs Watkins. Why not? I mean, I never meant for this ... for us to be like, you know, how it's turned out. She just arrived one day, and she was interested in what I was doing, the conservation work, and she hadn't got a job ...'

'She went to work for you, before there was any ... relationship?'

'That was how it started, aye.' Felix wiped his mouth with the back of a hand. 'I call her my plasterer – what she does really is mouldings, recreates original colours, experiments with limewashes. She just loves the feel of plaster.'

'I see.'

'Look, Mrs Watkins, I'm under no illusions about how long it's gonner last, but we're rebuilding that—' Felix nodded towards the barn. 'It was a ruin, and I'm determined to make it into a proper home for her. Like an ancestral home, kind of thing, for the ancestry she'll never have. She reads all these stories about folks living in country houses, and if I can give her that, things might be ... good. For a while.'

'You never heard from her mother again?'

'Not a word.'

'You'd never tried to find her?'

'Didn't know where to start. No idea where she was from. She had a bit of a Brummie accent, I remember, and she was mixed race – one of them must've been black. Fuchsia reckons she's dead.'

'Why does she think that?'

'Just a feeling. There's this kind of tribal mysticism in Tepee City, and she had a period of building fires in a clearing in the wood and looking for Mary in the smoke. Now she just mopes around ole churches and reads ghost stories. I was hoping, when the barn was finished, it'd be some kind of stability.'

Merrily looked at him, saying nothing. There was a sadness here. A longing, but also a realistic suspicion that it wasn't going to work out.

'If you can take away the fear,' Felix said. 'If you could just do that ... you know?'

'You think it's more than just this place – the Master House.'

'Look, I don't *know*. I believe something happened to her in that place, I just don't know if it's ... in her mind. I don't know, Mrs Watkins. I accept that these things go on.'

'What I mean is, you have a feeling for houses, but nothing seems to have ... I mean for you ...'

'It didn't have anything to say to me, good or bad. What I usually do, if a place is blocking me, is I'll spend a night inside, in a sleeping bag. You wake up in a house, you can somehow get a proper feel of it. I might've got round to that, but ... she didn't want me to. Look, I know what you're thinking, but ... it's just a job. Just money.'

'Right. Erm ... why's it called the Master House, do you know?'

'Not really. Bloke I spoke to said it goes back to the Templars who built Garway church. They had masters and grand masters, apparently. It *could* be old enough, I found fourteenth-century bits, maybe older.'

'Did you ask anybody if it was supposed to be haunted? Anybody locally?'

'A woman we talked to said it wouldn't be a surprise. Said it hadn't been a happy house.'

'Who was that?'

'Has a smallholding, edge of the hamlet. Sells free-range eggs and honey and herbs. Mrs Mornington ... Morningside. Something like that.'

'And the reason you won't go back now is purely ...'

'See it from my position, if you can,' Felix said.

Fuchsia came down the caravan steps then, wearing what looked like a bridesmaid dress with a bodice of white lace. The colours in her hair were like streaks of oil rainbowed in dark water.

Merrily felt a flicker of unease and glanced at Felix, but he was gazing across at Monkland church with its halo of gilded mist.

Pity this wasn't the church they were using. She had no history here.

Felix turned and saw Fuchsia and swallowed.

'Looks so much like her now it scares me a bit.'

'Her mother.'

'Aye.'

5

Who is This?

THE LAST TIME Merrily had been inside the Church of St Cosmas and St Damien, somebody had sacrificed a crow on one of the altars.

These things happened, just occasionally, after a church had been decommissioned by the C of E, left to fade into film-set Gothic.

Lifting cloak and cassock to climb into Felix's silver truck outside the caravan, she was remembering the crow's entrails arranged like intricate jewellery on the right-hand altar. It was a church with two of everything – twin chancels, twin naves – with a pulpit in the middle. *They might see this as representing a dualism*, Huw Owen, her spiritual director, had said at the time. *Left and right, darkness and light.*

This was in the very early days in Deliverance, and she'd blown it, been unable to handle the necessary cleansing of the church. Emotionally exposed at the time, her senses still snagged on memories of a fairly sickening job in the old General Hospital. Feeling clammy, palms itching, and then the explosion of coughing … and Huw, super-vising, ordering her out.

This was when she'd been advised to burn the vestments she'd been wearing, and she'd done that, in an incinerator behind the vicarage. Burned everything, except for …

Oh God.

… This cloak, the same heavy, woollen, cowled cape that she'd worn here on the night of her humiliation. Because it hadn't been at the General Hospital, it had seemed OK not to burn it. After all, they weren't cheap, these cloaks, the female clergy still a minority market.

But – never dismiss coincidence – it was better not to take it in. She began to unlace the cloak as the truck bounced down an eroded lane where torn shards of tarmac were crumbling like piecrust into the verges and Fuchsia's voice came cawing from the back seat.

'Are you High Church, then, Merrily? Anglo-Catholic?'

'Oh, well, I've never been one for labels, Fuchsia. You adapt … compromise where you can.'

Mix-'n'-match. Pick your own. Anything works now, in the new, flexible C of E.

'Do you have a statue of Our Lady in your church, Merrily?'

'No. But I've thought about it.'

'We have two in the caravan, now,' Felix said bitterly. 'One's above the bed. Makes you feel a bit queasy when you look up and the moonlight's full on it.'

'I also like to go to the cathedral in Hereford,' Fuchsia said. 'When it's fairly quiet.'

Merrily turned to look at Fuchsia, rocking in the narrow rear seat, her hair centre-parted, one hand holding a cream woollen shawl together at her neck, the other steadying the canvas zip-bag on her knees – the Deliverance bag. She'd asked if she could carry it.

'When it's quiet, Merrily. When there's nobody to say I don't *belong.*'

'Why would you think you don't belong?' Merrily said. 'Nobody has to sign anything.'

'I'm neither one place nor the other. That's how I feel.'

'I see.'

Everything had turned around. This was no longer just about an empty house with a presence. Now there was a human dimension, complicating matters in a way the Duchy of Cornwall wouldn't have anticipated.

… There are a few advisers I can call on, if necessary. But that's usually when there are people involved who might have problems – psychological … psychiatric?

Like an apparently intelligent woman with the manner of a small child – repeatedly clutching your name like a mother's hand in a bewildering department store.

'I've thought of joining the Catholic Church, Merrily, but they haven't got the old churches any more, and I like the old churches.

Especially St Cosmas and St Damien. It's open all the time. I can go in at night … at dawn, whenever.'

'And what do you do there?'

'Just sit there. It's a place of healing.'

'How long have you felt you needed healing?'

'Oh, it's not for me. It's for my mother.'

'You … won't remember your mother.'

'Oh yes.'

'But you were only a baby, when she …'

'I'm sure I do remember her. Part of her's in me, isn't it?'

'Have you … ever tried to find her? Maybe the internet?'

'I did once. There was another Mary Linden. It just got confusing.'

'Would you like me to … include your mother in the prayers?'

'It's too late, Merrily.'

'What makes you think that?'

'I just want you to make my aura strong, please,' Fuchsia said.

The mist was low and white among the pines around the little sandstone church. There might have been a proper village here once but it barely qualified as a hamlet now. A couple of dwellings sat fairly close, one of them a farm.

The church of St Cosmas and St Damien had a squat body and a timbered bell-tower, and its churchyard was raised like a cake stand. Supported by the Churches Restoration Trust, it apparently held just one service a year.

Felix left the truck at the side of the track and locked it. With the sun muffled like a coin in a handkerchief, Merrily, uncloaked and chilly, opened the gate into the churchyard.

'Perhaps we should tell someone we're here.'

'Nobody ever disturbs me.' Fuchsia handed her the bag. 'They probably take one look at me and think I'm a mad person.'

Shouldering the bag strap, Merrily saw Felix wince.

'Look,' he said quickly. 'I'll stay outside, yeah? Explain to anybody who shows up.'

'You sure?'

His look confirmed it. Merrily nodded, and Fuchsia drifted ahead of her, like a ghost in the mist, around the church to the arcaded wooden porch.

Is this safe? After several recent cases of exorcism turning up the jets under something combustible, you were forced to ask.

But this wasn't an exorcism; Fuchsia knew enough not to be asking for it. She'd wanted a blessing which was exactly what Merrily, under the circumstances, would have been offering, so no problem. Really, no—

'Fuchsia, before we go in …'

Fuchsia stopped just inside the porch, the mist hanging in shining strings from the Gothic points of its deep and glassless windows. Merrily caught her up.

'I want to get this right. Is it your feeling you might have brought something with you, out of the house at Garway?'

Fuchsia stood for a while, moistening her lips with her tongue.

'Something found me.'

'Something which … knew you already, do you think?'

Fuchsia said nothing. Her eyes gave nothing away.

Merrily said, 'When you talked about evil and also a feeling of death …'

The owl eyes didn't blink or flicker, the skin around them softly lucent.

'And about something moving … under the dust-sheets?'

'You mean, was I talking about something subliminal?' Fuchsia said. 'Something under the surface of my own mind? Are you asking if I'm mentally ill, Merrily?'

Merrily found a smile from somewhere.

'No,' she said. 'I'm not asking that. Let's go in.'

She remembered its intimacy, emphasised by the central pulpit, the two chancels like cattle pens. She remembered the harmonium and the discreet domestic medieval tomb of John and Agnes de la Bere, praying effigies modestly separated by John's shield.

Found herself picturing stone images of herself and Lol with his Boswell guitar between them.

'Candles.' Fuchsia held up a brown paper bag she'd found inside the pulpit. 'They're still here.'

'Yours?'

'Three left. And a stub. Sometimes I light them on one of the altars.'

'You have a preference?'

'The left-hand one. Because it's furthest from the door.'

'All right. Shall we make it just the one candle?'

'Oh – I haven't brought matches.'

'I've got a lighter.'

They didn't use the candlesticks provided, instead placing the candle stub in a tin tray, and Merrily lit it, praying within herself for assistance. They sat side by side, facing the altar from benches just inside the rood screen, Fuchsia in white, Merrily black-cassocked. It was less cold than she'd expected.

'You OK, Fuchsia?'

'Yeah.'

'You know what I'm asking?'

'There's nothing here now. There never is, in here. It's a holy site. A healing place.'

Merrily nodded, stood up.

'Shall I kneel down, Merrily? Before the altar?'

'OK.'

It didn't take long. Hands-on, very gentle.

'Father, I ask you now to cleanse and make new all things within the heart and soul of Fuchsia. To restore her to new life and a new relationship with you. To ... make her welcome.'

The lids were down over the owl-eyes. Wings of white light opening up in the window over the altar.

There was a small rustling from behind them, in the left-hand nave. Churches were full of small sounds. Merrily didn't look towards it, but was suddenly thinking of dust sheets wriggling and rippling like something malevolent under the skin, and it—

It needed more. Something – a vibration in the solar-plexus – telling her that.

She left Fuchsia kneeling there, the white dress tucked under her knees, the shawl hanging loose over her shoulders, keeping her in view as she moved quickly back to the bench and her bag, feeling for the smoothness of glass and bringing out the most Roman Catholic item in there.

The oil. Olive oil, extra-virgin, blessed by the Bishop, in a brown screw-top vial.

Fuchsia's forehead shone. Merrily bent and, with a forefinger, inscribed on it a cross, in oil.

'And if you could open your hands ...'

On the left palm, another cross.

'Oil of wholeness and healing ...'

And then the right, Fuchsia drawing a slow breath, eyelids fluttering.

'Watch over her, in the name of all the angels and saints in heaven. Keep guard over her soul day and night.'

All very solemn and slightly surreal. Merrily shivering slightly as Fuchsia's eyes opened and she was looking back through the chancel screen towards the harmonium and the doorway.

'Who is this?' Fuchsia whispered. 'Who is this who's coming?'

And laughed as lightly as her harsh child's voice could manage.

6

Stonewall

THE LOOK ON Sophie's face was beyond outrage, bordering on disbelief. Down in Broad Street, air brakes gasped.

Bishops came and bishops went, Hereford Cathedral remained.

And Sophie.

She sank down at her desk, almost fading into it like a ghost. Merrily shut the window of the gatehouse office, usually a refuge under the cathedral's calming façade, where the Bishop's lay secretary applied cold cream for the soul.

Today, the air up here was tainted with dismay, Sophie's snowy hair disarranged. Merrily had phoned her before leaving for Monkland, outlining the brief, and this was when Sophie had gone over to the Bishop's Palace to elicit some hard facts from Bernie Dunmore. And been unaccountably, shockingly, stonewalled.

Merrily sat down opposite her, with her back to the window.

'That doesn't happen, Sophie.'

'It certainly never has before. I actually thought at one stage that he wasn't going to tell me about *any* of it.'

All the time Merrily had been telling her about Fuchsia and Felix, Sophie had been rearranging the correspondence on her desk, lifting up the pile and stacking it like a pack of cards that she was about to shuffle. Finding things to do with her hands as if she was trying to stop them shaking.

Autumn at last: twinset time, but no real need for that extra scarf. The idea of Sophie feeling the cold was disturbing to Merrily; she stood up again as the kettle came to the boil.

'I'll make it.'

'I should perhaps take one sugar,' Sophie said calmly.

'Jesus.' Merrily pulled down the teapot and mugs. 'So … all in all, there's probably more to this than either of us knows.'

'You know rather more than I do.'

'Until last night, I didn't even know how heavily the Duchy was into the county.'

'I've made a point of finding out.' Sophie put on her chained glasses to consult a computer printout. 'The serious involvement with Herefordshire happened fairly rapidly. According to the Duchy of Cornwall's website, major investment here began with scattered segments of the once-vast estate, around Hereford and Ross, owned in the seventeenth century by Thomas Guy. Of Guy's Hospital fame.'

'I should know about this, shouldn't I?'

'Held more recently, of course, by the footwear magnate Sir Charlie Clore. And then, after his death, by Prudential Assurance, who sold it to the Duchy in, I think, 2000. This probably means there's now more Duchy investment in this county than anywhere outside of Cornwall itself.'

'Royal Herefordshire?'

'The showpiece being the very impressive Harewood Park. Which, of course, one can't miss because it's right next to the A49.'

'Why here? I mean, why Herefordshire?'

'Beautiful. Unspoiled. Perhaps the Prince wants to help keep it that way. He's famously keen on Green issues. Seems likely to ensure that the land will be treated sympathetically, with an eye to heritage, conservation and organic farming.'

'Hmm.'

'Nothing *overtly* sinister, Merrily. Nothing for, say, Jane to rail against. Which is why I can't understand—'

Sophie, cathedral person, confirmed royalist, closed her lips and turned her head, ostensibly fixing a clip in her hair.

'Nothing about Garway on the Duchy website.'

'Nothing.'

'Do you *know* Garway, Sophie?'

'Haven't been over there for many years. Not since our hiking days.'

38

'Hiking days?' Merrily blinked. 'Bobcap ... knapsack ... flask of soup. *You?*'

'I'm not in the mood, Merrily.'

Merrily sighed. 'Maybe you could tell me what you remember?'

'I remember the church. Small and rather strange.'

'Built by the mysterious Knights Templar.'

'In fact, one of the best-preserved examples of Templar architecture in the country. Especially since the London church was badly damaged in the Blitz. And there's a medieval columbarium nearby, said to be absolutely the finest of its kind anywhere.'

'Columb—?'

'Dovecote. The Templars kept doves and pigeons as a food supply. The whole area had, I suppose, a sense of isolation – self-isolation, in a way – that I wouldn't imagine has gone away. Not an area, I should have thought, that anyone visits without a particular reason. I printed out some general background material for you, Merrily. After the Bishop dropped what crumbs of information he deemed it necessary for *me* to have.'

OK, time to deal with this. Sophie hadn't seemed so screwed-up since Siân Callaghan-Clarke's attempt to turn Deliverance into a branch of social services. Merrily dumped two tea bags into the pot and brought the kettle back to the boil.

'What exactly *did* he say when you first mentioned it?'

'It's not so much a question of what he did or didn't say said as of what he did next. Which was to telephone Canterbury.' Sophie scowled. 'On his private line.'

'How do you know he did that?'

'About twenty minutes later, someone returned his call on *this* line.'

'Who?'

'Suffice to say, the voice was instantly recognizable.'

'Not—? *Aaah!*' Pouring boiling water into the pot, Merrily had scorched the back of a hand in the steam. '*Shit.* Sorry.' What was the *matter* with her?

'Some issue of Church politics here,' Sophie said. 'Obviously.'

'It isn't obvious to me.' Merrily held her reddening hand under the cold-water tap. 'All I can see is a conflict of loyalty over a woman who could well be emotionally disturbed.'

'You think the girl's delusional?'

'Don't know enough to say one way or the other. She has a complicated history. Seems to be looking for a kind of stability she's never had. Likes old churches and ceremony. You might've seen her in the cathedral. Big eyes. Doesn't smile.'

'And what were you able to do to help her?'

'Protective blessing. In church. With oil, which seemed appropriate.'

'You don't look entirely convinced.'

Who is this who's coming? Outside, she hadn't even remembered saying it. Merrily dried her hand on the towel.

'I'll keep an eye on her. Meanwhile, check out the house at Garway. Actually, I've got some stuff here ...'

She came back to the desk and brought out the folder that Adam Eastgate had given her, with the plans and a photo of what looked like a traditional Welsh longhouse, stone-built, one end extending into the barn or cowshed.

'We haven't had any reports about this house before, have we, Sophie? Nothing on the database? Even peripheral?'

'Nothing. I checked the files and correspondence going back to Canon Dobbs's time and earlier. You haven't been there yet?'

Merrily shook her head. She'd driven directly over to Hereford after picking up the Volvo in Monkland. Sophie brought out more printout.

'I looked up the Master House on the Listed Buildings database. It's given as fourteenth century, but they usually play safe so it could be earlier.'

'If it dates back to the Templar occupancy of Garway, which is what Felix Barlow reckons, that would be thirteenth century ... maybe very early fourteenth. I think the order was scrapped around then, wasn't it?'

'The order was officially – and rather brutally – dissolved in 1307. In France, anyway. This was less than two centuries after it was formed. The Templars would have survived a little longer in Britain, but not in any organized way.'

'And *would* they have been connected, in any way, with the Master House, given that head Templars were called Masters?'

'Possibly. In peacetime, they seem to have behaved like any other monastic community – farming the land, employing local people. As the house is still part of a farm, I phoned an acquaintance in the local NFU office. It seems to have belonged for *quite* some time – many generations – to the Gwilym family, whose land straddles the Welsh border.'

'Not heard of them. Should I have?'

'Very long-established. And rather affluent now, with business interests here in the city. They seem to have had financial difficulties in the early 1900s and had to sell the Master House, with a large package of land, to a family called Newton, who settled there for about fifty years. Finally moving out of the house itself in – we think – the late 1960s.'

'Why did *they* move out?'

'Nothing of interest to you. Upkeep, heating costs. They had no historical attachment to the Master House. Bought another farm nearby, with a more modern house. The Master House was later rented out to various people at various times. A riding stables, a commune of self-sufficiency fanatics in the 1970s.'

'And it's these Newtons who sold it to the Duchy?'

'The Grays now. An eldest daughter married into a family called Gray. They seem to have sold it to the Duchy with about ninety acres. Feeling the pinch, I gather. Had a very bad time during the Foot and Mouth in 2001, rather losing heart. When are you going?'

'Not decided yet. Possibly tomorrow. I'd hoped to persuade Felix and Fuchsia to come with me – doesn't make a lot of sense going alone. I can do a house-blessing and prayers, but who's going to say if it's achieved anything, with nobody living or working there to report back?'

'So you're going tomorrow, to stay for a few days.'

'I'm going for half a day, have a look around, talk to a few people locally and then come back to think about it.'

'The Bishop was insistent,' Sophie said, 'that you should have as much time as it takes to get to the bottom of this. I was asked to ring the Reverend Murray in Garway and reserve you a room at the guest house his wife runs. And, no, I don't understand it either.'

'Can't you stall him? Frankly …' Merrily poured tea '… it's hard to imagine Bernie Dunmore being so far – excuse me – up the Duchy's bum. Maybe I should talk to him.'

'He's in London, I'm afraid, until Tuesday. House of Lords.'

'Would be, wouldn't he? Still gives us three days. If you can copy some of this stuff, we'll present him with a full and careful report which he can safely dangle in front of the Duchy, the Prince of Wales, the Archbishop of— Are you *sure* he was talking to Canterbury about this?'

'I'm his confidential secretary, Merrily. Supposed to be.'

'So what are your personal feelings?'

Sophie was looking down at her desk. Sophie Hill, who *worked for the cathedral.* There was a pause in the traffic on Broad Street.

'Mmm.' Merrily nodded. 'You're probably right. The Church has always relied on the silence of its employees. No disruptive questions asked. Knowing your place. As you say.'

Sophie looked up, letting her chained glasses fall to her chest. Merrily avoided her gaze.

'I think,' Sophie said very quietly, 'that a lot would depend on whether the Prince of Wales knows about this.'

'Oh?'

'He has, after all, been known to express an interest in such matters.'

'Such matters?'

'You know.'

'Well, he's talked publicly about spiritual healing, organic farming, relationships with the land … and plants. If that's what you mean.'

'I think you'll find that it goes deeper,' Sophie said.

Merrily stood up, walked across to the door, opened it and looked down the stone steps.

'I don't think they've got around to bugging us yet, Sophie. We're quite alone.' She closed the door, came back and sat down. 'What?'

7

The Naked Cross

THE STEEPLES OF the two city-centre churches, St Peter's and All Saints, were far more visible in Hereford than the tower of the cathedral, which was in a corner, backed up against the river, not central.

It didn't hide, exactly, it just didn't show off.

It didn't have secrets, *as such,* just didn't go out of its way ...

Like Sophie.

'This relates to your late predecessor,' Sophie said.

'Dobbs?'

You could see him standing silently in the corner, face like an eroded cliff face. The man who had refused to be called a Deliverance minister. Who, until his last collapse, in the cathedral itself, had been the *Hereford Diocesan Exorcist.* Canon Thomas Dobbs, who wouldn't even open his front door to Merrily but had left a message for her in its letter box, succinctly conveying his thoughts on being replaced by a woman.

The first exorcist was Jesus Christ.

Interesting how rapidly the situation had changed since then. First Merrily, then Siân Callaghan-Clarke, canon of this cathedral, getting herself appointed Deliverance Coordinator, with plans to subtly secularise the service. Hadn't worked, and now Siân's ambitions were, allegedly, focused on the impending vacancy for Archdeacon.

'Sorting through Canon Dobbs's files after his death,' Sophie said, 'I came across a box file of press cuttings – I didn't bother you with any of this at the time; it seemed hardly relevant and you had enough problems. But he'd accumulated a substantial collection of newspaper and magazine articles about the Prince of Wales.'

'*Dobbs?*' Merrily rocked back in her chair. 'Dobbs collected stories about Prince Charles?'

'I don't mean photo spreads from *Hello*. These all have specific references to the Prince's spiritual life. For some reason, I filed them away in a storeroom in the cloisters.'

'Why would Dobbs be especially interested in Charles? I mean, this was presumably before the Duchy got into Herefordshire?'

'Certainly before they bought the Guy's Estate from the Prudential.'

'Is there any possibility that Dobbs knew him personally?'

'I don't know. I have no reason to think he did. I mean, he *may* have ... I really don't know, Merrily, it just brought it back to me, with all this ...'

'Could I have a look at the cuttings?'

'I've brought them up. You can take them with you when you leave.'

That night, Merrily called Huw Owen, who took it all unexpectedly seriously. Listen, he said, you must never trust the buggers. Never. Any of them. Not at this level.

Covering the phone, Merrily reached out a foot and prodded the scullery door shut. Jane, in a black mood, had Joanna Newsom on the stereo in the sitting room: California Gothic, cracked and witchy. Merrily lowered her voice.

'Who are we talking about – the Duchy of Cornwall or the royals generally?'

'It's not so much the royals, lass, as the C of E. The Church and the Monarchy have been an item for nearly half a millennium. But change comes fast these days. Some of our masters, as you know, have become a bit wary about a certain individual.'

'Let's not walk all round this. Charles.'

'Most of it dating back to his famous remark about the Monarchy – when *he* takes over – becoming Defender of the Faiths, *plural*. Muslims, Hindus ... *Catholics?* My God. Is this a safe pair of hands for the sacred chalice? It's backs to the cathedral walls, lass. Knives unsheathed in the deepest cloisters.'

'I've always liked the way you underplay a drama, Huw.'

Trying to psych out if there was even a hint of a smile on his cratered face as he sat by the racing flames in the inglenook of his eyrie in the Brecon Beacons. Smuggled out of his native Wales by his mother as a small child and brought up in Yorkshire, Huw was back in the land of his unknown father, supervising Deliverance courses for C of E clergy in a former Nonconformist chapel burned out by decades of hellfire preaching – the place where it had begun for Merrily, this weird ministry, not quite as long ago as it sometimes seemed.

'All right, maybe I'm exaggerating,' Huw said. 'I'm just warning you to watch your back. Where the royals are concerned – the royals and Canterbury – the smallest rumour can cause a seismic shift, and little folks like you can get dropped down the nearest crevice.'

'Thanks, Huw. I'll sleep so much easier tonight.'

'I'm just telling you.'

'So …' Merrily shifted the heavy bakelite phone from one ear to the other. 'Having established that nobody in ermine or a dog collar is to be trusted, what's your considered opinion of why Canterbury would need to be kept informed about a house owned by the Duchy of Cornwall that's alleged to be haunted?'

'Well, they wouldn't, would they?'

'Would they tell the Prince, or would they try to keep it from him in case he became too curious?'

'I think if he *is* curious, he's probably experienced enough now to keep it to himself. Happen what's more important – like your feller at the Duchy said – is that the press don't get wind of it. They'd hound the builder and then they'd hound you.'

'Mmm.'

'You ask me, this is just Bernie Dunmore covering his own back. Thinking how it might rebound on the Diocese if it all went pear-shaped.'

And it did go pear-shaped sometimes, no denying that. An inexact science, deliverance. Well, not a science at all, obviously …

'Everybody lives in fear nowadays,' Huw said. 'Way things are going, deliverance itself could be C of E history in a year or two.'

'And what would *you* do, Huw, if we all got the elbow?'

'I'd retire, lass. Take the pension, rent a little shack at the rough end of Sennybridge, with a back yard and a bog, and carry on with the job. No bureaucracy, no politics, no farcical PC synods. Just me and the naked cross.'

'Talking of which … Canon Dobbs.'

'Old bugger's dead.'

'Sophie's given me a collection of news cuttings he kept about the Prince of Wales and the Church and other connections. Why would Dobbs keep a royal scrapbook?'

'Traditionalist of the first order, Dobbs. Happen *he*'d started to notice the lad spreading his favours. I wouldn't worry about it. Concentrate on covering your own arse.'

'And your specific advice, as my spiritual director, would be …?'

'Keep all your cards on the table, face up.'

Merrily shook out a Silk Cut.

'Explain?'

'Stage one: find the former owners of this hovel and see what kind of *recent* history it's got. Forget the White Lady and the Phantom Stagecoach. The home movies you can do without.'

Home movies: Huw's latest euphemism for place-memories and trapped events that repeated themselves.

'And then … if it's just what the girl claims she saw and there's nowt blindingly obvious from the last few years, Stage Two would be to set up a low-key house-blessing for a specific date. Being careful, mind, to invite the local incumbent.'

'There isn't one. A retired guy's holding the fort.'

'He'll do. Also, you want at least one member of the family – the folks who flogged the place off to the Duchy, plus, if possible, someone from the family as owned it before. For many generations, you said?'

'So I'm told.'

'That would help, then. And finally – this is important – you must formally request the presence of an official of the Duchy of Cornwall. The higher up the better.'

'Wow.' Merrily sat back, lit her cigarette. 'Smart.'

'That way, you've acquitted yourself in full view, and they're all involved – all implicated.'

'Flawless.'

It wouldn't be, of course. It was never that easy.

'And what do you do after that?' Huw said.

'I don't know. What do I do after that, boss?'

'You bugger off out of it just as fast as your cute little legs will carry you.'

'What about the woman? Fuchsia. Aftercare?'

'Oh, aye.'

There was a lengthy, meditative silence. She imagined him staring down at his peeling slippers, their rubber soles smoking on the edge of the hearth.

'You do need to separate it,' he said eventually. 'If there's nowt particularly to support it at the house, you most likely *are* looking at a different problem. You said she was orphaned?'

'Abandoned. She's certainly had personal problems. Maybe the house brought something to a head?'

'Possible. How was the blessing?'

'Curious. There wasn't the normal sense of relief afterwards. In fact, she looked up, as if something might have followed us into the church. Said something like, *is something coming?* Something like that. And laughed. I mean, it's always a problem, isn't it? You can never be quite sure when somebody's winding you up.'

'Happen include her in your prayers when you do the cleansing. Something moving around under the carpet, was that what you said?'

'Dust sheets. I suppose a shrink would be talking about demons in her past that she's covered up. Perhaps she just has a Gothic imagination: the wriggling under the sheets, the face of crumpled linen. She's also obviously read a fair amount about healing and deliverance, because she knew exactly what she—'

'Hang on … Gimme that again, lass.'

'What?'

'Crumpled linen. A *face* of crumpled linen?'

'That's the image Fuchsia claims she saw when she turned around from the wall she was plastering. Poetic, in its macabre way. Although this would've been crumpled plastic.'

'Aye. Very literary,' Huw said. 'But, then, not surprising, really. It's a quote.'

'What?'

'M. R. James. Author of classic ghost stories in the 1900s?'

'Yeah, I know who M. R. James is.'

'I can even tell you which story it comes from. "Whistle".'

'What are you—?'

'"Oh, Whistle and I'll Come to You, My Lad" is the one about the university professor haunted by a malevolent entity which … I'd get hold of a copy if I were you, without too much delay.'

'You're saying …'

There'd been a book of James's stories amongst Fuchsia's collection in the caravan. Orange-coloured spine on the shelf by the wood stove. *Ghost Stories of an Antiquary.*

'All right, lass?'

'Let me get this totally right. You're telling me it's an actual phrase taken from one of M. R. James's ghost stories?'

Merrily dropped her cigarette in the ashtray and flopped forward, both hands around the old black phone.

Oh, bugger.

'*Bit* of a coincidence, eh? If you have any problems finding the story, give us a call and I'll scan a few pages and email them across.'

'Yes. Thank you, Huw.'

Shit.

Merrily tipped the phone very gently into its rest. Gazing at her reflection in the dark mirror of the scullery window and into a too-familiar void.

8

Heresy

This job …

People learned what you did, and envisaged desecrated graves, chalices of blood, night-long spiritual struggles with an indelibly black metaphysical evil, his satanic majesty, The Beast 666.

Their disappointment, almost invariably, was palpable.

So you've never really had to rescue anyone from actual demonic possession?

To which you'd shrug and smile awkwardly and admit that, rather than the coils of the Old Serpent, it mostly came down to the spirals of the subconscious mind.

This was the void – the thought that there might, in the end, be nothing there that psychology would not be equipped to explain. That people like Siân Callaghan-Clarke might just be right about the relevance of what you were doing.

The dark night of no-soul. What, in the end, you feared most, and a dampener on the spirit, as Merrily drove down into the Unknown Border, using a route she'd never travelled before: sunken lanes below the bare, abraded hillsides, wind-whipped, twisted trees.

Still England. It had to be; there, below the road, was the River Monnow, which *was* the border, failing to be crossed by a smashed and collapsing footbridge, fenced off, with a sign that said: *Danger*.

But if this wasn't Wales, neither was it truly Herefordshire, not with names like *Bagwllydiart* on the signposts. Rural Wales – almost all of it, now – was designated tourist country, while Herefordshire's own tourist country was Ledwardine and its neighbouring black and white villages in the north of the county and the lushness of the Wye Valley in the south.

The Unknown Border was only about an hour from Ledwardine and, sooner or later, it would be joining the New Cotswolds.

Not for a while, though.

And it certainly had never been, nor ever would be, East Anglia.

Jane had them all, natch. *The Penguin Complete Ghost Stories of M. R. James (1862-1936)*.

Sitting up in bed last night, under the blackened oak beams, with her dressing gown around her shoulders and the tawny owls fluting in the churchyard, Merrily had read 'Oh, Whistle, and I'll Come to You, My Lad', first published in 1904.

She couldn't possibly have read it before or even seen it on TV, because it really wasn't something that would ever allow itself to be forgotten, this story of Parkins, an academic on a golfing holiday on the Suffolk coast, and what he discovers there, and what discovers him.

Oh Parkins, says a colleague before he leaves, *if you are going to Burnstow, I wish you would look at the site of the Templars' preceptory and let me know if you think it would be any good to have a dig there in the summer.*

Templar preceptory. The only immediate connection with the village of Garway. *Preceptory:* the Templars' term for one of their communities, a description apparently unique to this curious order of medieval warrior monks.

But Burnstow, according to the author's own foreword, was based on a seaside town the whole width of England away.

Merrily had followed Parkins into the Globe Inn, where the only room available had two beds. Sure to be significant. As for the Templars' preceptory, all Parkins had found there was a series of unpromising humps and mounds ... Oh, and – in a cavity near the possible site of an altar – an old whistle.

On one side of the whistle it said:

QUIS EST ISTE QUI VENIT

Who is this who is coming?

*

If you weren't aware of Garway Hill, it meant that you were either on or immediately below it. She couldn't see a radio mast, only a row of houses like battered ornaments on a shelf, overlooking – a couple of fields away on the right – the Church of St Michael.

Welcome to GARWAY. Please drive carefully.

Like you had a choice in lanes like these.

Sanded by the low October sun, the church was aloof, in its own shallow valley. Saturday afternoon, nobody about. The folder containing the directions and the key of The Master House lay on the old Volvo's passenger seat. The house was supposed to be within sight of the church tower, but only just. *You should look for two white gateposts, one broken in half.*

Later, maybe.

If at all. Thanks to Huw Owen and M. R. James, the case was as good as closed. Fuchsia was making it up. Delusion was another possibility, but probably less likely, now.

A right turning brought Merrily to the entrance of the churchyard. No concessions here to the advent of the motor vehicle. Parking tight into the hedge, she climbed out through the passenger door, walking up, in jeans and a Gomer Parry Plant Hire sweatshirt, into a curving and shaded path leading to a mellow enclosure. A haze of greens and ambers, an awning of birdsong.

If you wanted to know about a place, always check out the church first. Feel its disposition: benevolence or disapproval or, more often nowadays, a mildewed resignation.

This one, she thought, was ... aware of her.

She walked up into the bumpy churchyard, under the tower: plain stone, simple pyramidal hat. And yet ...

Its origins are almost certainly Celtic. The earliest record of a monastery on the site is in the seventh century. Sophie's notes, from the internet. *But it is not until the arrival of the Knights Templar in 1180 that the history of Garway Church opens out ... and, at the same time, closes in.*

You could, apparently, still see the foundations of the original circular nave which the Templars had created in imitation of the Church of the Holy Sepulchre in Jerusalem – the extent of Merrily's knowledge of Templar architecture. She took a step back, looking up. The tower was square and unadorned, stonework like oatmeal biscuit, the lower half darker as if it had been dunked in tea. Two vertical slits near the top on each of the four sides were disconcertingly like all-round eyes. Watchful and mildly amused.

'I suppose, seen from above, it does look rather as though its neck has been broken. Like a chicken's.'

Merrily half-turned. He was standing alongside her, in walking boots and fishing hat, a two-tone nylon hiking jacket over his faded blue shirt and clerical collar.

'You see, the tower originally was entirely separate from the body of the church, which is why it's set at such an angle. The gap was bridged at a later date, as you can see. The arrangement would have looked less odd, one imagines, in the days when the nave was circular. I'm so sorry ...' He bowed his head. 'Didn't mean to sneak up. It *is* Mrs Merrily Watkins, I hope. Walking home from the pub when I saw the car, and you did look rather purposeful behind the wheel.'

'Mr Murray.'

'Teddy.' He bent down to her, putting out a hand. 'So glad. I realize this must be a terrible bind for you, but ... heavens, the *gossip* this sort of thing engenders. Usually among people who enter a church no more than twice in their lifetimes, carried in and out both times. Not really what one looks for in retirement.'

'No, I suppose not.'

Actually, the Reverend Murray didn't look old enough, or unfit enough, to be retired. Handshake firm, eyes vividly blue, and skin tanned to the colour of Garway's lower tower around the stiff white beard and the high bland dome of his forehead.

'Never been a particularly pastoral sort of chap, Merrily. When the girl turned up here asking for protection ... sanctuary ... I confess I was completely thrown.'

'You mean ... Fuchsia?'

'Fuchsia. Indeed, yes.'

'She came here to the church? To ask for sanctuary?'

Merrily remembered now. *The bloke at Garway, he was no help at all.*

'Sanctuary is perhaps too emotive a word. The builder chap was waiting in the entrance in his truck. The girl was rather vague, disoriented. I thought she was … Anyway, I brought her in and said a short prayer. You know the routine.'

'What *did* you think she was?'

'Beg pardon?'

'You said when you first saw her you thought she was …'

'Ah.' Murray straightened up, hands behind his back, looking up at the tower. '*I* thought – I'm *afraid* – that she was probably on drugs. A small percentage of the visitors here do tend to be what we used to call potheads. Found a chap the other week completely out of it, lying with his head under the holy spring. Harmless enough, I suppose, but not what one expects to see in a country churchyard.'

'Where's the holy spring?'

'My, we are getting down to business, aren't we? I'll show you, if you like. I can show you everything.' Teddy Murray extended an arm to steer Merrily towards the church entrance. 'It appears to be my principal role in this community: guide and interpreter. Much more my sort of thing – I have to say, with no little shame – than dispensing spiritual succour. Historian by inclination, I'm afraid. And the walks.'

'The walks?'

'For the guests. My wife's guest house tends to cater for people who like to tramp the hills in all weathers. I compile the handy route-maps. And I'm available to go along and point things out, when required. This …' The Rev. Murray turned and flung out an arm towards the guardian hills '… is God's own weekend retreat. I always say that. In fact it's in Beverley's brochure. *God's Own Weekend Retreat.*'

'Very, erm …'

'Presumptuous, I suppose. But there had to be some reason for the Templars to favour it, remote spot like this. Was it divine guidance? Sorry!' He put up his hands. 'One gets carried away. Do you *want* to know all this? I only ask because, as someone's bound to tell you, the Master House does seem to be contemporaneous with the Templars' occupation of Garway – although, despite the title, it does *not* appear to have been the home of the preceptor, or master.'

'So you didn't go back to the Master House? With Fuchsia?'

'Well … no.' Murray looked bewildered. 'She didn't ask me to. Hardly my property to intrude upon. Anyway, my impression was that you couldn't have dragged her back and, in the absence of a full-time minister here, I wasn't sure who it would be best to inform. And then events overtook me, and so— Paul. How are you?'

A man in jeans and a heavy work-shirt had come out of the church, leaning on a stick. There was a motorized wheelchair on the path outside; he stood looking at it with no great love. Teddy Murray took a step forward, and the man raised his stick.

'Bugger off, eh, Teddy?'

'Sorry.'

'Not ready for him yet, boy. Gonner have another bit of a walk round. Come back for the thing.'

Teddy nodded. They watched the man making his way up the path. He couldn't be more than mid-thirties, thick brown hair.

'MS,' Teddy murmured. 'What kind of luck is that for a farmer?' He opened the church door, stood aside for Merrily. 'You been in here before?'

'Never.'

No sooner were they inside than he'd closed the door, blew out a breath.

'Didn't want to introduce you, Merrily. Difficult. That's Paul Gray – he and his wife …' Teddy lowered his voice '… sold the Master House to the Duchy.'

'Oh.'

'Long story. Bad feeling. Not for me to … Still a bit of a newcomer. As, of course, is Paul, which is one of the problems.' He laughed. 'You can be here for three generations and they'll still call you a newcomer. Couple of families go back to the Norman Conquest. So …' Extending an arm. 'What do you think?'

'It's … unusual.'

'More than you know.'

Merrily nodded, taking it in. It was quite small but lofty and airy and filled with rosy light. The chancel was framed by a classic zigzagged and serrated Norman arch, wide and theatrical. Red velvet curtains were drawn across it, as if what lay beyond them was not for the unprepared. Something rare and sacred, Grail-like.

Or perhaps a body in a coffin?

Merrily shook herself. Too much M. R. James.

Teddy Murray nodded towards a banner with a crusader kind of cross, red and gold on white, hanging from the pulpit.

'Still a major presence, then?' Merrily said.

'The Templars? Yes, I suppose they are. Do you know much about them, Merrily?'

'Erm …' She looked up at the dark brown wooden ceiling, curved like the bottom of a boat and decorated with a small and regular galaxy of white stars. In a pocket of her jeans, the mobile phone began to vibrate against her left thigh. 'Maybe not as much as I ought to.'

Merrily placed a hand over the phone, and Teddy Murray leaned back against a pew end, looking down at her with what you could only describe as a beneficent smile, evidently all too ready to do what he was better at than dispensing spiritual succour.

'It's sometimes difficult to separate the truth from the lurid speculation,' she told him. 'Never a problem for my daughter.'

'I suppose,' he said, 'that few of us like to countenance the idea that the Templars guarded the secret of the bloodline of Christ through his supposed marriage to Mary Magdalene.'

'Oh, she's happy enough with that idea. I suppose what bothers *me* most is the idea of the Templars – or someone – guarding the secret resting place of his bones.'

'Let's not talk of heresy.'

'Let's not.'

'None of it, however, makes the Knights Templar less interesting,' Teddy Murray said. 'Follow me, Mrs Watkins.'

9

Funnies

WHEN MERRILY CLIMBED back into the car, the weather had changed; the sky had the deep grey lustre of tinfoil and a single slow raindrop rolled down the windscreen like a cartoon tear, and she just wanted to be home and lighting a fire.

She pulled out her phone. Lol would be on the way to his gig in Newtown, Powys, so it was more likely to be Jane.

It was neither, just a short text.

CALL ME.

MOB PLEASE

FB

A text from Frannie Bliss? If it *was* him, this was a first. Mobile would mean he didn't want to take the call in the CID room. She found his number in the index, but the signal was on the blink, so she reversed out of the church entrance and drove away from the village, uphill, pulling into a passing place, winding up the window against a rising wind.

'Nicely timed, Reverend,' Bliss said. 'You've caught up with me in the gents.'

'I totally refuse to picture the scene.'

'Not good enough, anyway. Too much of an echo. I'll call you back. Just give me a couple of minutes to … finish up in here.'

Echo?

Merrily sat watching the sloping landscape losing its colours in the gathering rain, compiling a mental inventory of all the curios that Teddy Murray had revealed in Garway Church.

*

Beginning with the green man, the familiar stone face with entwined foliage, inexplicably found in churches. This one was in the chancel arch and, with those stubby horns, he wasn't typical. There was also a cord or vine with tassels resembling fingers, so it looked like he was making a funny face at you, waggling his fingers at either side of his head.

What the green man had to do with the Templars Teddy couldn't explain, but this was a Templar church so it must have had some significance.

Everything in a Templar church was significant. They'd moved on to the matching long stones set into the chancel steps, the altar steps and one window ledge – these identified by Teddy as the lids of Templar stone coffins, now part of the fabric of the church. Teddy laughing, in his element now, the historian, the tour guide.

'Someone said you can throw the Templars out of the building, but you'll never get the building back from the Templars.'

Giving her the primary-school version, for which she'd been quite grateful.

The Order of the Poor Knights of Christ and the Temple of Solomon: founded in the early twelfth century, the time of the crusades, ostensibly to protect pilgrims to Jerusalem. The King of Jerusalem, Baldwin II, had allowed them to establish their headquarters at the al-Aqsa mosque, believed to be the site of the original Temple.

They'd begun, it was said, with only nine members, led by one Hugh de Payens. Monastic soldiers, red crosses on their surcoats, growing over the next century into something internationally powerful, influential and *very* wealthy.

Too wealthy and too powerful, by the thirteenth century, for the King of France, Philip IV, and the pet pope he'd acquired, Clement V, accommodated at the time in Avignon. The French Templars had all been arrested in a series of simultaneous dawn raids on Friday, 13 October 1307, accused of a black catalogue of heresies.

'Hang on …' It hadn't taken much calculation. 'Doesn't that mean it's exactly—'

'I'm afraid it does. Seven hundred years ago next Saturday. I was hoping we'd have a permanent minister in place by then, but it was not to be. It therefore falls to me to conduct some sort of memorial service for the poor chaps.'

'You don't sound totally enthused.'

'It is so obvious?'

'And the problem is ... what?'

'Fanatics, Merrily. The known facts about the Templars are relatively few – the amount of wild speculation has been quite monumental in recent years.'

'*The Da Vinci Code*?'

'And its source, *The Holy Blood and the Holy Grail*. All the preposterous theories undermining the central tenets of Christianity as we know it.'

'Mmm.'

Everybody knew about it now: the alleged bloodline of Jesus from his alleged marriage to Mary Magdalene, the female disciple whose crucial role was supposedly written out of the scriptures by the Roman Catholic Church. Jane had been quite taken with the idea that the real reason for the suppression of the Knights Templar had been their guardianship of this secret knowledge ... and the whereabouts of the tomb of Christ, unrisen.

Whether or not you accepted this, Teddy Murray had said, the charges against the Templars were surely made up.

'Like many of those levelled at various abbots by Henry VIII's people during the Reformation. What kings tended to covet most in religious organizations was their money.'

The last Grand Master of the Order, Jacques de Molay, had been burned alive in Paris, but the persecution had been less extreme in Britain, where most Templars had been allowed to join other monastic orders – except, apparently, the order of Hospitallers of St John to which the properties of Garway had been transferred.

De Molay was now seen as a martyr and Friday the Thirteenth ...

'Because of this? That's the reason for the whole superstition and a bunch of slightly distasteful movies?'

'Such is the received wisdom, Merrily. What rather bothers me is that the church promises to be packed. I've had letters from all kinds of organizations wanting to be represented – from Templar re-enactment groups to more ... shall we say more sinister-sounding societies.'

'Like what?'

Teddy had said there seemed to be a number of occult-sounding groups whose rituals were supposed to be based on Templar practices. He said he didn't know much about them. Merrily knew a little more, from Huw Owen's reading list. Supposedly ancient formulae handed down through Renaissance magical orders and then developed by the fashionable fraternities of the nineteenth and early twentieth centuries. Mainly bollocks.

'Lucky the anniversary is going to be a Saturday, then,' Merrily said.

'You think that will change anything? I don't. It's their first opportunity in a century to commemorate the suppression – and a century ago few, if any, of these theories were in the public domain.'

'Why here? There must lots of Templar churches all over the country. In fact—'

'Actually, no,' Teddy said. 'Nothing so perfectly preserved. The London temple, for instance, was wrecked in the Blitz. There's nowhere more authentic. Or more isolated and yet ... get-at-able.'

He'd unlocked the tower, dark and starkly atmospheric with its funeral bier and a magnificent medieval oak chest hewn from a massive log.

'Whose idea was it to have a memorial service?'

'So many people wrote in, we couldn't get out of it, Merrily. So I'm quite anxious that this business with the Master House should be dealt with before then. Do you think that will be possible?'

'Before next weekend?'

'Bad enough when the girl arrived. Wish I hadn't been here.'

Merrily had been forced to say that she'd do her best to get it wrapped. And if Huw was right that might be on the cards. She'd asked Teddy where the Master House came into the picture. One of the Templar farms, he'd said, that was all. They farmed sheep, as did the Hospitallers after them.

As did the locals today. Not much had really changed in Garway,

Merrily was thinking as the mobile chimed to indicate that DI Bliss had left the building.

'Raining hard in the police car park, is it, Frannie?'

'It's not raining at all, and I'm not in the police car-park. I'm off the premises entirely, and if it was known I was calling you I'd probably have a tail.'

'Sorry?'

Merrily was still thinking about the Garway Green Man who, having small, stubby horns, might be expected also to have a tail.

'All right, listen,' Bliss said. 'I may be touching upon something you already know about, but why would the gentlefolk that humble coppers like myself used to call the Funnies suddenly have become interested in you?'

'The Funnies?'

'I'm thinking specifically of a feller in an unmarked room at head-quarters who very occasionally creeps around this division when it's felt that national security might be at stake.'

Merrily rubbed vainly at the condensation on the windscreen. Without the engine running, it kept re-forming under her palm.

'You're talking about the Special Branch?'

'I hope you're on your own using language like that.'

'Frannie, are you actually saying the Special Branch are making inquiries about *me*?'

'I'm saying nothing, Merrily.'

She scrubbed furiously at the windscreen, starting to put it together, and it was ... it was beyond ridiculous.

'What are you doing, exactly?' Bliss said.

'Trying to see out of the bloody—' She sank back in her seat. 'I'm looking into something connected with the Duchy of Cornwall's invest-ments in Herefordshire. Would that explain anything?'

A short silence, except for a car engine somewhere and a clanging that became duller. What sounded like Bliss moving away from some-thing to a place of greater safety.

'That would *possibly* explain it, yes,' he said.

'It's nothing particularly contentious.'

'With respect, Merrily, how would you know?' Bliss paused. 'You want to explain? Being as we're old mates and those smart-arsed cloak-and-dagger twats get right up my nasal passages?'

'Well …' She thought about it, could see no harm. 'All right. The Duchy of Cornwall have paid good money out of the Prince's piggy bank for an old farmhouse which their favourite conservation builder is refusing to work on because his girlfriend says it's haunted.'

'That's it?'

'Sorry to disappoint. Obviously I'd *like* to be able to tell you that the vengeful spirit of Princess Diana's been seen around Highgrove in a—'

'Yeah, yeah.'

'But that's it, Frannie. That's the lot. As far as I know.'

'I see.'

'You don't, though, do you? Where's the threat to national security in that?'

'Maybe there's more to it than you know.'

'I've already been thinking along those very lines. These inquiries about me … is that still going on?'

'I don't know, Merrily. I've been off for a couple of days. I got this from Karen Dowell – now promoted to DS, by the way. They wanted your background, potted biog, any political connections and … Oh, yeh, they wanted to know about little Jane and her widely reported altercation with the Herefordshire Council over the proposed development of Coleman's Meadow.'

'Wha—?'

It was like yobs had strolled up and starting rocking the car.

'Calm down, Merrily, it's not so unusual. And it would've been pointed out by somebody fairly quickly that the kid's a force of nature, as distinct from a rural terrorist.'

'It doesn't matter, it's just—' Merrily sat up, dipping into her bag for the Silk Cut packet. 'The bastards! I mean, you know what else they've done, don't you? Someone's leaned on the Bishop, so that he's actually freed me up to … to devote all my attention to a minor issue which, the way it's shaping up, may not even be Deliverance business.'

'The Bishop's told you this himself?'

'Bishop Dunmore is conveniently away in London until Tuesday.' She lit a cigarette, opened the window to let out the smoke, which blew back in a blast of wind from Garway Hill, wherever *that* was from here. 'Sod this, I'm going home.'

'You're on this now?'

'Mmm.'

'Where?'

'Garway Hill.'

'Be a spectral sheep-shagger, then, would it, Merrily? All right, just remember we haven't spoken and you know nothing of this. If you need to speak to me, call the mobile. Using *your* mobile. As distinct from the vicarage landline.'

'You actually think—?'

'I'm just being careful.'

'Bloody *hell,* Frannie.'

'Stay cool, Merrily.'

Switching off the phone, she felt hunted, exposed, focused-on ... and just tired, brain-dead. *Sod it.* She took two angry drags on the cigarette and then put it out. Pulled her waterproof jacket from the back seat and walked out into the rain.

A lumpy grey mattress of cloud meant that she couldn't see the village or the church tower or anything much apart from the wind-combed coarse grass on the other side of a barbed-wire fence. Supposed to be going back to check out the Master House, but what was the point?

As Merrily was leaving the church, Teddy Murray had said, *We, ah ... we have a room for you, Merrily. I'm not sure what you ...*

I don't know, to be honest, Teddy. I don't live that far away, and I can't really understand why the Bishop feels the need to inflict me on you.

Oh, I think we both know what that's about. They want you to put the lid on something ... firmly. As regards my interpretive role, I suspect Mervyn Neale might have had a hand in it.

The Archdeacon. Been with the Bishop when the issue was raised by Adam Eastgate.

Mervyn and I have known one another for some time. He refers people to us – people looking for an open-air holiday. Not on a percentage basis, I have to add.

Well, she'd said finally, *I have a few things to sort out at home, so maybe I could ring you tomorrow.*

Pleasant enough guy, but Merrily had been glad to get away. His *interpretive* role suggested he'd been appointed by the Archdeacon as her native guide. Useful in some ways, but there was a sense of remote control that she didn't like.

The rain gusted into her face and drummed on the side of her hood. She let it come, shivering, thinking of the wind that had suddenly arisen when Parkins, the academic in the M. R. James story, had blown, experimentally, on the old whistle he'd found in the remains of the Templar preceptory.

Who is this who is coming?

A figure like wind-blown rags pursuing Parkins along the deserted beach. Making its final, most memorable appearance at night in his room at the Globe Inn. Arising under the sheets of the second bed and standing in front of the bedroom door, with its arms outstretched and its *intensely horrible face of crumpled linen.*

Although the dust sheets were plastic, you got the idea.

Merrily turned back towards the old Volvo, with the wind behind her.

10

Signposts

USING THE MOBILE from the scullery – this was insane – she called Sophie at home. Sophie's husband, Andrew, answered, *humphe*d a bit. Andrew, the architect and cathedral widower – they even lived in one of the cloisterish streets behind the close.

'Merrily.' Sophie had picked up an extension, Andrew humphing again and hanging up. 'I was half-expecting you to call this afternoon – the Bishop having suggested, in an email from the Palace this morning, that a preliminary written report might be quite useful.'

'And you thought, odd – he's never previously particularly requested a report of *any* kind on anything relating to deliverance.'

'Correct.'

It was almost dark, the grey-brown sky melding with the churchyard wall outside the scullery window. Still no rain here. Maybe Garway Hill had its own climate.

'Well, Sophie, it might all be academic now, anyway.'

Merrily put on the desk lamp and explained in some detail about Huw Owen's M. R. James revelation. Never any discretion problems here; next to Sophie, the grave was Broadcasting House.

'So the woman made it up?' Ice particles in Sophie's voice. 'The whole thing?'

'Either that or her perceptions have been conditioned by her reading habits, which seems unlikely.'

'Why?'

'I've no idea.'

'Presumably you'll go back and ask her.'

'Oh, yes.'

'That should be revelatory.'

'I'm almost looking forward to it, in a rather unChristian way. I'll try and get over to Monkland tomorrow after the morning worship. With or without a Special Branch tail.'

'I'm sorry, Merrily – I may have misheard.'

'You didn't.' Merrily looked at the cigarettes on the desk, decided against. 'Sources close to Gaol Street intimate I've been checked out by the security services. Jane, too – the heritage terrorist.'

'This is purely because of your unsolicited proximity to the business interests of the heir to the throne?'

'I don't know, Sophie.'

'But you're a minister in the Church of England.'

'That makes me harmless? Think about it.'

'The amount of surveillance in this country is becoming quite terrifying.' A pause. 'Incidentally, have you had a chance to read Canon Dobbs's file on the Prince of Wales?'

'Not really. It's on the desk here. I'll try and have a look later.'

'Well,' Sophie said, 'I realize we live in troubled times, but I think this has gone far enough. Leave it with me.'

'What are you going to do?'

'I think I'm going to call the Bishop in London.'

Sophie was probably the only person, outside his immediate family, with the Bishop's mobile number.

'I'm not sure that would really—'

'Will you be in tonight, Merrily?'

'Yeah, but I don't want to ruin *your* night. Or Andrew's.'

'Merrily,' Sophie said with some severity. 'This is what I *do*.'

Merrily sighed, pulled over the old black box file and opened it up. Unwrapped a wodge of A4 copier paper, held together by two rubber bands, the top page splashing two headlines.

CHARLES IN HEALTH STORM

TOP DOCS SLAM PRINCE OVER SUPPORT FOR 'QUACKS'

Both dated back to the early 1980s when the Prince of Wales, newly married to Diana Spencer, had been appointed President of the British Medical Association, the conservative and seriously cautious organization representing doctors in the UK.

The BMA was not into alternative therapy. In fact, the hatred of the association for practitioners who had not been through the System knew few bounds.

You would have thought these guys might have known better than to appoint, as their figurehead, a man whose famously healthy family had a long history of consulting osteopaths, homeopaths and various spiritual healers.

The first warning came at a dinner for the new President. In his speech, the Prince said how touched he'd been that the BMA should have even considered electing him, adding, *You may, for all I know, wish to get rid of me after six months.*

The laughter, Merrily thought, must have been hollow. She'd thought she remembered the row, but was now realizing that she couldn't have fully absorbed it, nor been knowledgeable enough at the time to recognize its significance.

One of the cuttings had an edited transcript of Charles's speech to the BMA.

It was dynamite, basically.

One of the least attractive traits of various professional bodies is the deeply ingrained suspicion and downright hostility which can exist towards anything unorthodox. I suppose it is inevitable that something which is different should arouse strong feelings on the part of the majority whose conventional wisdom is being challenged.

I suppose, too, that human nature is such that we are frequently prevented from seeing that what is taken for today's unorthodoxy is probably going to be tomorrow's convention …

Perhaps we just have to accept it is God's will that the unorthodox individual is doomed to years of frustration, ridicule and failure in order to act out his role in the scheme of things, until his day arrives and mankind is ready to receive his message … a message which he probably finds hard to explain himself but which he knows comes from a far deeper source than conscious thought ...

Merrily lit a cigarette. Amazing to think he'd actually said that to a bunch of doctors.

It got better – or worse, depending on your angle of approach.

Through the centuries, healing has been practised by folk healers who are guided by traditional wisdom that sees illness as a disorder of the whole person, involving not only the patient's body but his mind, his self-image, his dependence on the physical and social environment, as well as his relation to ...

Bloody hell.

... the cosmos. I would suggest that the whole impossible edifice of modern medicine, for all its breathtaking successes, is, like the tower of Pisa, slightly off-balance.

You could imagine some of Britain's leading physicians having to leave, at this point, to check their own blood pressure. Especially if they looked closely at the Prince's sources.

Merrily found an interview with Charles, which Dobbs, or someone, had marked down the side in what looked like felt pen.

It seemed that Charles – how had she avoided knowing about all this? – had become interested, apparently via the writings of Carl Jung, in the power of dreams, coincidence and what he called *signposts*.

In other words, the idea that individuals were open to guidance from ... elsewhere – the collective unconscious. The cosmos. That they should be alert for psychic pointers.

One of which had apparently manifested while Charles was in his study attempting to draft his speech to the BMA. He was quoted as saying.

It was the most extraordinary thing. I was sitting at my desk at the time and I happened to look at my bookshelf and my eyes suddenly settled on a book about Paracelsus. So I took the book down and read it, and as a result I tried to make a speech around Paracelsus and perhaps a re-look at what he was saying and the ideas he propounded. Wasn't it time to think again about the relationship between mind and body, or body and spirit?

Paracelsus. Rennaissance physician and … herbalist?
Also, an occultist of the Renaissance period. A magician.
Deep waters.

11

Because it was Raining

'As above ...' Jane did the arm movements '... so below.'

At least she seemed happier, the sullen face replaced by the concentration face. It always paid to consult Jane. They'd built a log fire in the parlour and eaten from trays, and Jane had produced one of her paperbacks with planets and pentagrams on the front.

'Paracelsus was just the name he adopted, OK? His real name was – this is interesting – Theophrastus Bombastus von Hohenheim, from which the word *bombast* is derived. Because that's the kind of guy he was. Always throwing his weight about and losing his cool. Got up people's noses.'

'Can we get back to "As above, so below"?'

'Paracelsus said the human body was like a microcosm of nature ... or the universe. Whatever. It's the basis of astrology. He had this theory that your main internal organs corresponded to individual planets? It made serious sense in the Renaissance. Still does, in a way.'

'He *was* an occultist, though?'

'Ah, see, that's a typical *Church* attitude.'

'Terribly sorry.'

'He didn't think of himself as an *occultist* – like, nobody did. It was science. Science and philosophy. It was like high learning. Cutting edge. Like, is Stephen Hawking an occultist? I can see where Chazza was coming from on this. Homeopathy operates on this microcosm basis, doesn't it?'

'I believe it does.'

'So you could consider Paracelsus as the father of alternative medicine. Except it wasn't alternative then, it was—'

'Cutting edge. State of the art.'

'Exactly. So does this mean the Duchy of Cornwall's going to be setting up a centre for alternative healing at Garway?'

'No, it … there's probably no connection at all. I'm just interested in why the late Canon Dobbs was interested in the spiritual development of Prince Charles.'

'Be a good place for it, though, Mum.'

'Garway?'

'With the Knights Templar. A lot of this started with them and their excavations of the Temple of Solomon. Most ritual magic, raising of spirits, all this, goes back to Solomon. And maybe the whole micro-cosm/macrocosm thing.'

'Sometimes I wish you didn't know all this,' Merrily said, and Jane smiled.

Happy … ish. Down on the rug, arms around her knees, watching baby flames scurrying from log to log. She'd be happier still if she knew she'd been checked out by the Special Branch, but perhaps this wasn't the time to enlighten her.

'I was over in Coleman's Meadow this afternoon,' Jane said.

'I thought it was all fenced off.'

'It is, but Coops has a key to the temporary gate.'

Coops?

Jane turned from the fire, picked up Merrily's look.

'Neil Cooper – the guy from the County Archaeologist's department?'

'Oh.'

'Actually, he's pretty pissed off. Been trying to leave for a while – too young, obviously, to be tied to local government. He'd like to be a field archaeologist. But he's afraid of what will happen at Coleman's Meadow if he quits now.'

'In what way?'

It had gone suspiciously quiet since the initial excitement over the discovery of the three long-buried megaliths in Coleman's Meadow. Jane had been euphoric about the stones, because the field was bisected by what she – and the great visionary Alfred Watkins before her – had considered to be a seminal ley line linking Ledwardine

Church with the Iron Age earthworks on the summit of Cole Hill, the village's *holy* hill.

Hills again. Always hills.

'OK,' Jane said. 'You know about rescue archaeology, right?'

'This is where archaeologists are given a specific period of time to excavate an area scheduled for development?'

'It's what most archaeology is these days, thanks to the rampant over-population that's suffocating Britain.' Jane scowled. 'Time we scrapped all family allowance if you've got more than two kids, so it's like ... three kids, no more benefits. Four kids, compulsory sterilization.'

'That's your personal concept, is it?'

Jane's politics could veer from extreme left to extreme right and back again within seconds. *Extreme* being the only constant.

'I don't know. We've got to do *something*, haven't we? Like I don't care what colour people are or what they worship, as long as there are *less* of them.'

'Fewer,' Merrily said.

'You clergy are just *so* pedantic.'

'But to return to Coleman's Meadow ...'

'Yeah, well, obviously it's our beloved councillor, Lyndon Pierce. Gomer should've buried that bastard with the JCB while he had a chance.'

'Gomer almost wound up in court, as it is.'

'He *wanted* to go to court. He told me. He wanted his day in court, so he could stand up and publicly accuse Pierce of corruption and get it into the papers. If you say something in court, you're like immune from getting sued for slander?'.

'Mmm.' It *was* interesting, the way Pierce had declined to give evidence and the police inquiry had been dropped. 'However—'

'OK.' Jane plopping down next to Merrily on the sofa. 'The situation is that Pierce and some of his fascist friends in the council's so-called *cabinet* want it *confined* to rescue archaeology. Which means Coops is allowed to get the site excavated and learn what he can from it and then they have to *give it back*. Like, take the stones away or something, and then give back the Meadow? So all that's left is like maps and stuff in a report?'

'And the housing estate goes ahead?'

'Which would be crass, soulless and a total crime. As well as, obviously, destroying the ley.'

'I'm with you there. What can we do to stop it?'

'OK, well, there's a small lobby inside the council, supported by the heritage guys and the tourist guys, suggesting that if the stones were re-erected they'd be the best prehistoric remains in the county and a major tourist attraction.'

'So potentially better for the local economy than an estate of four-bedroomed houses with double garages.'

'Means we get coachloads of tourists, but still the lesser of two evils.'

'So what are you proposing to do?'

'Nothing.' Jane's face had gone blank. 'Coops says it's best if I do nothing at present. Don't give Pierce any ammunition.'

'And you ... you're going along with that?'

'Coops is a very persuasive guy. In his quiet way.'

Merrily watched Jane selecting a new dry log for the fire, considering the options in the basket: the ash or the oak, fast burn/slow burn.

'Don't suppose Eirion called?'

'Wouldn't know,' Jane said, insouciant. 'Haven't had the mobile switched on all day.'

The call came just after ten. Jane was watching *Law and Order*, the one about sex crimes, Merrily's eyes closing when the mobile chimed on the arm of the sofa.

'Sophie rang me,' the Bishop said. Doleful.

'Two seconds, Bernie.'

Merrily took the mobile into the kitchen, where the cold air was like a razor. The Aga had swallowed two gallons of oil a day, but it had had its compensations.

'I suppose a grovelling apology's due,' the Bishop said. 'All I can say is that I kept nothing from you. Not intentionally.'

'That's reassuring. Kind of.'

'And I'm still no wiser, Merrily. Although, yes, I am now inclined to believe that the initial information I was given by Adam Eastgate is ... probably incomplete.'

'*Incomplete.* That's a very elastic word, Bernie.'

'Whether any concealment of information is down to the Duchy I would personally doubt. I don't think Adam's the sort of man to play a double game. However I, ah ... Sophie did say she'd felt obliged to tell you that we'd also had a call from, ah ...'

'A private number in Canterbury?'

'Yes, well, whoever it was from, I was advised that the best way of dealing with this might be simply to allow my Deliverance consultant to devote herself to uncovering what there is be uncovered. Without the usual constraints on her time.'

It was *Canterbury* who wanted the investigation?

'So – let's just clarify this, Bernie – there *is* more to it than a decidedly iffy haunting.'

'I'm assuming there is. I honestly do not know.'

'But someone in Canterbury does.'

'I'm not sure.'

'Bernie, we're not somehow ... indirectly working for the security services, are we?'

'Good God, Merrily ...'

'All right. Suppose I was to conclude that the ghost story was a fabrication.'

'You can do that?'

'It's a possibility.'

'Then please do it,' the Bishop said. 'Soonest.'

Afterwards, she felt exhausted, but couldn't settle. With the half-eight Eucharist tomorrow, she ought to be in bed, but ...

She made two mugs of hot chocolate, took one to Jane in the parlour then came back, sat down in the scullery and reopened the phone. Rang Felix Barlow and asked if it would be OK to come and speak to Fuchsia tomorrow.

'I know it's late, Felix, but I need to fit it into my fairly rigid Sunday schedule. I'm sorry.'

'Hang on, would you?'

Felix didn't sound happy. Merrily heard him moving back into his tin home, and thought there were raised voices. She drank some chocolate, lit a cigarette, still unsure of what to make of this. It wasn't unprecedented, but – if you excluded council tenants desperate to be rehoused – it was rare for anyone to invent a ghost story. Rarer still for anyone to transpose a relatively well known fictional story into a real situation.

After just over a minute, Felix returned and told Merrily that Fuchsia didn't want to talk to her.

'No offence to you, Mrs Watkins. She gets like this. Maybe leave it a few days?'

'A few *days*?'

'We'll get back to you, all right?'

'No. I'm afraid it's not all right. I'm under a certain pressure to get this sorted one way or—'

'*You're* under pressure ...' She heard the clangs of him hurriedly clambering down the caravan steps into the night, then his voice, up-close and frayed. 'Tell the Duchy we won't be touching that job now under any circumstances, all right?'

'But that—'

'Yeah, I *know* this is me burning my boats with them for ever, and that's some kind of madness, and I'm going to regret it for a long time, but that's the size of it.'

He was panting.

'Has something happened, Felix?'

'We've told you everything we can. Why do you need *us* any more?'

'Because ...' Merrily really didn't want to say any of this to him, she needed to put it directly to Fuchsia, but it was late and she was over-tired, and ... '... because I'm not sure you *have* told me everything.'

'I have to go now.'

'Where is she?'

'In the ... bathroom. Doing her hair. She got soaked.'

'Tell me one thing. Has anyone else been to talk to her about that house? Or to you?'

'Why would they?'

'I don't know.'

'You think Fuchsia's holding something back, is it, Mrs Watkins? Or do you think she's lying?'

'I think we need to discuss it again, that's all.'

'*You think she's lying, Mrs Watkins?*'

Oh God, why had she made this call? Why hadn't she thought about it first? Or maybe prayed for advice, sat in silence and listened to the voice inside.

'How's she been, Felix, since the blessing?'

Through the scullery's open doorway, the kitchen clock ticked off the seconds of silence in the phone.

'I think she's been back,' Felix said.

'Back?'

'To Garway. To the Master House. I had to go and collect some timber for the barn, and when I got home she wasn't here. Gone off in the van. When she got back it was dark. She said she'd been shopping in Hereford. Which is something she never does on a Saturday. Hates crowds.'

'How do you know she went back to the house?'

'Because we still got a key to the place. When I said I'd take it back to the Duchy, Adam said no hurry. Likely still thinking we might go back to the job one day.'

'And the key was missing?'

'It's back now. And, no, she won't talk about it.'

'All right,' Merrily said. 'How about I come over now?'

'*No!*'

'I think it might help.'

'It might help you, it wouldn't help me. If she won't let me go back to the bloody place because it's so evil, why did *she* go there again? You explain that?'

'I can't. I wish I'd known. I was in Garway this afternoon, too.'

'At the house?'

'No. I was at the church. I didn't go to the house.'

'Why not?'

Good question. *Because I'd decided I was being misused, under-informed, short-changed. Because I was pissed off. Because it was raining.*

'If I'd known she was there, I would have, obviously.' Christ, what a mess. 'Felix, can you ask her to ring me? Can you tell her it's very important?'

'All right,' he said. 'I'll try and get her to call you.'

'Any time. Doesn't matter how late.'

'Yes.'

On which basis, Merrily took the mobile to bed and kept waking up in the night, thinking she was hearing its electronic chimes.

Although she never did.

12

Ghosts and Scholars

USUALLY, AFTER A Eucharist, you were aware of subtle ambient changes: a charge of energy, a sharpening, a recolouring – on a fine day, shards of sunlight spilling between the apples in the rood screen, raising shivers of gold dust in the air.

This was not a fine day. When Merrily unlocked the church, under a sky like a gravestone, the interior had been unresponsive. Sixteen people had since taken Holy Communion. Afterwards, nothing much seemed to have altered. Or so she felt, blaming herself and her headache.

'I'm so sorry,' Shirley West said in the vestry, cradling the empty chalice like a sick baby. 'I'm so terribly clumsy. I just get nervous, I'm afraid, Merrily.'

'But you *didn't* knock it over.'

'I very nearly did.'

'Shirley, I nearly do most weeks. I've stopped worrying about it.'

You were often told that a Mass was supposed to be like perfect theatre, conducted with precision and …

'Grace,' Shirley said. 'I have no grace.'

'Shirley …' Merrily shook her head. 'That's not true.'

Which was a lie, but what could you say?

Shirley had come to live in Ledwardine a few months ago and had shown up in the church before the removal van had left. She was in her early forties, overweight, divorced, a bank manager in Leominster. She had family here. She'd come to virtually every service, moving up rapidly to giving out hymn books, arranging flowers and assisting, eventually, with the Eucharist.

Altar girl.

'Someone said in the shop,' Shirley said, 'that there's been talk of those old stones they found in the ground being put back up.'

'Mmm. It's a possibility.'

Merrily looked up from the chalice into deep-set brown eyes full of worried fervour.

'Shouldn't we be doing something to try to stop it?'

'Stop it?'

'The raising of heathen stones opposite our church?'

'Erm … well, you won't *see* them from the church, will you, Shirley? You've got the market square in between, and the market hall. Besides, I suppose they *were* here first.'

'And duly toppled over and buried. There was a Christian purpose to that, surely.'

'I think it was probably more to do with three big stones getting in the way of ploughing and haymaking.'

Evidently nobody had told Shirley about Jane's pivotal role in the discovery of the Coleman's Meadow stone row. Parish life. Complications everywhere.

'The thing is, Shirley, quite a lot of medieval churches were actually built on the sites of prehistoric stone circles and burial chambers.'

'Exactly. Burying the evil under the house of God, surely.'

'I'm not sure if pre-Christian necessarily means evil.'

'Our Lord was born into a world full of darkness. He was the Light of the World.'

'And, in fact, looking at it in a practical way, most archaeologists seem to think the early Christians put the new churches in the places where local people were used to worshipping.'

'I've never heard that.'

Shirley looked at her, eyes narrowed.

Merrily sighed.

'Nothing's ever quite as it seems,' Huw Owen said on the answering machine. *'Give me a call, would you?'*

Priests rarely phoned one another on Sundays.

Merrily had twenty minutes before having to go back for the

Morning Service. She'd only slipped home in the hope of finding a message from Fuchsia or, at least, Felix – she'd been worrying about it on and off since waking into the grey light. Suppose Felix had gone back into the caravan and told Fuchsia that she was being accused of lying?

Before calling Huw back, she tried ringing Felix. Phone switched off. For possibly the first time ever, she took the mobile back to the church with her, calling Huw from a damp bench in the graveyard, catching him in his Land Rover, between parishes. The signal wasn't brilliant.

'… Might be pu … oincidences …' Huw on the hands-free, breaking up. '… You should know … James collection … foreword mentions … based … ordshire … *call you back.*'

'Mobile, Huw – on the mobile!'

Getting interested glances now from fragments of congregation filtering through the lych-gate. In most parishes, the Morning Service was as good as it got, congregation-wise, Evensong having been dumped through low attendance. Here, mornings had actually been overtaken by the Sunday-evening meditation, even though the rumours of healing had long since died down. It was satisfying, a good reason to be able to be here tonight rather than at Mrs Murray's guest house in Garway.

Merrily waved to James Bull-Davies, a fairly impoverished remnant of the Ledwardine squirearchy, and his partner Alison Kinnersley who, when she and Jane had first come to Ledwardine, had been living with Lol. Always faintly troubled, Alison would return tonight for the meditation – alone. James wasn't into silence.

A nervous sun tested the clouds, and the phone chimed.

'"The Stalls of Barchester",' Huw said.

'Sorry?'

'M. R. James mentions in his foreword to the collected edition that his Barchester Cathedral was partly based on Hereford Cathedral. I'd forgotten that. Herefordshire was also the imagined setting for one of the later stories, "A View from a Hill".'

'I thought they were always set in East Anglia.'

'Sorry to complicate matters, lass.' No engine rattle now; he'd parked up somewhere. 'But it seems that James – Monty, as he was known –

came to relate to rural Herefordshire extremely well. You could even say it became a refuge for him.'

'You didn't know this before?'

'Of course I didn't, else I'd've mentioned it.'

'How come you know it now?'

'How does any bugger know owt these days? I Googled Montague Rhodes James and found an unusually erudite website called *Ghosts and Scholars*, devoted entirely to the man. How much do *you* know about him?'

'Hardly anything. He was an academic, wasn't he?'

'Divided his career between Eton – his old school – and King's College, Cambridge. Son of a clergyman, brought up in the parish of Livermere in Suffolk – moody sort of place, apparently, very inspirational. In later years, he reckoned there was only one area to match it.'

'Let me guess.'

'Aye. Specifically, the countryside around Kilpeck and Much Dewchurch. Four miles from Garway? Five?'

'Thereabouts.'

'The trail, however, does lead to Garway itself.'

Merrily pulled her cloak over her knees, wanting a cigarette. Watching an unexpected sunbeam stroking a mossy headstone. Where was this going?

'Monty never married,' Huw said. 'But he did have a close, though presumed platonic, female friend called Gwendolen McBryde. Widow of his good mate James McBryde, a talented artist, illustrated some of the early stories. Gwen was pregnant when he died, very young, and gave birth to a daughter. Mother and daughter moved to Herefordshire.'

'As youngish widows with daughters sometimes do.'

Oh, sod it. She pulled her bag onto the bench, found the cigarettes.

'Seems Monty would visit Gwen on quite a regular basis,' Huw said. 'Finding the countryside much to his taste, like I said. Monty was very fond of old churches and extremely knowledgeable about them. No big surprise that he'd visit Garway.'

'If you say so.'

'This is the point. After Monty's death, Gwen published a collection of his letters – *Letters from a Friend*. In one of them, James recalls a particular visit to Garway in, I think, 1917. Actually, there are two mentions of Garway, but one just in passing. The one you need to know about … Well, I've already emailed it to you. Best if you read it when you get back home.'

'Huw, for heaven's sake—'

'The woman who edits the website, Rosemary Pardoe, says Monty appears to have had, quote, *a peculiar experience* at Garway, the nature of which is, quote, *tantalizingly unclear*, but which he writes about with *typical spooky Jamesian humour.*'

'Saying …?'

'Read it when you get back. I don't want you thinking I'm embroidering it, winding you up. Some places just attract this kind of thing.'

'*Huw—*'

'Have to be off, anyroad. I've work to do, and so have you.'

And then he wasn't there, the bastard.

But if he'd thought it was *so* important, surely he'd have told her.

13

Couldn't Make it Up

AFTER THE SERVICE, when everybody else, even Shirley West, had gone, Merrily had a furtive cigarette with Gomer Parry behind the tower. Asking him what the feeling was in the village about the resurrection of the old stones in Coleman's Meadow. Maybe most people would actually prefer a new estate of executive homes?

'En't so much that, vicar,' Gomer said. 'Few more fancy houses en't the argument. Tip o' the muck-heap. It's who's in bed with Lyndon Pierce. Who wants to see the village turned into a town? Supermarkets and posh restaurants. And who's on young Janey's side.'

'And yours, Gomer. Let's not forget that.'

'Ar. I'll be doin' my bit, sure to, to see Pierce gets his arse kicked, vicar.'

The light was back, big time, in Gomer's wire-rimmed glasses, his white hair topping his weathered brown face like the froth on beer. Councillor Pierce had said Gomer Parry was halfway senile, an old joke who ought to be in a home. Gomer would need to be a long way into senility to forget that.

'Harchaeologists needs a JCB and a driver,' he said. 'Won't be no charge from me.'

'That's very generous of you, Gomer. I'm sure Jane'll see it gets back to the right people. Erm … you know Felix Barlow?'

'Barlow …' Gomer adjusted his cap, screwed up his eyes. 'Builder?'

'From Monkland. Knows Danny.'

'Ar. Met the feller a few times over the years. He don't build no mock-Tudor rainbow-stone crap. Don't build nothin' new at all, far's I can see.'

'Good bloke?'

'Oh, straight, I reckon. Liked a drink at one time, so I yeard. That'd be when he was married.'

'When was that?'

'Eight years, nine … I lose track. But I remember his wife. Oh, hell, aye, I remember her, all right.'

It started to rain. Merrily leaned into the base of the tower.

'You know Lizzie Nugent?' Gomer said. 'Widow, up by Bearswood?'

'Don't think so.'

'Husband left her with two kids and a twenty-acre smallholdin'. I was over attendin' to some ditchin' one day, early March it'd be, when the gales blows the roof off Lizzie's cowshed. Smashed to bits. So I calls a few people, see if we could get some galvanized, cheapish, and somebody puts me on to Felix Barlow. He comes round in his truck that same day, with these sheets off a shed he's took down, and we fixed the ole roof between us. Took us n' more'n a few hours, and when he found out Lizzie en't got no insurance he was very reasonable about it, was Felix, no question 'bout that.'

Gomer ignited his roll-up, hands cupped around it.

'We're havin' a cuppa with Lizzie afterwards when up comes this bloody great white BMW. Woman inside leanin' on the horn till Felix goes out. Givin' him hell, we could all of us year it. Folks in the next village'd likely year it – all this, what you doin' yere when you oughter be up at Lady So-and-So's? What you think you are, bloody registered charity?'

'This is Mrs Barlow?'

'Good-lookin' woman, mind. But it en't everythin', is it?'

'Erm … no. I suppose not.'

'Barlow goes around helpin' too many poor widows, where's the next BMW comin' from?'

'You met the woman he's with now?'

'The hippie? Never met her, no, vicar.' Gomer waved his ciggy. 'Feller's a bit alternative hisself, mind. Builder as en't into cheating his clients, that's alternative for a start, ennit?'

Merrily laughed.

'Knows the job, too. Could be in an office, collar and tie, directin' operations. But he knows that money en't everythin', no more'n a good-lookin' woman is.'

'She *is* a good-looking woman, as it happens.'

'The hippie?'

'And not much more than half his age.'

'Oh well.' Gomer shrugged, teeth crushing the ciggy. 'Just cause a feller spends all his time shorin' up ole buildings, don't mean all his tools is obsolete.'

Merrily blinked.

Merrily didn't know what M. R. James had looked like. The only face she could see in her mind was Huw's, framed by hair like dried-out straw, mounted on an age-dulled dog-collar and settling into a complacent conjuror's smile.

We must have offended somebody or something at Garway, I think.

'I *wondered* why you were so anxious,' Jane said, 'to borrow the M. R. James.'

Always a danger with emails. She'd been on the computer in the scullery, researching some aspect of stone rows, when Huw's mail had come through. She'd read it, looked up the references, been into the *Ghosts and Scholars* website.

'You couldn't make it up,' Jane said, still sitting at the desk.

Impressed, excited. Merrily walked to the window. *Oh hell.*

'Mr James *could* make it up, though, couldn't he? I mean, that was what he did.'

'Oh, Mum. It was a letter to his friend. Someone who obviously knew exactly what he was on about. He doesn't spell it out, does he? He knows she understands his point of reference.'

'Mmm. Possibly.'

Merrily read the rest of it.

Probably we took it too much for granted, in speaking of it, that we should be able to do exactly as we pleased. Next time we shall know better. There is no doubt it is a very rum place and needs careful handling.

No, the kid was right. You *couldn't* make it up. She could see why Huw had insisted on emailing the whole page from the *Ghosts and Scholars* website. Something had happened to M. R. James at Garway. Either something faintly curious which James's serpentine imagination had inflated into something disturbing. Or something *seriously* disturbing which James, in this otherwise routine letter to a female friend, was deliberately making light of.

The editor of the website had made a kind of pilgrimage to the area to track down the settings for the main Herefordshire story 'A View from a Hill'. Although the story seemed to be set in the general area of Garway, the village itself didn't appear to feature, even under a different name.

'I love this guy.' Jane was glowing. 'Greatest ghost-story writer ever. Because he just ... well, basically, he just ... he didn't do ghosts.'

'What did he do, then?'

'Entities. He did entities. Creeping things. Indefinable things, exuding ... malevolence. In traditional settings, like old churches and deserted shores and places with burial mounds. According to the website, he once said there was no point at all in writing about the supernatural if it wasn't evil.'

'Doesn't that kind of invalidate the Bible?'

'He meant fiction, Mum.'

'Wow,' Merrily said, '*there's* a step forward for you.'

'I mean *complete* fiction. Anyway, he wasn't exactly anti-religious. His old man was a vicar, in Suffolk. He was brought up in the Church. He might even have gone that way himself if he hadn't got into academic research and teaching and stuff.'

'And did *you* know he came to this area?'

'Well, no! I just *didn't*! It's incredible.'

'But you've read all the stories.'

'Erm ...' Jane fiddled with the mouse. 'Not *all* of them, to be completely honest.'

'You totally love him, but you haven't read all his stories.'

'OK … mainly, I've just seen the TV versions.'

'I don't remember us watching them.'

Remembered them being *on*. Usually around Christmas, and mostly before Jane had been born.

'Erm … I didn't mean *us*.' Jane's face had clouded. 'I saw them at Irene … Eirion's. His dad had a complete set of the videos, and we watched most of them one night, one after the other. It was … it was pretty good. We were on our own and we scared ourselves silly.'

'That must've been a long night. Watching them all.'

'Not that long.' Jane looked away. 'They only lasted half an hour each. Or a bit longer.'

Oh, Jane, Jane …

Merrily guessing they'd watched them tucked up together in Eirion's bed, when his parents were out.

'Anyway,' Jane said. 'The TV versions were obviously set in East Anglia or somewhere. To be honest, I bought the book but I only got round to reading a couple. And I didn't read the foreword, otherwise I'd've known about him coming here. Obviously, I'm now going to read everything. I'm going to find a biography. It's amazing.'

'Mmm.'

It was certainly a complication. Did Fuchsia know M. R. James had been to Garway? It was not unlikely.

'So …' Jane sat back, hands behind her head. 'What's your angle on this, Mum?'

'Oh, it … it's just somebody else who scared themselves silly.'

'In a house belonging to Prince Charles?'

'Did I tell you that?'

'Not directly, but I just happened to click on *history* …'

'And found the Duchy of Cornwall website.' Merrily nodded, resigned. 'Right.'

'Didn't mean to snoop, but this one was interesting. And you know it never goes any further, with me. Not any more.'

'I'd've told you all about it, if you'd asked.'

'I know, but … Anyway. Sorry. So, like, the house is at Garway, then. With the Knights Templar church. How did you get on to M. R. James?'

'Because ... there's a mention of a Templar preceptory in one of his stories – "Oh, Whistle, and I'll Come to You, My Lad".'

'That one is *really* scary. In the TV version, this professor, he's not what you'd call sociable and he just goes around kind of mumbling to himself on this grey beach, and then he—'

'Do you know of any more? Any more stories mentioning the Knights Templar?'

'No, but I could email this website and ask this Rosemary Pardoe, who obviously knows, like, *everything* about M. R.'

'OK,' Merrily said. 'Why not?'

Whatever had happened to M. R. James at Garway, he didn't *appear* to have used it in a story, but perhaps he had, in some less obvious way. If he'd been at Garway in 1917, it would have to be one of the later ones.

And Fuchsia ... whatever Fuchsia had seen or imagined or invented at Garway, she'd linked it to a story set in East Anglia, albeit with a Templar connection.

James had talked of next time. *Next time we shall know better.*

You sensed a residual fascination.

'*Holy shit ...*'

'Jane—'

'Look at *this* ... '

Jane had read further down, to where Rosemary Pardoe was passing on her own observations about Garway Church and its environs. Merrily leaned across.

'The dovecote?'

'Mum, did you *know* about this?'

'Sophie mentioned it. It's apparently the finest of its period in the country.'

'Oh, yeah, that too ... Now, read the rest. Go on.'

'It was built by the Knights Templar?'

'Probably. And then rebuilt by the Hospitallers who took over at Garway. Go on ... read it.'

Jane stood up. Merrily sat down.

As well as the ancient Garway church itself with its (semi) detached thirteenth-century tower, there is a huge dovecote on private property on the adjoining farm …

Its doveholes number a worrying 666.

'Oh.'

'When are you going back?' Jane said. 'And can I come?'

When she went upstairs to change into jeans and sweatshirt, Merrily took the mobile with her and called Felix again from the bedroom.

Unsure, now, of how best to approach this. It was all subtly turning around, M. R. James himself becoming a player, seventy or so years after his death.

As for the dovecote … if it had been there for the best part of eight centuries, it was a bit late now to start worrying about the implications of 666 dove-chambers.

'*The person you are calling is not available. If you would like to leave a message …*'

'Felix, it's Merrily. Could you or Fuchsia please call me. I need to talk about the …' She hesitated. 'The face of crumpled linen.'

Crumpling her cassock for the wash basket, she put on jeans and the Gomer Parry sweatshirt. The alarm clock said one-forty. Meditation was seven-thirty. She swallowed two paracetamol in the bathroom, came back downstairs to find Jane still hanging around in their chilly kitchen.

'Not got a meeting with, erm … *Coops* today?'

Jane shook her head. She looked less happy, her face a little flushed. There were crossroads in her life.

'Do *you* want to drive, then?' Merrily said.

PART TWO

This is wild frontier country with
an aura of barbarians roaming over
the adjacent border ...

Simon Jenkins, on Garway
England's Thousand Best Churches

14

As Above …

WHAT JANE KNEW about the Templars came, of course, out of paganism.

Those difficult months when she'd been a teenage goddess-worshipper, slipping out into the vicarage garden at night to make her devotions to the Lady Moon. Partly a rebellion thing – OK, understandable in an intelligent, imaginative kid who'd been dragged away to the unknown village where her mother had become a low-paid, low-level employee of the boring, set-in-its-ways, male-dominated, hierarchical Church of England.

Jane's paganism: partly about giving Christianity a good kicking.

Merrily watched her driving, back straight, hands textbook on the wheel, eyes unblinking. Remembering the all-time-low, a couple of years ago, with the heat of the old Aga at her back, a white-faced Jane rigid in the kitchen doorway, and their relationship trampled into the flagstones.

Nobody gives a shit for your Church. Your congregations are like laughable. In twenty years you'll be preaching to each other. You don't matter any more, you haven't mattered for years. I'm embarrassed to tell anybody what you do.

The rage had evaporated, tensions long since eased, but Jane's pagan instincts remained – tamer now, certainly, but still feeding something inside her that was hungry for experience; up in her attic apartment she was still reading books about old gods.

'Like, for centuries it's been accepted that the Templars were the guardians of arcane secrets – including the Holy Grail. I mean, who better? They were spiritual warriors. They put their lives on the line to protect sacred truths. They were like … the SAS with soul?'

'Who says the SAS have no soul?'

'Unlike the Templars, however, they're not known for their monastic celibacy,' Jane said.

They'd driven in from the east, less of a back door to Garway and better roads for Jane, who was hoping to take her driving test before Christmas. The sun was low and intense, a searchlight spraying the yellowing leaves on the turning trees. When you weren't driving, you got a more spectacular overview ... or underview, maybe; all you could see of Garway Hill itself was the top of the radio mast on its summit.

Changing down for a sudden incline, Jane let the clutch slip.

'Sorry ...'

'It's OK. Take your time.'

Jane, red-faced, pulled the car out of its shudder, the Volvo wheezing and protesting like an old dog being dragged out for a walk by a child who didn't understand.

'So if *The Holy Blood and The Holy Grail* concept is that the Grail is actually the suppressed feminine principle as, like, *enshrined* by Mary Magdalene, who was Jesus Christ's other half ... and don't look at me like that, Mum.'

'You don't know *how* I'm looking at you, your eyes are firmly on the road.'

'I can feel the self-righteous hostility.'

'It's not self-righteous and it's not hostility. It's just that all that's been discredited. Even the authors are now saying they were just testing a theory.'

'It doesn't change the fact that Mary Magdalene, whether or not she was Mrs Christ, represents the goddess figure which male-dominated Christianity suppressed.'

Jane's debating skills had become formidable, but how many times had they been here?

'Look ... I accept that there may be a hidden feminine principle. What I don't accept is Jesus and Mary Magdalene being an item, starting a bloodline. For which, when you look into it, there's no real evidence at all.'

'Aw, Mum, why do you have to deny the poor guy a sex life?'

'There you go. *The guy.* If he was just a guy, just another prophet who didn't rise again, didn't ascend into heaven … if you want to deny his *divinity* …'

'I don't want to deny anybody's divinity, I'm into divinity big time. But I don't see why women shouldn't have a share of it, whether it's Mary Magdalene or the Virgin Mary.'

'We won't argue now,' Merrily said. 'Take this bit slowly.'

Maybe she ought to be driving instead. The lanes were proving unpredictable, and there were more of them than she'd figured. More to Garway, too, than you imagined; flushed by the low sun, it seemed like a remote and separate realm. Like Cornwall was to England. Maybe the Duchy had recognized that aspect.

Jane glanced at a signpost which seemed to have been twisted round, so that *Garway* was pointing into a field.

'So Garway and Garway Hill are like separated, right?'

'Looks like it. I thought the church and a few cottages nearby were the centre of the community, but apparently not. You get these separate clusters … kind of disorienting.'

After half a mile or so, the landscape broadened out and they were into a random scatter of modern housing and an open stretch of common with a children's play area. Across the lane from the common was a pub of whitewashed stone with a swinging sign: a full moon in a deepening twilight sky.

THE GARWAY MOON.

'Cool sign,' Jane said. 'Artistic. Kind of pagan.'

'Why does the moon always have to be pagan?'

'You tell me. Does the Bible have much to say about it?' Jane relaxed into the driver's seat. 'This is very much my kind of place, Mum. It's like frontier country. On the edge.'

'It *is* frontier country. Those hills are Wales.'

'I actually meant *frontier* in the deeper sense. The Knights Templar move in, monks with horses and swords, and they stamp their presence on the whole area. Infuse it with mystery. I mean like, *why out here?* Unless … maybe it was considered a really good, obscure place to conceal secrets, practise arcane … practices.'

'Or they were just given the land. Maybe no better reason than that.'

'There's always a better reason,' Jane said.

'For you, flower, there always has to be.'

'Don't call me "flower". And don't tell me you're not curious, too.'

'I can be curious without having to subscribe to the whole fashionable Gnosticism thing.'

Jane slowed, as the road sloped past a modern-ish primary school on one side and a run-down village hall on the other.

'I don't see what's so wrong with Gnosticism. It's just saying that faith is not enough. The Gnostics wanted to *know*. They wanted direct experience of the reality of … something out there. God. Whatever. I don't see why you have a problem with that.'

'Anyway …' Not now, huh? Too weighty. '… I'd've thought you'd lived in the sticks long enough to know it's absolutely the *worst* place to keep a secret.'

'Yeah, *now*. But in medieval times, when almost nobody could read.'

'Including the Templars. Most of the Knights Templar seem to have been illiterate.'

'Mum, they were international bankers! People could stash money at one preceptory and withdraw from another.'

'Since when did banking demand literacy?'

'OK, then, maybe this was just where they came to carry on their own form of Gnostic worship, which the straight Church would see as heresy.' Jane pulled the Volvo over to the grass verge to let a tractor get past. 'Was that all right?'

'Except you should've signalled first, to let him know what you were doing. And why are we going up here?'

Inexplicably, Jane had taken an uphill right.

'Sorry. I thought …'

'I think the church was straight on down the hill. Never mind, carry on.'

It didn't matter. Merrily suddenly wanted to hug Jane. If the worst you had to deal with was theological debate …

'You OK, Mum?'

'Mmm.'

She felt the pressure of tears, deciding that when Jane wasn't around she was going to ring Eirion on the quiet, find out what had gone wrong between them. Just wanting the kid to be happy.

'This sort of location is actually more suited to the Cistercians,' Jane said. 'They liked to be *way* out on their own. But, see, that fits, too, because the Knights Templar were connected with the Cistercians. Through Bernard of Clairvaux? The top Cistercian fixer, smartest operator in the medieval Catholic Church?'

'I know who you mean. I'm just impressed at the extent of your knowledge.'

'It's in the medieval history syllabus – just. Our history guy, Robbie Williams, it's his period. So what happened, Bernard cleared up the problem the Templars had about being devout Christians and also having to kill people on a regular basis. Simple solution: he ruled that it was OK to kill non-Christians.'

'Especially Muslims,' Merrily said. 'A medieval interpretation, which now seems to operate in reverse. What's your point?'

'Comes back to paganism again. Of all the medieval monastic orders, the Cistercians were the ones who most reflected pre-Christian religion. The old ways.'

'*Some* sources might say that, but—'

'Come on – natural successors to the Druids? Sheep farmers who liked relative isolation and were into ancient sites and earth-forces and sacred springs?'

'Natural running water was very much prized in the days before taps,' Merrily said. 'And, sure, maybe they dowsed for it. That doesn't mean—'

'Garway Church has a holy spring, doesn't it?'

'It does. And if you can find somewhere to turn this car around we'll go back and check it out. No, not there. Jane, keep your eyes on the—'

'Did you *see* that sign?' Jane's head swivelling. 'On the house?'

'Mmm. I'm afraid I did.'

They'd passed a grey stone corner house which might once have been a pub and still had a big yellow sign on the side. *THE SUN.* A mystical golden sun, with a smug-looking, curled-lipped face and waving tendrils of radiance; below it were sunflowers and a naked figure on a horse. Merrily also noticed that the farmhouse almost opposite had a name plate: *The Rising Sun.*

'It's just an old pub sign, Jane, that's all.'

'Mum, it was like a giant tarot card. The Sun? And the Moon? This place had two pubs called The Sun and The Moon? That says *nothing* to you?'

'I'm … reserving my opinion.'

'I think I was probably guided to turn up this road.'

'You don't say.'

'As above, so below,' Jane said.

The holy well was at the bottom of the churchyard. Like most holy wells, it was disappointing. A trickle under the wall. Ribbons on a nearby bush, which could be down to either visiting pagans or local kids.

Jane crouched down, unzipping her white hoodie, holding cupped hands underneath the water. Merrily was reminded uncomfortably of the author Winnie Sparke, who had hung around the wells in Malvern, and what had happened to her.

'Jane, you know how much I really hate doing the mother-hen bit, but that water …'

Jane looked into her cupped hands but didn't drink the water. She smiled and dabbed some on her cheeks. Beyond the body of the church, the vertically-slit-eyed tower gazed down with what Merrily took to be a kind of benign cynicism.

'If we go back to the church, we can see the outline of the original circular nave. Templar trade mark. Designed in honour of the Church of the Holy Sepulchre in Jerusalem?'

'On the other hand …' Jane stood up and walked off to the edge of the churchyard '… if we go along here, we should be able to see the dovecote designed to commemorate the Beast 666.'

'It's on private land. We'd need to ask for permission.'

'Not just to *see* it.'

Jane – why else was she here? – was already walking across a marshy-looking field towards the fringe of a farm with barns, storage tanks, a galvanized shed and some kind of stone silo. Merrily, wrong shoes, as usual – *bugger* – stepping uncertainly across a boggy bit, following a shallow stream, while slowly realizing that the stone silo on the edge of the farmyard clutter was probably what they were looking for.

She stopped and confronted it: a squat round tower, like a sawn-off, roofless hop-kiln. The fading sun balanced on its rim, Jane shading her eyes.

'Doesn't look very evil from here,' Merrily said.

'Why should it be evil?' Jane turning in annoyance. 'That's just Christian propaganda. Anyway, recent translations of the Book of *Rev* from the ancient Greek suggest it might actually be six *one* six.'

'Not being much of a Greek scholar, I may have to continue to be wary of 666.'

'Whatever,' Jane said, 'it does suggest a kind of partly submerged mystical awareness, doesn't it?'

'It does?'

'Sacred architecture.'

'It's a dovecote.'

'Everything is significant. Another pointer to this whole hill being a store of arcane knowledge. I can't believe Coops and his guys haven't checked this place out. I need to ask him.'

'Jane, I think—'

Merrily shut up. Some mothers with daughters, it was pregnancy, abortion, drugs. If the worst you had to worry about was your kid creating a fantasy landscape ...

And Coops, of course. Maybe she ought to find out more about Coops.

'Fantastic energy here, Mum.' Jane began whirling around with her arms spread wide, eight years old again. 'Can't you feel it?'

'Not to speak of, no.'

The sun had tucked itself under the rim of the tubular dovecote, the ground dropping into shadow, and Merrily was aware of a damp pattering, as Jane said, 'You just don't want to admit—'

And then was staggering back, something long and grey and damp surging between them.

'God—'

Merrily lurching towards Jane through the wet grass, a woman's voice crying out behind her.

'*Roscoe!*'

When Jane sat down in the grass, it was on top of her, pinning her down, all over her face.

Tail waving, thank God. A woman with shoulder-length white-blonde hair threw down a short leather dog-lead.

'You *bastard*, Roscoe!'

The dog shifted from Jane, looked back at the woman, seeming bemused.

'Obviously thought she was offering to play with him,' the woman said. 'Is it racist nowadays to say the Irish wolfhound's the stupidest bloody creature on four legs? You all right, darling?'

'I ... sure.'

Jane had struggled upright, holding Roscoe's hairy head against a hip to prove that she wasn't afraid of him. If there hadn't been energy in the air before, there was now.

'Teach you to stand there in a place like this,' the woman said, 'calling out the Number of the bloody Beast.'

15

Fearsome Tradition

THE WOMAN PICKED up the dog-lead. She wore an ancient Barbour, flayed almost white in places, full of holes and flakily at odds with her rose-pink silk scarf. Her face was long and thin-lipped, and older than the Barbour, but by how much was anybody's guess.

'If we're on your land,' Merrily said, 'I apologize.'

Frowning at Jane, who was brushing herself down, smudged brown paw marks down the front of the white hoodie.

'It isn't my land, don't worry.' The woman patted her knee and Roscoe ambled over, and she attached his lead as a mobile phone beeped inside the Barbour. 'Not that ownership of *most* of the land around here isn't open to some kind of dispute. Excuse me a moment.'

Reining in the wolfhound, she dug out the mobile, pushed back her straight white hair and held the phone to an ear without turning or moving away.

'Mr Hinton, good afternoon ... No, not yet, I'm afraid. As you may not have noticed, it's *Sunday* ... Yes, indeed, I'm expecting the delivery in the next week and as soon as it gets here I shall bring it round ... Yes, I guarantee you'll love it. *Guarantee* it ... Money back, yes, absolutely. We'll talk again, Mr Hinton.'

The woman clicked off the phone, dropped it into a coat pocket.

'Farmers. They think *everybody* works on Sundays. The columbarium, yes, why *does* it have 666 chambers? Not often spoken of locally. As you see by its situation, we tend not to advertise our antiquities.'

'Why not?' Jane asked. 'It's supposed to be unique.'

'No idea.' The woman smiled, exposing a dark and raunchy slit between upper front teeth, setting light to deep-set but vivid blue-green eyes. 'But then I was merely born here. We tend, nowadays, to rely on outsiders – usually Americans – to explain all our mysteries. Where've you come from?'

Merrily told her Ledwardine, in the north of the county. Aware of time moving on, the need to take a brief look at the Master House before they left.

'You're no use at all then.' The woman patted her pockets. 'Haven't got a fag on you, by any chance? Slim chance nowadays, I know.'

'Actually, I have.' Merrily reached down to her shoulder bag. 'Only Silk Cut, I'm afraid.'

'That would be perfect, m' dear. Left my buggers on the mantelpiece, and I'm absolutely gasping. Thank you.'

She mouthed a cigarette and Merrily lit it for her and she swallowed a lungful of smoke, head tilted back to exhale it into the sky in the direction of the devil's dovecote.

'Lit up in the pub the other night in joyful contravention of the law. Chap looking at me as if I'd pissed on his shoes. *Bloody* government. How dare they?'

Merrily looked at Jane. Jane was wide-eyed and trying not to laugh.

'Ledwardine, eh?' The woman lowering her eyes to Merrily's *Gomer Parry Plant Hire* sweatshirt. 'And you evidently know the little digger chap with specs that you or I might use to track the canals on Mars.'

'I didn't realize Gomer worked so far out.'

'Needed new field drains in a hurry – ditches overflowing. Quagmire. My regular chap had packed it in but absolutely refused to recommend anyone local. He'd worked for the Grays, you see, and, oh my God, you can't work for the Grays *and* the Gwilyms. You were here yesterday with Murray, weren't you?'

'So fascinated that I came back.'

'Thought so.' Squinting at Merrily through the smoke and a frond of hair, nicotine-blonded, fallen forward, a worn elegance about her.

'Bad penny,' said Merrily.

'Oh, I don't think so, Mrs Watkins.'

And you thought the intelligence services in Ledwardine were fast. Merrily took a step back. The woman held up her cigarette.

'Not *habitually* nosy. But living here, one learns there are things it's as well to know about as not. So, yes, I do know who you are.' She snatched another puff, blowing the smoke out sideways. 'And what you do.'

'Not exactly a chance encounter, then,' Merrily said.

'No. Sorry.' The woman switched the cigarette to her left hand, putting out the right. 'Morningwood. Mrs.'

Free-range eggs and honey and herbs. The woman who'd told Felix the Master House was unhappy.

They shook hands.

'This is Jane. My daughter.'

'Of course. Girl involved in a fracas with the wretched Council. I applaud you, m' dear. Would have been there m'self, with a placard, but always too busy.'

Merrily sighed. 'Mrs Morningwood, this is all very impressive—'

'Darling, it's not impressive at all. Truth of it is, Roscoe and I happened to be padding quietly through the church precincts yesterday afternoon when Murray was kind enough to identify you by name.'

'You must've been … behind the church tower?'

'No wish to intrude.'

Merrily imagined Mrs Morningwood flattened against the stonework with a hand around the wolfhound's muzzle. Not that this would have been necessary; you couldn't help noticing how docile and obedient Roscoe had become since being … set on Jane?

'And the rest was down to Google. Directing me immediately to your Diocesan website. Deliverance? That's really what they're calling it nowadays?'

'Mixed blessing, Google.'

'Brass tacks, Mrs Watkins?'

'If you like.'

'All right.' Mrs Morningwood flicked away an inch of ash. 'Save some time, *I* ask you why you're here. You say, what's it to you, you prying cow? I then try to convince you that I might be able to assist in some way, being the nearest neighbour of whoever's attempting to live in that benighted hovel at any particular time.'

'The Master House.'

'So-called. And now, interestingly – or mystifyingly, perhaps – in the ownership of the heir to the throne. Should we feel honoured, do you suppose?'

Merrily said, '*Attempting* to live there?'

'If you were able to point to anyone who'd succeeded, you'd have a sight longer memory than me, m' dear. Am I to understand you've been invited to subject the place to some form of exorcism?'

'That's probably overstating it. We haven't even found it yet.'

'Want to find it now?'

'That was the original plan, but now we don't have much time.'

'Not much time is probably an advantage. An excuse to get out of there.' Mrs Morningwood patted her thigh, and the dog crept close. 'Follow me.'

The sun had been reduced to a reddening corona on the rim of the dovecote. They followed her back to where the Volvo was parked, up against the hedge on the edge of the churchyard. Then along the lane and into a lay-by concealing the entrance to a mud track.

All too easy to miss. Cigarette poking from her lips, Mrs Morningwood began pulling nettles away from the bars of a galvanized gate with her bare hands, a rural skill that Merrily had never mastered. Impressive.

'Entrance seems to seal itself up in a matter of days, even at this time of year. Make of that what you will.'

'Not you, Jane,' Merrily said, and Jane smiled and moved alongside Mrs Morningwood at the jammed gate.

'Mrs Morningwood, can I ask you something before I forget? Why were there two pubs around here called The Sun and The Moon?'

'Before my time, child.'

'I was thinking that the Knights Templar were well into astrology,' Jane said.

'Were they?'

'You don't know much about the Templars?'

'Problem at Garway …' Mrs Morningwood freed the gate, with a ferrous clatter, prising it from the post '… is separating fact from legend. You probably know the saying about the Garway witches. No? *There'll be nine witches from the bottom of Orcop to the end of Garway Hill, as long as water runs.'*

'And are there?'

'To my knowledge ... only me.' Mrs Morningwood let loose a short, throaty laugh. 'Herbs, darling. I grow various medicinal herbs. Make potions and flog them at the farmers' markets, two fingers up to the diabolical EC regulations.'

'Have you lived here all your life?'

'Except for the twenty years or so when I tried to separate myself, before the damn place reached out its suckers.' Mrs Morningwood pinched out the remains of her cigarette. 'Mother passed along, leaving me the cottage, which tied in roughly with the divorce. Came back to recover. That was thirteen ... no, *fourteen* years ago. God almighty. Shouldn't've reverted to the maiden name, that was the mistake. Slotted myself back into a fearsome tradition.'

Jane looked at her, waiting for it.

'*Always be a Morningwood on Garway Hill, as long as badgers shit on the White Rocks!*' Mrs Morningwood exploded into catarrhal laughter and flung open the metal gate. 'In you go.'

16

Watch Night

A SQUARE, RIDGED field, given up to docks and thistles. New thorn trees sprouting around the greying bones of the old. Woodland enclosing it on three sides hid many of the hills, and the only sighting point was the conical cap of the church tower.

'So many folds and hollows,' Merrily said. 'Hard to be sure exactly where you are.'

'You know Kentchurch Court?' Mrs Morningwood's arm, another of Merrily's cigarettes at the end of it, was signposting a heavy canopy of oak woodland. 'Down behind there. Home of the Scudamores. Normans who followed the Conqueror over here in the eleventh century. One of the sons married Owain Glyndwr's daughter, and they're supposed to have sheltered him when his rebellion went down.'

'And the Master House is ... where?'

'Close. Over the ridge.' Mrs Morningwood pushed the gate shut and plucked a twig from one of the holes in her Barbour, turning to Jane. 'Suppose I might as well tell you – those pubs, Sun and Moon?'

'Uh-huh?'

Jane stood on the mud track, a hand on Roscoe's grizzled head. Getting better at containing her curiosity.

'That's only half the story,' Mrs Morningwood said. 'Used to be a third inn. Called, as it happens, The Stars.'

'Wow.' Jane blinked. 'Really?'

'And ... if you continue past The Sun, you'll come to a white house which also used to be a pub. With the, I suppose, equally celestial name of The Globe.'

'*Holy sh ...*' Jane lost it. 'You're *kidding*.'

'Go and look on your way home. There's a small sign on the wall. *The Globe.*'

'Four astronomical pubs in one small area? This is amazing, Mrs Morningwood.'

'Yes, it *is* interesting, I would agree. When you've grown up with it, you don't think. Part of the fabric.'

'I'm sorry ...' Merrily kept on looking at the point of the church tower and the autumnal woodland glowing dully, like dying embers, under clouds the colour of old brick '... but did you say *The Globe?*'

At the first oblique sight of it, you thought of a fox dozing in the undergrowth.

Except they didn't, did they? Not out in the open, by day. Foxes didn't sleep like that.

They'd walked uphill for about fifty paces, cresting a rise with two oak trees on top, boughs locked like antlers, and then the house was in a hollow below them: sprawling side-on, low-slung and sagging in a frame of bleached oak, built of rubble-stone the muddy colours of Garway church. A tin-roofed lean-to had collapsed at one end, exposing arms of oak raised in a ragged V to the rafters.

There were the usual twentieth-century additions to the house itself, notably the dormers jutting from the old stone tiles, but you could see that they were already rotting – slates slipping, guttering hanging off, while the original oak endured.

'Sort of Welsh longhouse in one of its incarnations,' Mrs Morningwood said. 'Barn or cattle shed attached. Are you all right, Mrs Watkins?'

'I'm fine.'

If disoriented. Like she'd passed into a dream and then from one dream into another that was darker. *The Globe:* where did fiction begin? And why had Mrs Morningwood suddenly decided to pass on information that would make the place, for Jane, even sexier?

'Nice job on the roof, actually, Mrs Watkins. Timbers patched rather than replaced, and he had the foresight to use second-hand stone tiles. New ones might've been disastrous. The chap was good. Pity he couldn't stay.'

'What've you heard, Mrs Morningwood?'

'His girl was frightened.'

'He told you that?'

'Yes, he did.'

'You told him it was an unhappy house,' Merrily said. 'Would it be possible to explain further?'

Moving beyond the second oak tree, she saw a granary, with stone steps and a barn with a badly holed roof. Mrs Morningwood zipped up her cracked and fissured Barbour over the pink scarf.

'Last time I was in there was nearly fifty years ago. I was nine years old.'

'You lived next door and you haven't been in for fifty years?'

'"Next door"'s a relative term, darling. My cottage is six fields away, including one we let go to conifers, for purposes of concealment.'

'So you wouldn't see this house?'

'Word is the Duchy of Cornwall wants to turn it into craft work-shops, employing green energy. Good luck to them. I've nothing against Charles – been times I've even applauded the chap. Especially when he supports alternative remedies against the weasels of the medical profession taking their grimy little backhanders from the drug companies to cure us of non-existent ills. Cholesterol – who the hell invented cholesterol?'

Mrs Morningwood had sunk her fists so deeply into the pockets of the worn Barbour that you could see her knuckles through the holes.

'Do you know what a watch night is, Mrs Watkins? Or was.'

'Erm … maybe.'

'Most places it had faded out by the end of the nineteenth century. Garway's said to be the last part of Herefordshire to carry it on. Even so, it had almost vanished, even here, when it was reinstated by the Newtons.'

'This was the family who'd bought the place from the Gwilyms?'

'And how much do you know about that?'

'Not much. That's why I'm here. Learning history.'

'Fychan Gwilym,' Mrs Morningwood said.

'Sorry?'

'A name inevitably – and deliberately – mispronounced this side of the border. It all begins with Fychan. The Gwilyms, while not exactly marcher lords – being, of course, mainly Welsh – nonetheless had a substantial domain, and Fychan was their patriarch around the turn of last century. Notorious drunk, gambler, fornicator, wife-beater and, worst of all, a *very* bad farmer. Weekends, he'd take himself off to the fleshpots of Hereford and Monmouth. Weekdays, he'd be out hunting and gradually running the farm into the ground to pay off his debts.'

'When was that?'

'Early 1900s? Fortunately, one morning they found the bastard dead on the road to Bagwyllydiart. The eldest son far too young to take over, and the widow – much relieved, one imagines – rejected the local vultures, moved to a cottage on the edge of the village and shocked everyone by flogging the farm to the Newtons. From Off, Mrs Watkins.'

'How *far* off?'

'Over towards Ross, I believe. Well-heeled farming family, the Newtons, looking for a living for a second son. Gwilyms incandescent with rage. Hordes of them wriggling out of their holes. Imagine a raiding party of red-necked bastards, spitting and cursing – well, I exaggerate obviously, but such were the recriminations that the widow Gwilym found it expedient to leave the area altogether within the year.'

'This house was so important to the family? Or was it the land?'

'Oh, the house, principally. Ancestral family home, you see. Attempts to stop the sale, but it was legal, and once the Newtons were in they started buying more land – couple of fields here, bit of woodland there – gradually assembling a lucrative holding. Aware all the time, of course, of the Gwilym family closing in like Birnam Wood from the Welsh side – for many years in the ample shape of one Owain Gwilym, who had a farm near Skenfrith, ground extending almost to the border. Dedicated to getting the Newtons out and the Master House back. Not an ideal neighbour.'

'Sounds like the seedbed of a classic border feud.'

'Inevitably. Two farming dynasties head-to-head. Harassment … destruction of fences … smashing of gates … rustling of stock …' Mrs Morningwood sniffed in contempt. 'Farmers can be like children –

petty bullying and breaking one another's toys. Split the community down the middle. You were either for the Gwilyms or the Newtons. And the Newtons, during this period, had considerably more money and were generous to their local employees.'

'Always helps.'

'And they were clever. Always thinking of ways to weave themselves into the very fabric of the area, learning its psychology, absorbing its traditions – and *using* them. Which brings us back to the watch night. You remembered yet?'

'I think ...' Merrily flicked a wary glance at Jane '... that it was about ... keeping company with the dead?'

Mrs Morningwood folded her arms and hunched her shoulders, leaning her head back, as if to allow the memories to come sliding down like grain.

'Specifically, Felicity Newton. Only ever remember her as an old woman. Must've been close to a hundred when she died in the 1950s – and not many people made the century in those days. Her son, Ralph, head of the family, decided to make an event of it – in theory, to allow everyone to pay their respects. One can see now that it was designed to work as a kind of ritual homage, binding the village and the neighbouring farms to the Newtons. All I know is, it haunted my dreams for years.'

'You all had to see the body?'

'Darling, if only it had stopped there.'

Mrs Morningwood pointed down to the Master House, where the skeleton of a porch had been half pulled away from the Gothic-shaped front door of whitening oak. She described a square hall just inside, which had also served as the living room. With a large inglenook, in front of which the remains of Felicity Newton had been displayed.

'It must have been about eleven p.m. on a winter's night – I was quite excited, I'd been allowed to stay up. We walked across the fields, my mother and I – just across here. People going in before us, all dressed in black, leaving their hurricane lamps outside. People who all knew one another, but no one spoke. I remember there was a fire in the room, kept very low, the only source of light, apart from the one candle. Like a grotto, a shrine. We were allowed to enter in ones and twos, and each time the door closed behind us, so that we were shut in with the corpse.'

Merrily saw Jane discreetly rolling her eyes.

'First time I'd seen a dead 'un,' Mrs Morningwood said. 'The candle was in a saucer. Sitting in a mound of salt on a saucer placed on the chest of the corpse, which lay in its coffin on trestles in the centre of the room. The candle casting a quite ghastly light on the face. I remember – one of those frozen moments that resurface, for years, in nightmares – taking one look and being gripped by a horror that was *physical,* like a cramp in my stomach. Tried to run out, but then, from the shadows by the inglenook, a bigger shadow arose. Tessie Worthy, the Newtons' housekeeper. A large and formidable woman. I remember, as clearly as if it was yesterday, Tessie Worthy, in her big white starched apron, rising up and intoning, in this low rumble of a voice, *Everybody is to touch her.*'

'Gross,' Jane said, hugging the wolfhound.

'I remember my mother lifting me up and placing my hand on the withered cheek. I remember turning my head away when the smell wafted up at me – I'm sure if I went in there now I'd smell it again. Putrid. The faint but piercing stench of decay, mixed with the sickly smell of molten wax. I closed my eyes tightly. The face felt like the skin on a cold egg-custard.'

'This is an old Celtic thing?' Jane said, unfazed. 'Like corpse candles?'

'About keeping away evil spirits, m' dear. A light must remain burning in the room where the corpse lies, up until burial.'

'Until the funeral,' Merrily said, 'the spirit was supposed to be hanging around the house and shouldn't be left alone. That was the belief, I think.'

She looked down at the house, some of its windows leaded and framed with rusted metal, others just holes, like the sockets of eyes which had been put out.

'However, I do believe the Newtons used it as a kind of controlling device,' Mrs Morningwood said. 'Each hand on the dead cheek an unspoken gesture of allegiance. And, of course, almost everyone came – except, obviously, anyone called Gwilym.'

'How often did that happen?' Merrily asked. 'These communal visits to the Newton dead.'

'Twice? Three times? I don't truly know. I left home in my twenties. Couldn't wait to get out, to the big, exciting, non-superstitious city. By the time I returned, they'd moved out.'

'Left the house?'

'Built a new house, originally for a tenant, then improved and extended it, and then it became the family home. More convenient, easier to heat – or that was *their* story. The Master House was rented out, first to some people who tried to run a riding stables – and failed – and then to one of those 1970s good-life communes, posh kids with ideals but no morals. They'd gone, too, time I returned, and word was the Gwilyms were trying to buy it back. Gruffydd Gwilym, not a bad chap, actually, but the Newtons turned him away – rather see the house rot away than returned to the Gwilyms. And now, of course, there's Gruffydd's son. *Suckarse.*'

Merrily blinked, patting Roscoe, the wolfhound, who'd come to sit between her and Jane.

'Sycharth, actually.' Mrs Morningwood spelled it out. 'Some of us do know our Welsh pronunciations but can't resist taking the piss. Sycharth inherited earlier than expected, Gruffydd having been killed in one of those ubiquitous tractor accidents that occur on hill farms. Wouldn't happen to Sycharth – man's never even been on a bloody tractor. Big businessman, now, in Hereford. Property, restaurants. Latest is some abomination called The Centurion.'

'I know it.' Flash eatery on Roman Road. '*He* owns that?'

'A reversal of fortunes for both families. The Gwilyms back in the money, hard times for the Newtons. Suffered terribly during the Foot and Mouth of 2001 – which, of course, the despicable government allowed to spread, to shaft the farmers the way Thatcher shafted the miners.'

Merrily nodded. You heard this all the time. A conspiracy theory that would last for at least a generation.

'All governments are the same underneath. Final straw, though, for the Newtons. Farm was like a concentration camp after the war – smoke

and death. And the Newtons – hardly the powerful family I remembered, and it didn't get any easier. The boys wanted out, and that
might've been the end of it, had the eldest girl, Roxanne, not married
Paul Gray. Young farmer with ambition and enough family funds to buy
in. Actually started to turn it around … before he was diagnosed with
MS.'

'Ah. I saw him. Briefly. Trying to avoid his wheelchair.'

'He's fighting. Cursed, though. Farm was cursed. People still talk like
that, as I'm sure you know.'

'And the feud?'

'Never went away. Like a live electric wire under the ground, and
periodically someone would strike it with a spade. Sycharth pretends it's
all history. When the word leaked out about Paul's illness, he immediately offered to help by buying back the Master House and surrounding
land. Which might've been tempting if he hadn't been a Gwilym.'

'Didn't want to know?'

'But I think it did make them realize that this might be a good time
to sell … to the right buyer.'

'Ah.' Merrily nodded. 'Perhaps a respectable outside buyer with
plenty of money and no possible link to the Gwilyms?'

'I don't know the details,' Mrs Morningwood said, 'but it was clearly
the Grays who made the approach to the Duchy of Cornwall.'

'Mmm.'

'Knowing how keen the Duchy were on Herefordshire at the time,
having recently bought Harewood Park, not a dozen miles away.'

'Clever.'

'Oh, they've always been clever, Grays and Newtons both. If rather
unlucky.'

'And how do the Gwilyms feel about the Duchy?'

'One can only imagine. All right then, darling …' Mrs Morningwood
squeezed out her cigarette, tidily pocketing the stub. 'If you want to go
into the house, I won't detain you any longer. But at least you know
some of the background.'

'Yes. Thank you, Mrs Morningwood.'

'You have a key?'

'A very big key.' Merrily could feel its outline bulging her bag. 'Only problem now is, I've a church service to take at seven-thirty, back in Ledwardine.'

'Time for a peek, surely. I'm sure your God will protect you. Come along, Roscoe.'

'You're not coming?'

'Hens to get in before nightfall. Besides, I think I told you – I never go there.'

'Because you actually believe it's haunted or for some other reason that you ... maybe don't feel able to share?'

For just a moment, Mrs Morningwood looked almost thrown. Then she smiled.

'I trust the dog, Mrs Watkins. Once got carried away, in pursuit of a bunny, found himself within yards of the ruins. He froze for a moment – absolutely froze – then made the most extraordinary noise and came running back to me like the wind, tail well down. Walked pitifully to heel all the way home.'

She attached the leather lead to Roscoe's collar and then held out the looped end, first to Merrily, then to Jane.

'Go on – try him. See what happens.'

Jane looked at Merrily.

'Wouldn't be fair,' Merrily said.

17

The Inglenook

A YEAR OR so before moving to Ledwardine, Merrily had helped take the funeral of a youngish woman with psychiatric problems, wife of a local head teacher. Probably suicide but passed off, by a kindly coroner, as accidental death.

Up in Liverpool this had been, when she'd been a curate, and there'd been an open coffin, in the American tradition. And that had bothered her, and the fact that it bothered her was also worrying. Was she squeamish? Immature? Surely it was good to be as open as possible about death. Took away the fear. Touch a corpse, you'll never be afraid again.

They've made her look so composed, the husband had said. *After all her suffering and her confusion, I want everyone to see how together she looks.*

Together, yes. Like an expensive doll in a white padded gift-box. A classy ad for the embalmer's art, but you couldn't believe it had ever enclosed an animating spark.

This was the problem: the underlining of the finality of death, the erasure of the spirit, a lasting image of the recently departed in eternal rigid repose. Where was the promise of freedom, the *energy of release*?

Standing in the ruins of the Master House porch, gripping the big, rust-brown key, Merrily was still unsure how she felt about public displays of mortality. But one thing was certain: a single, eerie experience as a child would hardly be enough to keep someone as world-hardened as Mrs Morningwood at bay for a half a century.

'Weird about the dog,' Jane said.

'Maybe.'

'You think she was winding you up? You could've just taken her up on the offer, walked him down here yourself.'

'Wouldn't have proved anything. Most dogs don't like being suddenly taken away from their owners on the end of a lead. Perhaps she knew how he'd react.'

'Honestly ...' Jane scowled. 'You're always so *suspicious* of people. Is that really good for a vicar? I mean, I liked her.'

'*I* liked her, but I'm not sure how far I'd trust her. Everybody has an agenda, and she'd targeted us. There were things she wanted me to know. *That*'s suspicious.'

'And you a Christian.'

'Yes, it's very sad.'

Down in the hollow, the air was already purpling with dusk, the birdsong withdrawing into the trees. Two sparrows flew out of the eaves. Merrily looked at the oak front door.

'Makes you wonder why these Gwilyms wanted it back,' Jane said. 'It's going to cost a fortune even to patch it up.'

'I can understand that – if it's the family home since way, way back. And if this guy Sycharth owns The Centurion, he's certainly got the money.'

The house looked heavier close-up, less vulnerable, some of its lower stones like boulders. Jane picked up a stone tile fallen from the porch and propped it against the wall.

'So these Gwilyms are obviously going to be seriously pissed off about the Newtons or the Grays or whoever cut this deal with Charles's guys behind their backs.'

'Having to sit there on the other side of the river and watch the old homestead getting immaculately renovated. Turned into somebody else's business.'

'Would there be *any* chance of them ever buying it back?'

'Can't be ruled out, flower. The Duchy's a business, buying and selling property. If they can't make it work, they might sell it on. And the project certainly hasn't got off to the best of starts.'

Merrily was watching the top unrolling from a new can of worms. How influential *was* Sycharth Gwilym in Hereford property circles?

Had Felix Barlow ever worked for the Gwilyms? Had Felix somehow been got at? OK, that seemed unlikely but ... *God*, who could you totally trust? Who could you *ever* trust?

'So,' Jane said. 'We going in?'

She was standing, brown paw marks down her front, under the grey metal skull of a lamp over the front door. Fragments of glass embedded in its rim like splintered teeth. Merrily frowned.

'Perhaps not. Can't just look around and leave. First rule of deliverance: never walk away from an alleged disturbance without leaving God's card.'

'In case of what?' Jane said. 'A ghostly coffin in the hall, and the body suddenly sits up, with the pennies dropping from its dead eyes?'

'Wasn't *quite* how I was thinking.'

'You know what *I* think? I think you just don't want to go into a possibly haunted house with someone you think might still be half-pagan.'

'Things have changed. These days, I tend to credit the boss with being more broad-minded.'

'So go on, then. Unlock it.'

Jane's eyes were dancing erratically. It could be that she didn't actually want to go in. But she *was* Jane Watkins.

'Yeah. All right.'

Merrily put the key into a hole enlarged, probably, by generations of Gwilyns coming home from the pub in the dark. The key rattling around in there, failing to locate the tumblers. It took both hands and a lot of jiggling before the lock turned over and the door sprang loose and hung there sullenly, still needing a shoulder to shudder it open.

'House that doesn't want to be restored,' Merrily said.

'What?'

'Nothing.'

She stepped inside ahead of Jane, inhaling damp and plaster dust disturbed by the vibration. Two grimy leaded windows were set into a sloping wall, and the restricted light – brown and flecked, like the sediment at the bottom of an old medicine bottle – was barely reaching the shadows that crowded the corners of what seemed quite a big room.

Smelling wet earth, Merrily counted one, two three four … five doors, and the wall opposite jaggedly agape: a vast inglenook, the oak beam across it as rough and massive as the capstone of a cromlech. Primeval. Like the tree itself had fallen onto some waiting stones, been sawn off and the entire house built around it.

'So this …' Jane peering over Merrily's shoulder '… this is where they laid the old girl out?'

'Not here now, though, Jane. Sorry to disappoint.'

The only furniture was in the hearth, a rusted iron fire-basket the size of a small sheep-pen. In search of better light, Merrily walked across what seemed like worn linoleum ground into the earth to a narrow door next to the inglenook. When she unlatched it, greyness slithered down a stone staircase, half-spiralling behind the fireplace.

She didn't go up. She was cold, rubbing her arms through the too-thin sweatshirt, looking over her shoulder into an empty …

'Jane?'

'Down here. Couple of steps going down into … looks like the kitchen. Big hooks in the beams. Kind of a fatty smell.'

'Just … tell me when you're going somewhere, OK?'

'In case of what?' Jane came back up, pulling a door shut behind her. 'What's upstairs?'

'I don't know. I'd feel better with a torch.'

'If it was dangerous, they'd have warned you, wouldn't they?'

'I suppose.'

The only warnings had come, in that faintly teasing way, from Mrs Morningwood, Merrily scenting a set-up.

'Go on, then, Mum.'

Jane was behind her on the steps, the wooden handrail was hanging loose from the wall. Merrily didn't touch it.

Upstairs, they found a landing with no windows, the only light fanning from one door left narrowly ajar. Merrily put out an arm to hold Jane back – could be floorboards missing – before stepping tentatively into a long and dismal bedroom smelling of dead things in decay.

Bluish light from a single dormer, half-boarded. Wooden skeletons of two beds, at either end of the room.

'Like in the story,' Jane whispered.

'What?'

'"Oh, Whistle, and I'll Come to You". In Parkins's room at the … whatever the pub was called.'

'The Globe Inn.'

Jane turned sharply.

'Bloody hell! *That*'s why you—'

'It's just a bit coincidental.'

'In the circumstances, Mum, I'd say it's *seriously* coincidental.'

'It's … noteworthy.'

There was a paper sack up against one wall. Fuchsia's lime-plaster? Was this the room where she'd … *claimed* to have seen something wriggling under the …

The floor was bare boards. Felix had evidently taken his dust sheets away.

'Mum, why didn't you ask Mrs Morningwood about M. R. James?'

'Because there's a couple of other people I need to discuss it with first. And if you were to email the *Ghosts and Scholars* website we might learn a bit more from the experts.'

'I'll do that tonight. But if … like, if M. R. James admits something strange happened to him in Garway, maybe he actually stayed in the Globe Inn? That would surely—'

'He always stayed with some people not too far away. Let's not speculate, huh?'

'Whatever.' Jane looked around. 'Are you going to leave the calling card or what?'

'Can't decide what to do. It's just an empty house. In my limited experience, they need … people.'

'*They?*'

'Don't ask me what *they* are. However, I think – Huw Owen thinks – we might need to ask a few people round, interested parties. Although getting a Gwilym and a Gray into the same room might be problematical.'

'Why would you need to?'

'That seem a bit like meddling to you?'

Feuds were a pastoral issue, and she wasn't the parish priest. Maybe she needed to talk to Teddy Murray again, even though he was only a stand-in.

They checked out three other bedrooms of varying sizes, unfurnished. A bathroom with a cracked, discoloured bath and no water from the taps. A separate toilet that stank. Everywhere tainted by dereliction, in dire need of Felix Barlow.

But Fuchsia?

If Felix was right, something had brought Fuchsia back here yesterday. Fuchsia, who wanted to be blessed in the old-fashioned way. *Watch over her, in the name of all the angels and saints in heaven. Keep guard over her soul day and night.*

Fuchsia, newly blessed, had returned to a place she'd judged to be *full of death.* Nothing here was suggesting why.

Jane headed for the top of the half-spiral stairs, and Merrily followed her down, unsatisfied, mildly annoyed. The stone steps were worn smooth at the edges, slippery, some shored up underneath with bricks. Pointless doing a room-to-room prayer cycle; she didn't know enough of the history to have any kind of focus, and all she could feel in the air was the criss-crossing of private agendas. It was an unwelcoming old house, soured by neglect, and that was probably the extent of it.

Back in the big room, the light seemed stronger, but that would be just her eyes adjusting. She looked around, walked around the ingrained lino and then stepped inside the inglenook. Ducking, although there was no need to, under the vast beam.

The inglenook was almost a small chamber in itself. A separate place. In the sooty dimness, she found the remains of what must have been a bread oven, empty, and a matted tangle of grey bones, all that was left of a bird, behind the fire-basket. She looked up the chimney: glimmerings of light, but something blocking it – nests maybe.

'Nothing much here, Jane.'

'Sorry, Mum?'

Jane's voice coming from the other side of the room.

'I'm sorry,' Merrily said, 'I thought you—'

The sentence guillotined by the thought that if it hadn't been Jane who was with her in the inglenook …

'… Sort of passage, leading to a back door,' Jane called out. 'Kind of a washroom?'

Standing very still and fully upright, her back flat to the rear wall, Merrily let in a long, thin river of breath.

'… An old sink.' Jane's voice further away. 'Cupboards …'

'Jane, get—'

Merrily's throat spasm-blocked, her headache back, like spikes, like a crown of thorns, twisting in. The iron fire-basket gaped up at her like an open gin-trap while she scrabbled in the pockets of her mind for prayer. *Christ be* … Be, for God's sake, calm. Pushing back a sudden amazing panic, vile as a migraine, she closed her eyes, but it was like when you made yourself dizzy as child, and she felt sick, feeling the crumbling house turning slowly around her, grinding on the axis of its origins.

'*Christ be wi—*'

' *… with …*'

Only half-hearing the words – *St Patrick's Breastplate*, the old armour – but her lips were cold and flaccid and wouldn't shape them. There was a solid, substantial resistance, a flat, hard-edged *no*, and a rubbery numbness in her hands when she tried to clasp them together. And although the prayer was sounding in her head, it was distant, someone else's whispers, and she tried to turn up the volume, envisioning bright brass bells clanging in a high tower, but the sound was harsh and industrial.

Christ behind me, Christ before me …

A muted crackling down there: bird bones crunching under her shoes. When she opened her eyes in revulsion, there was a face in the high corner of the inglenook and it had stubby horns and a worm squirming from its blackened mouth, and Merrily recoiled.

'*Mum?*'

Jane's footsteps sounded on the ingrained lino. But she mustn't …

'Mum, look, I don't want to worry you or anything, but it's getting dark, and you've got your meditation in just over an hour? And I think we've both had enough of this place.'

Merrily wouldn't move. Or try to speak because, if Jane knew where she was, Jane would join her.

18

Listen

WHAT LOL LIKED best about the gigging was the coming home. Home to the mosaic of coloured-lit windows in the black and white houses, the fake gas lamps ambering the cobbles, sometimes the scent of apple-wood smoke.

He parked the Animal under the lamp on the edge of the square, well back from the cars and SUVs of the Sunday-evening diners in the Black Swan.

The truck had been Gomer's idea, watching Lol loading two guitars and an amp awkwardly into the Astra, together with all the one-man-band gadgets which contrived the drumming and the toots and whirrs and storm noises that audiences loved for the apparent chaos of it all.

Gomer had remembered that his sidekick Danny Thomas knew a reliable bloke who was selling his Mitsubishi L200. *Animal*, it said on the side. Gomer seemed to find this funny. He and Danny had converted the truck, building a watertight compartment into the box to accommodate the gear, fitting a metal roll-top cover you could lock, and Gomer had taken Lol's old Astra to recondition for himself: *Waste not, want not, Lol, boy.*

Lol climbed down, walked round the Animal in the late twilight and pushed back the roll-top under the lights, uncovering the case of the lovely Boswell guitar, handmade by Al Boswell, the Romani, in the Frome Valley, two harmonicas, shining like ingots in a black velvet tray, and the plastic thing that could make your voice sound like an oboe. Audiences everywhere – *Hello Hartlepool, Good Evening, Godalming* – seemed to warm to the homespun, the cobbled-together. They actually wanted to like you.

Taken him a long time to realize that. Nick Drake never had. Nick who, for God's sake, was so much better, all *he*'d felt was a paralysing isolation which had sometimes left him playing with his back half-turned away from the crowd.

Lol opened the case that held the Boswell. Paranoia, he knew, but he was always worried that the vibration of the truck might have damaged it. Many different kinds of wood had gone into its mandolin soundbox. It wasn't the kind of guitar you took out on the road, but he felt it was his talisman – receiving it from Al Boswell when his life was turning round, the songs coming through and Merrily, miraculously warm in his bed.

The guitar seemed fine. But, across the street, over the corner of the square, the vicarage had no lights.

Not how it should be. Before Merrily left the house to do the evening meditation, she'd always put on the globular lamp over the door. Always. Symbolic. Place of sanctuary. For Lol more than anybody. He pulled back the roll-top, locked it quickly, ran across the square to the vicarage gate. No visible lights in the house. No Volvo in the drive. Garage doors shut and bolted.

Lol felt the inner freeze of dislocation. She wasn't there, and she hadn't told him. He felt, for cold moments, like a stranger here again. Without Merrily, he *would* be a stranger, snatching moments of warmth only from his hard-earned applause, a furnace door opening and closing.

Stupid. Not as if they were married.

Maybe she'd left him a message on the answering machine? He ran back across the square to the terraced cottage in Church Street, unlocked his front door.

A haze of street light on the desk under the front window. Silence. No bleeps. Lol looked out into the street, up and down at the windows of Ledwardine, the mosaic of coloured squares now as unwelcoming as the ash in the hearth.

There would be a simple explanation. He was becoming neurotic, over-possessive.

Not as if they were married.

Yet, so often, with the nature of what she did, when he'd felt a wrong-ness there had been … something wrong.

He went back out to the square, to where he could see the body of the church through the lych-gate, the bunched shadows of people drifting through to an evening service with no hymns, psalms, lessons or sermon.

A vaporous glow from the church-door lantern. About to walk down, glancing back at the vicarage, he saw a blur of white, someone emerging from the gate, crossing the cobbles towards Church Street.

Lol made tea, and Jane seized her mug with both hands, carrying it through to the parlour with the burnt-orange ceiling, where Lol switched on the parchment-shaded desk lamp, leaving the curtains open, his initial relief burning away.

'You mean she's ill?'

'I don't know.' Jane's eyes glassy and anxious. 'Maybe.'

'Jane—'

'We were in a hurry, Lol. We got back late. I said I'd get on the computer, try and get some background.'

'On what? She is *in* the church?'

'Yeah. She dashed straight across. Left me to put the car away and feed Ethel and stuff.'

'So what's wrong with her?'

'Lol, I just … I don't know, all right? Maybe it's been coming on for a while. OK, it's been a heavy year, all the death, all the things she couldn't prevent. All the stuff that came to nothing. I don't *know*.'

'OK.' Lol sat down in the chair facing Jane on the sofa, a chill on the room. 'Tell me. In sequence.'

And she tried to, but most of it he couldn't really take in. The number of the beast and the pubs with the cosmic names, the spooky woman with the dog. And the farmhouse.

'When we came out, honest to God, Lol, she was white as … as a surplice. Like, trying to be normal – kind of, *let's not worry Jane*. Which only made it worse because it was so obvious. Like *I'm* going to be worried? Me? The pagan?'

'Worried about what?'

'And then we go into this field, and I get the full blessing bit. The spiritual body-armour, at sundown on the edge of a field? Like, *huh*?'

123

'She ever done that before?'

'No. But then I don't usually go with her on these jobs, do I? She said it was routine. Quite normal. Yeah, *right*.'

'And she's gone ahead with the meditation?'

'Mmm.' Jane nodded. 'I mean … maybe that'll help?'

Lol got her to tell him again – about the pubs and the dovecote and M. R. James.

'After you came out of the house, what exactly did she say?'

'She looked at her watch, and she's like, "Oh my God, we're not going to make it back in time." But you could tell that wasn't what was really bothering her, and if we were late why was she wasting time with all this blessing crap? Like, I'm an idiot? And all the way back she was like talking about other things – trivial things, in this brisk, practical way. Like she was trying to screen something out. Like she'd seen something in there, or realized something she didn't want to face up to.'

'And when you got back, was she still …?'

'Upset, yeah. That was obvious.' Jane drank some tea. 'She looked totally out of it, like someone who'd been in a car crash. But when we were actually looking around the place, she was fairly dismissive, a bit annoyed, like she'd been set up. She hates that, people treating her like she's some dim … vicar.'

Jane finished her tea, still looking starved and unhappy and maybe even resentful that some dim vicar might have picked up on an aspect of *otherness* that she'd missed out on.

'Lol …' Catching him looking at her. 'I think I've changed quite a bit the past year. I'd like to think I could help her. But she's still wary, you know?'

'I'll talk to her,' Lol said.

Lol padded past the font, unseen. Not difficult at the Sunday-evening meditation, when the front pews were arranged in a circle, and the only light was candlelight, vast shadows ghosting the sandstone walls.

About two dozen people had come – about normal. When the rumours of healing had been circulating, there would have been as many as a hundred, but it had calmed down now.

'... Idea that prayer's as much about listening ... means we have to think about what we *mean* by listening.'

No priestly trappings, no ceremonial. No smoke, no mirrors, no applause, no stamping for encores.

Merrily's gig.

She was sitting on the edge of the circle in her black jeans and sweat-shirt, hair tied back. Never a pulpit person.

'Because, when you think about it, we hardly ever really do it.'

Lol sank down a couple of rows back, in deep shadow, his eyes closing momentarily in relief. Feeling her voice: low, soft, conversational, unassuming, intimate. Half-guiltily fancying the hell out of her.

'If we're holding a conversation with somebody, even if we think we're taking in what they're saying to us, what we're actually doing is filtering it ... putting it through this sieve of our own needs, desires, fears. Thinking of what we *want* them to be saying, and also of what we're afraid they might *really* be saying. We're processing the words, analysing, alert for any subtext. Our minds are taking an active role, in other words. We're not *listening*. Does that make sense?'

Murmured assent. The people who came here on a Sunday evening were, by and large, not the ones who came to the family service in the morning. This was post-watershed.

'OK, then,' Merrily said. 'Do you think we should try listening tonight? Without filtering, without questioning or intellectualising? Without any attempts at interpretation.'

Someone said, yeah, they should go for it, and Merrily moved her wooden chair a little forward, into the candlelight.

'First, we need to go into the contemplative state, opening ourselves up. So ...' laying her hands, palms down, on her knees '... if we start with the relaxation exercise, beginning at the feet. Becoming aware of our feet. Curling our toes ...'

The scraping of a pew.

'Merrily ... I want to ask ...'

Merrily looked up.

'Shirley.'

'Is this in the Bible?'

'I'm sorry?'

'Does the Bible tell us we should be opening ourselves up to … messages?'

'Well … I think you'll find it's all over the Bible in one way or another. But when you say *messages*, I'm not sure we're talking about the same—'

'Messages from beyond? Is that in the Bible?'

'I could find you some examples, Shirley, but this wasn't really intended to be a Bible-study session as much as—'

'Only, it's what the spiritualists do, isn't it? Go into a trance and wait for something to come through. Don't get me wrong, I appreciate you're trying to do something different here, Merrily, to bring some of these people into the fold, but I'm an old-fashioned Christian, and I keep asking myself, is the church the right place for it?'

Merrily sighed, her breath fluttering a candle flame.

'Shirley, I take your point, but there's a subtle difference between spirituality and spiritualism – *spiritism*. What I'm— No, actually the difference is not that subtle at all, it's something entirely—'

'How do we know that what's coming through is from God? That it's not a dead person?'

Merrily's face was tilted into the candlelight, and now Lol saw the furrows and the strain.

'Or something evil,' this Shirley said.

Restive murmurs from around the circle. A groan. Lol just sighed. A fundamentalist – all she needed.

'Because when we approach it like this,' Merrily said, 'in this context, it's coming out of prayer and it's an act of faith. Shirley, if you could bear with me …'

'It's just that, in the dark, with a ring of candles, it doesn't feel right to me. I don't *like* opening myself up. How do we know there isn't somebody here who's brought something evil in with them?'

This time, when Merrily looked up, Lol was shocked at the pallor of her face.

19

Sound Like Jane

WHEN IT WAS over, Merrily held the snuffer over the last candle and then guided Lol through the darkness towards the south door.

'Didn't handle that too well, did I?'

Moving them both swiftly down the nave. She could find her way blindfold around this sandstone cavern – had even actually done that once, when she was new here; it had seemed necessary, having an intimate, tactile knowledge of the body of the church, her own sacred space, to which it had seemed desperately important tonight to get back.

Bad mistake. She felt sick. Better she hadn't made it in time than have to watch the so-called ground-breaking meditation service crumbling away into a pointless debate about the validity of replacing the traditional Evensong, hymns and all, with quiet and contemplation. More like a bloody parish meeting.

'I wouldn't care, Shirley doesn't normally come on a Sunday night. I mean, if she prefers the formality of a structured service, well, fine ...'

'Who is she?'

'Shirley? I think I mentioned her. Currently my most enthusiastic parishioner.'

'Oh. Yes, you did.'

Lol bumped into the prayer-book rack; there was the slap of a book landing on flags.

'Leave it, I'll find it in the morning. Why are we talking in the dark? How did the gig go? Oh hell, I'm so sorry, I've forgotten where ...'

'Newtown. Theatr Hafren. It was good. Almost full. The local record shop was selling albums in the foyer. They sold out.'

'That's *fantastic*. Come back to the vic? Have some supper with us?'

Lol didn't move. She could see his outline, head bowed.

He said, 'When she said that about ... someone bringing evil into the church ...'

'Lol ...' God, what was she supposed to say? 'Look, this is unchari-table, but I sometimes think Shirley actually comes to too many services.'

'You thought she meant you, didn't you?'

Merrily's fingers found the stone bowl of the font, pressing into its whorls and furrows.

'You've been talking to Jane, right?'

'Well, she came over just now. A bit worried. Told me about M. R. James and the woman who was saying she'd seen one of his ghosts. And the dovecote. And this Mrs Mornington ...?'

'Wood.' Merrily straightened up. 'Morningwood.'

'And how you came out of the house, white-faced, and wouldn't talk about it.' Lol was standing next to her now. 'Pretty much the way you're not talking about it now.'

Merrily leaned against the firmness of the font. She looked back along the nave, vaguely moonlit now. Like a straight path through woodland.

But there was no green man at Ledwardine.

'All right. I may have ... I saw something that wasn't supposed to be there.'

'Inside the house? The Duchy of Cornwall house.'

'It just looked ordinary. It felt ordinary. Until I decided, for some reason, to have a look inside the inglenook. It's quite a high inglenook. Someone like me can stand upright in it, and quite a lot of space all round. Like a small, black room.'

Her mind was already tightening. She'd hoped it might melt away in the meditation. But the meditation had never happened, and maybe that was just as well. Maybe she *had* brought something back and if they'd gone into the meditation it would've been contaminated. Maybe Shirley— *Oh, for God's sake ...*

'Go on.' Merrily felt Lol's hand on her arm. 'The small black room behind the inglenook.'

'There was a feeling of not being alone. I'm not talking about God or anything.'

'You're saying you actually felt something was with you inside this inglenook?'

'Something watching me. It's all a bit subjective. A feeling I'd been getting at Garway generally. It has a very peculiar atmosphere, I can't explain it. Even the church seems to have eyes. Ancient landmark, sentient landscape … Oh God, listen to me, I'm starting to sound like Jane.'

Lol was silent. There were cooling clangs from the heating, which had switched itself off.

'You know the green man?' Merrily said. 'Like you get in country churches? Stone face looking through foliage?'

'Mouthful of leaves and stuff.'

'Maybe an ancient fertility symbol. Several in Herefordshire. The one in Garway Church is moulded into the chancel arch, and … there's also this one inside the oak lintel over the fireplace in the Master House. Almost identical, I'd guess, but I'd need to check. I just looked up, there it was.'

'That's what you thought was watching you?'

'At the back, so only visible from *inside* the inglenook. You don't see him unless you enter his …'

'A secret green man.'

'And not in a church. I don't know of any ancient ones that aren't in churches, though maybe there are. And hidden away. Why?'

'This green man is what scared you? Why you'd turned white?'

'I haven't been feeling too great lately.' She pulled away from the font, couldn't deal with this now. 'Let's go.'

Outside, a wind had arisen, chattering amongst dead chrysanths in a grave-pot. Merrily pulled the church keys from her shoulder bag. The Master House key poked out, and she thrust it back.

Lol said, 'You now think something actually happened to this Fuchsia at the house?'

'I'd convinced myself she was pulling some kind of scam. The face of crushed linen, all that. I was coming round to thinking there was some entirely prosaic reason for Felix changing his mind, wanting out of the job. I was ready to confront her about it.'

'So what are you going to do now?'

'Confront her. But maybe with a bit more ... sensitivity. That is, I still think there's a lot she hasn't told me, but I'm no longer ruling out the possibility of something else.'

'What are you going to tell Jane?'

'I don't know.'

'You sure you've told me everything?'

'Lol, I'm going to ring them now, OK?'

Fumbling out the phone and putting the number in the frame.

They stood under the lych-gate, opposite the square, orange and green lights making lanterns of the leaded windows of the Black Swan.

Lol said, 'Why don't you call them in the morning?'

'They might leave early.' The ringing stopped. 'Hold on, he's—'

The voice in the phone said hello.

'Felix,' Merrily said. 'I've been trying to get you all day. Listen, I *really* need to talk to you. Both of you. Tomorrow morning if possible. Even tonight, if you're up for that. Take me about twenty minutes to get there.'

There was no reply, something quizzical about the silence.

'Sorry,' she said. 'It's Merrily Watkins.'

'Yeh. I thought it was.'

Oh *shit*.

'Frannie, I'm sorry, I must've put the wrong number in. More haste, less—'

'Who did you think you were calling, Merrily?'

'Just ... just a guy I've been trying to ...'

'Felix, you said,' Bliss said. 'That would be Felix Barlow.'

'How did *you* ...' Something jerked inside her chest. '*Frannie* ...?'

'Twenty minutes, then,' Bliss said. 'I'll be waiting.'

20

Supposed to be Sheep

THERE WAS THE usual small, sordid fairground under a frantic night sky, fallen leaves panic-dancing in the intersecting headlight beams from three cars and a dark blue van, all pointing at the caravan, engines growling. Flapping and crackling from the plastic screen they'd erected inside the tapes, to keep out the rising wind. A rich smell of churned mud.

The West Mercia Police travelling show.

'Fuchsia.' Merrily felt insubstantial, blown around like the leaves. 'Where is she? Please, can *someone*—?'

Nearly a dozen men and women, cops and crime-scene technos like worker ants in the grass, none of them answering her, all of them hyper: never let anybody tell you these guys didn't get a wild buzz from violent death.

'This *is* the feller?' Bliss was in a white coverall, what he liked to call a Durex suit. Flicking occasional questions at her like pellets. 'You're sure about that?'

All the motion only emphasizing the stillness of the big man in a heap, dumped like manure below the caravan's open door. *Oh God, oh God, oh God.*

'Yes.'

Was she sure? Under the hardened mud and the congealed fluids, his head was a different shape. Mouth half-open, dried blood caked around his nose, both eyes soot-black. Merrily forcing herself to keep looking at him, aware of Bliss watching her closely.

'This is the builder you were telling me about, right? Doing up the farmhouse for Charlie's outfit?'

'Yes.'

One of Felix's feet was twisted into the gap between two of the metal steps. A hand clawed the mud, poor guy trying to seize the earth one last time.

'A decent man, Frannie. Kind. Trying to do the best thing.'

'Really,' Bliss said.

'Do you know where Fuchsia is?'

Bliss said, 'Tell me again – why were you ringing him tonight, Merrily?'

'I was trying to arrange a meeting.'

'Sounded like an emergency to me,' Bliss said. 'Sunday night, very heavy day for the clergy, and there you were, prepared to drop everything and come rushing out here in the dark?'

'Yes.'

'What conclusions am I to draw from this?'

'I was …' Merrily sighed. 'How long have you got?'

'Till Billy Grace gets here.'

'The pathologist.'

'Which I hope is gonna be before flamin' daylight.'

Two crime-scene women were moving around Felix's body with evidence bags. Emotions uncoupled, not seeing a person, not looking for history much beyond the final act.

'Who found him, Frannie?'

'Dog-walker. Where would the police be without dog-walkers, eh?'

'What do you think happened?'

'That's for Billy Grace to find out.'

'Well, he didn't …' Merrily spun at him, furious '… just fall off the sodding step, did he?'

Segments of smoky cloud on fast-forward across the three-quarter moon. Bliss's eyebrows going up.

'My, we *are* fractious tonight, Merrily.'

'Yes.'

'It's interesting that you're so emotionally involved.'

'Interesting?'

'Significant, even.'

Bliss had his head on one side, red hair shaved close to the skull these days, to disguise erosion. Merrily looked away, over towards the edge of the field where Lol was parked, forbidden by some jobsworth copper even to get out of the truck.

'You need ...' steadying her voice '... to find Fuchsia. The house I told you about ...' How trivial and foolish this was going to sound. 'It was Fuchsia, who had the problem.'

'This is Fuchsia Mary Linden. The assistant.'

'And girlfriend. I keep asking if anyone's looking for her, and nobody— At first, I thought she was being, you know, disingenuous. I'm now more inclined to believe there's something to what she's saying, and I wanted to tell them that. Talk it all over again.'

Bliss scratched his nose, obscuring a reluctant half-smile.

'I'm loath, as ever, to go into the details of your frankly unenviable job, Merrily, but ... you're saying you were feeling a bit guilty?'

'I ... yeah.'

'When did you last talk to Mr Barlow?'

'Last night. On the phone.'

'And the girl?'

'Not since last week. When I met them here.'

'What's she like?'

'She's ... unusual.'

'Unusual. Yeh, that explains everything. I'll be sure to put that in my report.'

'Whimsical? Imaginative? In a childlike way. And beautiful, of course. And about twenty years younger than Felix. That what you were looking for?'

'This word *whimsical*,' Bliss said. 'Would that translate, for the rest of us, as *three sheets to the wind*?'

'What are you asking?'

Bliss didn't reply.

'You *have* got people out looking for her?'

'We've gorra couple of people out there, yeh.'

'You're sure she's not ... somewhere close?'

An image of Fuchsia crouching, big eyed, between tree-roots in the woods.

'Sure as we can be,' Bliss said.

'You actually think *she* did this, don't you?'

'Can't deny that the domestic solution would save us a lorra graft.'

'What was he hit with?'

'Could be one of his own tools. I'm never one to pre-empt the slab, Merrily, but when the head's swollen up like that, battered out of shape, you're looking at multiple skull fractures. And, no, you wouldn't generally get that falling off the steps into a field. The killer must've been … very, very angry.'

A fourth vehicle had appeared next to the dark blue van. A cop shouted across to Bliss.

'Dr Grace, boss.'

'Must be a bad telly night.' Bliss turned to Merrily. 'You ever think, on these occasions, that our fates might be entwined, Reverend?'

'Every time there's one of those occasions, Frannie, I just … Look, when you find Fuchsia, will you let me know?'

'If I can,' Bliss said. 'And we'll probably need to talk about this at length, maybe tomorrow. Thanks for dropping by, Merrily.'

'Yeah.'

Walking back across the field, hands jammed into the pockets of her fleece, Merrily looked behind her once and saw, on the very edge of the headlights, the gaping maw of the bay in the barn that Felix had been renovating for Fuchsia. To bring her stability.

'Shit.' She wanted to scream it into the wind. '*Shit, shit, shit …*'

Jane's mobile played the riff from Lol's 'Sunny Days' and she tightened her lips and ignored it. Wouldn't be Mum; she'd call the landline.

Ethel, the black cat, prowled the scullery desk. The mobile stopped. Jane clicked on the email address from the *Ghosts and Scholars* website, put in the message she'd drafted, read it through one last time.

Dear Ms Pardoe

Sorry to bother you, but I wonder if you might be able to help me. After reading on your website about M. R. James's unexplained 'strange experience' at Garway Church, on the Welsh Border, I wondered if you could throw any more light on it.

I live in Herefordshire and went with my mother to Garway today and, to me, the mystical influence of the Knights Templar could still be felt very strongly there after all these centuries. M. R. James's story 'Oh Whistle, and I'll Come to You, my Lad' has a Templar preceptory in it, and we were wondering if the story could have come out of whatever M. R. James experienced at Garway.

Like me, you were also intrigued by the medieval dovecote with 666 dove holes. Do have any ideas why this might have been?

Anything you can tell me would be very gratefully received.

Perhaps we might be able to help with your own researches too, one day.

Yours sincerely,

Jane Watkins

Seemed OK. Didn't give too much away.

Jane sent it.

Feeling a lot less excited than she had when she'd composed it. Since then, Mum had been back with Lol – Mum looking totally like death, this time – and then they'd both gone out to this place at Monkland. Mum apologetic, as usual – could Jane get herself something to eat? Jesus, what about *her*? Like, when was *she* going to eat? Mum was clearly losing weight. She looked like a small bird after a long winter.

Jane picked up *Ghost Stories of an Antiquary*, one of two books she'd brought down from her apartment. She put it down again. 'Oh, Whistle' was actually quite a bleak story, full of solitude. The guy didn't die or anything, but the effects of what he'd seen would be hanging over him for the rest of his life.

She saw – the image still as vivid in her head as if it had been on the computer screen – Mum walking out of that derelict farmhouse into the early dusk. Walking with her shoulders stiffened and her spine kind of pulled in, like she knew there was something very close behind her. Her face like yellowing paper.

Never seen her quite like that before. Never. And it was unnerving because, in one way, she needed Mum to be basically sceptical – as resistant to the paranormal, despite her job, as Jane was to the strictures of the Church.

Mum as a buffer against her wildest ideas. Giving Jane the freedom to explore because there was always that framework of stability. Maybe she was really afraid of growing up into a world where a mature and intelligent woman was visibly and seismically shaken by the irrational, trying to conceal her fear from a kid ... who was no longer a kid.

Jane turned, with a reluctance she recognised as unusual, to the second book on the desk. Ella Leather's *The Folklore of Herefordshire*. In the index, under Garway, she'd found the line about nine witches and also a page reference for *The watch after death*.

On page 120, Mrs Leather listed the places where:

> It was customary, until a few years ago, for the household to sit up all night when a death had occurred. They did not sit in the same room as the corpse, but elsewhere, the idea being that the spirit of the dead person was still in and about the house, and the people said, 'it was for the last time, it was the last night'; so no one went to bed. But at Orcop and Garway, the watch is still kept, so Martha S— who lived on Garway Hill, assured me. 'Only if it was somebody you cared about,' she added, 'not for strangers.'

So, as for bringing comparative strangers into the same room as the body ... The Newtons had obviously bent the rules in their own best interests, picking up on what came next. Maybe they'd even read this very account, published for the first time in 1912.

> ... Usually, among the country folk, a light is kept burning in the room where a corpse lies every night until burial; a pewter plate of salt is placed on the body; according to Martha S—, the candle should be stuck in the middle of the salt, heaped up in the centre of the plate.

Seriously creepy. Jane shut the book. It was too quiet in here. Picking up the mobile, she got up and walked to the scullery window, looking out at darkness and a wall, pressing *one* on the keypad.

You have three new messages. To listen to your messages ...

She hesitated, staring into the little square of light, before pressing *one* again.

First new message, received at thirteen forty-three today.

'*Jane, it's … Oh, shit, you know who it is. For God's sake, I've left about seventeen messages …*'

Five actually.

'*… I know there's nothing wrong with the phone, which means something wrong with YOU. I even tried ringing the landline, thinking I'd ask your mum – yeah, yeah, I know how much you'd hate that, but I'm a bit beyond caring. Only it's always the bloody answering machine.*

'*I mean, have I done something? Have I done something I didn't know about? Has somebody told you I've done something? Just— You don't even have to ring me back. Just leave a message. I'll close down the phone for the rest of the night so you don't risk speaking to me. Just leave a message, Jane. I mean, Christ, we've been, like, together for two years? That's longer than a lot of marr— Oh … fuck it!*'

Jane stared into the phone for a long time before switching it off.

The builder was dead, his girlfriend missing.

Most of this Lol had already put together out of fragments of chat heard from the open window of the truck, watching the shadowy scurryings around the screened-off caravan. Guessing what was coming when Merrily returned. Just not sure – as a failed psychotherapist and a derivative songwriter finding a little success a little too late – how best to handle it.

'Maybe you need a good manager.' She was rubbing her eyes wearily. 'A tour-organizer. Whatever the word is.'

'I really don't think so.'

'Or just a roadie to carry the spare guitar.'

'You're tired.' Lol started the engine, flicked on the headlamps. 'You haven't eaten since lunch. Or, as it's Sunday, knowing you, maybe even breakfast.'

'It's still Sunday?' As they bumped into the lane Merrily loosened her seat belt, as if there was pressure in her chest. She hadn't yet reached for a cigarette. 'Couple of weeks ago … I lay awake counting up all the people who've suffered in some unnecessary way, or died – unnaturally – in spite of all my prayers and entreaties and …'

'It's supposed to be sheep, Merrily,' Lol said gently. 'I suppose counting corpses *will* eventually get you to sleep, but the dreams are going to be altogether less pastoral.'

'She had the blessing, Lol. The full bit. Holy water. Oil.'

'We could drive into Hereford now, and you could go round administering blessings at random to people in the street, but some of them would still get into a street fight, cause a road accident or something.'

'So what's the point? What's the point of any of it?'

Lol was silent, pulling on to the main road, speeding up as Merrily stared out of the side window. On the way here, she'd told him about the ritual in the little, disused church, the girl suggesting something was coming – Merrily's discussions with Huw Owen leading to her discovery of the fictional origins of that line.

This constant tension between her faith and an equally-necessary scepticism must drive her half-crazy at times. Like now. Her face was still turned away from him, watching the night.

'You keep thinking, what if the Church is actually reaching the end of its useful life? And every day it gets harder to answer that persistent, nagging question: If there *is* a God, why does he allow so much suffering? Well, my children, the truth – the bottom-line, heartfelt truth – is, I'm buggered if *I* know.'

'You're thinking—' Lol braked hard for a badger ambling across the road. 'You're thinking of that guy … Michael Taylor, that his name?'

The Yorkshireman who, back in the 1970s, told his local priest he was possessed by evil spirits and then, having been subjected to a night-long exorcism, went home and murdered his wife. In the most horrific way possible with bare hands.

Merrily shook her head, probably meaning she hadn't been thinking about the guy for a whole half-minute

'It was a *blessing*, not an exorcism,' Lol said. 'There was no question of possession, was there?'

'I did at least two things wrong. *One*, I didn't involve Felix.'

'In the blessing? Would he have even wanted to be involved?'

'*Two*, I had a chance to go to the house yesterday, and I didn't. I decided it was probably bullshit.'

'But you had every reason to think that. You talked to Huw Owen and he—'

'I was careless. Cynical.'

Traffic was sparse, this area still managing to stay a decade or so behind the rest of the country. High in the cab, Lol saw, in a dip on the left, the lights of the perfectly-formed-around-the-green, black and white village of Dilwyn. He tried again.

'Even if you'd gone to the house yesterday, there's no certainty you'd have felt any reaction. That isn't how it works, is it?'

'I don't know how it works. Nobody knows how it works.'

'Maybe the woman didn't kill him,' Lol said. 'They don't *know* it was her, do they?'

'They know something. I'm fairly sure there's something Bliss wasn't revealing. It's how they operate. Never tell anybody anything unless it serves a purpose.'

'When they find her, you need to talk to her. Bliss would arrange that, wouldn't he?'

'She didn't want to talk last night. And why did she go back to Garway? Why did she go back after the blessing? Evidently, he didn't want to tell me that.'

'Merrily …'

'Should've thought.'

'Please,' Lol said. 'Just …'

He slowed for the sign that said LEDWARDINE 3, trying to shut out the whingey voice of the fundamentalist woman, Shirley West.

How do we know there isn't somebody here who's brought something evil in with them?

The road curved towards the village, the hump of Cole Hill forming under the half-clouded moon and the steeple rising out of nowhere like an ancient rocket petrified on its pad.

Crises of faith, Merrily would say, when she wasn't in the middle of one, were part of the deal; they could only strengthen your faith, in the end.

Until, Lol thought, you had one too many.

He parked easily on the square. The diners had left and the lights of the Black Swan had dimmed. There was nobody about. He turned to Merrily, not touching her.

'You, um … want me to come in with you?'

21

Lesser Creatures and Birds

IN THE EARLY light, Merrily let Lol out by the vicarage back door, so that he could use the garden gate to slip, unseen, into the churchyard. Creeping between shadowed headstones and out the other side into the old orchard which had once enclosed the village like a nest around eggs.

The secret ways of Ledwardine.

Merrily, in her bathrobe, watching from the landing window as Lol emerged from the alley by the new bistro, onto the square. Vanishing into Jim Prosser's shop – called Eight Till Late but usually open by seven – and coming out with a morning paper.

There was no real need for this game any more; everybody must know by now. Yet she had the feeling that it was expected, a matter of decorum, a village thing.

No sex, anyway, just needed warmth. Whatever gets you through the night and the recurrent images of wide-eyed, big-eyed Fuchsia: *'Will you bless me?'*

'You look like the Lady of Shallot or something,' Jane said.

Appearing at the top of the stairs, already dressed for school, face shining, hair brushed.

'Wasn't she last heard of lying in a barge or something?' Merrily said. 'Kind of ... dead?'

'Before that, she was a seriously messed-up person.'

Messed-up? Right.

'Erm ...' Jane had waited up last night, knew the worst. She was leaning against the stair-rail with her blazer over an arm '... I've just been listening to the news on Hereford and Worcester. They said a man's body had been found near his caravan at Monkland, and the cops were treating it as suspicious.'

'It is.'

'They didn't mention a woman.'

'Good.'

'Mum …' Jane came down to the landing. 'Look, I'm not stupid. I can put the pieces together.'

'If not always in the right holes.'

'Are you OK? I'm serious.'

'I've been thinking maybe I should take a hairdressing course, open a little salon in Lol's front room.'

'Mum—'

'Do something useful.'

'You need a holiday.'

'Mmm. I've been thinking about Garway Hill. Nice views.'

'So do it,' Jane said. 'I mean it. If you want to go over there and deal with whatever needs dealing with, I'll stay here with whichever loopy, militant-lesbian cleric they want to dump on the parish.'

'Jane, I was just—'

'And I'll help however I can. Checking stuff on the net, ringing people, whatever you need. I … well, I just wanted to say that. Any religious differences don't come into it. I want to help. No ulterior motive, I swear it.'

'I never thought there was, flower, but—'

'I looked up some stuff in Mrs Leather last night. Left the page refs on your desk.'

'Thank you. Maybe I'll get a chance to read them when you've gone to school.'

Merrily set off downstairs, Jane right behind.

'I bet you didn't sleep much last night, did you? And not because Lol was here.'

'Yeah, well, thanks for your concern, however …'

'For Christ's sake, Mum, your guy's had his head smashed in. That must be—'

'Something I wish I hadn't had to see, yes.'

'And, like, not the only thing? I saw your face when you came out of that house.'

This wasn't going to go away, was it?

'Look … I've told you. I'd seen something that was in the wrong place. The green man – we don't know what it means, but it's an odd, symbolic, medieval thing, and it isn't usually, if ever, found in houses. So it was unexpected, just a bit of a shock.'

'Bit more than that, if you ask me.'

'The jury …' Merrily stopped on the stairs '… is still out, all right?'

'There are some things you just don't want to face up to. You're a priest but you're afraid to confront the reality of, like, metaphysical evil. Even when it's possibly caused violent death. I'm just putting two and two together.'

'And making thirteen. Violent death, in my limited experience, is caused by people.'

'Sure, but what causes the people to cause the violence?'

'Let's just get some breakfast, or you'll be late.'

Merrily carried on to the bottom on the stairs, listening out for the bleep of the answering machine, but all she could hear was Ethel crunching dried food, rocking the bowl on the stone flag.

'Oh, the other thing,' Jane said, 'I emailed the M. R. James site last night, while you were out. About the dovecote and the Templars? So like if something comes in for me don't feel you have to wait till I get home. Just open it.'

'Thank you.'

Jane looked at her. That look got shrewder every year; all you could do was stare back and hope you came through.

'Breakfast,' Merrily said.

'I'll make it,' Jane said. 'And I'll make yours, too, and I'm not going to school until I've watched you eat it.'

No overnight messages on the machine and no early calls. Local people had come to accept that Monday was a vicar's day off, usually the only one. By the time Merrily had read Mrs Leather's account of the *watch after death*, the computer's in-box was showing what looked like an actual email amongst the spam.

> Dear Jane,
>
> Thanks for your mail. Garway is certainly the most mysterious and intriguing place I've ever visited in my quest for MRJ. I'm afraid I can't throw any particular light on the dovecote mystery apart from pointing out, as you probably already know, that, before the suppression of the order, the Knights Templar were accused of denying Christ, rejecting the Mass and the sacrament and spitting on the cross. These charges may have been fabricated, but the possibility of the order becoming corrupt in later years cannot be ruled out.
>
> The dovecote, as it stands today, seems to have been largely rebuilt by the Knights Hospitaller, who succeeded the Templars at Garway, but I don't know of any satanic scandal attaching to them.
>
> Re. your question about 'Whistle', I'm afraid I have to disappoint you. Whatever happened to MRJ at Garway seems to have occurred in 1917, a good thirteen years after the publication of the story (it was probably written in 1903). He may have visited Garway before *Ghost Stories of an Antiquary* came out in 1904, but there is no record of it that I know of. He doesn't seem to have found any reason to come to Herefordshire until the widow of his friend James McBryde moved there with her young daughter in 1906.

So that was that. Merrily sat back, unsure if she was disappointed or relieved that, despite the Templar connection and the Globe Inn coincidence, 'Oh, Whistle, and I'll Come to You, My Lad' could hardly have been inspired by whatever happened to M. R. James at Garway Church nearly fourteen years later.

Remiss of her not to have checked those dates herself.

And Fuchsia, the face of crumpled linen, it had all turned around again: more evidence that whatever had happened to Fuchsia had happened inside Fuchsia's head, whether creatively or otherwise. It was not unlikely that Fuchsia had even made those same connections with 'Whistle'.

Time to talk to Huw Owen again. As she glanced at the big black phone, it rang.

'You in, Merrily?' Bliss said.

'What's it sound like?'

'You're not still ratty …'

'Make that confused and upset.'

'Will you still be in in half an hour or so?'

'Have you found her?'

'I'll have another bloke with me,' Bliss said.

Background buzz suggesting the CID room rather than the car park. His tone – and the fact that he was ringing on the landline – suggesting she might need to exercise caution.

'Who?'

'You'll like him,' Bliss said. 'He'll make you laugh.'

'You still haven't told me whether—'

The line went dead. Merrily sat holding the empty phone, staring blankly at the rest of the message on the screen.

Incidentally, if you didn't know this, Gwendolen McBryde's daughter was also called Jane, and MRJ was very fond of her. This may well have been because Jane, something of an artist like both her parents, was fascinated by the supernatural and creepy things generally. So when MRJ says 'we' caused offence at Garway, he may well be referring to the, by then, teenage Jane and possibly her mother as well as himself. It occurs to me that you might like to read Michael Cox's biography of MRJ, relevant pages of which I've attached.

Good luck with your investigations; do let me know how you get on!

Rosemary Pardoe

Merrily sat up, clicked on the attachment, bringing up two scanned pages from *M. R. James, An Informal Portrait*. The first began by examining the possibility that the lively and affectionate young widow Gwendolen McBryde had been rather attracted to her late husband's best friend, a man who had helped her through difficult times and been conscientious about his role as Jane's guardian.

Monty had been entirely relaxed at the house, Woodlands, in south Herefordshire, treated with 'affectionate and admiring indulgence' by his host. Gwendolen had recalled him doing impersonations, putting on funny accents and once reading aloud from *A Midsummer Night's Dream* to a background of nightjars.

He'd also once read the lessons at nearby Abbeydore. According to Gwendolen, he had a beautiful voice which, when he read aloud, *lent you his understanding*. At Abbeydore, *it gave me an unreal feeling as if some saint held forth to lesser creatures and birds.*

As for Gwen's daughter ... well, it seemed she was *very* much Monty's kind of kid, producing lots of delightful drawings of unspeakable entities emerging from gaping tombs.

So Rosemary Pardoe's suggestion that it was the daughter who'd been with Monty James in Garway seemed to be on the money.

Oh God. When in Herefordshire, M. R. James had stayed with a widowed single mother with a teenage daughter who was into creepy things and was called ... Jane.

Into the bleak morning, after the night of cruel tragedy, came the brittle sound of cosmic laughter.

She thought of Bliss. *He'll make you laugh.*

And what he'd said on the phone when she was in the car on Garway Hill.

What they used to call the funnies.

Oh hell.

'This is Jonathan Long.' Bliss hooked out a chair at the refectory table. 'One of my colleagues.'

All the time she was making them coffee, Merrily kept glancing at Bliss, but there was no eye response; he didn't look happy. She felt the tension rolling in her stomach, hard as a golf ball.

Jonathan Long – rank unspecified – looked several years younger than Bliss, perhaps very early thirties. He didn't look like a cop, maybe a young academic, a lecturer in something dry and exact like law or economics. His body was thickening, and he wore a dark grey three-piece suit. A cop with a waistcoat was rare these days, a *young* cop with a waistcoat entirely outside Merrily's experience.

'I gather you've known Francis for some time,' Long said.

'Way back. Since he had a full head of hair.'

Tension throwing out flippancy like feeble sparks. Long didn't smile. Neither did Bliss. Long had spiky black hair, and a light tan; Bliss needed to avoid the sun in case his freckles turned malignant.

'We were hoping, Mrs Watkins, that you might share some of your impressions.'

Long's accent was educated and still fairly refined; seemed unlikely that he'd spent much of his career confiscating crack pipes and bundling binge drinkers into blue vans. It also seemed unlikely that he was going to identify himself as Special Branch.

'About what, Mr Long?' She sat down opposite them. 'Theology? Contemporary music?'

'Specifically, Fuchsia Mary Linden.' Long examined his coffee. 'Do you have cream, by any chance?'

'Erm … no, sorry.' All right, playtime over. 'You've found her, right?'

'Yeh,' Bliss said. 'We've found her. We *think* we've found her.'

His usually foxy eyes were dull as pennies. Sudden sunlight dropped from the highest kitchen window like a splash of cold milk.

'We're still waiting for the dental report,' Jonathan Long said. 'But it's unlikely to be anyone else.'

22

Collecting Beads

HAD SHE, ON some level, expected it? Had she looked down on Felix's body last night, dumped like a heap of building rubble on his own doorstep, and somehow known she was seeing only half a tragedy?

I didn't know whether it wanted me out or it wanted me dead, Merrily.

A train in the distance, rattling through the night. The coffee going cold in front of her while the horror came out in short, sick spurts.

'On the southern line. The London train, via Newport.' Jonathan Long's voice light and casual, as if he was reading from a passenger timetable. 'Just under half a kilometre from what I understand is known as the Tram Inn level crossing.'

'Past the big feed place with the silos,' Bliss said.

The full significance of it crashed in on Merrily like a rock through a windscreen. She pushed her chair back, a raking screech on the stone flags.

'She laid her head …?'

'On the line,' Bliss said. 'I don't know how people can do that, meself. They just think of the train roaring unstoppably out of the night. Never a thought for the poor bastard driving it.'

Watch over her, in the name of all the angels and saints in heaven. Keep guard over her soul day and night.

'You knew last night, didn't you?' Merrily stared at him. 'You knew when we were at the caravan.'

This word 'whimsical' … Would that translate, for the rest of us, as three sheets to the wind?

'Don't look at me like that, Merrily. We knew a woman had been hit by a train, that was all. What do you know about her?'

'Not much. But then, in some ways there isn't much that anyone knows.'

'We have names of adoptive parents, but we haven't spoken to them yet.'

'You even found them?'

'I'm— We have someone working on it.'

Merrily told them about Fuchsia's mother, Tepee City.

'How did you get an ID, Frannie?'

'Car keys in her pocket. A van parked near the Tram Inn, registered to Felix Barlow.'

'Tepee City,' Long said. 'That's well into Wales, isn't it, Mrs Watkins? A Welsh-speaking area.'

'Yes. Why?'

'A significant amount of old-fashioned Welsh nationalism in that area, I think.'

'Not much in Tepee City itself, I'd've thought. Alternative communities are usually immigrants. What's your point?'

Like he was going to tell her, this smooth git with his secret agenda. Merrily just wanted to throw him out, throw both of them out and take herself down to the church to scream abuse at God.

'This house,' Long said. 'The Master House. Fuchsia was instrumental in getting Felix Barlow to pull out of the contract?'

'She was the reason he pulled out.'

'Because she thought it was haunted.'

'Because she said she'd sensed a ... an evil there,' Merrily said, reluctantly.

Long smiled the kind of smile where you couldn't have slid a butter knife between his lips.

'From your conversations with her, can you think of any other reason why she – or anyone else, for that matter – might not have wanted that house redeveloped?'

'You mean a *sane* reason? No. I can't.'

Wasn't God's fault. Merrily gripped her knees under the table. She was incompetent. Smug, self-satisfied, lazy. She'd spotted the unconvincing elements, the lines from M. R. James, and missed all the danger signs.

When he came home it was like it was all over him. I made him shower and then I burned all the clothes he'd been wearing. Just out there, Merrily. I poured petrol on them.

'So what did you …?' Long was steepling his fingers. 'Francis has tried to explain your role in the, ah, Diocese, but what precisely did you *do* with this woman?'

'Are you actually leading the inquiry, Mr Long?'

'Mr Bliss is leading the murder inquiry, I'm dealing with a side issue which may or may not be connected.'

'Do you want to explain that?'

Jonathan Long said nothing. Merrily played with a teaspoon, let the silence drift for a few seconds, looked at him.

'So would that … would that be one of those *we ask the questions* kind of silences?'

'I did try to tell you on the way here, mate,' Bliss said. 'This is a woman who isn't invariably attracted to the enigmatic type.'

Long's gaze settled for a moment on Bliss, and then he turned back to Merrily.

'You performed an exorcism? Or whatever you prefer to call it.'

'Oh, for heaven's sake—' Merrily dropped the teaspoon into her mug. 'We have an escalating series of responses, and exorcism is so far up the ladder we usually get vertigo before we … She had a blessing. In a church. That's it.'

And it shouldn't have been. There should've been follow-up. Aftercare.

'What was your opinion of her, Mrs Watkins?'

'What?'

'Give me a picture.'

'She was intelligent, in her way. Intense. Seemed certain about what she'd experienced, but I was … keeping an open mind.'

'You thought she might be delusional.'

'Or making it up. Some people do.'

'But you went ahead, all the same.'

'At the blessing stage, we can afford to be … a bit uncertain. For the heavier stuff, you need permission from the bishop. It's also likely to involve a psychiatric assessment.'

'And do you think psychiatry might have been appropriate in the case of Fuchsia Mary Linden?'

'I don't know.'

'Any suggestion of previous violence? On either side.'

'Her and Felix? No. I mean, are you *sure* she did this?'

'Merrily,' Bliss said. 'As I'm apparently leading the inquiry, I'll make an executive decision to spell it out for you. We're waiting for forensic. Even the dental stuff isn't straightforward. When a train's – I'm sorry – when a train's run over someone's head, it's like collecting beads from a broken necklace. No, we *don't* know she killed him and there's a possibility we never will, for sure. We haven't found a weapon. But it's one of those situations where the press statement is likely to say that we're not looking for anybody else. That any clearer?'

'Thanks. No … I can't see any reason she'd want to kill Felix. My impression was that she very much needed him in her life. Her rock, if you like. An old family friend, a link going … way back. *She*'d gone in search of him. She seems to have wanted security, a proper home.'

Didn't want to mention either umbilical cords or paying for art college. Might tell Bliss later, but not in front of Jonathan Long.

Not for her to pass on Mrs Morningwood's stories, either. Not to this guy.

Long nodded. 'Right then.' He stood up. 'That's probably all for the present … unless …'

He glanced at Bliss, who came more slowly to his feet.

'If you think of anything else that might be relevant, Merrily, you know where I am.' Bliss smiled. 'Jonathan … well, nobody really knows where Jonathan is.'

When they'd gone, Merrily poured Long's coffee, untouched, down the sink and rang Huw Owen in the Brecon Beacons. No answer. She called Sophie at the gatehouse. Engaged.

She wasn't ready to go to the church.

She ought to sit down and think about it, sensibly.

She didn't feel sensible. There was a possibility – no getting round it

– that she could, in some way, have prevented this. All of it. If she hadn't been so blasé, so easily deflected. She fumbled a cigarette out of the packet, started to light it and couldn't get a proper grip on the Zippo. No use saying it had all been out of her hands; she'd let it slip through them, fall to the flags, smash.

The phone was ringing in the scullery. Merrily dropped the lighter, went to the sink and splashed water on her face. Towelled it roughly and went through to the phone.

'Ledwardine Vicarage.'

'Adam Eastgate, Merrily, at the Duchy. Listen, have you heard the radio news this morning?'

'Kind of.'

'I've been trying to get some sense out of the police.'

'Erm … I was over there last night. Not long after they found him. I'm so sorry, Adam.'

The big black phone was full of a charged-up silence.

'The police've just been here,' Merrily said. 'I'm afraid …'

'Jesus, Merrily, I could never in a million years have imagined—'

'No. Me neither. I'm not sure if you know this, but Felix's girlfriend Fuchsia is also dead. Found on … on the railway. Not yet officially identified, but I don't think there's any doubt.'

'Christ almighty. So, how … how did Felix die?'

'He had head injuries. Adam, I'm sorry. I didn't see any of this coming, either. And I ought to have.'

'Come on, that's *easily* said, Merrily. We could all say that. Hell, I knew him better than any builder we ever used, he was a canny fella, I liked him a lot, but … Jesus, this is not real. This is complete madness.'

'Yes.'

In her head, Merrily was in the car again on Garway Hill, on the phone to Bliss, irritably deciding not to check out the Master House. *Sod this, going home.*

'I'll have to get word to the Man,' Adam Eastgate said. 'He always admired Felix's work.'

She heard him breathing steadily. Pictured him standing by the window in the Duchy's barn, looking out towards the Welsh border hills and Garway and wondering how this might rebound. Heard him clearing his throat.

'Merrily, I've got to ask. Does this connect, in your … your view of things, to the Master House?'

'Be stupid of me to say it doesn't. But not, I'd guess, in any way that would interest the police.'

'So it won't come out at the inquest or anything, about …'

'Inquests tend to stick to the cold facts.'

'Right.' Eastgate paused. 'Well, I don't know what to say. Have to … get another builder.'

'Yes.'

'I don't know how to react to this. Was she crazy? I mean, that's the issue, isn't it?'

'I don't know. At first I thought it was something like that, but now I've been to the house, and … I don't know. There's a lot of history.'

'What do you suggest?'

'Me?'

'The Bishop referred it to you, Merrily.'

'Yes.'

Remembering how she'd reacted, telling Lol, *I don't* want *to go and stay in Garway for a week.*

'You think it's over, Merrily? You think it begins and ends with this disturbed woman?'

'No,' Merrily said. 'Not really.'

23

Corruption of Muhammad

WHEN SHE WENT out by the back door, it had turned into the kind of October day that made global warming seem like a scare-story, cold air seizing her arms through the thin sweatshirt; she didn't care.

She walked through into the churchyard, the way Lol had left at dawn, the sun now pulsing feebly in a loaded sky. Self-disgust oozing rancid fluid into her gut.

We have to think about what we mean by listening. Because, when you think about it, we hardly ever really do it.

She hadn't. She hadn't really listened to Fuchsia.

Smug, sanctimonious, hypocritical bitch.

'He don't look happy, do he?' Gomer Parry said. 'The ole sun.'

He was sitting, gnomelike, on the headstone of Minnie's grave, his head on one side, as if he was listening for faint sounds from below the soil. When Minnie died, they'd both had new batteries in their watches and he'd buried them together in a small box under her coffin.

The watch after death.

'You OK, Gomer?'

'En't too bad, vicar.' He stood up. 'Ole Min'll be sayin' I'm makin' the place look untidy again.' He peered at her. ''Ow're you?'

'Had better days.'

'Felix Barlow, is it?'

'How did you hear?'

'Danny rung me. Hour or so ago.'

'What are they saying?'

'Usual. Never mess with a mad hippie, kind o' thing.'

'And Danny?'

'Reckons there's likely things we don't know and en't never gonner find out. 'Bout Barlow and that woman.'

'He'd known her since she was born. Literally.'

'Knowed her ma. When her moved in, some folks put it round he was the girl's ole man.' Gomer shook his head. 'Feller starts doin' well for hisself, always some bugger ready to pull him down the gutter. Don't take it to heart, vicar, I reckon you done your best.'

Merrily stared at him. Didn't recall telling Gomer anything about her dealings with Felix Barlow and Fuchsia.

'The ole church, vicar.' Gomer dipped a hand into his top pocket, pulled out his ciggy tin. 'St Cosmo's?'

'Cosmas,' Merrily said. 'And St Damien.'

'Ar, them's the boys.'

'Bloody hell, Gomer, it's a disused church … remote.'

'Exac'ly. You wasn't exactly dressed for not gettin' noticed, place like that. You like a nun, her like a bride. Word gets round.'

Like a bride. Fuchsia in the white dress. The candle and the bigger light from the window over the altar. The light in Fuchsia's wide-apart owl eyes. No light now, no eyes, no head.

'Go back in the warm, eh, vicar?' Gomer said. 'You're shivering.'

'I'm OK. I just …' She stared at the dull sun. There was something else. 'Gomer, you did a drainage job in Garway – for a Mrs Morningwood?'

Gomer stiffened, shut the ciggy tin with a snap.

'Muriel?'

'Sorry, I don't know her first name.'

'It's Muriel,' Gomer said.

'Just that we met her, Jane and me, the other day.'

'Oh ar?'

'And when she heard we were from Ledwardine, she mentioned you.'

Gomer said nothing. He looked wary. Merrily blinked.

'This is, erm … where you usually tell me something interesting. Some little anecdote.'

'What's to tell?' Gomer sniffed. 'Got her own smallholdin'. Keeps bees, chickens. Does this toe-twiddling treatment thing. And herbs.'

'Yes, I knew some of that.'

'And her's popular with the farmers.'

'In what way?'

'Well … knows her way around, ennit? Lot o' the ole farmers don't. Don't like computers, paperwork, London, Europe. Hell, don't like Hereford much neither.'

'No.'

'Plus, add to the list the council and the Min of Ag, whatever they calls it now.'

'She helps farmers deal with red tape?'

'Knows how to talk to shiny-arsed buggers with clipboards, that's the basic of it. Farmer's got hisself a problem with some official, don't know how to harticulate it, he calls Muriel. Officials'll back down, write it off as a bad job, see, soon as deal with Muriel.'

'And this is official, is it? I mean, does she do this kind of thing as … you know … some kind of agricultural consultant?'

Gomer laughed, started coughing and fitted a ciggy in his mouth, still laughing, still coughing.

'I see,' Merrily said.

'Go and get warm, vicar. That's the best thing.'

Robbie was complaining that his coffee would be ready. Couldn't this wait? But Jane persisted; these guys were sometimes inclined to forget they were getting paid fairly decent money to feed young minds.

'I suppose you've been reading some trashy novel,' he said.

'No, Mr Williams,' Jane said. 'I've been to Garway Church.'

Robbie sat down again, behind the history room desk.

'Have you now?'

'Seriously interesting place.'

'Yes, it is,' Robbie said. 'Spent many a day there, fully absorbed.'

Morrell, the head, had introduced this system where sixth-formers got to call teachers by their first names, like they were your mates. It just led to awkwardness, in Jane's view, and this was a view clearly shared by the head of history, who refused even to reveal his first name. It had always been *R. Williams*. So, obviously …

'Right …' Jane pulled up a chair. 'So if anybody could answer my questions about Garway and the Templars …'

For you, Mr Williams, the mid-morning break is over.

'Damn and blast,' Robbie said mildly. 'Dropped myself in it there, didn't I?'

He had to be coming up to retirement. Sparse white hair, tweed jacket, comfortably overweight and, unlike most of his smoothie colleagues, so determinedly uncool that he almost *was* cool.

'You see, it's not exactly very big, that church,' Jane said. 'But so full of mysteries.'

She wasn't going to tell him she hadn't been into the actual church yet, due to them running into Mrs Morningwood and everything. Anyway, no problem, she'd been on the common-room computer, and there were two or three websites with stacks of pictures of the church's unique features – the Templar coffin lids in the floor, the enigmatic carvings, the remains of the circular nave …

Robbie took off his brown-framed glasses, looked at the ceiling.

'Thing is, Jane … there's an awful lot of twaddle talked about the Knights Templar. Always has been. Supposed to be magicians and guardians of famous secrets, but in reality they were uneducated and illiterate, most of them. Weren't even monks, in the true sense, simply a religious brotherhood who observed various disciplines and went out into the world to fight people.'

'But they obviously knew about magic and astrological configurations and things.'

'Not "obviously" at all, girl. Magic, in medieval times, was a high science, chronicled in Latin and Greek. Hardly for the illiterate.'

'Yeah, maybe *one* kind of magic, but, like, what about all the hedge witches and the local conjurers? You're saying *they* were intellectuals? I mean, there was always like an *instinctive* element, surely. Like, something that was passed down?'

'An oral tradition. Perhaps. I'm merely saying that the ornate web of mythology woven around the Templars was precisely that.'

'But you don't *know* that. You don't know that they hadn't—'

'They've became a very convenient repository for ludicrous conspiracy theories, and you need to remember that I—'

'But you don't know that they didn't develop some instinctive spiritual feel for—'

'—teach history, Jane, not New-Age theology.'

'OK, history.' Jane focused. 'The Templars were linked to the Cistercians, right?'

'That's one theory.'

'And the Cistercians were known for being close to the earth, in like a pagan way? Always settled in remote places where they could be self-sufficient. And *they* studied the stars and they were well into landscape patterns and stuff.'

'To an extent.'

'And *that* wouldn't've been written down in Latin, would it? And … OK, if the Templars weren't into magic, what about all the charges that were proved against them? Secret rituals at night?'

'The charges were *not* proved, Jane. The Pope, Clement V, actually declared that they were *un*proven, but decided to dissolve the Templar order anyway because these accusations had brought it very much into disrepute.'

'But if you—'

'Ah, Jane …' Robbie Williams sat back, arms folded, smiling almost fondly and shaking his head. 'You really are a most unusual girl. Hard to think of anyone else in your year who displays the smallest curiosity about anything not actually involved with achieving the necessary qualifications. And I'm not being very helpful, am I? Why don't you tell me where you're going with this? Or hoping to go.'

For the first time, Jane felt her engine stall. Couldn't tell him *that*. Stick to questions. Teachers always liked questions.

'There's only one pub left in Garway, right?'

'The Moon.' Robbie patted his comfortable stomach. 'I do know my hostelries.'

'Did you know there used to be another three, called The Sun, The Stars and The Globe?'

'I *didn't* know that. How interesting. Do you know how far those names go back?'

'Well, I … haven't had a chance to check it all out yet. But it does suggest there's some astrological tradition in the area, doesn't it?'

'Astronomical, anyway. Then again, it may be simply that some chap opened a pub called The Moon, and another chap set up in opposition and called his The Sun. And so on.'

'Yeah. I suppose.'

'Sorry, Jane. What else have you found? The dovecote with 666 compartments? Your guess is as good as mine on that one. Could be a coincidence, could be someone's idea of a joke or it could be rather sinister. Who knows?'

'How about the green man?'

'Ah,' Robbie said.

A bell at the end of the passage signalled the end of break-time.

'The stone face carved into the chancel arch,' Jane said quickly. 'And nobody knows what it really means … even though they're fairly common in churches.'

'Yes. Is the green man of Celtic origin or early medieval? And does this one even qualify for the title?'

'How do you mean?'

'A green man is, by definition, a *foliate* face – leaves and vines coming out of his mouth and his nose and whatnot.'

'Yes.'

Jane had a picture of it in her head, from one of the websites. The blank eyes, the stubby horns …

'But what's interesting,' Robbie said, 'is that the specimen inside the chancel arch at Garway appears to have no foliate embellishments whatsoever. No representation of greenery emerging from its mouth – instead, what, on closer scrutiny, is quite obviously a thick, studded cord with tassels at either end. I admit that's puzzled me, too.'

'What could it mean?'

'Well now …' Robbie leaned forward in his chair; he smelled quite strongly of mints. 'If we return to the list of charges against the

Templars, they were, if you recall, accused of worshipping an idol. In the form of a bearded male head.'

'Yeah! Of course ... It was supposed to have powers?'

'It was also said to have a cord wound around it,' Robbie said.

'Holy sh—' Jane slid to the edge of her chair. 'So that face could be—'

'*Baphomet.*' Robbie raised both arms and joined his hands behind his head. 'It came to be known as Baphomet. A name for which there seem to be several explanations, the most common of which is that it's a corruption of Muhammad. And the Templars, during the Crusades, would obviously have been much exposed to Islam.'

'The Templars could've been secret Muslims? This could be a kind of Islamic idol?'

'The Muslims don't *have* idols, Jane. And if we pursue that theory, we also tend to stumble over the word "worship". While the Muslims afford their prophet the very greatest respect, they only *worship* Allah.'

'Maybe the Pope or somebody put a spin on that. Because, like, messing with Muhammad, that would be serious heresy, right?'

'Obviously, it *would*. However, since those days – in the West anyway – Baphomet seems to have acquired a rather darker image. Satanic, even. Demonic, anyway. Which is where it rather departs from the medieval historian's sphere of expertise, so you'd need to research that at the library.'

'But, like, the fact that the head's set into the chancel arch, the entrance to the holiest part of the church ...'

'If that *is* Baphomet ...' Robbie put on a slightly twisted, conspiratorial smile '... is he guarding the altar? Or is he drawing attention *away* from it? Think, for instance, which side it's on.'

'Well, erm ...' Obviously she hadn't seen the actual thing, only the picture, which was close-up. 'I suppose that would depend which side you're approaching it from.'

'It's only visible from one side Jane. The side facing you as you walk in. Putting it very firmly on the *left*.'

'Oh.'

'Sinistral, as it were. The left-hand path. Hah! Now *I*'m getting carried away. And my coffee will be completely cold.' Robbie rose from his chair. 'I do so hate cold coffee.'

'I'm sorry, Mr Williams. But you've been really helpful ...'

'I suppose I really ought to have asked you why you're so interested in all this.'

'Maybe I'll tell you sometime.'

'Might, on the other hand, be better if I never knew, Jane.'

She watched him plodding across to the door, his battered briefcase under an arm, and couldn't believe how, after rubbishing all her other ideas and dismissing the Templars as some kind of thick thugs, he'd suddenly come out with something as weird and disturbing as this. She came to her feet.

'*Oh ...*'

Robbie stopped, neck hunched into his shoulders as if she'd thrown something at him.

'Just one more thing, Mr Williams. Have you ever heard of a green man or a bearded head or whatever ... that *wasn't* in a church? Say, in a public building. Or a house?'

'Can't say I have. And, unless it was in a chapel, that would strike me as unlikely.' He turned and looked at her, his eyes narrowing. 'Why? Have *you* seen one somewhere else?'

'No, no.' Jane slid her chair back under one of the desks. 'I just wondered, that's all.'

This time, the phone was picked up at once.

'Gatehouse.'

'Sophie, it's me. Look, I'm sorry about this, but—'

'I know. It's been on the radio. No more brutal form of suicide, in my opinion, than to lay one's head in the path of a train. The engine driver is usually traumatized. I did try to ring you. I don't think the Bishop knows yet.'

'It brings up the question of going back to Garway.'

'Oh,' Sophie said. 'I doubt he'd want that now.'

'I think *I* want it.'

'Merrily, some people appear to be locked into a tragic cycle, and whatever we—'

'A cycle I just might have broken if I'd known more.'

'Yes, you would think that.'

'I need to understand, as far as I can, what happened.'

'That's surely for the police to establish. Or the coroner.'

'Superficially.'

'And you think this would need a full week?'

'I don't know. I've had another message I can't really ignore. I'll explain when I know a bit more.'

'You want me to tell the Bishop?'

'Please.'

'I'll see if Ruth Wisdom's still available … Merrily?'

'Mmm?'

'I think you need to be very careful,' Sophie said. 'This may go deeper than either of us had imagined.'

Merrily made some tea and took it into the scullery. Lit a cigarette and stared unhappily at the answering machine for a minute or so before rewinding the last message. The one waiting for her when she'd come in from the churchyard.

'*Mrs Watkins. Morningwood. Come and see me, will you, darling?*'

A pause, then

'*Someone didn't do a terribly good job, did they? Was it you or was it me? Or is something dreadfully amiss?*'

24

Invaded Space

'BACK OFF, MERRILY,' Huw said. 'You're not thinking, you're reacting.'

She said nothing. Over by the door to the hall stood two overnight bags, packed. She didn't have a respectable suitcase.

'Let it lie, lass. Attend to your parish, go into the church morning and evening for three days. Contemplate. Let things settle. And *then* look at it again.'

'I've just been to the church. It wasn't a great success. I was probably too emotional.'

'My point exactly.'

'Anyway,' Merrily said, 'it was already too late.'

She was on the mobile in the kitchen. Using the mobile too much, thanks to Bliss and his paranoia.

'So you think you had a bit of a psychic experience, do you? That's what this is all about.'

'No, what it's about is that two people are dead. For reasons it seems unlikely anybody will ever be able to explain. Except possibly me. After a fashion. And too late. Because I was putting my home life and my parish and my personal comforts before the job I agreed to take on. Because I was being lax and lazy.'

'Wrong attitude, lass.'

'Mopping up, Huw. It's just mopping up. And a miserable attempt at penance. I won't exactly enjoy it, but I don't think I really deserve to.'

'Mopping up?' Huw's voice rose, uncharacteristically. 'It's *digging* up. It's disturbing the ground, it's exposing live wires. A little woman with a bucket and spade?'

Spade. Wires. Mrs Morningwood talking about the sometimes-dormant feud between the Gwilyms and the Newtons/Grays: *Like a live electric wire under the ground, and periodically someone would strike it with a spade.*

'I've told you what to do,' Huw said. 'Talk to the vicar of Monkland or whoever's attending to the funerals, and the bloke standing in at Garway. You then have a Requiem at Garway Church, followed by a blessing – or something a bit heavier, but don't overdo it – at the house. Two priests, plus interested parties. Bang, bang … out.'

'And if it goes on?'

'What … deaths?'

'I don't know. They bring in another builder, who happens to have a heart attack, whatever. I need to find out what's there.'

'Merrily, there's *masses* there. It's *always* going to be there. Garway's layered with it, that whole area. Tantalizing little mysteries. Codes nobody's going to crack and symbols and forgotten secrets. And occasionally summat flares. So you tamp it down and you walk away and, with any luck, it won't flare again in your lifetime.'

'You're saying it's too big to deal with?'

'Too big, too deep. It's Knights bloody Templar. Folks've been obsessing over the buggers for centuries. You don't need it.'

'One week.' Merrily looked across at the overnight bag. 'I'm giving it one week, max.'

She'd phoned Teddy Murray. 'Oh dear,' he'd said, all vagueness, the kind of minister who held garden fêtes and came to tea. 'I was told it was all off. Never mind, I'm sure we can organize a room. Do everything we can to ensure your stay is as painless as possible – think of it as an autumn break in God's weekend retreat.'

He clearly hadn't known about Felix and Fuchsia.

'All right.' Huw did one of his slow, meditative sighs; she thought of him pushing weary fingers through hair like waste silage. 'Tell me again. Tell me what happened to *you.*'

'I'm *not* going into it again because it sounds stupid and if anyone told it to me I'd react the way you're reacting.'

'Oh, for— Listen. Don't get me wrong, Merrily. I accept that summat happened. You've been doing this long enough to know the difference and it'd be patronizing of me to suggest otherwise. Give me the physical symptoms.'

'I don't—'

'You bloody *do*.'

'All right, couldn't breathe, heart going like an old washing machine.'

'And?'

'And the feeling of being … I was transfixed. It was like I'd invaded his space and had to take the consequences.'

'It felt evil?'

'It was … without heart. I thought it had some kind of worm coming out of its mouth, but it was rope or something fibrous. There was a sense of naked contempt. And a sense that it was …'

'Alive?'

'I was trying to pray. As you do. The Breastplate. Second nature. And I couldn't get the words out. Couldn't, you know, *form* the words. Jane was calling to me from across the room, and she might as well've been miles away. There was just me and him. I'd invaded his space, he … invaded mine.'

'How'd he do that?'

'It was just an instant, a microsecond of insidious cold, a … a penetrating cold.'

'Sexual?'

'Jesus, Huw!'

'Was it?'

'The so-called green man …' Merrily stifled the shudder, leaning back hard '… carries a lot of associations, some of them fertility-oriented, therefore—'

'Therefore it's all subjective. Jesus wept! You go in with that kind of namby-pamby academic attitude, you're stuffed before you start. You're a priest. You either treat it as a level of reality, or you back off. Which is what, as your spiritual director, I'm formally suggesting that you do.'

'You're spending too much time in your hellfire chapel, Huw.'

She listened to him breathing. Shut her eyes, bit her lip.

'I'm sorry.'

'Let's lay it out,' Huw said. 'A woman kills her lover and then tops herself, and you're worried it's because of something she picked up at this house. That correct?'

'I think … that it's a question that needs an answer. And a question that neither the police nor the coroner are ever likely to ask.'

'Even though the only experience in that farmhouse she told you about was a not-even-thinly-disguised scene from a famous ghost story by Monty James?'

'I can't explain that. Doesn't help, either, that the story predates James's visit to Garway by about fifteen years.'

'And bears no relation to your own perceived experience.'

'No.'

Frannie Bliss's face had appeared at the kitchen window, peering in, hands binoculared against the glass. Merrily pointed in the direction of the door, making turning motions to indicate that it was open.

'Ever think summat's playing with you?' Huw said. 'The way a cat plays with a bird?'

'You trying to scare me or something?'

She'd noticed he'd said bird. Unlike mice sometimes, she thought, birds don't escape.

Bliss said, 'I'm not here, all right?'

'You're asking me to lie for you again?'

Merrily filled the kettle. Bliss sat down and stretched out his legs under the table, hands behind his head.

'He really bothers me, that bastard. They all do.'

'Jonathan?'

'If that's his name.'

'I thought you knew him.' Merrily sat down. 'I thought he worked out of a little office at headquarters.'

'No, Merrily, that's Bill Boyd. We've learned to put up with Bill. Jonathan came up from the capital last week, apparently to look into a certain issue. One of the less-publicized aspects of nine-eleven and seven-seven and the rest is that we get to see a lot more of his sort. Lofty, superior gits in expensive suits.'

'*What* issue?'

'You're not the first to ask.'

'You're expected to work with him, and you don't know what he's investigating?'

Bliss glanced at Merrily, an eyebrow raised.

'I didn't like to ask him directly, Frannie, if he was Special Branch, in case he realized we'd been discussing it.'

'I'm grateful, Merrily.'

'So ...' She half-extracted a cigarette and then pushed it back. '*He*'s not investigating a haunting, is he?'

'I think it's reasonable to assume,' Bliss said, 'that he's looking into a perceived threat against the Heir to the Throne.'

'I don't think I understand.'

'Applying my renowned deductive skills, I'm working on the assumption that they – the Duchy of Cornwall – have received certain communications. Could be anonymous letters, untraceable emails, text messages – lot of options in the technological age.'

'Locally?'

'Or at their head office, wherever that is. But *relating* to here, that's clear enough.'

'Posing a direct threat to the Man?'

'Maybe suggesting – if I'm reading between the right lines – that the Duchy is acquiring too much property in this part of the world.'

'But who would that be likely to bother? And what can they do about it anyway? It's probably just a crank.'

'Merrily, Al-Qaeda might just be five towel-heads in a cave with a computer, a video camera and a mobile phone.'

'It's crazy.'

'It's the world we're trying to go on living in.'

'All right ...' Merrily let her chin sink into her cupped hands. 'Long did ask a particularly odd question, didn't he, when we were talking about Fuchsia and Tepee City? He said isn't that a Welsh-speaking area full of Welsh nationalists?'

'*Old-fashioned* Welsh nationalists, was the term he actually used.'

'Why would he think Welsh nationalists are concerned about the Prince of Wales buying property in Herefordshire, *England*?'

'Doesn't make a lot of sense, does it, Merrily?'

'And anyway, the days of Welsh nationalist terrorism, such as it was, are *long* over.'

'If he really thought there was anything in it, he certainly wouldn't've mentioned it in front of you. Oh, Merrily …' Bliss bounced his heels alternately off the stone flags, like a kid '… you don't know how much it pisses me off when there's something high-level going down in my manor that I don't know about.'

'You think I can help, or you're just here for sympathy?'

Bliss smiled. Merrily leaned back, folding her arms, thinking it out.

'OK … if someone is suggesting that the Master House – for reasons we can't fathom – is one acquisition too many, was this before or after Felix Barlow told Adam Eastgate that this was a house that didn't want to be restored?'

'After would be my guess.' Bliss nodded at the overnight bag in the corner. 'What's with the luggage?'

'Going to Garway.'

'Why?'

'Need to.'

Merrily pulled over the padded folder containing Adam Eastgate's plans for the Master House. When she upended it, a plastic bag fell out, resealed like a police evidence bag. She pulled it open and shook out the key onto the table.

'You don't find too many like this nowadays, do you, outside of churches?'

'And prisons,' Bliss said. 'You're not staying *there*, are you?'

'Too scary. And the central heating's not working.'

'Come on, Merrily, the truth.'

'Why I'm going back? Apart from, every time I close my eyes, seeing Fuchsia Mary Linden swimming towards me, asking to be blessed in the old-fashioned way?'

'That's it?'

'And all the things we might have found out if I hadn't been so smug and sceptical. Things that would never come out at an inquest. I'm assuming an inquest is going to be where this ends.'

'The media have indeed been told we're not looking for a third party,' Bliss said. 'And, frankly, if it was so much as suggested that the third party might turn out to be the kind of third party I suspect *you*'re looking at then I think we've made a sound decision.'

'Assuming the forensics support the obvious conclusion that Fuchsia killed Felix and then herself … how important is it to you to find a motive?'

'It's obviously *tidier*, for us, Merrily, if we can find evidence of domestic strife and/or mental imbalance.'

'You tried to find the mother, by any chance? Mary Linden.'

'We've got the birth certificate, and the name tallies. As does Tepee Valley. But the mother's name is less poetic than "Linden". Mary Roberts.'

'What about the adoptive parents?'

'Moved on, some years ago. We're trying to pin them down, but bloody hippies, they could be anywhere. We're continuing inquiries, but we don't have the manpower to make too much of it.'

'If you get anywhere … would there be stuff you're able to share? Sometimes it's easier for the police to get information than somebody like me with no obvious reason to inquire.'

'Equally,' Bliss said, 'there are situations where it's easier for a harmless cleric to learn things than a copper.'

'Does that mean we're looking at an arrangement? You tell me what you've learned from relatives or anyone else, I tell you … what I can.'

'What you *can*?'

'Look at it this way, Frannie – most of the stuff I wouldn't feel right divulging is going to be stuff that would embarrass you anyway. *And* the coroner.'

'You're so cute, Merrily,' Bliss said.

'I'm a professional. It's odd how people seem to forget that.'

Bliss smiled, shaking his head.

'Particularly me,' Merrily said.

After a lunch of soup and a cheese sandwich, she rang Uncle Ted, the senior churchwarden, to explain that she might be away for a few days.

He was out, so she laid it gratefully on his machine. Uncle Ted was still resentful of Deliverance, although he must know that without it she'd probably wind up with another four parishes and Ledwardine would see even less of her.

She rang Lol, but he must have already left for tonight's gig, somewhere in South Wales. She'd try his mobile later. She ought to go and lie on the bed, try and recharge, but there was too much to do in a very short time.

Looking up *Morningwood* in the phone book, she found just one entry and called it on the mobile.

'Poor girl,' Mrs Morningwood said.

Nothing about Felix. Just *'Poor girl.'*

'I'm … coming over. Either tonight or early tomorrow. Will you be around, Mrs Morningwood?'

'In and out, darling. Never far away. Always there around nightfall to shut the chicks away.'

'And you're … where?'

'Coming in from the Hereford side, past The Turning – know where that is?'

'No.'

'Ask. Three hundred yards, sign on the right, *Ty Gwyn*. Short track.'

'OK. If you're not in, I'll keep trying.'

There was an uncertain pause. Mrs Morningwood cleared her throat.

'Reason I called earlier … Spoke about you with a friend, Sally, in the Frome Valley.'

A momentary fog; you ran into too many people in this job.

'You met, it seems, under difficult circumstances, relating to gypsies,' Mrs Morningwood said.

'Oh … Sally Boswell?'

At the hop museum. Her husband, Al, had made Lol's most precious guitar. Mandolin soundbox and about a dozen different types of wood. Lol revered Al. Al revered Sally.

'Known her for quite some years, darling. She confirmed what I'd sensed when we met. That you are rescourceful and trustworthy.'

'That was very kind of her. Mrs Morningwood, can I—'

'No, come and see me. I'm wary of phones.'

And she'd gone. Suddenly nobody was trusting phones. It was getting like the old Soviet Union.

Merrily dropped the mobile in the in-tray, picked up Dobbs's Charles file and read an unidentified cutting – looked from the typeface and the length of the paragraphs like one of the quality broadsheets – about the Prince's diet. How, aged around thirty, after seeing how some pigs were treated, he'd vowed to become vegetarian. Dropped red meat, taken up raw vegetables, lost weight and developed a rather ascetic appearance.

He'd still gone shooting, though. Some family traditions must've been hard to shed, especially with a father like his. But the interest in organic farming had grown out of it, with impressive results.

How relevant was any of this stuff? If there'd been anything immediately pertinent in the Dobbs file, Sophie would have spotted it. Merrily slid the papers back into the file as the phone quivered before it rang.

Sophie herself.

'You have … a locum.'

Her voice was not so much dry as arid.

'That was quick.'

'Merrily, I'm afraid that it isn't going to be Ruth Wisdom.'

'Oh.'

'Ruth has unexpected domestic ties,' Sophie said. 'Consequently, I had to put out a round-robin email. Which, I'm afraid, was answered within … a very short time.'

'I did point out, didn't I, that Jane will still be here? I mean, she's got her own apartment in the attic, but— it's not a bloke, is it?'

'I'm very sorry, Merrily,' Sophie said. 'You really won't like this, but it was out of my hands.'

25

Monster

WHEN JANE GOT off the school bus, there was a silver-grey car she didn't recognize outside the vicarage.

She walked over. It looked like one of those hybrid jobs that ran partly on urine or something, cost an arm and a leg but the driver was guaranteed a martyr's welcome in eco-paradise. Very tidy inside, a pair of women's leather gloves on the dash.

Jane went back to the market square, wishing whoever it was would just sod off. Needing some time, undisturbed, with Mum, because what she had in her airline bag was likely to be of serious and sobering significance.

Normally, if you had a free period in the afternoon, you spent it wiping out any outstanding homework essays. Jane had had two free periods and had spent them both, plus most of the lunch hour, on one of the common-room computers. Feeling she had something to prove. To Mum and … maybe to Coops, who she hadn't seen for a few days. But she intended to, soon.

She looked around the square for Lol's cool truck. Not there. He must've left for his gig. Jane felt a kind of dismay. While it was good that Lol *had* gigs, better still that he'd found the balls to *do* gigs, inevitably it was pulling him and Mum in different directions. And although they did their best neither of them, in all honesty, was what you could call a strong and decisive person.

Outside the Eight Till Late, a news bill for the only evening paper that reached Ledwardine, the *Star*, read:

DOUBLE DEATH RIDDLE OF BUILDER AND GIRLFRIEND
The girlfriend, too?

Jane froze. Literally froze, hard against one of the fat blackened oak pillars holding up the market hall.

She could remember, quite clearly, a time when shocking death had given her not a shiver but a *frisson* – subtly different, fizzing with a forbidden excitement. Back then, death had not, essentially, been about loss. Even – God forbid – the death of her own dad, because it had happened, when Jane was quite young, in a high-speed car crash with a woman next to him who had not been Mum.

Then they'd moved to the country, and death, in Ledwardine, had resonated. It was so much closer – as close as the churchyard just over the garden wall, where funerals were conducted by her own mother, before burial in a grave dug by Gomer Parry. Whose wife, Minnie, had gone, in the hospital in Hereford. His nephew, Nev, in a fire. And there was Colette, the friend Jane had first got drunk with, on cider, both of them paralytic under the tree in Powell's Orchard where old Edgar Powell had blown his brains out at the wassailing. And, worst of all, Miss Lucy Devenish, Jane's friend and mentor and inspiration … but not for very long before her moped had been on its side in the main road under Cole Hill.

The fragility of life. Random cosmic pruning. One snip of the big secateurs. And then what?

Sometimes, she wished she had Mum's faith. Always assuming it really was faith. She pictured Mum standing at the landing window in her frayed robe, staring bleakly out into the drab, grey morning.

This guy, the builder. Obviously Jane hadn't known him, or his girl-friend, but out here he was much more than a cheap cliché on a billboard – *Death Riddle* – tapped onto a screen by some cynical hack in a town where the air was always singing with sirens.

Out here, where it was quiet and death resonated, he'd been part of the fabric, working the sandstone and the timber and the Welsh slate.

And the girlfriend. Mum was not going to be easy to live with tonight.

Now the stuff in the airline bag, the printouts – from, admittedly, some fairly lurid websites – felt like some kind of porn. Not the kind that could get you banned from using the computer for the rest of term, more insidious than that.

Unnerved by the billboard, switching the bag from her left shoulder to her right, Jane crossed to the vicarage.

She'd seen the woman somewhere before, she was fairly sure of that. Fiftyish and elegant, heavy hair with a dull sheen like pewter, serious grey eyes, dark grey suit. Dog collar.

Mum said, 'Jane, this is Siân.'

Mum was looking, to be honest, frazzled, her skin close to grey, standing at a corner of the refectory table, like the kitchen wasn't her own. Which of course it *wasn't*. The Church owned it. The Church owned everything. Owned Mum.

There was a case in the hall. A real leather traveller's case, with stickers, next to Mum's old overnight bags.

Siân? Jane stared at the woman. The woman smiled in this bland way. Perfect teeth.

Holy shit. It had to be Siân Callaghan-Clarke.

'Siân's going to be looking after things here for a few days,' Mum said. 'As you, erm, suspected this morning, I need to go over to Garway, sort some things out.'

This was the woman who, only a few months ago, had nearly destroyed Mum after getting herself made diocesan Deliverance *coordinator*. Callaghan-Clarke's view of Deliverance seemed to be that it was totally about helping deluded people to seek treatment – bringing in this smooth shrink as part of the *Deliverance Module*. At least *he*'d gone, and the last time Mum had mentioned Callaghan-Clarke it was to say that she'd been keeping a low profile lately, not interfering, never going into the office.

But Mum was inclined to take her eye off the ball.

'Jane is fairly self-sufficient, Siân. She has her own apartm— a big room on the second floor. And a lot of studying to do. So, with all the parish business, you probably won't get to meet a lot. Anyway ...' Mum smiling inanely '... here she is.'

Jane just stood there, like struck dumb, Ethel doing a figure of eight around her ankles.

'Hello, Jane,' Callaghan-Clarke said. 'I've heard *such* a lot about you.'

Black farce. Mum had collapsed into the old captain's chair in the scullery. The door was shut, Jane with her back to it.

'Have you gone insane?'

Callaghan-Clarke was upstairs in the guest room, unpacking her fancy case of Italian leather covered with stickers from international church synods, and it was a big house where voices didn't travel ... so, like why, in God's name, were they *whispering*?

'Nothing I could do,' Mum said. '*Fait accompli.* Ruth Wisdom couldn't make it, Sophie asked around by email, Siân offered.'

'Sophie *accepted* that?'

'If she'd said no, how suspicious would that have looked? Siân's ... highly placed in the Diocese. *I* wouldn't want Sophie to get on the wrong side of her over something like this.'

'I have to stay here with this monster?'

'She's not a *monster*, Jane. She's just an ambitious, very smart, ex-barrister with ... some kind of calling.'

Mum started to laugh. One of those laughs where things really can't get any worse.

'Your builder guy,' Jane said. 'There's a news bill outside Prosser's. It says the girlfriend's ...'

'Yes.'

It was worse than Jane had expected. Immediately, she was imagining doing it: one ear squashed into the cold steel track, the other exposed to the enormous saw-bench scream of the oncoming train. Did she lie facing it, watching the lights? Or was she turned away, feeling the vibration inside her brain, her whole body hunched and tensed, foetal? What could make a fairly young and apparently beautiful woman batter to death somebody she'd loved and then have herself demolished, her face ground into fragments of bone, shreds of tissue?

Jane pulled the plug on it. She dragged over the other chair and sat down.

'Why does Callaghan-Clarke want to come here? Like, what's the ulterior motive?'

'Jane, there—'

'I'm not a kid any more, Mum, I can keep my mouth shut and I've been around this situation long enough to get a feel for seedy C of E politics. *Why?*'

'OK,' Mum said, 'to look at it charitably—'

'Oh, yeah, sure, let's all be terribly *Christian* about it—'

'To look at it charitably, *first* … Maybe she just wanted to help out, knowing this was a job that the Bishop's keen we deal with efficiently and it would need to be a woman.'

'She wants to be the first woman bishop, right?'

'Archdeacon, apparently. In the short term.'

'What?'

'The present Archdeacon's coming up to retirement, possibly next year. Becoming Archdeacon would be a good stepping stone to a Bishop's Palace, when that becomes a possibility for a woman.'

Jane thought about this. As she understood it, the Archdeacon was like the Bishop's chief of staff, the Head of Human Resources in the Diocese. He – or she – organized priests.

'The Archdeacon's in charge of like not replacing vicars who retire or burn out, so the rest of you can all have seventeen parishes each? The Bishop's axeman. Or woman.'

'Something like that.' Mum wasn't laughing now. 'The word is – according to Sophie – that Siân's shadowing Archdeacon Neale for a month, using the time to put together a new game plan for rationalizing the Diocese. I've known for a while that I could be affected.'

'But you *can* say no to more parishes, can't you?'

'I can. But I'm on a five-year contract, which may not be renewed if I don't agree with whatever they propose. No getting round the fact that I'm one of the very few to have only one church. Because I've also got Deliverance.'

'She wants to figure out how to turn you into the Vicar of North Herefordshire, with South Shropshire, and no time for Deliverance?'

'Who knows?'

'You sound like you don't care.'

'What can I do, anyway? Siân's view has always been that Deliverance should be spread out over quite an extensive team. So you have a larger number of clergy with rudimentary training in aspects of healing and deliverance. Like the way – stupid analogy, but it's all I can think of – a percentage of police are firearms-trained. Many more now than there used to be.'

'And you'd …' Jane was dismayed '… you'd actually go along with that?'

'*I* think too many armed cops can be dangerous. Better to have a handful who know when not to shoot. But I didn't get ordained to become Deliverance Consultant.'

'You're good at it. I don't care what you say.'

'Anyway, it might all be academic. She may not become Archdeacon. And there's nothing she can do in a few days.'

'You reckon?'

'Just stay cool, disappear into your apartment, feed the cat and don't get into arguments.'

'*Me*? Arguments?'

'Please?'

'I'll try not to antagonize her. But I *will* be keeping an eye on her.'

'Just don't make it too obvious.'

'Discretion is my middle name.'

Mum smiled this weak kind of *if only* smile. Her face looked drawn-in, blotchy.

'You know what?' Jane said. 'You shouldn't be going to Garway, you should be going to the doc's.'

'There's nothing wrong with me.'

'Have you looked at yourself?'

'Just need a good night's sleep.'

'No, you just don't want to give Kent Asprey the satisfaction of having you at his mercy.'

'I'm all *right*. Probably one of those twenty-four-hour bugs. Be fine tomorrow. Why are you hugging that case?'

'You weren't fine yesterday.' Jane took her airline bag over to the desk and unzipped it. 'Look, I'm sorry, but I'm afraid this isn't going to help you sleep.'

Mum stiffened.

'What've you done?'

'No, it's not ... I was talking to Robbie Williams. The head of history?'

'I know.'

'He's a medieval historian, and he knows a lot about the Crusades and the Knights Templar.'

'Jane, you didn't—?'

'I didn't say a word about you. I just said I'd been across to Garway and got interested. Bottom line is, I asked him about the green man, and he said he thought the one at Garway Church was a representation of ... something else.'

Jane pulled out her plastic document case and opened it out. All the stuff she'd printed out from the net.

For some reason – Sod's Law – it opened to the crude engraving of the dark and devilish bearded figure with a goat's head and cloven hooves, wings and a woman's breasts and a candle burning on its head between the horns.

Mum went, 'Oh, for God's *sake* ...'

26

Scarecrow for the Vulgar

AN IMAGE OOZING calculated perversity. Paint it in blood on the wall, in the soiled sanctity of some abandoned crypt: the Devil, the Antichrist, the Beast 666. The oldest enemy.

Introduced into the vicarage, inevitably, by little Jane.

Merrily's first instinct was to cover it up with the mouse mat, take it away, but that would be playing into its ... hooves.

Don't let Siân see it. Siân, whose upper lip would pucker in distaste – not revulsion, no nervous fingering of the pectoral cross here, merely *distaste* at the *medievalism* of it.

Only, it wasn't medieval. Nineteenth century, probably.

Merrily propped up the plastic folder against the computer and gazed into the smudgy smirk of the goat/man/woman/demon. The face of bored decadence. The face of look-at-me-I'm-so-twisted-and-satanic-and-don't-you-just-love-it?

The red and black ink had blurred, making it look even more perverse. Hints of blood and lipstick.

'It's an old printer and I probably whipped the paper out too fast,' Jane said. 'You've got to be a bit careful about what you download, Morrell has occasional dawn swoops. Anyway, this is the work of Eliphas Levi. You *have* heard of him?'

'Heard of him?' Merrily turned wearily to Jane. 'Flower, I've worn his jeans.'

Jane scowled. Merrily smiled fractionally.

'Sorry. Yeah, I have heard of him. French occultist, late nineteenth century or thereabouts, who, under his real name, was an ordained priest. Although he and the Catholic Church became increasingly estranged – didn't help when he ran off with a sixteen-year-old girl. Like Aleister Crowley, who claimed to be his reincarnation, he really wanted to be a rock star but, unfortunately for both of them, rock music wouldn't be invented for another century.'

'I hate it when you're flip,' Jane said. 'Although I realize it's essentially a defensive thing.'

Merrily felt the thickness of the file. Must have taken Jane quite a long time to collect all this.

'Sorry. You've gone to a lot of trouble. Yeah, I suppose you could be pointing me in a direction I hadn't thought of. Both Levi and Crowley, as I recall, were, at some stage in their murky careers, into what they saw as the tradition of the Knights Templar.'

'If you already know it all I've been wasting my time.'

Jane snatched down the copy of the engraving, looking quite hurt. Merrily sighed.

'I've probably forgotten most of it. Remind me.'

'That woman will be down soon.'

'No, she won't. She'll see the value of giving us some time to talk before I leave.'

It was like this: in 1307, with no crusades on the agenda, the Poor Knights of Christ and the Temple of Solomon were no longer even pretending to be poor. They were multinational bankers: a wealthy, powerful, secretive and formidable presence.

The guardians of too many arcane secrets – that was Jane's view of it, but to orthodox historians they were simply a threat to the French monarchy. And the Pope. This Pope, anyway, Clement V, based at Avignon and therefore under the protection of the French king, Philip IV. A puppet Pope.

Jane talked and it all came back.

How the list of charges against the Templars was drawn up, or dreamed up, nobody could quite say, but it was impressively damning: they denied Christ, they didn't believe in the Mass, they practised sodomy and exchanged obscene kisses on being received into the Order. They were taught that the Masters of the Order – none of them ordained priests – could absolve them from sin.

And they worshipped this bearded head, which came to be known as Baphomet. Mr Williams had told Jane that the name was seen by some sources as a corruption of Muhammad, but Merrily vaguely remembered other interpretations.

'It was quite clever,' Jane said. 'If you look closely at the charges, you can definitely see where some of them are coming from.'

'Yeah, I know. The denial of Christ could mean that they were simply denying the *divinity* of Christ because they were supposed to have known the so-called truth: that he'd died, leaving behind his girlfriend, Mary Magdalene and their family. On the same basis, you have the rejection of the Mass, because – allegedly – they knew there could be no transubstantiation.'

'Right. And then we come to the head.'

'OK, tell me about the head.'

'Probably goes back to the Celtic *cult* of the head,' Jane said.

'I hadn't heard of that connection.'

'The Celts saw the head as the receptacle of the spirit, right?'

'Mr Williams thinks the Templars actually *did* worship the head?'

'Or maybe just recognized it as *symbolic* of something? Consider the fact that the Templars were linked to the Cistercians and gnostic sects.'

'Here we go ...'

'And other guys who weren't stupid enough to reject centuries of pre-Christian knowledge of nature and harmony with the land and ... and a lot of other practical stuff that you can't get *in any way* from the Bible.'

'Yeah, yeah, I'm sure it must've been symbolic of *something*. However, if the bearded head represents *that* revolting joke' – Merrily jerked a thumb at the engraving of the horned beast with the candle on its head – 'then it really doesn't say a lot to me about mankind's links with the earth. Especially as it also features in black masses and is often found above the altars of satanic temples.'

'You haven't actually read Levi, have you?'

'Somehow, that thing with the teenage girl kind of said it all for me. But go on ...'

'What it basically comes down to ...' Jane shuffled papers '... is whole centuries of superstition, smears and misrepresentation. It's a hieroglyphic representing male and female and illumination – the candle? It's also Pan, the goat-foot god, the spirit of nature. OK, listen to this: "The symbolic head of the Goat of Mendes is occasionally given to this figure and it is then the Baphomet of the Templars and the Word of the Gnostics ... bizarre images which became *scarecrows for the vulgar*."'

'So only thick people think there could be anything evil here. And the Church, of course.'

Jane shrugged.

'Well, thank you, flower, you've converted me. I'll pack in all this Christian crap, put up a Goat of Mendes poster in the hall – only ten dollars from the Church of Satan and All Fallen Angels, Sacramento – and once I've popped into the church and spat on the altar—'

'All right ... you can mock.' Jane stood up. 'I'm just trying to show you what you're dealing with, that's all. There are two sides to everything.'

'So the Garway Green Man is actually Baphomet. Mr Williams thinks that?'

'He knows Garway church, and he thinks it makes sense. And if what you found inside the inglenook at the Master House was a replica of the Baphomet in the church ...'

'You didn't tell Robbie Williams about that?'

'No, I just asked about it in a general kind of way.'

'Only I would hate any of this to get back to your beloved head teacher, because if Morrell thought I was involving you, a minor, in what he regards as my unscientific, primitive and superstitious occupation ...'

'It's OK. I don't think Robbie Williams likes Morrell either. And in case ...' Jane's gaze softened. 'In case you were fearing the worst, even *I* would be a bit wary of bending a knee to Baphomet. Or the Goat of Mendes.'

She came over, and Merrily half-rose and then they were spontaneously hugging. Ridiculous. Embracing your heathen daughter because she'd granted you the concession of drawing the line at actual devil worship.

More probably, Merrily guessed, it was the formal sealing of a pact against what was upstairs.

'Jane, look … I'm sorry. It was a bad night, and it's not been a great day. I don't really know what I'm supposed to be doing. Going over to Garway – it could be a wasted exercise. Even Huw Owen's telling me to back off, because whatever happened there concerns ancient secrets that aren't going to get cracked. Definitely not by someone like me.'

'He actually said that?'

'I don't think he meant it in any mystical sense. I think he was saying I'd just tie myself up in knots, getting nowhere. And when *you* come home and hang all this on me, with the saintly Siân upstairs …'

Merrily was feeling almost painfully tired. Tired and inept. Huw was probably right: tamp it down, walk away and, with any luck, it won't flare again in your lifetime.

'Listen, there's one final thing, Mum. Jacques de Molay?'

'The last Grand Master of the Templars.'

'I think there's an engraving of him here. I've got it … *there* … He looks a bit like Baphomet himself, doesn't he?'

Merrily looked at the drawing of the figure with the cross on his surcoat. Dignified but defiant. Che Guevara. Or maybe just the quiet one from some electric-folk band in the 1970s.

'He was burned at the stake?'

Jane nodded. 'After refusing to confess to sodomy, sacrilege and the rest of it. Most of the others who were arrested did confess after being threatened and tortured. But De Molay insisted to the end that he was a good Christian. He said he wanted to die facing the Church of Our Lady. But – get this – before the flames took him, he said that God would avenge him. He said the Pope and the King of France could expect to see him again before too long.'

'I know. De Molay's dying curse. Where's this going, Jane?'

'Neither the King nor the Pope lasted a year. And Jacques de Molay became this kind of cult figure. Still is, apparently.'

'Yes.'

'There was some guy in the French Revolution,' Jane said, 'and when they guillotined Louis XVI he was like, *This is for Jacques de Molay.*'

Merrily thought she could hear footsteps on the stairs and stood up. Felt, for a moment, slightly dizzy.

'Suppose I'd better show Siân around.'

'Hang on,' Jane said, 'I haven't *told* you, yet.'

'Sorry. Only—'

'And this isn't, like, supposition or legend or anything. This is official history. I think it was 1294.'

'All right.' Merrily paused, holding the door handle, aching for a cigarette. 'What happened in 1294?'

'That was the year Jacques de Molay came to Garway,' Jane said.

27

Bev and Rev

SETTING OUT A place by the window in the whitewashed dairy, now the guests' dining room, Beverley Murray glanced at Teddy across the table, and you could almost see it happening: this smouldering issue reigniting in the air between them.

Then Beverley went back to the cutlery tray, and Teddy said, 'If handled discreetly, I think it would be sensible. Discretion being the operative word.'

'When was there—?' Beverley letting the cutlery clink more than was necessary. 'When was there *ever* discretion in a place like this? Sometimes I think that damned radio mast picks up everything we say and broadcasts it into everybody's living room.'

'In which case, Merrily needs to get it all done and dusted before too many people find out.'

By 'too many people' Teddy presumably meant some of the cranks likely to descend on Garway next weekend for the Templar memorial service.

'Quick as I possibly can.' Merrily was not feeling up to an argument. 'As soon as I can establish what we're looking at.'

Meaning *help me here*. Teddy prised out a reluctant chuckle.

'Merrily has a most unenviable job. Bumps in the night being an area most of us tend to steer clear of. Too many pitfalls.'

'If there's a crisis in the parish, Teddy tends to take himself for a walk,' Beverley said.

She was maybe ten years younger than Teddy, one of those brisk, practical, short-haired blondes who'd become a familiar breed in these parts, like the golden retriever. Their farmhouse was eighteenth-century, a block of sunburned-looking stone wedged into the hillside half a mile beyond the church, ruinous outbuildings scattered below it like scree. *The Ridge: Dinner, B & B. Walkers welcome.* Two public footpaths intersected below a terrace with tables and green and yellow umbrellas.

'Balm for the soul, this landscape.' Teddy was in thick socks, still carrying his walking boots by their laces. 'You'll start to feel it soon, Merrily. Take away that anxious frown.'

'Teddy!'

'Well, it's true, Bevvie.' He turned to Merrily. 'Sorry if I'm being tactless, but I have to say I don't think I've seen anyone alter as dramatically as you have in just a few days. Well, yes, sudden death ... inevitably a shock to the system. But it's not your fault, my dear, *not your fault.*'

'Yes, well ...' Merrily said, 'Maybe a good night's sleep ...'

'Or, as I say, a good walk. Oh, I know Bevvie thinks I'm an *avoider*, but the countryside calms and strengthens. One of the functions of a parish priest is to remain centred and ... essentially placid.'

'He means *passive*,' Beverley said. 'In other words, uninvolved. Male priests think there's some sort of dignity to being remote. One of the benefits of having girls in the clergy is that at least they aren't afraid of getting their feet wet. Women get involved, men go for a walk. He does yoga, too, I'm afraid.'

'Basic stuff, but it keeps one in trim.' Teddy dumped his boots by the door. 'Like to enjoy this place for a couple more decades. That so wrong?'

'I mean, obviously we're delighted to have you here, Merrily,' Beverley said. 'If only the circumstances were different.'

'Yes. Thanks.'

If only. Merrily was the sole guest, although a party from Germany was expected at the end of the week. There were no-smoking signs in the dining room, the lounge, her bedroom and the en-suite bathroom.

'At the end of the day, I'm afraid I really don't see,' Beverley said, 'why this community has to be dragged into something which might be terribly sad but is also sordid, sordid, sordid. Bad enough that Teddy's forced to conduct a service next Saturday for a bunch of ... anoraks, I suppose. But nothing to do with the Knights Templar is *terribly* healthy, it seems to me. The activities they were accused of ... well, no smoke without fire, that's my view.'

Outside the window, rolling shadows chased the last of the sunlight out of a patch of woodland.

'I can ... understand how you feel,' Merrily said carefully.

When she'd rung from the vicarage, thinking she'd go to Garway in the morning, Teddy Murray had invited Merrily over for supper. Jane, listening to her vacillating, had held up both palms, pushing: *go*.

And it *was* the only way, she realized that now. Time-consuming, but if you went in cold you learned no more than the police would, or the media. Interviews. Statements. On the record, therefore restricted.

Really, it was about listening. As she'd said at the Sunday meditation, not quite getting through to Shirley West. Merrily shivered, not the first time, Beverley noticing at once.

'Cold, Merrily?'

'Oh no. Not at all. Goose walked over my ...'

After a light supper – *Vegetarian? Not a problem, grow our own* – the three of them were sitting around a glass-fronted wood stove in the lounge, which had rough panelling and a small cocktail bar, like a pulpit, in one corner.

'More coffee, I think,' Beverley said, reaching for the pot, and Teddy, having collected more of Bev's sidelong glances, discreet as neatly folded notes, made another approach.

'How much of a public affair does this have to be, Merrily?'

'Well, I won't be selling tickets.'

'No ... ha ... I think what I'm asking ...?'

'Eight people, max. That's what I was thinking. You, me, a representative of the Duchy, a couple of friends or relatives of Felix and Fuchsia and – tell me if you think this is going to be a problem – members of the two families who've owned the place. The Grays and the Gwilyms.'

'Oh Lord.'

Teddy's white-bearded chin sank into his chest, and Merrily pined for a lie-down and a cigarette. She sat up.

'A bit ambitious, do you think?'

'They don't speak to one another, you know.'

'I did hear that.'

'Family feuds in this part of the world can be very bitter indeed and go on, literally, for centuries.'

'It's not a joke.' Beverley was filling cups. 'Personally, I think it might cause more trouble than any of this is worth. There's still a lot of super-stition in this area, and this is almost encouraging it. I mean, how can a house ...? It seems more than a little absurd.'

'Yes.' Merrily nodded. 'I suppose it does.'

Later, when Teddy had gone for his evening stroll, she joined Beverley in the kitchen. Stainless steel, halogen lights. Ultra-functional, no dust, no stains, no dark corners. Beverley wiped down a worktop with a damp cloth.

'I didn't want to be offensive, Merrily, and I'm still a churchgoer of sorts but do you *really* think the atmosphere of a place can affect the way someone behaves? Make them do something horrible?'

'I suppose I have to say yes, sometimes, in a way, but—'

'And that you can do something about it?'

How were you supposed to answer that? Tell her about the times you awoke in the night and wondered if you weren't just patching up the fabric of a great big ancient but flimsy construction that was, in fact, completely hollow?

Merrily closed her eyes momentarily, finally admitting to herself that she wasn't very well. Couldn't be pre-mentrual, she wasn't due for another ... ten days?

'You OK, Merrily?'

'I'm fine. The thing is, I thought at first it was going to be nothing. I thought the Bishop was going over the top in asking for a full inquiry. Then two people die.'

'Yes.' Beverley threw the cloth into one of three sinks. 'Something you said earlier worried me a little.'

'Mmm?'

'When you said there should be no more than eight people at this ... ceremony. And that one of them should be Teddy. How necessary is that? I suppose what I'm saying – and please don't tell him we've had this conversation, he'd be angry with me – is that I'd really rather you did it without him.'

'I see.'

'No, you don't. What you see is a fit, healthy, athletic man who walks at least five miles every morning before breakfast. You don't see what I saw when he was the rector of our village near Cheltenham.'

'How long ago was this?'

'Six years? That's how long we've been married, anyway. I was recently divorced at the time – when I first met Teddy. And my son was abroad – gap year before uni.'

Beverley said she'd had room to breathe for the first time in years. She'd been awarded the house in the divorce settlement, and there was a recent bequest from an uncle. But she'd only been forty and on the lookout for a meaningful job.

'I was thinking of going back to nursing, but that's a thankless task nowadays. NHS hospitals are like meat-processing plants.'

Beverley switched on the dishwasher and then, mercifully, dimmed the lights. She stood looking out of a small square window towards the glowing of distant farms. Telling Merrily how she'd started going to church, helping out, spending time with the rector. Much as Merrily had when her own marriage had been coming unstitched. The difference being that it had led Merrily into a personal calling and Bev into a project called Teddy.

'His workload was becoming ridiculous, poor man. Four large parishes in Gloucestershire, and the phone never seemed to stop ringing. And then the main church was broken into five times in two years. You get that, too, I imagine.'

'Not so far.'

'Then you've been very lucky. The final straw was a wave of absolutely awful vandalism. Well, not just vandalism – desecration. Gravestones pushed over, defaced, strange symbols chiselled into them. And one night someone broke in and actually defecated in the church, which was horrible, horrible, horrible ...'

'And a police matter, surely?'

'You'd think so, wouldn't you? It's only when it actually happens that you find out that, unless the damage is very serious or someone's been hurt, the police really aren't interested in the slightest. They might show up and take a statement, looking rather bored, but you never hear from them again.'

'How long did this go on?'

'Couple of months, intermittently. There was supposed to be a neighbourhood watch in the village, but they were only interested in protecting their own homes. Teddy would be out patrolling the church-yard himself at all hours of the night. One night, he almost caught someone and was knocked to the ground. What *is* happening in our society? Sometimes they're *killed*. Priests killed outside their own churches!'

'We've been lucky in this part of the world. So far.'

'I suppose that's one advantage of a place where everyone knows everyone else. But, to cut a long story short, he more or less had a break-down. Constantly tired – you'd see his hands trembling, dropping the prayer book at service. When the graves were desecrated, some people in the parish were talking about – well, it was inevitable, I suppose ...'

'What – Satanism?'

'That sort of thing. Whatever it was, it wasn't pleasant. It left a nasty taste. Teddy seemed to age about ten years. I ... found myself looking after him. It's what I'm good at, I suppose.'

'He, erm ... he wasn't married then?'

'His wife had died some years before. Car accident. The Church was his life, if you could call it a life. And in the parish ... the *nerve* of people. The way some of them reacted when they found out I was divorced! I mean, it was hardly a major scandal. One night, I said, for God's sake, why don't you pack in this stupid, *stupid* job, and let's move to somewhere they don't know us and start a guest house. I *did* know what I was doing, by the way – my parents were hoteliers.'

'He got early retirement?'

'After I threatened to go to the press. Overworked, overpressured, underpaid and under threats of violence?'

'Literally?'

'There were threatening phone calls. Didn't I say? Untraceable these days, people make them from cheap mobiles. But … he got early retirement, and we wound up here. Not *quite* my idea of an idyll, but the people are OK, they don't judge. "Bev and Rev", that's what they call us in the pub. We thought of having it on the sign outside, but that would be a little *too* cosy.'

'He seems OK, now.'

'I tease him about his walks, but it's really done him the world of good, the four years we've been at Garway. Learned all the history, guides people around, leads expeditions, and able to keep his hand in with the church. Just our bloody luck that the vicar would have to leave and there'd be an unexpected hiatus before the next one takes over, and Teddy would feel obliged to stand in full-time. And that it should coincide, God help us, with *this* madness.'

It wasn't clear whether she meant the Master House problem or the Templar service. Maybe both.

'What sort of service is he going to give them?'

'We still haven't given up hope that someone else might take it on.' Beverley looked at Merrily, eyes steady. 'I don't suppose …?'

'Beverley, most of what I know about the Knights Templar I got from Teddy the other day. All he needs is an ordinary service with a couple of customized prayers, a sermon about the need for religious tolerance and … I dunno, "Onward Christian Soldiers"? Beverley, would it be OK if I—?'

'Your exorcism service … someone prone to stress-related problems, that could be damaging, couldn't it?'

'Well, it … it's been known. But in the vast majority of cases it—'

'So if you do need an extra minister at your, whatever you call it, deliverance, perhaps you could call in another … exorcist or something?'

Merrily nodded wearily.

'Sure.'

She'd end up doing it on her own in the dim, mould-smelling room, the atmosphere swollen with historic hostility, the Baphomet grinning in the inglenook.

'Is that all right?' Beverley said.

'Of course. Would it be OK if went to bed. I'm feeling a bit …'

'Oh, I'm so sorry, you must be absolutely exhausted. It's obviously been a difficult couple of days.'

'Just a bit tiring,' Merrily said.

As always when you were feverish, there wasn't much sleep that night. Strange bed, a hard, fitness-freak mattress. Getting up around two a.m., feeling hot, and leaning out of the first-floor window. Cold air on bare arms, murky night obscuring distance so that the end of the cigarette, feebly glittering against the moonless sky, was like the tail light of a passing plane.

Before bed, Merrily had called Jane on the mobile. Jane said Siân Callaghan-Clarke had been very friendly, not at all what she'd imagined. They'd actually talked for a couple of hours, about Siân's time as a barrister and Jane's problems finding the right career plan.

'Erm … great,' Merrily said.

'Hey, Mum, it's not my fault she wasn't being a bitch.'

'I never said a word …'

'That meaningful pause said it all.'

'You remembered to feed Ethel?'

'Like Ethel would let me forget? Mum, don't—' Small hiss of exasperation. 'How's it going there?'

How *was* it going? Merrily peered down the valley, into vague dustings of light. There was a prickling of fine drizzle now, on her arms. She pulled them in, stubbing out the cigarette on the stone wall under the windowsill, feeling cold now, and hollow and disoriented. No sense of where she was in relation to the top of the hill with its radio mast or the hidden valley of the church, the *rum* place where M. R. James believed he'd caused some offence.

This was not an easy place.

Jacques de Molay had located it, though.

In 1294, the last Grand Master of the Order of the Poor Knights of Christ and the Temple of Solomon had sailed from France, then ridden across southern England to visit the remote preceptory at Garway. According to Jane's internet research, nobody appeared to know why he'd come or what he'd done here. And if there were no crazy theories on the net, last refuge of the extreme ...

She shut the window, groped her shivery way back to bed. Please God, not some bloody bug.

Woke again, from a darkly vivid dream in which the tower of Garway church was with her in the room. The tower was standing in the far corner beyond the window, its vertical slit-eyes solemnly considering her. Guarding its secrets, knowing hers.

She sat up violently in bed, the duvet gathered around her. The moon had come out, sprinkling talcum-powdery light on the wardrobe.

The wardrobe, no more than half a century old, was roughly the same shape as the church tower and had twin vertical ventilation slits, high up in each door, black now.

You could go crazy.

Merrily lay down again, rolling herself in the duvet, turning her back on the wardrobe, stupidly grateful that The Ridge was not The Globe and the room had only one bed.

When she walked on to the square in Ledwardine, a crowd was gathering, but nobody was looking directly at her, although she was collecting meaningful sidelong glances from people like the Prossers, James Bull-Davies, Alison Kinnersley and Shirley West.

It was a deep pink dusk and the lights were coming on. Lol wouldn't be at home, of course, he was off on a gig somewhere. So why was there a filtered light in his cottage in Church Street?

She walked across the square, getting out the key he'd given her, but she didn't need it, the door was slightly ajar. She went in.

There was a dim light in the hallway and low music coming from somewhere, the song 'Cure of Souls', from Lol's album, the one he'd written about her before they were together:

> *Did you suffocate your feelings*
> *As you redefined your goals*
> *And vowed to undertake the cure of souls ...*

Over the music came the throaty notes of slippery female laughter. Dripping down the stairs, like a pouring of oil, was a shiny, black, discarded dress.

Merrily, heartbroken, ran out, back onto the square where they were burning Jacques de Molay, his cold eyes fixed on hers through the darkening smoke as his white smock shrivelled up, turning brown.

She awoke sweating and shivering, no light in the sky.

PART THREE

Mystery is a way of saying that we
do not fully understand what it is that
we are experiencing or talking about
but nonetheless we know it to be real
and not false. It is not about trying to
evade important questions as to how
or why or what.

Kenneth Stevenson
*Do This. The Shape, Style and Meaning
of the Eucharist.*

28

Suicide Note – Kind Of

MRS MORNINGWOOD, HAVING beckoned her into the window, now appeared to see something worrying in Merrily's eyes.

'You're not at all well, are you?'

'I'm fine.'

'Shoes off,' Mrs Morningwood said.

'Look, I—'

'Lie down on the chaise longue. Put that pillow behind your head, the other one under your back where the springs have gone in the middle.'

Mrs Morningwood wore jeans and a military sort of jumper, ribbed, and a pale lemon silk scarf. Her hair was down and looked freshly washed. Merrily tried to focus, saw the blur of a timelessly handsome woman no longer over-fussed about what she looked like. A clock was ticking somewhere. The room had cream walls, a bentwood rocking chair, an ebony desk and a black cast-iron range with a fresh log on a glowing bed, Roscoe the wolfhound lying full length below it, longer and hairier than the rug he was on.

'I'm sorry …' Merrily looked around for the clock, confused. 'What time is it now?'

'I should think coming up to midday. Clock's in the kitchen. We don't allow time in here.'

Midday. Oh my God.

She'd had breakfast at nine – most of a boiled egg, one slice of dry toast – watching Teddy Murray cheerily loading his knapsack, off to plan out a circular ten-mile walk for the German party next weekend, Bev inspecting Merrily, practical, blonde head on one side. 'Are you *sure* you're all right, Merrily?'

She'd gone back to her room, lay down for a moment on the bed ... woke up over an hour later, in a panic. Rushing into the bathroom, washing again, brushing her hair and stumbling down the stairs – nobody about, a radio somewhere playing Classic FM, but it still brought back celloed strands of 'The Cure of Souls', that reproachful song. She'd ring Lol, just as soon as she got back. Wasn't his fault – *her* dream, her paranoia. Slipping quietly out of the front door, which had steps down to the lane, forgetting for the moment where she'd left the Volvo, only remembering where she had to go in it. *Past The Turning three hundred yards, sign on the right, Ty Gwyn. Short track.*

An end of a terrace, two tiny white-rendered cottages at one end knocked together, set well back from the road, overlooking fields and woodland under a pocked and mottled cheesy sky. Didn't really remember getting here.

Mrs Morningwood had pulled up a piano stool with a black velvet seat to the foot of the chaise longue. Arranging a blue woollen travelling rug over Merrily's legs. Bending over her feet now, reading glasses on her nose. Separating the toes and then running a thumbnail along one sole; it felt like a Stanley knife. Blanking out the pain, Merrily scrabbled for a question unrelated to her state of health.

'Why did Jacques de Molay come to Garway?'

'Who?'

'Templar boss.'

'Haven't got a heart condition, have you?'

'Not that I'm aware of.'

'Should've asked before I started. Remiss of me. Jacques de Molay. I suppose it's more or less established that he *did* come here. About twelve years before his unfortunate death, I believe.'

'Where would he have ...? *Oh my—*'

'Your stomach, darling. Tight as a drum. Intestines wound up like a watch spring. And then something implodes. I think you're rather close to an ulcer. What've you been doing?' Mrs Morningwood stood back, deep lines in her long face, all her features hard-focused in the sunless light. 'You really weren't aware of this? At all?'

'No, I … *God!*'

'It'll get less painful after a while. At first, you know, I was thinking premature menopause.'

'What?'

'No stigma. Sometimes happens to girls in their twenties. Probably isn't. Probably plain stress. Never had reflexology before?'

'Well …' Rolling her head in the pillow '… Not quite like this. Not the seriously painful kind.'

'Some so-called practitioners are merely playing at it. Feelgood, massage-parlour stuff, bugger-all use to anybody. Sorry, darling, what was your question?'

'De Molay. I was trying to ask you where he might have stayed. When he was here.'

'You really need to rest. A holiday. When did you last have a holiday?'

'Four years? Five? I don't know, we weren't living here then. Another lifetime.'

'I can feel other people's problems curled up tightly inside you, stored away in little sacks.'

The Stanley knife again, biting into the side of a big toe.

'Sacks that swell,' Mrs Morningwood said.

Merrily shut her eyes. This was not going the way it was supposed to. The plan had been to walk in, eyes wide open, go for some straight answers: *Mrs Morningwood, you didn't just accidentally bump into Jane and me the other day, you had an agenda and presumably still have. Why did you court Jane with your revelations about the four pubs and the heavenly bodies? Why were you so keen that we should check out the Master House while you buggered off?*

The pain faded. She let her head sink into the pillow. With her usual uncompromising dynamism, she'd staggered up the path, under a wooden pergola still lush with vines. Still trying to find a doorbell or a knocker when the door had opened and she'd virtually fallen over the threshold.

'I suppose you're thinking of the Master House,' Mrs Morningwood said. 'It would make sense of the name, certainly. Doubtless the sort of grand celebrity occasion they'd have wanted to commemorate.'

'Nobody know for sure?'

'So little from that period was written down, Mrs Watkins. Not exactly known for their illuminated script, the Templars. Didn't keep diaries or ledgers, far as I know.'

'Being illiterate couldn't have helped. No word-of-mouth, old wives' tales about *why* de Molay came?'

'He was presumably inspecting the preceptory. Why does it interest you?'

'Trying to get a handle on the place, that's all. To what extent it's connected to the Templars.'

A log collapsed in the range, gases spurting, Merrily starting to sweat.

'Good.' Mrs Morningwood didn't look up, working on a toe with both hands, like peeling a plum. 'You're probably full of toxins. I'd hate to even inquire about your diet.'

'Mostly vegetarian. Bit of fish.'

'Bit of this, bit of that, *I* know. A vegetarian diet needs to be carefully organized or there'll be deficiencies. Looks of you, I bet you don't even bother to eat at all half the time.'

'You find life isn't something that happens between meals.'

'Life, my darling, needs to be battered into shape.'

'Easier said than— *Oh, for* ... I thought you said it'd get less painful.'

'I expect I lied,' Mrs Morningwood said.

When Merrily awoke, still on the chaise longue, the light in the two windows was blue-grey and the light in the cast-iron range was molten red, like the crater of a live volcano. Like the sun through the glass of red wine she'd been given. The sun had been out then, when she'd drunk it. Gone now, the sun and the wine.

Mrs Morningwood was rocking gently in the bentwood chair, smoking. Merrily raised herself up on her elbows.

'What was in it?'

'Nothing much. Valerian, mainly.'

'What's that do?'

'A remedy for nervous debility. Unclenches the gut. Promotes sleep, quite rapidly sometimes.'

'You didn't tell me that.'

'Of course I didn't tell you that – you'd've buggered off.'

'This wasn't supposed to …' Merrily's head fell back. 'How long have I been here now?'

'Why are you so obsessed with time? You've been here as long as was necessary.'

'Right.'

'Don't get up yet, Watkins, you might fall over.'

Couldn't have if she'd wanted to. Merrily felt limp and disconnected and distictly odd but not in a bad way. And not, as she'd feared, in a drugged way. Something seemed to be vibrating inside her, like a motor idling.

'Where did you learn all this stuff?'

'The basic herbalism – and it *is* basic – was from my mother and she had it from *her* mother and so on.'

Always be a Morningwood on Garway Hill, as long as badgers shit on the White Rocks.

Right. Merrily felt like someone abducted by aliens, taken away to the mother ship, physically investigated, brought back. Mrs Morningwood supervising the experiment.

'Wasn't *complicated*, darling. Bad diet, insufficient sleep and nervous stress. You'll sleep well tonight, probably wee quite a lot first, mind. And after that it's up to you. The reflexology, picked that up in London. Seemed to be something I could do, almost from the outset. Technique might go back to ancient Egypt – who knows that the Templars didn't bring it back from the Middle East? Although it's not, as far as I know, in the traditional repertoire of the nine witches of Garway.'

'Garway's loss. I expect.'

'You feel better.'

Merrily eased herself up again, nodded slowly, very aware of the movements of her neck, the fulcrum of bones.

'I feel – a bit worryingly – relaxed.'

'Smoke if you want to. Why *worryingly* relaxed? You feel guilty about relaxation?'

'Teddy Murray says it's a function of the clergy to appear totally placid at all times. I realize that's his excuse for spending hours strolling the hills, but maybe there's something— How much do I actually owe you, Mrs Morningwood?'

'Owe?'

'It's going dark, I've been here over half a day—'

'Lots of other tasks were performed in between. You just didn't notice.'

Mrs Morningwood arose from the chair, went over to the range. There was an earthenware teapot on the hob. She detached a brown mug from a hook.

'But since you mention recompense, sadly from your point of view I'm not much of a Christian, so yes, I have every intention of extracting payment in kind.'

'Oh.'

'What brought you here – feeling of failure?'

'Partly.'

'What could you have done?' Mrs Morningwood brought over the cup, steaming. 'It's only tea, weak as gnat's piss, and I can assure you there's nothing in it that will send you back to sleep. What do you think you might have done to save either of them?'

'Could've believed her. Thank you.' Merrily sipped, holding the mug in both hands, swinging her feet tentatively to the floor. 'Although I had no reason to at the time.'

Drinking the weak tea slowly, telling Mrs Morningwood how Fuchsia had claimed to have been haunted by something which, it transpired, had been invented by M. R. James.

'Interesting.'

'You've read that one?'

'Oh yes.'

'And you knew James was in Garway?'

'My grandmother met him. And the girl – his ward, Jane McBryde. But that's by the by. So Fuchsia Mary Linden borrowed Monty's seaside ghost. How very imaginative of her.'

'What's that say to you?'

'Only that she didn't want to tell you – or Barlow – what actually happened to her in the Master House.'

'Which was?'

'How should I know?'

'She wanted me to bless her, give her protection. Before she came back here.'

'And then, afterwards, she returned and battered Barlow to death. What do you know about Barlow's history?'

'Not a great deal.' Merrily thought about it; where was *this* going? 'He spent time in a tepee community in West Wales where he met Fuchsia's mother, who was already pregnant. Felix was a bit in love with her and also, I think, felt sorry for her. He said she was … fragile. And he seems to have accepted a role as a kind of godfather … guardian. Tragically sealing his own fate, if you want to be—'

'Tepee community,' Mrs Morningwood said.

'Tepee City. In Cardiganshire.'

'Why did Barlow go there?'

'Gap year was all he said.'

'No such thing in those days, darling.'

'I think he was probably being ironic. It was just a year between leaving school and having to do something responsible connected with his dad's building supplies business. Which maybe didn't seem very appealing at a time when everyone else seemed to be sleeping around and taking exotic drugs.'

'Did he …' Mrs Morningwood sat on the piano stool '… mention being a part of any other community? Before Wales?'

'No, he didn't. What are you thinking of?'

'*I'm* thinking of the one that was in occupation at the Master House in the 1970s, when the Newtons were repeatedly leasing it out.'

'Don't know anything about it.' Merrily finally brought out her cigarettes. 'Some kind of good-life smallholding – did *you* tell me that?'

'Good life? Not me, darling. Bastards couldn't even grow their own dope. The house was leased by the Newtons to an *honourable* – son of some minor member of the Midlands aristocracy. Newtons were well pleased, at first. Not realizing he'd turn out to be the kind of dissolute, overprivileged hooray hippie that could turn … I don't know, Sandringham into a shell in a matter of weeks.'

'Anybody I've heard of?'

'Shouldn't think so. Lord Stourport?'

Merrily shook her head.

'Endless rumours about the things that went on there,' Mrs Morningwood said. 'Orgies and the rest. Nude bathing in the Monnow. Place would probably've been burned to the ground, result of some discarded spliff, if there hadn't been a rather timely police raid. Result of which Lord Cokehead was sent down for three months or so. Lease effectively terminated.'

'So why would Felix Barlow have been *there*?'

'Most of the hoorays couldn't replace a washer on a bloody tap, so anybody who was halfway practical was welcome to move into one of the sheds, drugs on the house, long as he brought his tools. That's what I was told, anyway – wouldn't know anything for sure, all this happened while I was … away.'

'Well … Felix was indeed a very practical man, but I'm not getting why you think he would've been at the Master House. In fact …' Merrily sat up, the cigarette halfway to her mouth. 'What *is* your angle on this, Mrs Morningwood? Where are you actually coming from? Like, what did you mean when you said on the phone that someone *didn't do a terribly good job*?'

Merrily slumped on to the edge of the chaise longue. Her body felt weak but the low vibration was still there and went cruising up into her head, bringing on a dizziness.

'Steady, girl. You got the works, you know.'

Mrs Morningwood turned and threw the remains of her cigarette, with practised accuracy, into the heart of the fire.

Merrily lay back against the pillows. The windows had dimmed, crimson caverns opening up in the iron range. Roscoe, the wolfhound rose up and stretched, his front legs extended, revealing the black smudges of old burn marks on the rug where he'd been lying.

Mrs Morningwood stood up and moved across to the ebony desk. Sound of a drawer sliding open. She bent and drew the piano stool towards the well of the desk, switching on a green-shaded oil lamp converted to electricity.

Placing a fold of paper on the floodlit blotter and beckoning Merrily over.

'Sit there. Won't take you long to read it. I have to go and shut the chickens in for the night. Toilet's back into the hall, second left. You'll probably need it now you've been on your feet.'

Merrily sat looking down at the paper, pooled in lamplight, apple green. She opened it out.

'What is it?'

'A suicide note,' Mrs Morningwood said. 'Kind of. With hindsight.'

29

Like a Ghost

SITTING ON THE lavatory, bent over, elbows on her knees, head in her hands, Merrily was holding the first sentences in her head.

People say death is like sleep.
I just hope they're wrong. Sometimes I think I must be very close to death
and I hate sleep more than anything.

It wasn't the original, that was clear. There was no address, and – she'd looked at the bottom – no signature. Mrs Morningwood, or somebody, must have copied it into a computer.

When she came out of the downstairs bathroom, a bit fresher, Mrs Morningwood had returned and was stripping off her old Barbour, hanging it in the whitewashed hall, fluffing up her hair – the first conspicuously feminine thing Merrily had seen her do.

'You've read it?'

'I had to stop. Had to … go.'

Mrs Morningwood nodded, and Merrily went back to the desk in the living room.

You wouldnt know me Muriel. Theres nothing of me no more I am so thin
and my head feels like a rotten egg sometimes and what can you do with a
rotten egg except get as far away from it as possible. But you can't, can you,
if it's inside your head day and night and all your dreams are addled. (See,
I remember all about eggs. They were the good times.)

Merrily looked up.

'This is a girl?'

'Poor little darkie.'

Mrs Morningwood came over to the desk. Brought out a small leather photo album and began thumbing through it.

'It was what people called her. Almost a novelty in the 1970s, a black girl in these parts. Mixed race, actually. Used to come here on holiday with her parents, in a caravan on a farm at Bagwyllydiart. *There.*'

The photo, its colours faded, showed two girls sitting together on a five-bar gate.

'That's ... you?'

'Frightening, isn't it?'

The young Muriel, willowy and lovely, linking arms with the other girl, who was laughing so hard that her face was fuzzed and her white hoop earrings had ghosts.

'They were from Coventry. Black father, white mother. They didn't appear one year and then we heard the parents had broken up. Learning later – from the poor kid herself – that she was being interfered with by the mother's new man. She'd've been fifteen or sixteen. Ran away a couple of times, finally hitch-hiking to just about the only place that had good memories for her.'

'Here?'

'Twenty quid in her pocket. Got picked up by the chip man – there was a chap in Monmouth ran two or three fish-and-chip vans, came out to the villages one or two days a week. He recognized her, picked her up, gave her a job in his shop in Monmouth, let her sleep in the room over the top. Until his wife found out.'

'Oh.'

'It was probably quite innocent. She'd never have told, anyway. He was there when she needed help. Upshot of it, she turned up at our door, ended up moving in. Would've been on the streets otherwise.'

I'm sorry to keep on at you but you were always strong and I dont know anybody else I can tell who wouldn't just hate me more.

'You didn't try to contact her parents?'

'So she could go back and get fiddled with again? Not a chance, darling. She asked us not to, anyway, and she was sixteen or seventeen, we knew that. Besides, I was going to London, had a job lined up with a distant relative, theatrical agent. She filled the space.'

Mrs Morningwood took the photo back, put it in the album, left the album on the desk and went back to the hob.

'House was only half as big then. I suppose she was here nearly a year. My mother found her a post as housekeeper – not live-in. Farmer called Eric Davies whose wife'd walked out because she couldn't stand the isolation and Eric's refusal to take a day off. Go on – read the rest.'

I'm writing this now because theres times when I still think I can get rid of it if I want to. Like Oh its not that bad it's only your body and look at the money your getting.

'I take it this is not about Eric Davies.'

'Hardly. That came later. We exchanged letters for about a year. Most of them more coherent, I have to say, than this one. She was actually an intelligent girl, resourceful. Adaptable.'

'So this is referring to the Master House, is it?'

Mrs Morningwood chose a wooden block from the log basket, wedged it into the fire and talked about the Master House commune. Two or three couples there originally, but there was always room for more bodies in the five bedrooms and outbuildings. Then two of the women left and one of the men. Eric Davies, meanwhile, had been made aware of gossip – he was in line for chairman, or president or something, of the local branch of the NFU and someone had discreetly pointed out that perhaps Mary Roberts was not good for his image, middle-aged farmer with a little darkie on the premises several hours a day.

Merrily said, 'Mary Roberts?'

'I don't know where she got the name Linden from. Perhaps she thought it sounded pretty.'

'Bloody hell,' Merrily said. 'You're absolutely sure about this?'

'Soon as I saw the girl with the builder. Look at the photo again. Look at the eyes.'

The eyes were blurred in the picture, but the size and the separation … well, maybe.

'If I had one of her a couple of years later, even you would be in no doubt. Fuchsia, the first time I saw her and Barlow, they weren't here to work, just look around, so not in overalls. She was even wearing the same kind of clothes as Mary had. Highly coloured. As if she'd seen some old photos of her mother and gone out of her way to recreate the image. Barlow was asking about the house and I tried to help him – rambling on in a state of slight numbness, trying not to keep staring at the girl. Hell of a shock, Watkins. Like seeing a ghost.'

'Did you say anything?'

'No. I needed to know if *she* knew. Needed to get her alone. The name, you … that was the clincher. Mary's few possessions included a decrepit, much-thumbed paperback copy of *Titus Groan*. Mervyn Peake? Leading female character?'

'Fuchsia.'

'Pretty conclusive.'

'And did she know?'

'Never got her alone to ask. Barlow came back alone some days later telling me she'd been troubled by something in the house. Wouldn't go into details.'

'You didn't tell him you may have known Fuchsia's mother?'

'Of course I didn't.'

Mrs Morningwood bit her lip.

'You'd better tell me the rest,' Merrily said.

When you dont go to bed no more because they come to you in your sleep thats pretty bad isnt it . And when you wake up it's like your body is not yours no more, it's their's. They can make your arms and legs move about and make you see what nobody should have to see. Well thats when you think you must be getting close to the end of this sick life and thank God for that.

'I'd actually wanted her to come to London with me,' Mrs Morningwood said. 'I was working for a magazine by this time, making better money – in the process of moving to a flat in Clapham. But, for reasons I didn't know about at the time, she declined. I … didn't make proper arrangements for the forwarding mail so may have missed a couple of letters from her. And then that one arrived … five months after it was posted.'

'That does not sound good. At all.'

'I phoned my mother straight away, and of course it had all gone wrong – Mary had been staying away for several nights at a time, and then a whole week. Having taken up, it emerged, with one of the Master House people. And taken various drugs, obviously. Possibly, judging from the letter, LSD or mescaline.'

You wouldn't recognise me now. Youd walk past me in the street, I probably look like some old bag out the gutter. I went into Hereford once, into the shops but I could sense like a shadow behind me all the time and once it touched me and run its fingers down my back and I turned round and I screamed GET AWAY GET AWAY FROM ME and people did get away they all crossed the road thinking I was drunk or doped up and that was awful. I really need normal people not to hate me like your mum does now.

'And your mother hadn't told you any of this?'

'There was … a distance between us at the time.'

Mrs Morningwood was smoking again, the room clouded, Roscoe prowling.

'"*Thinking* I was doped up", Merrily said. 'She's saying fairly categorically here that she was neither drunk nor stoned.'

'Then *what?*' Mrs Morningwood said. 'How would you explain the rest of it?'

I went into the Cathedral but it didnt feel right, it was too big and quiet and I had to keep walking round to be near people because I dont like being on my own in a big empty place and then I found I was standing in front of the old map. You know the one called something in Latin and these disgusting things were grinning out at me and the shadow was leaning over me like when the sun suddenly goes in and you feel cold

'The old map.' Merrily looked up. 'The *Mappa Mundi*?'

'Displayed in the cathedral in those days.'

'Yes.'

Hereford's only world-class treasure. Medieval map of the world, now on view, along with the historic chained library, in a recently constructed building of their own in the cathedral grounds. Merrily had seen it a few times, never really had time to study it. Remembered the bizarre drawings around the primitive topography – a bear, a mermaid, a griffon, a unicorn. Didn't remember any of them as grinning or obviously disgusting, but …

and I mustve screamed out or something because there was this man in black clothes and he said I've been watching you he said I can see your in trouble let me help you and I screamed at him GET AWAY GET AWAY GET AWAY YOUR EVIL.

I think it was just that he was in black clothes I thought he must be evil. He gave me a card to get in touch with him but I never have, whats the use.

One of the cathedral canons? Might even have been Dobbs, the exorcist.

'She must've been looking a bit deranged to get that kind of approach.'

'Evidently.' Mrs Morningwood nodded. 'What does it suggest to you?'

'Extreme paranoia? Which obviously could be linked to drug use. Did the police find any acid? If she was still tripping, she might look at the Mappa Mundi, with all these mythical beasts, and it becomes like a nest of monsters or something.'

'I've never seen an inventory of what they found.'

'I could probably get some background. There's a cop I know—'

'No!'

Mrs Morningwood backing away, well out of the pool of light, leaving Merrily blinking.

'Sorry?'

'What's the point of involving the police? They're not going to find her now, are they? Not going to be remotely interested.'

'*Find* her? I thought she was—'

'I don't *know* she's dead. I simply never heard of her again. Nobody I know ever did. We even tracked down her mother in Birmingham. Not interested. Didn't seem to *care*. Nobody cared. Except me, because I could've saved her. Could've got her out of there.'

'But *somebody* obviously did …'

Mrs Morningwood's face was grim amongst the shadows.

'Mary came back to my mother, apparently unwell. Stayed for four days. Quiet, penitent. And … my mother would awake in the morning to hear her throwing up. Coming to the obvious conclusion. Which she put to Mary. When she got up the next morning, Mary had gone. For good.'

'Didn't leave a note or anything?'

'Only this one. Which took weeks to find me. I came back at once, but of course it was all too late.'

I expect you guessed I'm writing to ask a favour. You were always so strong
Muriel and I cant go back on my own.
You see I've got a baby now.

30

Directionality

NOT THAT JANE was fooled or anything. This woman was a former barrister. Barristers defended people they knew were guilty and prosecuted people they guessed were innocent. You didn't need to watch much TV to know that.

You didn't trust barristers, you paid them. And if someone else was paying, you'd mean less than nothing to them. They'd take you apart with merciless precision and discard the bits.

OK, Siân was a priest now, but you could still sense this kind of – to borrow a stupid word from one of those hi-gloss US forensic shows – *directionality*. Focus. Everything she said was coming from somewhere down in the small print of her personal agenda.

Like, when Jane was showing her round the vicarage, entering the nest of rooms around the back stairs, Siân going, 'It's awfully large, isn't it? For just the two of you.'

Translating as, *Even in its present condition, we could flog this place for well over half a million and put you in a bungalow.*

With no attics and no apartment.

'Well, you know, I used to think that, too,' Jane had said, 'but that was before we had to take people in. Like deliverance cases? People who think they're mad? Need a big house for that, so nobody can hear the screams.'

Knowing as soon as it was out that, if she'd been in the witness box, Siân would have dismantled her. Having studied all the cases in her capacity as Deliverance Coordinator, she'd know this was not even loosely true. Well, except for …

'Like, Dexter Harris?' Jane pointing at the blackened oak beam where

a door had once hung at the bottom of the stairs. 'That was where he …
you know …'

'Yes, I heard about that. Regrettable.'

'Mum had to do the necessary, for quite a few nights afterwards, to
make sure there was no, like, detritus?'

'Yes, I'm sure she *would* have felt that was necessary.'

Like, *Your mother is a superstitious idiot.*

It really hadn't been easy last night, having to watch what you said all
the time, looking for the loaded questions. Now, with dusk and rain
seeping in, Jane, in her old parka, airline bag over a shoulder, was
standing between the oak pillars of the market hall, looking across at
the vicarage, psyching herself up before going home. Except it wasn't
really home at all, right now, was it?

After school, she'd slipped into Leominster in the vain hope that
Woolies might have any CD by Sufjan Stevens who, she'd just discovered, was sufficiently like Lol to be interesting. Catching the last bus
back to Ledwardine, predictably Sufjanless, she'd realized this had been
just an excuse to shorten the evening.

The hardest bit of all was when Mum rang and Jane, taking it from
the privacy of her apartment, had been like, *Oh, no, fine, she's really quite
nice. We had a long chat about how she'd wanted to be a barrister from the
age of about eight.*

Mum trying hard to conceal her dismay, Jane going, *Hey, Mum, it's
not* my *fault she wasn't being a bitch.* Knowing that if she'd come out
with the truth, Mum would be on edge the whole time, imagining this
cataclysmic row exploding, Jane screaming at Siân. Mum imagined her
daughter was still fifteen or something and had no subtlety. But Jane
was changing. She had to.

During the lunch hour, she'd called the vicarage from the school
library stockroom, borrowing Kayleigh Evans's mobile in case Siân
checked. Getting the answering machine and deepening her voice,
sounding posh, she'd asked for the time of the *wonderfully inspiring*
meditation service and would it really be all right if someone from
outside the parish attended, she'd heard it was always so *packed.*

A few more calls like that, carefully spaced, would do no harm at all.

Maybe a toned-down Scottish accent next time. Go careful, though, because this woman was …

… *oops,* coming out.

Jane stiffened. It was strange, almost surreal, watching another woman cleric emerging from the vicarage drive. Siân had on a dark belted coat, unbuttoned, over her cassock, the dog collar luminous and her pewter hair gleaming in the lights from the square. Walking purposefully, with *directionality*, up towards the church through sporadic rain.

On the edge of the square, Siân was ambushed by Brenda Prosser from the Eight till Late. Nobody else was about, so Jane could hear most of what they were saying.

'Yes, I am indeed,' Siân said. 'We couldn't leave Ledwardine without a priest for a whole week, could we?'

'Well, you know, I hadn't seen her since church on Sunday,' Brenda said, 'and I thought she might be ill or something. She works a bit too hard, I think, sometimes.'

Well, thank you, Brenda.

'Merrily is very conscientious,' Siân said. 'Now, I know you're at the shop, Mrs Prosser, and I fully intend—'

'Oh, quite a few years now, Mrs Clarke. Came over from Mid-Wales, we did, when my husband was made—'

'Only— I hope you don't think I'm being terribly rude, but I did arrange to meet someone at the church at six o'clock, and I've just realized I'm going to be *late.*'

'Oh, I'm sorry—'

'No, it's not your—'

Meet someone? Hadn't taken her long to get her feet under the table, had it? And why not meet whoever it was at the vicarage?

Unsettling as the situation may appear, trust your instincts, listen to your inner voice and by next week's climactic conjunction of—

Jane's horoscope in the *Sunday Times.*

Right. Sod this.

Pulling up the hood of her parka, transferring the airline bag to her left shoulder, she came out from behind the pillar, walking directly towards Siân and Brenda. And then, drawing the fur trim across her face, she was gliding anonymously past them towards the end of the square. Crossing the street, slipping under the lych-gate and running through the spitting rain down to the church, calculating that the lower door would be unlocked because Tuesday night was choir practice.

It always felt better sidling in by the smaller door. OK, she might be coming around to accepting the sense and the structure and the basic morality of Christianity, but she couldn't imagine ever going the whole way, not even when she was old and scared; it lacked thrills, wasn't sexy.

And yet its buildings were, somehow. The church yawned around her, that sudden sense of live air you never quite got used to. The secondary lights were on, high in the rafters.

Jane didn't move until she was sure that all the pews were empty. Then padding down the aisle, listening for footsteps, voices. Sliding into the Bull Chapel. Always a good place to hide; if anyone came in, you could slide around the wooden screen to where the organ was and then out through the chancel.

The effigy on the tomb of Thomas Bull, long-dead squire figure, had a naked sandstone sword by its side and, instead of the eyelids being humbly lowered, the eyes were wide open, part of this self-satisfied half-smile.

Lowering herself into the only pew, Jane smiled back: *Don't smirk at me, pal, your family counts for zilch these days.*

Siân's meeting, she was thinking maybe Uncle Ted. Retired solicitor – maybe he'd even worked with Siân?

Ted in senior churchwarden mode was a hypocritical old sod, suspicious of Mum's deliverance role, for ever whingeing that she should be devoting all her energies to the parish. Ted would love that the village was getting increasingly upper-middle-class, and given the choice between ancient stones and executive homes in Coleman's Meadow ...

He'd sell you down the river. Jane patted Tom Bull's eroded cheek, hoping his bones were twisting and tangling up in fury. *Turn this chapel into a wine bar.*

She jumped as the main doors creaked, and they came in together, the famous acoustics soon making it clear that this wasn't Uncle Ted.

31

No Smoke

THERE WASN'T MUCH doubt at all, any more, was there?

'Let me try to understand this,' Merrily said. 'Mary was writing to you from Tepee City.'

'Yes.'

Mrs Morningwood was squatting on the floor now, arms around the dog, face in deep shadow, Roscoe panting. Merrily picked up the letter.

'She wanted to meet you back at Garway. She wanted you to go with her to the Master House – because you're the strong one. And yet you read this … and it doesn't seem right.'

It's in my dreams, Muriel. I thought I'd got away but I cant. When I was having the baby it was terrible, the dreams I was having then I cant tell you. Rachel who was looking after me said it was just the hormones and they got Rick who was a priest to pray with me and it was all right for a while but then it started again after the baby was born.

'She's had a very bad time at the Master House and yet she wants to go back?'

'She needs to deal with it,' Mrs Morningwood said. 'And now it's different. Now she isn't the only one affected.'

The baby cries too much. The baby cries day and night. I cant get no sleep and when I do the dreams start.
The baby cries whenever shes <u>WITH ME</u>. Thats not how it should be! It really frightens me! Please help me Muriel! Theres nobody else I can go to to do what I need to do.

'You agreed to meet her? You replied saying you'd—'

'I didn't waste time replying, I came back. Drove across to West Wales, found this rather pathetic community, boiling their drinking water from the ditches. She'd left. Nobody knew where she'd gone. They weren't terribly helpful.'

'Nobody told you about a baby, then.'

'Not a word. Probably thought I was a spy from Social Services.'

'And you never heard from her again.'

'Nobody did. And then, of course, while I was in Wales, something else happened. The police carried out their famous dawn raid on the Master House, removing quantities of drugs ... and the future Lord Stourport.'

'*Just* Lord Stourport? He carried the can?'

'Couple of others, I think. Nonentities. There were said to be some more people involved in the activities, but not living in. They may have got away minutes before the police broke the door down. A dawn raid tends to be less effective when its targets are habitually not going to bed *until* dawn.'

'Have you still got the original letter?'

'Somewhere. It was getting worn with repeated, agonized readings, so I retyped it, word for word. Preserving the erratic application of the apostrophe, as you may have noticed.'

'And this is all of it? I mean, is this *all* she said? No explanation of exactly what happened to her at the Master House.'

'No, it ... perhaps she'd explained in a previous letter that went astray. That seems the most likely explanation.'

'Or that she didn't want to put it in a letter anyone might read. Or that she couldn't bear to write about it. What's all this about money? *Look at the money your getting.*'

'I don't know.'

'The people at the Master House seem to have been paying her. For what?'

'Evidently not merely as a housekeeper.'

'No local gossip about it?'

'Of course there was gossip. Sex, drugs, orgies. But nobody really *knew*.'

'What about Lord Stourport? What's happened to him?'

'Became some kind of rock-music promoter, putting on concerts and festivals and making a ridiculous amount of money. Last I heard of him he was languishing at his family seat in Warwickshire – I think he acceded to the title within a few years of coming out of prison. I actually wrote to him once asking if he remembered Mary Roberts. Had quite a polite, civilized reply – under the circumstances he could hardly deny he'd been at the Master House – saying there'd been quite a number of young women at the house over the months and, to his shame, he didn't really remember their names.'

'That figures.'

'Lying, I don't doubt, but, darling, what could I do? You know what always haunted me?'

'The thought that Mary might have gone back to the Master House without you?'

'You're very perceptive.'

'It's …' Merrily shrugged '… It's what would've haunted me, too. Look, the only thing that occurs to me – if she's out there, she's likely to have heard about what happened to Fuchsia. I shouldn't think it's made that much impact in the national press, but it's not a common name, is it, Fuchsia Mary Linden, and if Mary *is* out there …'

'You mean if she's still alive.'

'You're fairly sure that Fuchsia was conceived at the Master House?'

'Almost certainly.'

'So her father could be Lord Stourport himself? The story Felix gave me was that the father had gone to America. But that's the sort of thing Mary might just *say* to forestall questions. And *you* were obviously wondering about Felix himself.'

'I was simply thinking of reasons why the girl might suddenly have wanted to smash in the skull of the man she was living with.' Mrs Morningwood waved an unlit cigarette. '*Might* she simply have found out, coming here, that Barlow was at the Master House at the same time as her mother? The same time, in fact, as her mother got *pregnant*?'

'With the worst will in the world, I really don't think we're looking at an incestuous relationship.'

'Some strange and complex alliances are formed, Watkins. I merely floated the possibility.'

'Yeah, well, I feel fairly confident about sinking it. If Felix was Fuchsia's father, why would he tender for the building contract at the Master House in the first place and bring her with him? Wouldn't a few people have recognized him?'

'Hmm.' Mrs Morningwood sniffed. 'Stourport's people didn't exactly mix in the community, but I take your point. It would have to be unusually perverse – especially whilst employed by the Duchy of Cornwall.'

'Who were the other girls Lord Stourtport mentioned?'

'I ... I've no idea. I suppose you didn't *have* to be able to change a washer to get a bed at the Master House. You could also be a woman. And probably didn't have to be all that good-looking either, towards the end, when everyone was perpetually stoned.'

'No idea where Mary got to, between walking out on your mother for the last time and turning up in Tepee City? She must've been introduced to the community.'

'I have no idea. Tell me – why do *you* think Fuchsia did it – killed Barlow?'

'Don't know. It's why I'm here. Partly.'

Roscoe hauled himself up, stretched and wandered over to Merrily, tail waving. She stood up.

'He wants me to go. Would it be his dinner time?'

'You're *very* perceptive,' Mrs Morningwood said.

'I wanted to be a vet when I was a kid. And then discovered about all the pets they had to put down.' She patted Roscoe, didn't need to bend. 'It's surprising how well behaved he is, isn't it, when he's not in a churchyard?'

'Good icebreakers, dogs.' Mrs Morningwood smiled, disarmingly girlish in the glow from the range. 'Had to get your attention somehow. I thought – and still do – that you would be my best bet for finding out ... not only what happened to Mary, but ... other things I can't quite put my finger on. The girl showing up like that, after all these years ...'

'And then you made sure you *kept* our attention by telling Jane just what she wanted to hear about the mysteries of Garway.'

'It was all true.'

'What – including the gruesome tale of Mrs Newton laid out in her coffin to be pawed by the whole village?'

'That was true … in essence. Garway was almost certainly the last village in Herefordshire to maintain the Watch Night traditions.'

'So which bits did you exaggerate?'

'Well, it … wasn't the *whole* village. Just a few neighbours. But I really *didn't* like the place and like it even less since Mary disappeared. Whatever you propose to do there, it needs it. What *will* you do?'

'I was thinking some form of Requiem Eucharist.'

'A Mass?'

'A service for the repose of the dead. Thinking originally of Felix and Fuchsia but, from what you've said, we could be looking at something more extensive. Mrs Morningwood, look … thank you for all you've done. I do feel better. If a bit tired.'

Face it: without the reflexology, she'd most likely be on her way home by now, driving slowly, popping aspirins.

'That's normal, that's good. You need to come back in a couple of days, have it topped up … and, of course, tell me what you've found out. This Requiem Eucharist – would that aim to deal with what one might term evil residue?'

'Evil residue?'

'Those accusations of heresy and idolatry against the Templars – no smoke without fire. We get people here, a handful every year, poking around, taking measurements in the church. Freemasons, some of them, believing themselves to be the inheritors of the Templar legacy. Idiots in robes, sometimes. Think about what might've destroyed Mary's sleep. What they were doing to her. What continued to throw a shadow over her wherever she went.'

'Well …' Merrily picked up her bag. 'The Eucharist can be very powerful. I need to go away and think about it.'

They walked out of the cottage, Roscoe between them, into a greyness of fields, a blackness of woodland. Two windows were lit up at Mrs Morningwood's end of the terrace, the rest of it dead, like a neon sign in which most of the letters had fused.

'What are the neighbours like?'

'Absolute worst kind.' Mrs Morningwood snorted. 'These are all holiday cottages. We were isolated in Garway at one time, but now it's getting just like everywhere else – local youngsters priced out by London lawyers and stockbrokers and junior government ministers here for an average of about three weeks a year. Three out of four in a single terrace, all so-called weekend cottages, and the bastards wonder why we have a housing crisis. Answer is, we don't, we're simply top-heavy with self-indulgent second-bloody-homers.'

Merrily stood looking back at the terrace. An empty holiday home conveyed its own distinctive form of dereliction. But then, what right did she have to moralize, her and Jane rattling around in their seven-bedroom vicarage?

'I can't get my bearings up here.' Eyes adjusting now, she looked away, along the limited horizon, hills concealed by the woods. 'Where's the church?'

'The church – *this* church – is always closer than you think,' Mrs Morningwood said. 'Go carefully, Watkins.'

32

Hysterical Frenzy

'... For agreeing to meet me, Canon.'

A woman.

'My pleasure. That's what I'm here for.'

'You see, it's difficult—'

'And let me say that, although I'm only here for a few days and you don't really know me at all, you can safely tell me *anything* you would have told Merrily.'

Safely. Jane glared at Tom Bull. *Oh yeah.*

'Mrs Clarke—'

'Look, it's all *right*.'

'No ... this is *about* Merrily, you see.'

Jane stood up quickly, her back to the wooden screen.

'I think we'd better sit down,' Siân said firmly, and Jane, well out of sight, automatically sat down again, before realizing.

'I've agonized about this, you see,' the woman was saying, really intense. 'When I heard that a very senior minister had taken over for a few days, I knew what I had to do. I said to myself, you're not going to get a better opportunity than this, are you? In fact, to be honest, I thought ... well, I thought this was a sign from God.'

'I see,' Siân said.

Oh sure. Like *she*'d believe in signs from God. Jane stood tensed against the wooden screen, airline bag at her feet, hands clenched into fists, pushing at the pockets of her parka, listening to it all coming out, this senseless stream of totally unfounded bollocks. No sublety at all, no restraint, no ... no basic intelligence.

'... I know people were beginning to have their doubts when she reduced the number of hymns at the morning worship from three to two. Hymns are traditional, aren't they? Songs of praise we all know. And the church I went to before, there was *always* an evensong.'

'Well, yes,' Siân said, 'I'm afraid quite a few parishes have had to dispense with it, mainly due to falling congregations, especially in the winter. Many people really don't like leaving their firesides and, indeed, in some places, simply don't feel *safe* any more going out after dark. Especially the elderly.'

'But replacing it with this so-called service of meditation?'

'It seems to be rather popular.'

'But it's not *Christian*, is it, Canon Clarke? It's *eastern religion*, that's what it is. Sitting there in a circle with candles, men and women, dressed in … in casual clothing, so-called opening themselves *up* …'

'Well, you know, there *is* a fairly well-established tradition of Christian medi—'

'Not in the Bible!'

'Well that depends on how you— However—'

Siân, you had to give her some credit, was doing her best, but you could hear the woman's voice rising higher, when she wasn't getting the reactions she'd obviously expected, the accusations getting wilder, crazier. Jane getting madder.

'… And I think what offends many of us is the way she makes no attempt to conceal her private life, which is not … Well, she has a boyfriend, see, and there's no doubt – no doubt at all – that they're sleeping together out of wedlock. A priest! What kind of example is that setting to young people?'

Jane fought for control. All the time and energy she'd spent bringing Mum and Lol together, and this small-minded—

'At least, she's *one* of the women he's sleeping with. He's a so-called musician, see, a *rock* musician of some kind, and we all know the level of their morality.'

'I'm sorry, Shirley, I'm not sure I understand precisely what you're saying here.'

Shirley?

'Well, I'll tell you, Canon. My brother overheard some young women talking in the Black Swan. They were drunk, as so many of these young women are today, and one of them said she … well, there are words I will not use in church, or anywhere else, but she seemed very much to be implying to her friends that she'd had *sexual congress* with this man.'

Jane froze up, Thomas Bull smiling at her, and she wanted to kick his smug face in. The despicable, small-time *viciousness* of this village. Anyone who really *knew* Lol. But they didn't want to, did they? They just watched from behind their curtains and muttered and fantasized.

She wanted to storm out there, snatch this bitch out of her pew, point out that people like her were the reason the Church was dying on its Celtic foundations, losing what was left of its real spirituality. Haul her to the door and throw her out.

'And the smoking. It's not nice, is it? There's no excuse any more, all the help that's available. It's a sign of weakness. I've seen her smoking in the churchyard, with the gravedigger. It's a public place. I could have them arrested.'

Jane let her face fall into her hands.

'… And you *do* know, I suppose, that she's supporting these people who want to reinstate a pagan temple?'

'I'm sorry,' Siân said. 'A *pagan* temple?'

'In the field where they were going to build a housing estate? Starter homes for our young people.'

Executive homes, you ignorant …

'Nobody can tell me that those stones were not buried for a good reason.'

'Oh, the *stones*,' Siân said. 'I see.'

'You would expect our parish priest to oppose that on principle.'

No reply from Siân. She must surely have realized by now the level of insanity she was dealing with here.

'And if it wasn't for the daughter …'

'Jane?'

'The daughter – well, that explains a lot.'

'You've rather left me behind here, Shirley.'

Shirley.

Shirley West. Mum had talked about this woman a few times, Jane only half-listening because this had been Mum as doormat: feeling obliged to help someone whose attentions had become kind of smothering. Just another vicar-hugger, Jane had figured. And all the time, behind Mum's back ...

'Put it this way,' Shirley West said. 'How often do we see the daughter in church?'

'I'm afraid I don't know.'

'Never!'

Jane had to hold on to the screen to prevent herself from walking out there and going, *Not* quite *never*.

'Believe me, Canon Clarke, she's had a terrible time with that girl. Hated the idea of her mother becoming ordained and has just ... gone out of her way to make her life a misery. *Impossible* to control, absolutely *no* respect ... and this is not gossip, Canon, I've had this from a respected public figure. This girl and that old man who digs the graves and smokes, they were very nearly arrested for vandalizing the building-site in Coleman's Meadow, did you know that? She was in a kind of hysterical frenzy.'

'Shirley, I ...' Siân paused. 'Regrettable as all this might be, I'm afraid you'd probably find similar situations in the homes of over half the clergy in this diocese. Most teenagers go through a period of rebellion against their parents' values. The only *consolation* being that if children are left to make up their own minds, without being pressurized, they will often find their own way into what we still like to think of as the fold.'

'But is it?'

'I'm sorry ...'

'*Is* it a rebellion? Because Merrily is involved with the other business, isn't she? Ghosts and the demonic.'

'You mean deliverance.'

'Which is to do with the occult. I've been in the vicarage, Canon Clarke, I've seen the occult books on the shelves.'

'Well, she's had to study all that, Shirley. She's had to go into areas of study that many people would find distasteful.'

'But does *she*?'

'I don't understand.'

'Does *she* find it distasteful? I've talked to people about this. I have many Christian friends all over the country. My information is that this is a job that's always been done by men before. She was probably the first woman exorcist in the country, that's my information. And she's also the first that I – or any of my friends in the church – have known to introduce this so-called meditation. This opening up of a congregation to unseen presences.'

'I don't think you'll find it's *that* uncommon nowadays. As for deliverance being a male preserve, just a few years ago, the whole ministry—'

'*I* think we have to look at all these things together – the interest in exorcism ... the meditation ... the pagan temple ... and the near-Satanism practised by the daughter. And see what it adds up to. I think it adds up to a terrible danger.'

The silence was so absolute that Jane could hear her own breathing. Jesus, this was not a joke.

She made eye contact with Tom Bull, his bearded face openly malign. Jane thought of the green man and Baphomet, anger giving way to a kind of fear of the unknown. Fear for Mum, out there on the unknown border, Lol gigging somewhere miles away. Their little nucleus fragmented, and she was alone here, in this supposedly sacred place, this sanctuary, watching the poison dripping into the chalice.

Shirley West said, 'I think before Merrily goes around encouraging people to open themselves up, she needs to take a good look inside her own family. Don't you?'

And then Siân, who so far had been displaying a reasonable attitude to this insanity ... Siân blew it.

'You'd better tell me everything,' she said.

33

Turn Over Stones

OVER DINNER – RAIN rolling down the dairy's main window, silent as tears of old grief – Merrily asked the Murrays how much they knew about the Grays and the Gwilyms.

'Our friends either side of the great divide,' Teddy said.

Lifting his wineglass, as if in a toast, his silhouette a magic-lantern show on the white wall behind him in the lamplight.

'Not that you'd know it,' Beverley said. 'They sound exactly the same. Not as if the Gwilyms have Welsh accents, let alone *speak* Welsh. Well, certainly not … Oh, I *never* know how to pronounce that man's name.'

'Sycharth, Bevvie. We're inclined to say *Sickarth*, but it's *Suckarth*. Yes, it's an odd thing. If someone lives just a few yards over the border in what might seem to be a very English part of Wales they become determinedly *Welsh* Welsh. Perfectly affable chap, though.'

'Not that we see much of him,' Beverley said, 'since his business has become more Hereford-based. Rich enough now to have a farm manager.'

'And his family owned the Master House,' Merrily said.

'Since medieval times, I believe.' Teddy nodding. 'I can certainly tell you something about *that*.'

His version tied in with Mrs Morningwood's. As a result of the sudden death of the head of the family, the house had been sold around the turn of last century. The wife, embittered at the way she'd been treated over the years, had got rid of it almost before anybody noticed.

'Causing an awful fuss, but there was nothing the Gwilyms could do,' Teddy said.

'But the Master House is in England.'

'Well, yes, Merrily, but a part of England that seems to have been more Welsh, in its time, than many parts of Wales. In religious terms, particularly. Both early Welsh Christianity and Welsh Nonconformism in the nineteenth century have their roots hereabouts. And, of course, if Owain Glyndwr's rebellion had been successful in the fifteenth century, the border would have been redrawn, putting this whole area in Glyndwr's new, independent Wales. You *do* know about Glyndwr's connection with this area?'

'He's supposed to have retired here, after his campaign collapsed.'

It had always seemed odd to Merrily that Glyndwr should spend his last years in the border area where he'd caused maximum damage, burning down most of the major castles. You'd have thought he'd feel safer in some Welsh heartland.

'Hidden away, more like, with a price on his head,' Teddy said. 'A celebrity outlaw. His daughter, Alice, had married a Scudamore from Kentchurch Court, and they might have helped to conceal him. He was never caught, he just disappeared. There *is* a legend that he once hid out at the Master House – but, then, lots of places claim that connection.'

Beverley said, 'It's the sort of legend I imagine some of the Gwilyms liked to pretend was actual history.'

'And they've been trying to … reacquire it?' Merrily said. 'I mean, the Master House?'

'Periodically, yes. I'm not sure how bothered Sycharth is now.'

'I heard he was totally hell-bent on getting it back.'

'Well, you *could* be right.' Teddy shrugged. 'I don't know. How are your plans going, as regards, ah …?'

'Still thinking it would be good to get the Gwilyms and the Grays under that roof. Especially as it no longer belongs to either of them. No better time to heal old wounds.'

'Would you like me to have a word?'

'With?'

'The Grays, at least. They come to church – Paul in a wheelchair now, poor chap. My feeling is that *they* were more than glad to get rid of that house. Whether you believe in some sort of spiritual malaise or not, they haven't had much luck. The question is, will they come if the

Gwilyms are going to be there? I don't know. I'll talk to them. I'll do what I can.'

'Thank you, Teddy.'

'If I tell them someone from the Duchy of Cornwall will be there?'

'I'll try and talk to the land agent tomorrow.'

'Not the, ah, Duke himself, presumably.'

'At a rite of cleansing?'

'Quite.' Teddy smiled. 'Although *that* would certainly bring both families out of their cupboards, wouldn't it?'

'It would also bring the Special Branch out of theirs,' Merrily said. 'And, on the whole, I don't think my nerves would stand it.'

Earlier, sitting on a corner of the bed at The Ridge, with the bedside lamp on, she'd called Lol on spec, a bit surprised to catch him in.

'I've been back all day,' Lol had said patiently. 'Last night's gig was Brecon. Thirty miles?'

'Of course … sorry.'

'Old hippies and young soldiers, mainly.'

'What?'

'Brecon. It's a garrison town. Plus a few girls who couldn't have been born when Hazey Jane started.'

'Groupies?'

'In Brecon?'

The power of bad dreams. Merrily closed her eyes. Sometimes you could punch yourself in the mouth.

Lol said, 'Been watching Canon Callaghan-Clarke familiarizing herself with the village landmarks: church, market hall, Black Swan, Gomer Parry …'

'*I'm* sorry. Couldn't even let you know we were getting her. Events … overtook.'

Lol had met Siân only once, last spring, during a tense and troubling evening in Ludlow Castle, when Siân had finally been exposed to the blurred reality of deliverance. Not a comfortable night, for any of them.

'Not a problem,' Lol said. 'I kind of thought you'd wind up going. Under the circumstances.'

Not a problem? *Why* wasn't it a problem?

'Lol, I'm sorry, it's ... I'm still a bit tired. Got up feeling lousy and wound up having foot-reflexology. From this Mrs Morningwood. It was ... strange.'

'But it worked?'

'Something worked. I think. It's just knocked me out a bit. After some moments of rare clarity, I'm tired and confused again, but yeah, I feel better. Don't knock it.'

'Merrily—'

'Never straightforward, this job. You turn over stones, things crawl out. You ever come across Lord Stourport?'

'Lord ...?'

'Stourport.'

'Well, we've obviously exchanged nods at various receptions,' Lol said. 'Buckingham Palace garden parties, that kind of ...'

'You've never heard of him, then.'

'No.'

Merrily took a long breath and told him, in some detail, about Lord Stourport's time at the Master House, his supposed connections with the music industry. About Mary Linden nearly thirty years go. It was good to talk about it, to bring it out of the dreamlike fug of the day.

'We think she was abused.'

'Abused how?'

'Don't know. Don't know anything for certain. Or even if there was an element of fantasy. Drug-fuelled. I mean, it was a very long time ago but I really, *really* don't like the feel of it.'

'How about I ask Prof about this guy,' Lol said.

'Prof. Of course. That would be ... What the *hell* is that?'

Her head wouldn't process the clamour, but its vibration brought her to her feet.

'You OK, Merrily?'

'It's ...' She started to laugh. 'It's a dinner gong.'

And no time to hang out of the window to smoke half a cigarette.

'A period boarding house,' Lol had said. 'I so envy you.'

*

There *was* a strained kind of formality about the Murrays. As if she was a child they were in the process of adopting.

'If you don't mind me saying so, Merrily …' Beverley was putting out nut roast; why did non-veggies always think it had to be nut roast? '… You seem rather … sleepy. I was quite worried about you this morning. Now, you don't look unwell, but you do look exhausted. And Teddy, *please* don't say anything about the powerful air of God's own country.'

'Actually,' Merrily said, anything to get this sensible woman off her back, 'I had some treatment today.'

Telling them about Mrs Morningwood. No reason not to. Presumably it was a legitimate business, the reflexology.

Beverley frowned. Teddy looked intrigued.

'It was effective? Because I've often thought of consulting her myself. A lot to be said for preventative therapy. Beverley's not so sure, though, are you, Bevvie?'

Beverley didn't reply until she'd finished serving the nut roast, the onion gravy and the veg.

'It's nothing to do with alternative therapy, which I'm sure has its place. I just never know quite what to think of Mrs Morningwood.'

'In what context?'

Merrily realized how hungry she was, the body craving food, even nut roast. Beverley sat down, pushing a strand of blonde hair away from an eye.

'Oh, you hear things. Put it this way, if Teddy *was* to go I'd certainly make sure I went too.'

Merrily's fork froze just short of her lips.

'Something of a man-eater,' Beverley said. 'That's what they say, anyway.'

'*Mrs Morningwood?*'

'Always strikes me as a little … threadbare for that sort of thing. Eccentric, deranged. The way she drives around in that big Jeep, taking corners too fast. Sorry, I didn't mean deranged, I think I meant *disarranged.*'

'Can't say anyone's said anything to me,' Teddy said. 'Apart from you, of course, Bevvie.'

'Well, they wouldn't, now, would they?'

'Blimey,' Merrily said.

She ate slowly, aware, it seemed, of every spice in the roast. Aware of herself eating – that element of separation which sometimes came with extreme physical tiredness when the senses, for some reason, were still alert.

Gossip. There was, unfortunately, a place for it; it was often the most direct route to ... if not the truth, then something in its vicinity. She looked at Beverley.

'Who are we talking about, then? Mrs Morningwood and ... who?'

'Oh dear.' Beverley pouring herself some water from a crystal jug. 'I wish I'd never ...'

'Ah, now you've started ...' A slightly sinful sparkle in Teddy's blue eyes. 'Can't not tell us now, Bevvie.'

He knew, of course. Merrily watched their eyes. They must surely have had this discussion before. Now they were having it again for her benefit, passing on something they thought she ought to be aware of. Especially if submitting to further reflexology.

'Farmers. I was *told*,' Beverley said.

'Farmers *plural*?' Merrily blinked. 'I mean ... how plural?'

'Well ... at least two, certainly. I suppose she has that sort of rough ... edge that I imagine a certain kind of man would find attractive. Admittedly, always farmers living alone. And it never seems to lead to anything. No evidence that she's after anyone's money, if you see what I ...'

'An independent sort of woman,' Teddy said. 'Was she ever married? I'm never quite sure.'

'In London,' Beverley said. 'She was in London for over twenty years. Long enough to lose her local accent, certainly. But she came back, unmarried, re-adopting her maiden name, and whatever she gets up to ... is a question of roots, I suppose. They go back many generations in Garway, the Morningwoods. Whatever they do is accepted.'

'Whatever *they* do?'

'Well, her mother ... oh, I hate this.'

Beverley drank some water. Teddy leaned back.

'It's all right, *I* know. The family has quite a history of what are now known as *alternative* remedies. Folk remedies. What were known as wise women. There's an old tradition of nine witches of Garway, and her mother and grandmother were more in that mould. Allegedly.'

'They were ...' Merrily looked up '... considered to be witches?'

'They dispensed herbal remedies. They were also said to – no way to dress this up, I'm afraid, Merrily – assist girls who got themselves into trouble.'

'Oh.'

'Used to be a local social service, didn't it? No great need for it now.'

Merrily remembered Gomer Parry's uncharacteristic reticence on the subject of Mrs Morningwood.

Beverley looked down at her plate.

Lord Stourport – Lol was surprised to find out that he *did* know him. Well, knew *of* him, mainly – they'd met, briefly, maybe a couple of times.

'I never realized,' he said on the phone to Prof Levin. 'Jimmy Hater.'

He'd called around nine p.m., when Prof habitually took a coffee break from whatever album he was mixing. Often, he would work through midnight, the cafetière at his elbow. An addictive personality, but caffeine was safer than the booze of old.

Lol said, 'I remember he always sounded kind of upper-class, in comparison with most of the others.'

'Real name James Hayter-Hames,' Prof said. 'If you were rock 'n' roll management in the punk era, that was *not* a good time to let it get out that your family was even posher than Joe Strummer's. Hayter on its own, however – that was a strong and impressive name to have. Especially if you left out the "y".'

'I didn't even know about the "y" for a long time.' Lol recalled a stocky, strutting guy, Napoleonic. 'I used to think it was a completely made-up name, like Sid Vicious. You ever produce anything for any of Hayter's bands?'

'Produced, no.'

'Engineered?'

'For my sins. Post-punk death-metal. Not my favourite period, Laurence. Bearable at the time, with three or four bottles of red wine, God forbid, on the mixing desk. That era, I like to draw a curtain across it. Death metal – mostly foul. Jimmy Hayter – a twat.'

'Still?'

Prof said, 'Once a twat …'

'Where does he live? I mean, is he accessible?'

'Yes and no. He inherited the pile eventually, of course. It's a responsibility. Nobody wants to besmirch the coat of arms. On the other hand, the family seat gobbles wealth. And farming, even big-time farming, doesn't pay half the bills any more. So the earl, whatever he is now, he keeps his hand in, and when the roof falls in on the orangery or something he puts on a festival. On the very fringe of his estate, naturally. The house a mere dot on the horizon.'

'Where *is* the house?'

'I dunno, someplace south of Brum. Stratford way, possibly. I could find out.'

'Death metal,' Lol said. 'A lot of occult there?'

'Generally pseudo. Guys on Harleys, with skull rings and *slash-here* neck tattoos. So … occult … this would be a Merrily inquiry, would it?'

'Would he talk to her, do you think? Say, on the phone?'

'On the phone, Laurence, he won't say anything worth the price of a cheap-rate call. And, frankly, the last thing you want is to expose a woman as appealing as little Merrily, with or without the dog collar, to Jimmy Hayter. Especially with his lovely wife, her ladyship, living a lavishly subsidized life in France, her physical role in his life complete … and, from what I hear, bloody grateful for that.'

'Would he speak to *me*, do you think?'

'Why should he do that?'

'Maybe in the interests of … I don't know … keeping the past where it belongs?'

Lol had the map book open on the desk in the window, marking out the route to a village he didn't know, outside Gloucester. Tomorrow night's concert: a big pub with a folk club, the kind of intimate gig which, on the whole, he preferred. He pushed the page under the lamp. How far from Stratford? Forty miles, fifty?

'The situation is, Prof, that in his youth Jimmy Hayter seems to have been part of a commune. In a farmhouse down on the Welsh Border. Some of what they might have got up to … it would help Merrily to know about that.'

'Might have got up to?' Prof said. 'What's that mean? Do I like the sound of that? I don't. What does Merrily say?'

'She says it gives her a bad feeling.'

'Never dismiss a woman's feelings, good or bad,' Prof said, and Lol could hear the clink of the beloved and necessary cafetière, the slurping of the brown elixir. Then a silence, then, 'Jesus, Lol, you need to understand, you must not threaten this man.'

'Don't take the glasses off, then?'

'Laurence, listen to me. Jimmy Hayter … stately home, dinner parties with the gentry, but the guys with the skull rings and the *slash-here* tattoos, they still dig his garden, you know what I'm saying?'

34

Shaman

Teddy was right, it had once been an accepted rural service, like blacksmithing, and there had been an opportunity for Muriel Morningwood to talk about it and she hadn't.

My mother would awake in the morning to hear her throwing up. Coming to the obvious conclusion. Which she put to Mary.

Merrily lay on the bed, gazing up at the wardrobe. Just a wardrobe, mesh over its ventilation slits, nothing like Garway Church.

There was a different light, now, on Mrs Morningwood Senior's motherly concern for Mary Linden. Finding out about Mary's pregnancy, would she have offered to terminate it, or what? What had actually passed between them to cause Mary to leave the Morningwood house before morning?

Need to know. *Did* she need to know? Was this important? You kept turning over stones and uncovering other stones. At which point did you back off?

There were times when deliverance could seem like the most rewarding role in a declining Church, but it was also the most ill-defined.

It was not yet nine p.m. Needing to think about all this, Merrily had accepted Beverley's assessment of her level of fatigue, taken herself upstairs. Had a shower, put on a clean T-shirt, lay down, her body instantly falling into relaxation … but her damn head just filling up with questions, anomalies …

Tomorrow she'd need to talk to Sycharth Gwilym. Might find him at his farm, or it might mean driving into Hereford.

Before or after facing up to Mrs Morningwood? This time, no flam, no bullshit.

She sat up. There was an electric kettle on the dressing table. She prised herself from the bed, filled the kettle in the shower room. And, of course, she needed to call Jane, perhaps talk to Siân, make sure everything was OK. Sitting on the side of the bed, she switched on the phone, and it throbbed in her hand.

Message.

'Merrily, it's Sophie. Could you ring me at home?'

Sounding strangely close to excited, Sophie said she might have solved the mystery of the cuttings.

'Cuttings?'

'Canon Dobbs, Merrily.'

'Oh … sorry.' Hell, the cuttings. On hands and knees on the carpet, Merrily pulled one of the overnight bags from under the bed, dug out the plastic folder. 'I was just … going through them again.'

'In which case, you've probably noticed several mentions of the late Sir Laurens van der Post.'

'Yes.' Scrabbling through the papers. 'That's, erm …'

Uncovering an article enclosing a picture of this benign-looking old guy with a grey comb-over, side-on to the camera: PRINCE'S GURU: SAGE OR CHARLATAN?

'You haven't read them, have you, Merrily?'

'I …' Merrily sighed. 'I haven't read them all. Things have been complicated. Just inconveniences, really. But time-consuming.'

'Do you know *anything* about van der Post?'

'This and that.'

Van der Post, Laurens: white South African who bonded with the bushmen of the Kalahari studying so-called primitive belief systems and showing what Western societies might learn from them, while drawing public attention to the horrors of apartheid.

A war hero. But known primarily, in later years, as a close friend of the Prince of Wales. A seminal influence.

'The Church wasn't happy,' Merrily recalled, 'when Charles decided he should be William's godfather. On account of van der Post's own belief system being not strictly C of E. Correct?'

'He believed that all religions were, essentially, one,' Sophie said.

'Which possibly accounts for Charles's declared intention of becoming Defender of *Faiths*, when he becomes king?'

'Which almost certainly *does* account for it. The extent of van der Post's influence can never be overstated. He was extremely mystical in a way that I suspect your ... daughter would understand.'

'Pagan?'

'That would be too simplistic. He died in '96, at the age of ninety, having been far closer to the Prince in his crucial formative years than, I would guess, anyone in the Church of England. You'll find details in the cuttings about the time they went together into the wilderness of Kenya and van der Post imparted his knowledge of ... I suppose the word "shamanism" would not be inappropriate.'

'It's coming back to me. Closeness to the land, anyway.'

'And the alleged ... spirits of nature. Evidently a very powerful experience for a young man. They were camping out in a very remote area, without guards or detectives. And there, if you want to look for it, lies the basis of this much publicized – and possibly much misrepresented – communication with plants. It might have sown the seeds of the Prince's passion for conservation and green issues generally.'

'Interesting.'

What was also interesting was the way Sophie – who *worked for the cathedral* – talked about it, with no hint of condemnation. As if even the fringe-pagan became less obnoxious, for her, if it happened to be championed by royalty. If it ever came to a stand-off between the Church and the Crown, whose side would Sophie be on?

'But where's it leading, Sophie?'

'It leads,' Sophie said, 'directly to Canon Dobbs. When he first came over here in, I think, the late 1920s, van der Post became a farmer in Gloucestershire for some years. Canon Dobbs grew up near Cirencester. My information is that he might even have worked on the van der Post farm as a boy, during holidays.'

'Who told you that?'

'I've been speaking to a retired clergyman – nobody you would know, so don't ask – who knew Dobbs years ago. He said Dobbs would often talk about a South African farmer he'd known before the war who had helped to awaken his spiritual faculties.'

'If they stayed in contact, Sophie, that doesn't totally add up. Dobbs's attitude to spirituality, while not exactly fundamentalist, was certainly tightly focused.'

'Merrily, you only encountered him at the very end. We're talking about the 1930s, when he was a boy, and Laurens van der Post a young man. They may not subsequently have followed the same spiritual paths, but in their questing years … Anyway, they were exchanging letters almost until van der Post's death.'

'You know this for a fact?'

'I confirmed it about an hour ago, with Mrs Edna Rees. You remember her?'

'Yes, I do.'

Dobbs's housekeeper in Gwynne Street who had once told Merrily he hardly spoke to her. A cloistered existence in his later years.

'She sometimes, in his absence, managed to clean his office,' Sophie said. 'And she remembers the letters.'

Merrily recalled Mrs Rees. Stolid West Herefordshire countrywoman. Shrewd.

OK, crafty.

'She read these letters?'

'As Canon Dobbs was apparently shutting her out – unnecessarily, she felt – I would guess she saw it as justified. How far she understood them is another matter. The parts that stuck in her mind, inevitably, were the references to the late Princess Diana.'

'By *Dobbs*?'

'It's been widely reported, since, that Sir Laurens was not entirely in favour of that marriage. Once describing the poor child as, I recall, *a pinhead*.'

'Sharing his opinions with Dobbs? Elderly men conspiring against Diana?'

'So it seemed to Mrs Rees.'

'A big Diana fan, I'd guess.'

'Until then, she hadn't really known who Laurens van der Post was.'

'When *was* this?'

'Early nineties, I would guess. Mrs Rees made it her business to find out about him – afterwards, of course. And although she insists she never discussed the correspondence with anyone from that day to this, I think she was rather glad to have finally unloaded it all on … someone.'

Someone who *worked for the cathedral*. And who – humiliatingly excluded, for the first time, from the Bishop's confidence – would be bitterly identifying with Mrs Rees's dilemma.

'Well,' Merrily said, 'it's certainly fascinating from an historical perspective, but—'

'There's more. Mrs Rees believes something was entrusted by Sir Laurens to Canon Dobbs – information, perhaps even a package of some kind. Canon Dobbs never actually accused her of reading his mail, but a locksmith arrived one day to change the locks on his study door, and this time Mrs Rees never found the keys.'

'Any idea what it was?'

'There was one significant reference in the last letter she saw from Sir Laurens. He … believed he was under surveillance.'

'Well, that would figure. Anybody that close to the heir to the throne, the security services would be bound to check him out.'

'Yes, I suppose.'

'I don't know what to say about this, Sophie. It's intriguing, but unlikely to have any bearing on what I'm supposed to be dealing with. It's all getting too crowded for me. I just want to strip it down to the basics, get the right people in one room, hold a suitable service. I'm just a small-time cleric in the sticks – let's not get too ambitious.'

'Oh,' Sophie said.

'What?'

'The Bishop's here.'

'With you now?'

'Standing in my porch. I can see him through the window.'

'He usually show up this time of night?'

'No. I'm going to have to go and let him in.'

'Of course you are.'

Jane said everything was absolutely fine which, if you knew Jane at all, meant that everything was very much not fine.

'Can you talk? I mean, is Siân there?'

'She's not far away.'

'What's wrong?'

'Nothing I can't handle.'

'Jane, I don't want you handling *anything*.'

'Mum, have you seen the Baphomet again? I mean, have you been back to that house?'

'Don't change the subject. Do I need to come back to deal with anything?'

'Of course not. Don't even think about it.'

'If you need any advice,' Merrily said, 'you go to Lol, OK?'

'Sure. When he's here. Listen, if you're going to, like, cleanse that place, it's going to be a problem, isn't it?'

'What is?'

'The Baphomet. You'll be taking it on. Some kind of power symbol that maybe goes back to Celtic times? The Baphomet is also a representation of the great god Pan – nature at its most merciless and ferocious. I'd be a bit careful.'

'You watch too many weird DVDs, Jane.'

'Yeah, well, even practising Satanists have to relax sometimes,' Jane said. 'Goodnight, Mum. Sleep well.'

35

Unleashed

THE SLEEP, AS Mrs Morningwood had predicted, had been deep, and there were no clinging dreams. The muted chimes of the phone awoke Merrily. She rolled out of bed, the mobile clutched, like some throbbing fledgling, in her hand. Dislodging the bedside table, the lamp wobbling, her watch falling, and then the Bishop saying, very clearly, 'Merrily, I'm going to ask you to wind this up.'

She sank down to the floor.

'Give me a moment, Bernie.'

On hands and knees, patting the carpet for her watch. The window was flushed with pink and orange. What the hell time was it?

'I'm sorry if you're not yet up and about,' Bernie Dunmore said, 'but I wanted to catch you before you went anywhere. After all, you didn't even tell me you were doing this.'

'Doing what?'

'Didn't tell me that you were going to stay at Garway Hill.' His voice distant, abnormally formal. 'In fact, my information—'

'I couldn't. You weren't there.'

'—My *understanding* of the situation was that you'd found some obvious discrepancies in this pitiful woman's story which had rendered further inquiries unnecessary. You told me yourself last Saturday that you could prove fabrication.'

'That's not … I'm afraid that's not true, not any more. And as for not knowing I was coming here …' On her feet now, couldn't believe this. 'You *wanted* me to come and stay at Garway. Remember? Full attention? *Need to get you a locum?*'

'I may have overreacted,' the Bishop said.

'That was what I thought at the time, but it's a bit, you know … it's a bit late now.'

'Late?'

'Two people died?'

She walked barefooted to the window, the valley rising into view then plunging into a mist that was opaque, like set honey. She was wide awake now, and she didn't understand.

'Merrily, let's be sensible about this.'

'I'm trying—'

'I do know about the deaths. I also know of no one, apart, it seems, from yourself, who is connecting them, in any way, with these alleged disturbances at Garway.'

'Bernie—'

'Furthermore, I do *not* believe that it would be in the best interests either of the Diocese or the deliverance ministry if it were to become known that *we* were making something out of this. Do I really need to remind you why having Deliverance linked with the taking of life, whether it's suicide or murder or, in this case, God forbid, *both*, is—'

'No. You don't.'

'Good.'

'And the subtext here is what, Bernie?'

'Just come home,' the Bishop said, as though she was abroad. 'Administer a blessing, if you think it's necessary, and then come back. There are other issues we need to discuss. Organizational issues. *Reorganization*.'

'Of parishes?'

'Merrily, I don't want to get into this over the phone, it's very early days, and you know how I feel about it. I generally think you've been doing a terrific job under less than ideal conditions, and I don't *want* to see your position prejudiced …'

'Is this something to do with Siân Callaghan-Clarke? Does Sophie know about it?'

'It's nothing to do with Siân, essentially, and I talked to Sophie last night—'

'*Essentially?*'

'—And asked her not to telephone you until I'd spoken to you myself. I've also, in the meantime, spoken to the Duchy who are a little worried about what might have been unleashed.'

'*Unleashed?*'

'You, Merrily. We unleashed *you*. Or rather I did.'

'I …' She rubbed her eyes; maybe she wasn't actually awake. 'I'm sorry, would you mind spelling this out for me, Bishop? Preferably in big coloured nursery letters?'

'Traditionally …' Bernie Dunmore hesitated; his uncertainty was almost audible. 'Traditionally, the role of the deliverance ministry has been in the way of … of administering balm to what might be seen as an open wound – a psychic wound, if we must. You've displayed a tendency to go beyond the brief. Which, in normal circumstances, is not necessarily a bad thing. However …'

'You're saying you don't consider these to be normal circumstances. This case might be tiptoeing around the edges of national-security issues. Which are obviously more important than the little lives of ordinary people.'

'Merrily, please don't make this more difficult than it—'

'Has a detective called Jonathan Long been to talk to you, by any chance?'

'No. I've never heard of a detective called Jonathan Long.'

'All right.' Merrily sat down on the bed. 'I accept that you might not be able to tell me if he *had* been round. But if you could listen for just half a minute? Yes, initially, the evidence did suggest an element of scam. But now … now I feel strongly – and sometimes you have to run with feelings – that there's something that needs looking into.'

'Then let someone else look into it.'

'You really think someone else is going to?'

'That's not your problem.'

'I can't believe you said that. Look, give me one more day, and I'll submit a written report which I'll email to Sophie so it's on your desk by ten o'clock tomorrow. It will explain exactly why – with the underlying issues here – I feel this is not something we can, in all conscience, ignore.'

'Merrily, you clearly haven't been listening.'

'And – as you've accepted that there should be at least a blessing at the Master House – there's at least one person I need to talk to before I can organize it.'

'And that would be …?'

'His name's Sycharth Gwilym.'

'Mrs Watkins,' the Bishop said, 'the only thing I want to see on Sophie's desk tomorrow morning is the Reverend Murray's bill. Tell him we'll pay him for the full five days.'

'This is totally—'

'I most certainly don't want you to talk to anyone else. Please humour me. Pack your case.'

'Bishop, be honest. I think we've always been honest with one another. Have you been – how can I put this? – *got at*?'

'Don't be ridiculous.'

Merrily saw her watch glinting underneath the bedside table, bent and retrieved it, peered at the face and was initially relieved. It wasn't yet ten minutes past seven. She knew the Bishop always rose early these days, but this was …

'I'm sorry,' Merrily said. 'That was a bit offensive.'

Dead silence.

He'd hung up.

Christ.

Jane had been down since seven. In the cold kitchen, fully dressed for school. She'd fed Ethel, put the kettle on, was spooning tea into the pot when Siân Callaghan-Clarke appeared in the doorway, wearing a silk dressing gown – sea green, very expensive, almost swish.

'Good morning.'

Jane took a breath.

'Actually,' she said, 'I'm not sure it is.'

She'd avoided Siân last night, claiming that she had essays to do and escaping to the apartment, where she seemed to have lain awake half the night, replaying the drab, whiny voice of Shirley West. Listening to edited highlights of her own history, twisted by an expert.

Siân walked into the kitchen, pulled out a cane chair near the head of the refectory table and sat down, gathering her robe across her knees. This was where Mum would have lit a cigarette. Siân didn't move. Jane pulled down two mugs.

'Sorry. I've forgotten. Is it one sugar?'

'It's no sugar, Jane.'

'Right.' Might have guessed. 'I've only just put the kettle on, so it'll be a minute or two.'

'Thank you.'

'OK,' Jane said. There was no clever way of dealing with this. 'Here's the situation. I was in the church last night, while you were talking to that woman. I was in the Bull Chapel. Behind the screen.'

'I know,' Siân said.

Jane stared at her. Siân's sleek metallic hair was brushed back from her face, which had surprisingly few lines, even first thing in the morning, and no expression. A barrister face.

'I was mildly concerned …' a barrister tone of voice '… when you didn't get off the school bus at what I'd been advised was the appointed time and I didn't like to leave the house until you were home. I know you aren't, strictly speaking, my responsibility, but I did think it wise to wait until the last possible moment. When I eventually saw you on the square, I decided it was safe to leave. And when you walked directly past me and Mrs … I'm sorry, I …'

'Prosser.'

'Yes, of course. When you walked directly past us – particularly Mrs Prosser – without saying a word and with your face concealed, I rather anticipated your intentions.'

Shit.

'Look,' Jane said, 'I just …'

'You were curious.'

'I was suspicious.'

'Why?'

'Because, I …' Jane tossed the spoon onto the worktop. 'Oh, for—'

'Come and sit down, Jane.'

'I'm not going to apologize.'

'What have you to apologize about? You were simply – I would guess – trying to protect your mother.'

Jane said nothing. Siân steepled her fingers.

'Jane, there are certain issues on which Merrily and I are unlikely ever to agree but, for what it's worth, I suspect the level of my regard for her somewhat exceeds the level of hers for me.'

Siân's smile was kind of wan and regretful. Jane didn't know how to respond and didn't.

'I realize that I would hardly have been her first choice for looking after the parish,' Siân said. 'She was probably dismayed?'

'Erm, yeah.'

Jane sat down, near the bottom of the table. Couldn't get anything right at the moment, could she? Walked right into this one, thinking she was going to nail Callaghan-Clarke first thing in the morning, while her senses were fuddled.

As if.

The tables had been turned, Jane stitched up like a unreliable witness in the box. Stitched herself up, in fact. Mum might almost have predicted it last night: *Jane, I don't want you handling anything.*

Siân Callaghan-Clarke, practised in silence, just sat there. Waiting for you to dig yourself further in.

'OK ...' Jane proceeded with extreme caution. 'If you knew I was there, in the church ... why did you get her to go through it all? All the stuff about me being a not-so-closet pagan, worshipping the goddess in the vicarage garden.'

'Do you?'

'No. I mean, I did once, maybe a couple of times, in a half-hearted kind of way, but not any more. And, like, all the stuff about me having an altar in the attic and, like, chanting and trying to raise dark forces, that is total crap. I wouldn't do that. I mean, OK, I thought about it ... an altar. But only as a kind of a focus point. I didn't ... I mean, I was just a kid.'

'A teen-witch?'

'Never *that* much of a kid, Siân.'

'My apologies.'

'And, for heaven's sake, it's not *satanic*, is it? She's making the funda-
mental mistake that all these ignorant fundamentalists— I mean,
Satanism's just a perverse reversal of Christianity. It doesn't even qualify
as any kind of paganism.'

'Yes, Jane, I have read my deliverance handbook. And – since you ask
– the reason I invited Shirley to pour out everything was that *I* thought
it might help if we both knew the extent of it. There's one in every
parish, Jane. Often more than one – a faction, even.'

'Sorry?'

'Probably harmless most of the time, but she needs watching. She
might well be used, for instance, by opponents of the plan to re-erect
your standing stones in Coleman's Meadow.'

'Right.'

'Although I wouldn't imagine it would improve their case to any
great extent.'

'No.'

'Well …' Siân sat back. 'And there was I, feeling rather pleased with
my success at drawing Shirley out in a way that perhaps wouldn't have
been open to Merrily. I'm sorry you felt the need to put a rather
different interpretation on it.'

Jane sagged in her chair.

'But I'm glad you brought it up this morning,' Siân said. 'It says
something about you.'

'Like that I'm a totally immature idiot who shouldn't be allowed
out?'

'I think the tea should be almost brewed by now,' Siân said. 'Would
you like to pour for us, Jane? And have you eaten yet, or were you
waiting for me?'

Jane stood up and went over to the worktop. Taking the opportunity
– which the bloody woman had obviously deliberately just given her –
to hide her reddening face.

'I just want to say, in case you were wondering …' talking into the
mugs '… All that stuff about Lol and other women …'

'It's nonsense, of course.'

'You …' Jane looked up. 'You do believe that?'

'I met Mr Robinson once,' Siân said. 'He wasn't what I might have expected.'

'No. No, he isn't. Look ...' Jane started talking, in this great, hot rush, before she could stop herself. 'Why are you really here? Why did you offer to come?'

'Why do *you* think I'm here?'

Lawyers. Always elegantly turning your questions around.

All right, then.

'Mum thinks ... that there's a possibility they're putting together some kind of carve-up? And that she's going to end up with about eight parishes and lose the deliverance thing. Or it gets divided up and, like, run by a committee?'

'I see.'

'I don't suppose I should've said that, but, you know ...'

'Why not? It's true.'

'Oh.'

'There *is* such a proposal, and I *have* been asked to make an unofficial report.'

'Oh.'

'I'm sorry.'

'Right.'

Siân shrugged.

In the end, the bedroom had been too small to contain Merrily's emotions. She came out of the shower room and dressed in a hurry: jeans, sweatshirt, trainers. Within ten minutes, she was at the foot of the stairs, sliding back the bolt on the front door of The Ridge, letting herself out into a breeze swollen with rain.

It wasn't cold and, physically, she was feeling much better. Still slightly ... well, not weak exactly, but a bit tender, a bit raw.

Oh, come *on* ... *very* bloody raw.

The blowing rain was stinging Merrily's face. Like the Bishop's veiled threats.

Threats? From good old easygoing Bernie Dunmore? Could she possibly have misheard?

I don't want to see your position prejudiced.

No. It wasn't even subtle. It wasn't veiled at all.

And she'd thought she knew him. Thought he was a friend. But a friend would have said, *Come over and we'll talk about this. There are some things I can't say on the phone.* He hadn't said that. He hadn't wanted to talk about it at all. There were *other issues* they needed to discuss. Of an administrative nature.

And if it was hard to fire an incompetent vicar, it was a lot less complicated to remove a deliverance consultancy from someone who tended to go *beyond the brief.*

The mist was lifting over the woods in the valley, the landscape forming in a watercolour wash as Merrily walked down the steps to the parking area and the intersecting footpaths, one up to the hill, one down to the church. Behind her the steep, tawny house was silent. Nobody about yet. No real need to be; she was the only guest, and she hadn't exactly been demanding an early breakfast.

Maybe, by nine, she'd feel up to talking to people.

And then what?

She could go, on her own, to the Master House, suitably attired and equipped with holy water. A straightforward room-by-room blessing. An end to it. Or merely a reprieve, because Bernie Dunmore would know there'd be no easy retrieval of their old relationship.

On which basis, she might just as well ignore the bastard's instructions and go in search of Sycharth Gwilym.

Angry now, but she cooled it. She unlocked the Volvo, reached behind the driving seat for her waterproof and then, on impulse, tossed it back and climbed in, switched on the engine and let the car slide away, down the hill.

Merrily drove slowly, although there was no other traffic around, not even a tractor or a quad bike. She was looking for a lay-by, a field entrance, a patch of grass verge wide enough to park on. She needed to sit alone somewhere. And listen.

... This sieve of our own needs, desires, fears ... what we're afraid they might really be saying. We're processing the words, analysing. Our minds are taking an active role. We're not listening.

In a service with no sermon, it had probably been the best sermon she'd delivered all year.

She needed to listen. She took a left turn, high hedges either side, trees still laden with a summerload of leaves. The point of the tower of Garway Church, with its bent cross, appeared over the trees.

Why not?

Weighted as it was with the density of the Templars, it was still a church, and Merrily wondered if it was open yet.

Never did find out, though, because that was when the dog ran in front of the car.

36

Only Darkness

SHE'D PULLED HARD into the verge, a thorny hedge screeching against the Volvo's side panels, its scratchy mesh compressed against the window. Finishing up in a cage of brambles, with a back wheel in a shallow ditch and the engine stalled.

Oh God, no ...

She'd been travelling at well under thirty m.p.h., but the road was wet and the brakes were spongy. She'd slammed on and gone into a skid on the overflowing verge of grass and mud, letting go of the steering wheel as she was flung back into the seat, the frayed belt slipping and cutting into the side of her neck.

What was she doing in the bloody car, anyway? Driving off in a self-righteous fury. *Resentment. Inflated self-esteem. They can't treat me like this.*

Releasing the belt, she inched painfully across the slanting seat, over the gear lever and the handbrake, to reach the passenger-door handle, pushing the door open.

Climbing out and staggering around to the front of the Volvo, Merrily went down on her knees, half-sick with dread, looking underneath.

Couldn't see. The grass was still knee-high on the verge, around the bumper. She had to lie down on the wet tarmac, edging between the front wheels and ...

... Face it, there was unlikely to be more than one Irish wolfhound in this part of Garway.

'*Roscoe?*'

With one wheel in the ditch, the other on the edge, the big car was tilted in the undergrowth, its belly hard into the muddy bank. Impossible to squeeze underneath; she just about managed to push her left arm under, feeling around in the soaking foliage.

'Roscoe!'

Nothing moving under there, only … multiple stabbing pains in her left hand and up the inside of her wrist told her she'd grabbed a handful of nettles.

This was no use, basically; she'd have to get back in and try to shift the car. With extreme care.

Warm breath on the back of Merrily's neck made her body retract, twisting over onto her side. Like they always did when you were on the ground, he thought she wanted to play; he was standing over her with his nose above her ear, poised and quivering.

'Oh, Jesus, Roscoe—'

Collapsing into the road in a moment of wild relief, head in her arms, before pulling herself up. The dog waited, panting. His coat was messed up, matted, spiked and sodden, a thorny twig trapped in his collar. He'd been through hedges and perhaps a stream.

Merrily pulled herself up, clothes wet through, cold and clinging. There was no sign of Mrs Morningwood, and it seemed unlikely that she habitually turned her dog out in the mornings to take exercise in fields full of sheep.

Detaching the thorn twig, Merrily slipped a hand under Roscoe's collar. He squeaked.

'What've you done?'

She ran her hands down his flanks; at some point he squirmed away, as if in pain, but eventually let her lead him to the car. Tried twice to jump in; she had to help him into the back seat before dragging herself back through the passenger door.

The easy bit. She started the engine, one wheel spinning, another spurting mud and the old chassis creaking and moaning as she fought to wrench the Volvo out of the ditch.

Lol had set the alarm. Best to leave early; he had no knowledge of Warwickshire, only its awful motorways.

Prof Levin had called back just short of midnight, as the ashy-pink embers of last night's hastily built fire had been quietly crumbling into the hearth.

'Get a pad, Laurence, I'll give you the directions.'

'You ... actually called him?'

'I phoned his office, left a message and he was back within half an hour. Must be some call-referral system.'

'I'm impressed,' Lol said.

He'd always known Prof had some serious clout in this business, but even so ...

'Hayter and me – first time we'd spoken in some years. I knew he'd get back, if he was in the country, if only because he was always on at me to tell him what happened at the Abbey on the anniversary of Lennon's murder.'

'You told him *that*?'

Lol knew two other people who'd been involved in this notorious, myth-soaked session. Neither of them, nor even Prof, had ever disclosed what had taken place, and it wasn't something that had ever bothered Lol. The dark, narcotic side of the music business, like parts of the Old Testament, was best left alone if your faith was shaky. So this – telling Hayter – was above and beyond, and it spoke less of Prof's friendship with Lol than his admiration for Merrily and what she did. The explicit nature of which, Prof would often say, was not something on which, as a recovering alcoholic, he ever wanted to dwell.

'I told him some of it, Laurence. He won't put it around, if only because everybody knows he wasn't there.'

'But he'll see me?'

'And you will see him, that's the downside. Eleven-thirty in the morning. You get half an hour. You don't get lunch. You owe me one, needless to say.'

'I think I do.'

'You also owe it to me to listen. I may have said this earlier – Hayter, if he's doing business, prefers to deal with people in the flesh, rather than talk on the phone or exchange emails. This is because he needs to have them exposed to the full awesome glory of his repellent personality. But do not make the mistake of thinking this is all special effects, you know what I'm saying?'

Lol shook his head.

'You still there, Laurence?'

'I'm nodding,' Lol said. 'It's because my mouth's gone dry with fear.'

'It's not a joke. And be sure you call me afterwards. If you still have fingers to push the numbers.'

Now, memorizing his route from the map book, Lol looked at the clock on the desk. He needed to call Merrily, to find out exactly what she wanted to know from Hayter, but it was probably too early. He'd leave it an hour and, meanwhile, get on the road.

His stuff was still in the hall where he'd left it yesterday. The Guild acoustic amp, the Takamine jumbo, the exquisite lute-shaped Boswell, the harmonicas and the little drum machine. Loading and unloading the truck without injury to the kit was getting to be a serious chore. He just couldn't imagine years of this.

He put Merrily's number in the frame on his mobile.

Merrily had never really looked at the Morningwood house in the light of day, too fever-ridden yesterday morning to take it in. With its shambling pergola, its rampant chicken wire and its chaos of sheds, it was an almost comical contrast to the manicured holiday homes at the other end of the terraced row.

The only one of them, though, with any signs of life: the smoke like a curl of wispy hair above the chimney stack, the clutter of free-range chickens.

But if Morningwoods had been on this hill as long as the badger shit on the White Rocks, it hadn't always been here at Ty Gwyn. This row couldn't be more than a century and a half old, its angles too sharp, doors and windows too regular, too uniform for real age.

The rain had stopped, but dirty pink clouds were still bunched like muscles over the hills. Not a promising day. The car window was halfway down, Roscoe's snout halfway out, his head up against Merrily's hair. She could hear the chickens from the sloping land behind as she drew up in front of the two end houses. Blocking the lane, but it was a dead end; apart from Mrs Morningwood, it seemed unlikely that anyone else would be here until next spring.

'Roscoe, I'm going to leave you in the car, in case she's out looking for you or something. OK?'

Maybe this visit was meant. She thought about the Prince of Wales, his attention to coincidences and *signposts*.

It was just gone seven-thirty. At the front door, she looked around for a bell or a knocker. Sense of déjà vu – at this stage yesterday, she'd been ill and the door had been opened for her. Lifting a fist to beat on the panels, she thought she could hear movement from the back of the house … or one of the others, the holiday homes?

She glanced along the terraced frontage of emptied hanging baskets, smokeless chimneys. At Mrs Morningwood's end of the block, there was a long fence reinforced with chicken wire, lining an unmade drive leading to a carport with a roof of galvanized sheets.

Under the carport was the back end of an old black Jeep Cherokee. Merrily glimpsed a figure moving along the side of the garage towards a barn or a stable.

'Mrs Morningwood?'

She stopped, up against the house wall. The figure kept on moving, looking back just once, on the edge of the barn.

It didn't look like Mrs Morningwood. It didn't look like a woman. It didn't seem to have a face, only a darkness.

Come on, this didn't mean a thing. It didn't mean a thing that the back door was ajar, like another door had been last summer, or that curtains were drawn across two downstairs windows, like on the days of funerals when she'd been a kid.

But still Merrily drew a long breath, and still it came back out as *Jesus, Jesus, Jesus*, half oath, half prayer.

And, because she really didn't want to, she went in.

Entering the kitchen to the smell of something overboiled and a rumbling, refrigerator or a Rayburn, overlaying a sound from deeper into the house, like a roll of carpet being dragged across the floor.

Call out? She opened her mouth to do it, but no sound came.

A door was half-open to the living room – the treatment room where she'd spent most of yesterday. Merrily stayed just short of the doorway. A dimness in there and a drifting smell, salty and sour. A smell that had not been apparent yesterday, a smell she half-recognised and …

OK, phone.

She pulled out her mobile, switched it on and then plunged it back into her hip pocket, cupping both hands over the bump. One day she'd figure out how to mute the electric piano chord that told you – and everybody else – that the phone was awakening.

Waiting. Mobiles these days, all this techno, they took for ever to boot up. In the living room there was a gap at the top of the drawn curtain which lit a triangle of blue-white across the room, like a flickering sail on dark water, and then it vanished. She took out the phone again, pressed the nine key three times, didn't send it. Not yet.

The darkness pulsed and jittered. Someone was fumbling about in there. Merrily was feeling around for a light switch when something fell over with a *bong*, and then a sharp, tight shattering of glass jerked her back into the doorway.

Halfway down the wall, her hand found the metal nipple of the switch, and she flipped it down.

'Come *any* closer …' a voice high and cracked '… and I shall take out your—'

The light flickered on, a frosted bowl, flat to the ceiling, exposing a woman crouching in a corner.

Merrily said, 'Oh dear God.'

'—Take your throat out.'

Mrs Morningwood was a cramped detail from an engraving of hell, her hair crimson-rinsed, thick ribbons of dark red unrolling from her scalp, collecting in her eye sockets, blotching on her bared teeth.

Both her hands were bleeding freely around a shivering tube of jagged glass.

'Mrs—'

'Get *back*!'

The glass shuddered in her hand, and Merrily saw that it was the smashed chimney from the green-shaded oil lamp, its tip serrated but the whole thing cracked, cutting into the hands that gripped it.

She saw the brass body of the lamp on the carpet at the end of its flex. The darkwood piano stool on its side, blood-flecked. The log basket overturned, leaving the rug cobbled with logs. The bentwood rocking chair still in motion, as if someone had just stood up.

Mrs Morningwood was wearing a pale blue nightdress. She was squinting through the blood, trying to divert a river away from an eye and making a red delta across a cheek and over her chin, spatters sporadically blossoming, like wild roses, on the blue nightdress.

It seemed likely that she couldn't see who was with her in the room because her eyes were full of blood.

'It's me,' Merrily said. 'Merrily Watkins.'

Mrs Morningwood held on to the lamp-glass.

'He's gone,' Merrily said.

She crossed the room, watching the jagged lamp-funnel – now in Mrs Morningwood's right hand.

'I saw him running into the trees. I think he had a hood … black bag over his head, with eye holes. Just let me—'

'No. Don't touch me.'

Merrily said, 'I'm getting an ambulance … all right?' She opened up the phone. 'Just …'

'No!' Mrs Morningwood edging crablike around the wall. 'Go away. Forget you ever came here.'

'Who was he?'

'There was nobody.'

'Mrs Morningwood, I saw him. I saw him running towards the barn.'

'Forget it. What are you doing here, anyway?'

Reaching the chaise longue, Mrs Morningwood tried to heave herself up. Sudden, frightened pain came out in a compressed mouse-squeak from the back of her throat.

Dragging a handful of tissues from a Kleenex box on the desk, Merrily moved across, kneeling down beside her. Mrs Morningwood turned sharply away with a snort, tossing her head like a horse, blood bubbling in her nose and on her exposed and blueing throat you could also see red indents, which …

'Jesus Christ, you've been—'

Mrs Morningwood felt at her throat and winced.

'Did most of this myself.'

And she probably had, with her nails.

Trying to prise his fingers away.

'Put that *fucking* thing—' Bloodied hands clawing out; the phone dropped to the carpet. '*Leave it!*'

'We need the police, Mrs Morningwood.'

'*Shush!* Was that …?'

'It's all right, he's *gone.*'

But suppose he hadn't?

They waited, listening. Merrily was aware of the clock ticking in another room. Out in the car, Roscoe barked once. Mrs Morningwood's head jerked up.

'The dog …'

'In the car.'

'Dog's all right? I thought—'

'He's fine. I picked him up in the lane.'

'Thank you.' Mrs Morningwood's bloodied head fell back into the pillows on the chaise. Big bruises on her thin arms were almost golden in the light. 'Thank you, Watkins. Owe you … a whole course of bloody treatment.'

She started to laugh and sat up and went into a spasm of coughing and had to spit out some blood into the wad of tissues. Merrily pulled out some more from the box.

Could be internal bleeding.

'You have *got* to let me get you some help.'

'Help myself, darling. What I do. Get me a cigarette, would you? Mantelpiece.'

'Just—'

'Wouldn't give the bloody doctors the satisfaction. One other thing you might do …'

'Just listen. Please. We can't put this off, he's going to be miles away if we don't—'

'Lock the back door.'

'All right, but—'

'And then go into the bathroom and turn on the shower for me, would you?'

'It's a crime scene, Mrs Morningwood. You've been subjected to a … a savage bloody … We need an ambulance and we need the police. There's no way you—'

'You're wasting your breath, darling. Not as if they're ever likely to get the bastard. Take you in, strip you down, probe your bits, accuse you of lying …'

'There'll be DNA.'

'He was *masked*. Wore surgical gloves and a fucking condom, he—' Silence.

Merrily gasped. Mrs Morningwood began to laugh again, with no humour, the blood already drying in the deep lines in her face.

PART FOUR

There are many symbols that are not
individual but collective in their nature
and origin. These are chiefly religious
images, their origin so far buried in the
past that they seem to have no human
source.

Carl Jung

I don't think a man who has watched
the sun going down could walk away
and commit a murder.

Laurens van der Post

37

Threadbare

Siân said, 'You'll need to explain this again.'

'Can't. Sorry. Not my decision. Look – sorry – the signal's not great. I'm sorry.'

'You're in the car?'

'I'm coming back.' Keep it short; less chance of voice-shake. 'Bishop's decision. I think he should be the one to explain. I'm baffled, frankly, Siân, but he makes the rules.'

If Merrily was quieter inside now, it was the result of an hour's violent scrubbing of the floor, the walls and the legs of furniture. The painstaking removal of sticky blood from the fabric of the chaise longue. The careful and complete incineration of a blue nightdress in the range. A full hour of scrubbing and squeezing until her hands hurt and her knees were abraded from the flags.

So calming, these domestic chores.

The car was at the side of the track, engine running. Merrily sitting, quite numb, looking directly in front of her at the rain-greyed hills and thanking Siân for looking after things, saying how very grateful she was.

Playing a part.

Now would be the time for Siân to point out that she was still, if only nominally, the deliverance coordinator for this diocese and therefore entitled to the facts. But Siân said nothing for several seconds.

'So you want me to leave, Merrily.'

'Obviously, had we known it was only going to be a couple of days, there wouldn't have been any need to bother you. Or anybody. I'm really sorry.'

Siân was smart, would pick up any stray nuance, any hint of the spiralling descent into madness represented by the woman sitting stiffly beside Merrily.

Like a badly wrapped parcel: outsize sunglasses, the scarf around her discoloured, swollen face, the cracked Barbour storm-flapped over the pink silk scarf covering the lesions on her throat.

'Ah … there will probably be issues for us to discuss,' Siân said, 'after you talk to Jane.'

'Oh.' Merrily laughed lightly. 'I won't ask.'

The other, still-visible damage: two black eyes from the fists, two deep cuts just above the hairline from falling against the piano stool, a split lip, a broken tooth. It was what they did: first, they beat you into semi-consciousness. It was about violence, more than sex, most experts agreed on that.

Siân said, 'If you'd like to talk about the Bishop's attitude, I can wait.'

'I am so pissed off about this,' Merrily said, 'I don't think I want to talk to anybody for quite a long time.'

She'd phoned The Ridge, not tarting it up for them either. The best lies were always the bald truth: the Bishop had told her to come back at once. She was bewildered and resentful and trying to conceal it. She'd have to return sometime for her things. *Sorry, sorry, sorry.* And Teddy was like, I really don't think I could cope with your job, Merrily.

'So Garway … that's over,' Siân said.

'Yes, it's over.'

'Against your advice.'

'I wasn't asked for my advice.'

'All right,' Siân said. 'I think I'm getting the message. I shall leave.'

'I'm sorry.'

Merrily released the clutch and nosed the Volvo slowly out into the road which led past the area known as The Turning, above the church. Beside her, Mrs Morningwood mumbled something.

'Mmm?'

'Over. You said it was over.'

'Yes, well, the lies have been coming so much easier since I was ordained.'

Which was cynical and untrue and she didn't know why she'd said it. A sidelong glance showed her Mrs Morningwood trying to release a laugh through lips liked diced tomato. It seemed to be getting harder for her to speak.

'Stronger woman than you look, Watkins.'

'I don't think so.'

'Have I thanked you?'

'What for?'

Mrs Morningwood laughed. The fear and the pain glittering in her eyes. along with the fury. Fury, almost certainly, at herself, for letting someone do this to her, Merrily feeling much the same.

'Just don't …' Squeezing the wheel. 'I must've been temporarily insane to go along with this, and it's done now. But there is no way I'm going to forget that you have been—'

'In a car accident,' Mrs Morningwood said.

She'd shut herself in the downstairs bathroom, showering in water so hot that Merrily, scrubbing the floor, had heard her screams, all the rage that would find no other form of expression.

'How long do you intend to keep this up?'

'You want to hear me sob? You think there's something wrong with me, something unnatural, that I'm not sobbing my heart out? You think I'm … unwomanly?'

On the back seat, the wolfhound whimpered. He'd been kicked, Mrs Morningwood said. Trapped in the door and then kicked. They'd examined him between them. No bleeding, nothing broken.

Merrily said, 'I don't understand you, that's all. There's something about you I don't understand.'

'And have no need to,' Mrs Morningwood said.

Before the shower, before the scrubbing and the burning, she'd said, 'If you report this I shall deny it.'

'Oh sure.' Merrily starting to lose it too, by then. 'That'll work. People just won't look at you. They're tactful like that, especially in the country. Pride themselves on minding their own business. Are you *crazy*?'

'I shall simply go out and run the Jeep off the road and leave it sticking out of the hedge with my blood on the seat and the steering wheel. No-one will dispute it, and they won't get close enough to be able to.'

'Insane.'

'I've done it before. Crashed the car, that is. Police find out, they'll just think I was drunk. Police always like to think you were drunk.'

'Why? Why are you doing this?

'You have no need to know.'

'I have an increasingly urgent need to know. In fact, seems to me that the only reason you could have for covering this up is because you recognized the man who attacked you and you don't want him arrested, because ... I don't know. But *you* do.'

Rape, violence, it was usually the husband or partner. All those times when the police knew about it, urged the conspicuously injured party to give evidence, and the victim refused. It seemed unlikely that Mrs Morningwood had ever before been a victim.

She said, 'You're wrong. I do not know who it was.'

'But you don't think it was just a random thing, either, do you? Have you been followed? Stalked? Seen anybody hanging around the house?'

'No.'

'What are you not telling me?'

No reply.

'What if I tell the police what I found?'

'You wouldn't do that. You're implicated now. Cleaned up his mess.'

'What if he does it to somebody else?'

'He won't.'

'This man you don't know. What if he comes back?'

Silence.

'Either you tell me exactly what happened,' Merrily had said, 'or I ring my friend in the police, who knows me well enough by now to—'

'All right. But you'll be the first and last to hear this.'

Muriel Morningwood got up at first light, as usual, letting Roscoe and then the chickens out into the mist.

Her attacker had simply followed her back into the house, trapping the dog with the door, kicking him back out, slamming the door.

He wore camouflage clothing, no skin exposed, and what had been most frightening about him was not the hood with the eyeholes, but the flesh-coloured surgical gloves, one of them coming at her face as she turned and then there was an explosion in her left eye and she'd been thrown into the living room, punched repeatedly in the mouth, stomach, mouth again. Slammed to the floor, her scalp raked on a corner of the piano stool, hair filling up with blood, as he knelt astride her and put on the condom.

She was a strong woman, very fit. Self-sufficient. Prided herself on it, always thought she'd be able to defend herself. What you never accounted for was the effect of shock – the way the body, untrained, was shocked into a kind of inner collapse by sustained, unrelenting, extreme violence.

The sound of the car had stopped it. He'd lifted himself, listening and she'd managed to scream. He'd been kneeling over her, holding her down with both hands and when she opened her mouth, he'd slammed a hand across it, freeing one of her arms, and she'd punched him as hard as she could in the balls, and he'd uncoiled in agony, clutching himself with both hands, and she'd squirmed away, blinded by the blood, just as the footsteps had sounded on the path.

She'd thought he looked at her once, through his eyeholes, and then he wasn't there, only the smell of his sweat, his fluids, her own blood.

It had been obvious to Merrily that if she hadn't shown up when she did, Mrs Morningwood would, by now, have been waiting for Dr Grace, the pathologist. And something else was also clear.

'You can't stay here.'

'Where would I go?'

'I live in a big house.'

'Oh, no.'

'There's no alternative, Mrs Morningwood.'

'There'll be other people.'

'Only Jane. And, at the moment, a woman priest who's standing in. I'll need to tell her to go. Is there anyone who can look after things here?'

There was a couple, graphic artists from the village, reflexology patients who'd helped out once before when Mrs Morningwood had

had to go away. She'd got Merrily to phone them, explain that she had to travel to see a patient urgently, in Devon. No problem, they'd come and look after the chickens and anything else, morning and night, until further notice.

When Mrs Morningwood had brought down an old brown case, Merrily had one last try.

'I know a good copper. A decent guy.'

Mrs Morningwood had held out her cigarette to Merrily's lighter, both hands trembling.

'Wasting your breath, darling.'

'He was on foot,' Merrily said. 'Where could he have been going when I saw him?'

'Anywhere.' Watery blood soaking into the wobbling cigarette from lips failing to grip. 'Over the hill and far away.'

38

Doormat

On the way here, Lol had glimpsed a signpost and braked. At the next junction, he'd turned round and gone back. Sat in the cab of the truck, gazing at the three words on the sign. A name with only one meaning. A place of sorrowful pilgrimage.

He hadn't realized that he was going to be so close. No time now, but there would be no excuse on the way back. He'd turned round again and driven on into the Warwickshire countryside, and now the Animal was in an off-road parking area a short way from the castle lodge.

A burger van was opening up at the far end. The big man in the long tan leather coat evidently knew the burger guy because he walked past him without a glance, directly to Lol's truck, and Lol lowered his window.

Five times he'd attempted to call Merrily on her mobile. It was always switched off. He'd left two messages, the first one explaining he had a chance to talk to Lord Stourport and how far did she want him to go? The second one saying that if she didn't call back within twenty minutes he was going to be late.

'Yow got business here, pal?' the man in the leather coat said.

Lol told him he had an appointment with Lord Stourport in – he looked at the dashboard clock – twelve minutes?

The man, who had gelled hair and chewed gum, asked for his name and Lol told him, and the man nodded and went back to the lodge. Lol sat back and waited and kept seeing the signpost in his mind's eye.

He'd never been there. He'd spoken to dozens of people who *had* been, some travelling hundreds of miles. But, all these years, he'd avoided it. What good would it do now?

When his phone rang, he didn't even look at the caller's number.

'Merrily.'

'Uh, no. Lol, its me … it's Eirion, it is.'

'Oh,' Lol said. 'Hello, Eirion.'

'I'm sorry to bother you, but I figured you'd probably be gigging at night. Saw a piece on you. In *Mojo*? They'd reviewed your gig in Oxford, did you know?'

'No, I didn't. Eirion, look—'

'It was pretty good.' Eirion's South Wales accent kicking in, usually a sign of nerves. 'It was this guy who'd seen you in Hazey Jane when he was young. He said Hazey Jane were never quite as good as they might have been. Or as good as they would be now if they'd had the quality of material you're producing at the moment. Something like that.'

'Well, that's …'

'Pretty positive.'

'… Not really the reason for your call, is it?'

'Er, no,' Eirion said. 'No, it isn't.'

This would have to be about Jane who, according to Merrily, had not heard from Eirion for a couple of weeks and was thinking she'd been dumped. And he'd love to find out something that might help, but this really wasn't a good time.

'Eirion, could I call you back? I'm expecting—'

'Lol, *please* … could you give me just two minutes? *One* minute.'

'Well … yeah, OK. As long as it—'

'Only I rang the vicarage, see, I was going to ask Mrs Watkins, but this other woman answered. Is there something wrong, Lol? Have they – you know – *gone*?'

'Where?'

'Gone. Left.'

'Good God, no.'

'Then why isn't she returning my calls, Lol?'

'Jane isn't returning your calls?'

'See, I didn't want to bother you with this, it's not like she's your daughter or anything, but I'm going crazy here, man.'

'Well, you know … this is difficult, but the impression we were given was that, now you're at university ... your lives had kind of taken different paths?'

'I'm at Cardiff! It's less than an hour and a quarter away. I come back every weekend. I mean, you know, I could've gone to Oxford.'

'You *could* have?'

'They'd accepted me. It was a bit borderline, but they said yes.'

'You turned down Oxford so you could be nearer to Jane?'

'My old man's still fuming. Weeks before he'd even talk to me.'

'I didn't know,' Lol said.

'No, you wouldn't.'

'Does Jane know?'

'I told her ... I said they'd turned me down.'

'Eirion!'

'Don't say anything, will you?'

'I don't— How many calls have you made?'

'To Jane? Bloody dozens. Her phones's always switched off, and I leave messages and she doesn't call back.'

'I didn't know.'

'She's with someone else, right? It's this bloody archaeologist, isn't it?'

'I ... I don't know.'

'You know he's married, don't you? *And* he's nearly thirty. I mean, he's *married*. All right, Jane, she can be ... you know ... I mean, you know what she can be ...'

'Yeah.'

'And yet ... you know what I mean?'

'Oh yes,' Lol said.

'Sorry, I shouldn't be hanging this on you.'

'I'll talk to her, OK? I'll find out something. Look, I'll call you back ... maybe tomorrow?'

The man in the leather coat was standing outside the lodge, beckoning, pointing to the gates. Telling Lol it was time.

The vicarage was immaculately tidy, and Siân had made a coal fire in the parlour and banked it up. This was thoughtful; Merrily rarely lit a fire before evening.

Upstairs, the guest room looked like Siân had never been there. It was at the rear of the house, overlooking the old Powell orchard. The sun had come out and ripe apples gleamed like baubles. Roscoe plodded around on the oak boards, and Merrily's move to replace the duvet cover with a fresh one got a dismissive wave of the hand from Mrs Morningwood.

'Don't bother, it'll only be stinking of this stuff by morning.'

Jars and bottles, some labelled, were set out on the pine dresser with a glass and a spoon. She'd accepted a cup of weak tea, declined food. Merrily sat on the edge of the bed.

'At the risk of—'

'*No.*'

'I'm thinking, primarily, of the head injuries. The doctor here, he's not exactly a fan of alternative remedies, but he could at least put your mind at rest.'

'You mean *your* mind. It's not necessary. I don't have a skull fracture, and even if I *did*—'

'He doesn't need to know what happened to you.'

Knowing, as she said it, that she was wrong. Kent Asprey *would* need to know and, while Mrs Morningwood might get away with her story about the head injury, how many people emerged from car crashes with strangulation marks?

'Sooner or later this is going to hit you, Muriel.'

'Is that supposed to be a joke?'

'No, I wasn't thinking. I'm sorry. You get some rest, I'll pace around for a couple of hours.'

When she turned at the door, Mrs Morningwood was standing by the window, a wounded smile on damaged lips. Or maybe not a smile at all, just the wound. It just *had* to be someone she knew.

'And no, you won't wake up to find police at the bedside,' Merrily said.

'Thank you.'

'You need anything, just—'

'I won't. Equally, if you need to go out to attend to your parish affairs, go ahead.'

'Right.'

Merrily went unhappily downstairs and through the kitchen to the scullery. Sat down and stared at the blotter on the desk, trying to be impressed by Mrs Morningwood's resilience, but becoming only more mystified, not to say horrified by the bloody woman's ability to contain the rage and the pain which ought to be taking her apart.

Merrily felt useless, ineffectual and – Jane had been right – some kind of doormat. She'd … for God's sake, she'd just *cleaned up a crime scene.* This monster was out there, and she'd mopped up his mess, destroyed any usable traces of his DNA, and she …

… needed to pray and couldn't.

Her palms were moist with sweat and she couldn't summon the will even to put them together. A kind of barren coldness in her chest. A sense of desertion, as if something had vanished from her life.

Like the meaning of it. Like a basic feel for the spiritual validity of her job, her role in this black farce. Like any kind of self-worth.

She made herself look up Adam Eastgate's number in the index. Maybe, if she hadn't been so flattened by the Bishop's early call, she'd have stood up to Mrs Morningwood, made her see some sense.

Stood up to a woman who'd been beaten up and raped? Made her 'see sense'?

Merrily shook her head almost savagely, as if this could crumble the sludge in her brain so that the fragments might resettle into some random but interpretable pattern. Then she lit a cigarette, picked up the black bakelite phone, abruptly replaced it, reverted to the mobile and made the call.

'No, the Bishop didn't phone,' Adam Eastgate said. 'He came to see us, Merrily. At home.'

'He came to your home?'

'Said he was passing – I live over at Burghill, not the kind of place you just happen to pass. What he had to say made sense, I suppose. A pity, mind.'

'He told you … what, exactly?' She was aware of her stomach contracting. *Close to an ulcer.* 'He suggested that it might be dangerous to be connected with a murder and suicide?'

'More or less.'

'For the Church or the Duchy?'

'I think he meant for us, but that would be our problem, wouldn't it?'

'Maybe suggesting it would not look good if it got out that I'd administered a blessing for Fuchsia, in a disused church, just a short time before she killed her partner? Did he say that?'

'Close.'

'And if it got out that I'd been involved at the behest of the Duchy of Cornwall ...'

'He might have said something like that as well, aye.'

Merrily had expected a reluctance to answer her questions, but it wasn't there. Eastgate wasn't obviously eager, but he wasn't erecting barriers.

'Did the Bishop tell you I'd come to the conclusion that Fuchsia had made the whole thing up? So it had all been for nothing.'

'My information is that the inquest will be told that the girl killed Felix and then took her own life while the balance of her mind was disturbed. I think that's the official wording.'

'So, erm ... did you then tell the Bishop that you didn't want us to take it any further?'

'No. I didn't say that.'

'Oh.'

'I liked Felix. I was wishing I could turn the clock back to the time we were first offered the property by the Grays. If I could unmake that deal, I'd be a happier man.'

She remembered him standing by the window in the Duchy's barn. *We don't often make mistakes.*

'Adam, when you bought it, did you know about the feud with the Gwilyms? That is, did you know the Grays were offering it to you specifically because they wanted to keep it out of the hands of the Gwilyms? That they wanted it to go to someone richer, more remote ... impregnable. Someone who couldn't be leaned on to sell it. Did you know any of that?'

'Not then, no. I learned some of it later, and I've since had a long chat with Paul Gray. Yesterday, in fact. Mr Gray's got his problems, as you may know.'

'Yes.'

'He told me he didn't want them compounded by an old feud. He didn't want – if anything should happen to him – for his wife to be left with it.'

'The feud.'

'Or the house. He wanted to apologize for unloading an unhappy place on us. He'd considered us as – like you just said – rich and remote. Hadn't realized that local people would be involved.'

'An unhappy place.'

'Well, he's not had much luck, has he? In that situation, mind, you can get a bit irrational. I told him we were taking steps. I was sorry for the man. Sorry for all of us.'

'This was *before* the Bishop …?'

'Obviously. It was … disappointing, the Bishop's attitude.' Eastgate spoke slowly, edging around something. 'I wasn't expecting that. Left us in a bit of a dilemma.'

'Has it?'

'As you know, I was in two minds, from the start, about involving the Church, but I'd told them I liked the look of you, and it couldn't do any harm.'

'Told who?'

'You must've realized there'd be people I needed to keep informed. And when the Bishop backed off, I referred the whole thing up. That is, to my immediate boss in the Duchy.'

'Right.'

'And he referred it further up.'

'How *much* further?'

'I think you know what I'm saying.'

Blimey.

'When was this?'

'First thing this morning. You should expect a call, Merrily.'

'From …?'

'I was asked to provide what information I could about you. I'm telling you this in case someone mentions it. I wouldn't like you to think we were going behind your back.'

'Thank you.'

'Somebody went on your website, found a lot about deliverance, not much about you personally.'

'Low-key, Adam. Part of the brief.'

'Your daughter's been a bit of a feisty lass, mind.'

'That isn't on the website.'

'No. It isn't.'

'If you're talking about the stones in Coleman's Meadow,' Merrily said, 'for what it's worth, I'm behind Jane all the way. I'm sorry if—'

'No, no, that's good, Merrily. That was well received. Part of our heritage. I was going to say that, meanwhile, someone else was consulted. A senior person in the Church who knows you. Thinks a lot about you, as it turns out. Anyway … you should expect a call.'

'Who was this you spoke to? In the Church.'

'Merrily, I'm just the land agent.'

'Expect a call, you said?'

'Aye.'

'Is this a call for which I need to wear my best cassock? As it were.'

'No.' Eastgate laughed. 'That's not how it works.'

When she stood up, it felt as if the scullery floor was tilting beneath her feet, and she had to get out of here, and the damn mobile was chiming again.

'*Yes.*'

'So what's the weather like over there, Reverend? Bracing?'

'Hello, Frannie.'

'The way you snapped "*yes*", just then … are my detective's acute antennae picking up an element of stress, or—?'

'What do you want?'

'Just I hadn't heard from you in a while. Wondered if you'd tripped over anything that might interest me – even mildly – in the impenetrable jungle that is Garway.'

'You mean you've finally won the fight against inner-city crime in Hereford and you're at a loose end?'

'You know, Merrily ...' Bliss paused. 'Experience has taught me that these small displays of facetiousness on your part often conceal a profound anxiety.'

'I'm a Christian. I don't get profound anxiety.'

'So nothing's happened that you might need to tell me about.'

'Nothing special at all,' Merrily said, God forgive her.

39

A Place in the Country

'LOL ROBINSON,' JIMMY HAYTER said. 'Remind me, have we met?'

'Um, very briefly at Glastonbury, way back. We only played there once. On a very small stage. You wouldn't remember.'

'Nah, I *wouldn't* remember. I don't like Glastonbury.'

Lol said nothing. He hadn't imagined there was anybody who didn't like Glastonbury.

What he was sure of was that he didn't much like this room, with its lofty cathedral windows and an elaborately carved ceiling bulging with lumpen cherubs blowing trumpets. Victorian Gothic. Unsubtly different from the original soaring, arboreal Gothic, in Lol's view. Built not so much to elevate as dominate.

Intimidate, even.

'Levin – he back on the piss, Lol?'

'Is somebody saying he is?'

Lol had a four-seater sofa to himself, about the size of his truck. He'd shuffled himself to one end, hunched forward so that his feet would actually reach the floor. Lord Stourport was in a well-worn leather armchair, close to the vast open fireplace, half a tree trunk sizzling there like a whole pig at a pig roast.

'Just he wasn't very lucid on the phone,' Stourport said, 'about what you wanted.'

'He drinks coffee. It was probably a caffeine high. And maybe I hadn't explained it very well.'

'Let's hope you can now, then, cocker.'

Hayter had a leg thrown over one of the arms of his chair, revealing a small split in the crotch of his jeans. He was squat and overweight, but not too much of it was fat. His hair was dense and white and wedged on his forehead, a weighty awning over his deep-set penetrating dark brown eyes.

'This is not easy, Jimmy,' Lol said.

Hayter's eyebrow lifted at the familiarity, probably on account of this was not Jimmy's drum, *this* was the seat of Lord Stourport.

Very Hayter, all the same, this Victorian fake. More powerful, in its heavy-duty way, than some authentic medieval castles rendered romantic by time and erosion. Very death-metal. Lol had counted four staff, including the guy in the leather coat and a gardener in a greenhouse, and he wondered if there was also a formal butler somewhere, in a butler suit, like the guy in the *Celeb* strip in *Private Eye*.

'So you've come up from Herefordshire,' Hayter said. 'Where your girlfriend is the official exorcist. Working for the council or what?'

He wasn't smiling. Hard to work out whether he was taking the piss or this was genuine ignorance. Best played down the line.

'The Diocese. The Bishop. She's an ordained priest.'

'Right.' Stourport nodded. 'So if I rang the Bishop's office …?'

'You want the number?'

'No, I'll trust you. What's she do, basically?'

Lol told him, patiently, about the cure of troubled souls and troubled premises. Like the Master House at Garway.

Lord Stourport leaned back, contemplating the cowboy boot on the end of the leg over the chair arm.

'I'm a bit hazy. Would that be the tumbledown shit-hole a bunch of us rented for the summer, way back?'

As if Prof hadn't told him and he hadn't already done some hard thinking.

'I heard it was you who paid the rent,' Lol said. 'And it was quite a bit longer than a summer.'

'Summers could last for a couple of years, back then,' Stourport said. 'Back when we were young.'

'I think this one got a bit autumnal. Quite quickly.'

Hayter's eyes refocused.

'You're not here to try and blackmail me, are you?'

'No,' Lol said. 'Sincerely I'm not. I'm just hoping you could give me some background. It's like … people are saying it's disturbed now, but is there any history? My friend, sometimes people ask her to clean up a place, and they're making it up for some reason. Or there's an element of delusion. Or they're not telling her the whole story.'

'How would I know the whole story?'

'Maybe you wouldn't. But you were an outsider living there. No local pressure to cover anything up.'

'She goes to that kind of trouble?' Stourport wore a grimace of disbelief. 'A priest?'

'Either you do the job properly …'

'Because if you're bullshitting me …'

'Why would I?'

'… Because if you *are*, I should just tell you, any hint of anything I say to you appears in the press, you are truly fucked, cocker. I'll come after you. Well, not me *personally*, obviously, but someone.'

'You've found that approach helps, generally?' Lol said.

'Sometimes it does.' Stourport waved a languid hand. 'Go on. Ask what you want.'

'Did you get any feeling the place was – I have to say this – haunted?'

'Could be.'

'Really?'

'It was *old*. I mean, *this* pile's old, after a fashion – built on the site of the original Norman castle – *and* it's haunted. Shapes seen out of the corner of an eye, on the stairs, in the long gallery. Nobody should give *me* that all-in-the-mind bullshit. But I would have to say this house isn't haunted like *that* house was haunted. Or maybe the drugs were too new and lovely, then.'

Lol smiled. Stourport brought his leg down from the chair arm, inched the chair closer to the fire.

'Doubt if I'd've got through it without the drugs, thinking back. Who's living there now? Let me guess – couple of gay hairdressers from Islington, weekends only.'

'Nobody's living there at the moment. But it's been bought by the Duchy of Cornwall.'

'*Has* it, by God?'

'The plan is to restore it. Sensitively.'

'*Right.*' Lord Stourport shifted in his chair. 'Now you're starting to make sense. They have weight, those guys. And money.'

'And there are complications.'

Lol told him about the deaths. No reason to hold any of that back, not as if it hadn't been in the papers. Stourport drew in his lips like he was about to whistle, but he didn't comment.

'So you're just the boyfriend,' he said when Lol sat back. 'You don't meddle yourself?'

'Are you kidding?'

'You mean this is all for … *lerve*?'

Lol shrugged lightly.

'We've been educated out of all that nonsense, the aristocracy. I tell you, Robinson, most of us were mightily relieved when punk came in and we no longer had to babble on about peace and *lerve*. Except for poor Charles, of course, who's at least half-hippie. Never could stand the man, personally, but if he's had the Master House unloaded on him one can only sympathize. What will she do, this woman of yours?'

'She'll say some prayers. Bless the premises. Or maybe organize a small service, a Requiem for the people who died, with people there who might still have problems with the house and people who had problems with it in the past. You could come if you wanted.'

'No thanks.'

'Your commune's been mentioned, anyway.'

'It was never a commune. Nothing so formal.'

'Can you tell me about it?'

'I can tell you what I remember, but what I remember might have very little to do with what actually happened.'

'Like that, huh?'

'Very much like that, cocker.'

On the sunlit square, Merrily felt like a tourist. The last couple of nights were probably as long as she'd spent away from here since they'd moved in. You came back, it made you blink – the black and white houses and shops unexpectedly exotic in the Lucozade light of an autumn morning.

Or was that because she was afraid she was going to lose it all? Didn't even feel safe in her own house any more.

Which *wasn't* her own house. Which was the Church's house. The Church, as represented, in her life, by the Bishop. The Bishop behind whose back …

She was alone on the square, a few people around the shops, none of them close enough to have to greet – God, had it come to this? She slid into the familiar sanctuary of the market hall, took out her mobile, switched it on to find it frantic with messages.

There was a bunch of calls from Lol, who was on his way to … *where?* She listened. She called him back at once. His phone was switched off, she left a message: 'Lol, I don't *know* what it's best to ask Lord Stourport. This is getting messier than you could ever imagine. All I can say, just play it by ear, maybe don't even mention Mary Linden, because I've only had that from one source which I … don't entirely trust. I'm sorry.'

And then there was Sophie: two cautious *call me back* messages from her. Merrily called the gatehouse.

'Are you alone?'

'For the moment. Merrily, I need to apol—'

'Doesn't matter. I understand. Sophie, did *you* tell the Bishop that I'd finally concluded that Fuchsia had made it all up?'

'Well, it's certainly what he *wanted* me to tell him.'

'When was this?'

'Last night. When he arrived on our doorstep in a state of some agitation. He instructed me quite formally not to call you until *he* had. I gave him until nine-thirty then I began to leave messages. I'm sorry, Merrily, he's still my boss, however … eccentric he's become.'

'Well, look, I'm back at the vicarage, and there've been some developments, which I'll explain in due course.'

'You sound upset.'

'I'm OK. I'll explain it face to face, when the Bishop's not on your back or mine. You said he was agitated. Why? Like he was getting pressure?'

Sophie didn't reply.

'I'll tell you something else. He suggested that the Duchy itself would be happier if I forgot all about the Master House. He indicated he'd had this from Adam Eastgate. It wasn't true.'

'I see.'

'Who might be leaning on him, Sophie? Could it be Canterbury?'

'I certainly haven't taken any calls from Church House, but that means nothing. Ah—'

'Who else? Come on, Sophie, who else can you think of with any influence over the Bishop? Who the Bishop might be *intimidated* by?'

Sophie said, 'Perhaps I could call you back a little later, Reverend Longbeach.'

'Oh.'

He was there. He'd walked in on her. Merrily killed the line and walked out on the other side of the market hall, emerging next to a grey car parked tidily in its shade.

She'd wanted to ask if Sophie knew – or could find out – who exactly had been tapped for information about Hereford deliverance ... and her ... and Jane. Who was the other minister consulted by the Duchy?

Well, obviously this described Huw Owen. But Huw would have told her. No way Huw would not have told her.

She'd call him anyway. She scrolled through the list on the mobile. She should call him now.

And then Merrily closed up the phone with a snap. Stood staring at the grey Lexus parked next to the market hall, noting, on the back seat, a lavishly labelled case of Italian leather. Siân Callaghan-Clarke's gloves on the dash.

'We were not kids,' Lord Stourport said. 'That's too easy. We were young, voracious adults, the world spread out in front of us like a picnic. We had the power of youth. And that *is* a power, because it comes without responsibility except to yourself. Well, that's commonplace now, that's almost the norm – Crowley's line, *Do what thou wilt shall be the whole of the law*, that's every fucker's motto now, nobody thinks twice. Back then, it was new and risky and seductive.'

Lol was quite fascinated by the way Stourport/Hayter would uncon-
sciously switch from officer-class drawl to street-hard pseudo-cockney
without a breath in between.

'Actually, it was quite a sad time for a lot of them,' Stourport said.
'The hippie dream all gone to shit, with nothing to replace it, no real
energy. Everybody seemed to be sprawled around, stoned and directionless. It never bothered me. I was quite happy to be stoned and
directionless for a while.'

'When *was* this?'

'Seventy-three, seventy-four. I'd dropped out of Cambridge in
disgrace but with a portfolio of music-biz contacts par fucking excel-
lence, and a working knowledge of how to make money that would
subsequently win the reluctant respect of even my old man – living here
in faded splendour, buckets catching the drips, sitting in his overcoat in
winter watching his black and white TV surrounded by old masters.
Imagine the ignominy of having your heritage saved by the ill-gotten
millions of the disreputable punk impresario son. Poor old bastard
never recovered.'

'How long've you been here?'

'Fifteen, sixteen years. It was sudden, really. Ironically, living a warm,
damp-free existence seemed to do for the old man's health. But of
course all this was still far into the future when we moved into the
Master House.'

'How did you find out about the house?'

'Can't remember. I mean, it was that time when bored young people
of my generation would look up and go hey, let's start again, let's go out
into the sticks, be pioneers. Ronnie Lane decamping to Shropshire,
touring in a gypsy caravan, bucolic bliss – that was a myth as well, of
course, even if you've got the money, if you have land it needs to be
worked. Scores of idle freaks lying in the grass – a *spade*? What's that
about?'

The man in the leather coat put his head round the door, looking
pointedly at Lol, but Stourport waved him away.

Lol said, 'Did you know anything about the history of the place when
you took it? The Knights Templar?'

'Robinson, I knew *nothing* about the Knights frigging Templar. Had a flat in London with my girlfriend at the time, Siggi, and we had a lot of parties which were – as we used to say – busted by the pigs, on no less than three occasions. It was getting tiresome, and my friend Pierre Markham – you know who I'm talking about?'

'No.'

'The merchant banker? Never mind. Anyway, it was Pierre who said why don't we get a place in the country? Well, I'd been born in a place in the bleeding country, so the idea held no particular magic for me. Besides which, although I had plenty of readies, I didn't really have a lump sum to put down on a property, but Pierre's saying, "No, we *lease* somewhere" … That was Siggi and me, Pierre and his lady, and a guy called Mickey Sharpe who was basically our dealer, kept us supplied with whatever we needed. In quantity.'

He flung his leg back over the chair arm, lounging back, slowly shaking his head.

'Actually, I remember now. What put us on to the Master House, it was just an ad in *Country Life* or *The Lady*. It didn't actually *say* No Hippies, but it probably did no harm at all reverting to being The Hon. until the deal was done. Anyway, we move into this hovel – throw some money at it, scatter the sheepskins and the Afghan fucking rugs, set up the important item, this monster B&O stereo. And … it was summer and life passed in a bit of a haze. Mickey had a van, and he'd go off to London and come back with the stuff, early mornings, and we had a secret stash we called the Grotto of Dreams, as you did in those days.'

'What broke the idyll?'

'What makes you think it broke?'

'They always do,' Lol said.

'This one didn't *break*, it just got diverted. Got a lot more intense very quickly. After some weeks we discover this guy called Mathew is living with us.'

'You *discover* he's living with you?'

'He was just there. You know? People came and went. Any problems we had, plumbing and whatever, Mickey would fix it for some guy to attend to it. Mickey was an excellent man, he'd go out and find the right people, the ones on the fringe who, in return for a small package, wouldn't spread it round that we were, you know, dangerously subversive. Then this guy Mathew – Mat, with one T, he was very particular about that – your name, the number of letters it had – very important, the numerological correspondences, all this shit.'

'Bit mystical?'

'*I* thought, at first, he was just some fucking gardener Pierre'd hired. This messianic-looking guy – not much older than any of us but he had the look. Mat Phobe, he called himself, obviously not his real name. But who used their real names in those days? You called yourself what you thought you ought to be called, what would reflect your spirit. So it was a while before we became aware that Mat Phobe was actually in charge of us all.'

'How do you mean, "in charge"?'

'Yeah, exactly. I don't believe we knew. You did one weird thing, weirdness became the norm. Especially if you were getting a buzz. But the Templars – it was Mat knew about the Templars. We'd all been down this weird little church and wandered around, but it hadn't meant that much to us. There wasn't all this shit about the Templars all over the media in those days. Medieval history wasn't cool. *Stone Age* was cool, the golden age of ley lines when the land was irrigated by mysterious energies that could blow you away. We knew all about that, but we knew diddly-squat about the Templars. Except for Mat.'

And so it came out, Lol wishing there was some way he could record it all for Merrily.

Mat came and went. He'd go off for weeks at a time and come back with some new idea. Mat had said they were sitting on energies the like of which they couldn't imagine. Mat had said the Master House was at the centre of forbidden secrets, all this stuff that gave a deep and wonderful significance to their lives when they heard about it, stoned.

He'd told them about the Templars being suppressed because of their advanced esoteric knowledge. He knew about Jacques de Molay, Grand Master of the Order, coming to Garway in 1294. Mat was convinced de Molay had stayed in the Master House. He was also convinced that the Grand Master had brought something with him.

Lol sat up.

'Like what?'

'He reckoned Garway was … I dunno, the chosen place? He said this guy Jacques could already see the writing on the wall, knew that all these kings and popes were suspicious of the Order and jealous of their wealth and their influence and the secret knowledge they had – all this *Da Vinci Code* shit.'

'*Is* it shit?'

'Probably. But we had no point of reference back then, anyway – the book that raised the whole bloodline of Christ issue, *The Holy Blood and the Holy Grail*, wouldn't come out for several years.'

'So are you saying Mat knew something of this *before* it was in the public domain?'

'Oh man …' Jimmy Hayter raised his eyes to the cherubs '… you listened to that guy, you thought there was nothing he didn't know. He had all these charts and symbols and glyphs and astral correspondences and all this impenetrable balls. He was the high priest, the adept. Looking back, I can see that he was probably full of shit, but we didn't question it at the time because the women found it, shall we say, very alluring. At first.'

'So what did he think he was going to find?'

'Treasure. Money … gold. Whatever. The Templars had massive wealth. They were a multinational enterprise. They ran a banking system across Europe and the Middle East. Mat'd got it into his head that de Molay had chosen Garway as a hiding place if the deal went down in France. Garway made sense, he'd say, because it was not only remote, it was on the Welsh border and the Templars were well in with the Welsh. And the Scots – they rode with Robert the Bruce at Bannockburn.'

'Mat thought there was Templar treasure stashed at Garway?'

'He thought we were sitting on it.'

'At the Master House?'

'The *Grand* Master House. Which was built soon after the church, just far enough away that nobody would suspect.'

'And he thought the treasure was still there?'

'Oh, Jeez …' Jimmy Hayter laughed. 'We were all over the place after that, tapping walls, looking for signs and symbols. Pierre and his woman, whatever her name was, they'd gone by then, and some other guy was there and I remember him being chased out of the church by the vicar after taking a crowbar to one of the long stones that were originally the lids of Templar coffins. I remember Mat gave him a talking-to, and then he gathered us all around and he said we were going about it all wrong. He said the only way to find out the secret was to get onto the Templar wavelength.'

Suddenly, Stourport was back, and his face seemed less relaxed now, his eyes harder.

'That was when it got intense. That was when we started on the magic.'

40

Frail

MERRILY WENT BACK to check on Mrs Morningwood, listening outside the door of the guest room. All she could hear was Roscoe, padding around on the other side. Once, he growled.

Twice she went back out to the square, and Siân's car was still there. Just after midday, she rang Huw Owen from the scullery and asked him straight out if he'd been approached by the Duchy.

'I never thought you had so few friends, lass. No, it's not me.'

'Then who?'

'Doesn't have to be somebody you actually know. Could just be somebody as knows *you*. Somebody as knows exactly what you've been doing the past couple of years. Could even be Merlin the Wizard.'

Huw's name for the Welshman who was Archbishop of Canterbury. Huw seemed oddly – for Huw – fond of him, which might have been down to their shared affection for The Incredible String Band, old Celtic hippies sticking together.

'Help me out here,' Merrily said. 'What are they likely to want?'

Huw said. 'You might remember what I told you about royalty and the Church. Reference to seismic shifts and little folks getting dropped down crevices?'

'I remember.'

'Follow your conscience but watch your back.'

'And did it work?' Lol asked. 'The magic?'

He could feel the atmosphere hardening. He felt like he was stirring cement and running out of water to soften the mix. Soon Jimmy

Hayter's memories would become clogged, Lord Stourport less accommodating, and when his curiosity about Merrily ran out it would be time to go.

'It was *magick* with a "k",' Hayter said.

'Aleister Crowley put the "k" on the end, didn't he?'

'A tosser.'

'But an influential tosser,' Lol said. 'I'm told.'

'My dear friend ...' Stourport heaved himself up on an elbow. 'If you thought I was going to tell you what we were *doing* ...'

'Well, I did, actually,' Lol said. 'Hoped, anyway. It was a long time ago, after all.'

Crowley. Lol remembered a discussion he'd once had in a flat in Ross-on-Wye with a woman called Cola French who had hung out with some weird people and had told him about ...

'The OTO? That was something to do with Templars, wasn't it? *Ordo Templi Orientis*?'

Stourport eyeing him balefully now, sitting up in the chair.

'Somebody's been talking, have they?'

'I was just thinking Crowley ... Templars ...'

'Crowley was into them, yeah.'

'And Mat Phobe was into Crowley?'

Stourport said. 'You want a drink?'

'No, thanks, I'm working tonight.'

'All the more reason, my dear.'

'Not when you're your own roadie.'

'Jeez, you poor, sad bleeder. Why do you bother?'

Lol shrugged. Stourport was quiet for a while, looking up at the cherubs with their trumpets. Then he got up and went over to a Chinese lacquer cabinet with dragons on it, came back with a heavy glass and a squat bottle of tequila.

'All right.' He sat down again. 'But don't take any of this as gospel – I was only half there.'

It was clear that the rambling reminiscence was over. Hayter was being monitored by Stourport now, and there was more care, less free-flow as he talked about Mat Phobe telling them how the Order of the

Poor Knights had been officially stamped out, its churches closed, its assets seized, its leaders burned.

How, in spite of this, it had never really gone away. The Templars had gone underground under different names, their secrets passed on through Rosicrucianism and Freemasonry and some of the magical orders which had manifested in the late nineteenth and early twentieth centuries. Yeah, including the OTO.

'He said he could show us,' Stourport said. 'He said we'd never look back. That was when Pierre split. He'd had a bad experience. We got up one morning and he was flailing around, saying we were all evil and we were laying ourselves open to eternal damnation – he'd been brought up as a Catholic and it taints you for life.'

'What had you done?'

Stourport shook his head. Lol thought about the girl called Cola French, who had worked in a bookshop.

'The OTO was into sex magic.'

Cola French had said, *You use the build-up to an orgasm to channel and focus energy for a particular purpose and then … boom.*

'With women,' Lol said, 'or men. Or on your own.'

'Two out of three was good enough for me. Mat said we could employ supernatural … this sounds like utter shit now, but you have to remember the chemicals we were absorbing. He said we could follow a path to enlightenment. Focus our will-power, strengthened by sexual tension. Like, for instance, the Templars had this girdle kind of thing they wore in bed as an aid to chastity. He showed us how to use something similar, only this was to prolong an orgasm.' Hayter smiled ruefully. 'A guy who thinks he can show you how to come for ever, you'll follow him anywhere.'

'What was his background?'

'Never knew. Narcotics make you incurious. He was just there, you know? And, yeah, we might have plumbed what some people may consider the depths of depravity, except it didn't seem like depravity at the time. Me, I was up to here with peace and *lerve* and ready to get steeped in the dirty stuff.'

'I'm not really getting this,' Lol said. 'How it ties in to the location …

the Master House. How was this leading you to whatever you wanted to find?'

Lord Stourport sipped his tequila. Sun flooded one of the vast Gothic windows.

'You call something up and you ask it. A spirit, a demon. You do a ritual to invoke whatever you think can tell you what you want to know. I remember there was a blood sacrifice once – Mat sent Mickey Sharpe to steal a cockerel from one of the farms. I didn't care too much for that, fucking blood was everywhere. That was when Siggi split. I think Mat was glad. Siggi was getting a little flaky.'

'So that was just the two of you left? You and Mat Phobe. Two men?'

'Oh, none of *that* stuff, old boy. Anyway, other people were there by then. Mickey had discovered a source of ...' he smiled '... Farm girls.'

Lol said, 'A *source*?'

'Country girls who knew their way around. Country girls are under-valued, as if they're naive or something compared to your hard-nosed city chicks. Not the case. Bulls and cows, rams and ewes, they've lived with it since they could walk. Not easily shocked, is what I'm saying. We were not corrupting innocents.'

'Who was this? You, Mat ... this Mickey?'

'I remember Mickey thought that, given the circumstances, he ought to be paid more. I remember that.'

'What did you do?'

'Paid him, of course. After all, we were paying the girls.'

'Paying them to ...?'

'Go a little further. And keep their mouths shut ... well ...' Hayter chuckled. 'Some of the time. No problems there, like I said. They'd never seen that kind of money before. I want to stress this: no corrup-tion of innocents.'

'You make it sound like they were ... working girls.'

'And that wouldn't happen in the sticks, would it?' Stourport put his glass down on the edge of the stone fireplace. 'Don't knock it, Robinson, it has its uses.'

So they were paying local girls to take part in ceremonial magic involving sexual practices – the kind of practices you wouldn't get your own girlfriend into no matter what she'd taken.

He said, 'How could you be sure they wouldn't talk about it?'

'Put it this way: they never did. You wouldn't want to, would you? Not if you'd been paid more for a couple of nights than you'd normally earn in a month. And like I said, country girls … and none of it was illegal, they weren't under age. I was more worried about the men. I didn't want any more men, but Mat … there was one guy Mat was keen to involve. I thought he was a pain in the arse. Fortunately, he didn't live in.'

'Local guy?'

'Oh yeah. His family used to own the house. Had a name that was ridiculously Welsh. He didn't *sound* Welsh. Mat soft-pedalled him for a while, until it was clear he was up for it. He didn't smoke so we gave him pills and got one of the girls to bake hash brownies, which loosened him up a lot. We got him talking about the house and what had happened there … I remember one night, him saying to me, "You think *you*'re a nob … I'm royalty, man." He was a pompous shit. Bloody Welsh and their upside-down inferiority complex. Didn't even sound Welsh.'

'What did he mean, royalty?'

'Oh … his family was descended from the Welsh princes, all this bollocks. But Mat was interested. He constructed some kind of ritual this bloke had to be at the centre of. Some necromantic thing, to put him in touch with his ancestors. We taped it. Candles and incense and a magic circle and a tape recorder. He went into some sort of trance, and all this balls came out in Welsh. He swore he couldn't speak Welsh. Actually quite shattered, I remember, when we played it back to him.'

'This was in the house?'

'This was in the main room, yeah. Maybe you need to talk to *him*. Wish I could remember his name. William something-unpronounce-ably-Welsh? Tell your lady to talk to him, if he's still alive. Make the bastard squirm.'

'So did you ever manage to contact his ancestors?'

'I don't know. I had to go back to London to meet my father who I did *not* want coming down to Garway. Get out the suit, drive up to

London. Would've stayed in London, if I'd had any sense, but I was keen to get back. Still had the hots for one of the girls, who'd been away and come back.'

'One of the farm girls?'

'Nah.' Stourport sniffed. 'The farm girls, they were … they didn't … they weren't bothered. They weren't *fazed*. They just accepted it. And the money, of course. No, this was actually a black girl. Strange as it may seem, I'd never had a black girl. At the time.'

'Such sheltered lives people had, back then,' Lol said. Stourport scowled.

'Wasn't to be, anyway. I'd been back from London one … no, maybe two nights, when the Herefordshire Constabulary paid us an early-morning call.'

'I think I heard about that.'

'Pulled me and the faithful Mickey. Bastard Hereford magistrates sent me to jail. Served nine weeks. A nightmare. Mat and the Welsh guy got away … and the black girl. She was the only woman there at the time. I didn't think about this then, but maybe it was a blessing for her, she was getting quite frail. Didn't have the stamina of the other slappers.'

'They used her in rituals? Sex rituals?'

'Robinson, watch my lips and remember this: all I did at the Master House was pay for the drugs and expend some testosterone. The so-called magic passed over my head. I didn't believe in it, then, and I don't believe in it now. It was libidinal spice.'

'So you never found the gold. Or whatever it was.'

'Need you ask?'

'What happened to the tapes?'

'Mat took them, I suppose. If I should come across one, I'll let you know. Or anything else that occurs to me. Just write down your phone number on there.'

Hayter picked up a folded copy of *The Independent* from beside his chair, tossed it at Lol, who wrote down his mobile number. The chances of Hayter getting back to him were about as likely as *Alien* going platinum. He looked up.

'So the girl—?'

'She was black. It was a novelty. She was … succulent.'

There was a coldness in the room and it seemed to gather in Lol's spine and he sat back against a cushion. Stourport finished his drink and didn't pour another.

'Don't expect me to go any further than that – not that any of it's spectacularly obscene in comparison with some of my later escapades. Most of which have been extremely well chronicled, as you know.'

'What happened to them? The ones that got away.'

'Dunno. I was in the slammer. A nightmare. You couldn't even get decent dope in British prisons back then.'

'You didn't hear from Mat?'

'No. Dead, now. Somebody told me he'd gone out to the Middle East or somewhere and he'd died or been killed. I wasn't sorry. He was a cold bastard.'

'What about Mary?'

'Dunno where she went. I was in the pokey, like I said. When I came out, just about the last place I was likely to go near was the Master House. In fact—'

Lord Stourport broke off, slowly put his glass back on the hearth and looked out from under his shelf of white hair, levelling at Lol a steady gaze that went on for a long time. All the time it took for Lol to realize that he'd said the name Mary and Jimmy Hayter had only ever mentioned a nameless black girl.

41

Time of No Reply

On the back of the stone, it said:

NOW WE RISE

AND WE ARE EVERYWHERE.

'Where are you now?' Merrily was asking in Lol's ear.

'In a churchyard. Under an oak tree. Tried to call earlier but your phone was busy. All the time.'

On the grave, in front of the stone, strewn like the fallen petals of plastic flowers, Lol had counted fourteen plectrums.

Above them, on the small, grey memorial, a blunted plectrum of stone in the grass, the names of MOLLY DRAKE and RODNEY DRAKE and their dates.

At the top, the name of the son who had predeceased them both. His dates: 1948 – 1974.

'Churchyard, where?'

'Um, Tanworth. Tanworth in Arden. In Warwickshire.'

Pause.

'Lol, that's …'

'Nick's village.'

'Oh God, Lol.'

'It's OK.' His glasses had misted; he took them off. 'It was on the way. I saw the signpost. Had to stop, obviously, never having been. Maybe – you know – avoiding it.'

'Of course you had to stop.' Slightly awkward pause. 'What do you … I mean, what's it like. You know, the …?'

'Very quiet and modest, really. Not unhappy. Listen, there are things I need to tell you. Lord Stourport.'

'You saw him? I tried to reach you.'

'Um … you won't find this edifying.'

Lol put his glasses back on, took out a folded tour-schedule, full of the notes he'd scribbled in the truck, back near the burger van, and told her what he'd learned from Jimmy Hayter.

Standing next to the grave of Nick Drake and his parents, decent, prosperous residents of this increasingly wealthy village, while the sun was hiding in the oak tree, making an autumn bonfire amongst the turning leaves.

Merrily made notes on the sermon pad.

She wrote down the names:

PIERRE MARKHAM

MICKEY SHARPE

SIGGI—?

MAT PHOBE?

DE MOLAY – TREASURE?

With a kind of mental shiver, she wrote down,

CROWLEY

OTO

And then,

GROTTO OF DREAMS???

And, in rapid sucession,

BLOOD SACRIFICE … COUNTRY GIRLS.

… PAID

Underlining this, remembering Mary's letter: *it's only your body and look at the money you're getting.*

Because he was safely out of there, in the sanctuary of the Tanworth churchyard, at the shrine of his first tragic hero, she was able to smile at the way Lol had blown it, dropping Mary's name when Stourport had referred only to a black girl.

She wrote,

FRAIL.

And then, finally,

SYCHARTH????

Amid the distaste, an unexpected fizz of excitement as Merrily put down her pen.

'Lol, did Lord Stourport miss something when he was in London, do you think?'

'I can't help wondering if he even *went* to London,' Lol said. 'Or if, whatever happened towards the end, he was effectively dissociating himself from it. Giving himself an alibi. And the way he was stressing that he was only in it for the sex, wasn't really involved in the ritual magic.'

'Was that true, do you think, or just a blokey thing to say?'

'Well, it *was* blokey, but … the sex, the magic, I don't think you can divide them. I think he *did* get off on all that. You sensed a kind of pride. After a while, he was enjoying talking about it – his decadent youth, before he had the responsibility of property and a title dumped on him. I think he'd do it again tomorrow if there was another Mat Phobe around to set it up.'

'But he never went into detail?'

'No. You'd probably be looking at whatever rituals Crowley did in that context.'

'Templars. He was always intrigued by the Templars.'

Thinking of the time, while she was waiting for the first deliverance course at Huw Owen's chapel in the Beacons, when she'd been reading heavily about magic, and Crowley in particular. All the books came back to Crowley, his attempts to raise spiritual and demonic entities, representing various energies – sexual arousal going hand-round-cock with higher consciousness. His ambition to become godlike.

In a seedy kind of way.

She remembered once making the mistake of reading in bed about how, at his *abbey* in Sicily, Crowley had supervised a ritual which involved a woman having sex with a goat, culminating in Crowley cutting the goat's throat so that the blood washed over the woman.

It was about the magical energy of blood. Crowley liked to call them Scarlet Women, and that was how they'd end up, the sick bastard.

'The Welsh guy,' Lol said. '*He* must've been there at the end.'

'Yes. That's your big discovery, Lol, and I'm truly grateful for this. I need to talk to the guy, don't I? If it's who I think it is.'

Was she going to talk to Sycharth, in defiance of the Bishop?

Oh yes. Oh God, yes.

Lol said, 'You foresee him reacting with the same kind of half-suppressed glee as Jimmy Hayter?'

'Not exactly. He's a big businessman in Hereford now. He owns the Centurion on Roman Road.'

'Do *not* go on your own.'

'What's he going to do, sacrifice me?'

'You need a witness.'

'I just want to invite him to a small service.'

God, was she still going to *do* that? A deliverance swansong?

'You're not going today, are you?' Lol said.

'I'll call him, make an appointment.'

'Get Sophie to do it. Makes it seem more official.'

Merrily said nothing. It would take too long to explain.

'You're OK, aren't you?' Lol said. 'I mean, you're feeling all right?'

'I'm feeling surprisingly well. *Surprisingly* well. What time will you be home?

'Gig's at nine.'

'Decent gig?'

'Not bad.'

'Do this one for Nick,' Merrily said. 'You know what I mean? And when you get in, come round. I don't care what time.'

'Well, then.' Lol knelt down next to the grave. 'Made it at last.'

Two blokes in the same business, one who went down, one who – having begun his career by shamelessly copying the other – had somehow come through.

This was silly. Embarrassing. Futile. Not only did he not know what to say, he wasn't even sure who he was addressing. He was now over a decade older than Nick had been when he'd died alone in his bedroom in a big house in this village, from an overdose of antidepressants.

301

Having already overdosed on cannabis and commercial failure. The house was called Far Leys, and apparently was quite easy to find, but Lol had decided that he wasn't going to.

If Nick Drake was alive now he'd be nearly sixty. What would he *sound* like now?

Now we rise and we are everywhere.

Could hear him breathily singing those words on the summery 'From the Morning', the last song on the last album released in his lifetime.

Like a prophecy.

The last one. His songs had always been full of dark prescience, if you wanted to hear it – as if he'd seen the design of his short life laid out in symbols. He was the *fruit tree* that would only flourish when his body was in the ground, when the *pink moon* had taken his life after the years of the *black-eyed dog* howling at his door, asking for more, giving nothing.

This man who could stand in silence for two hours on the periphery of a party, like a half-formed apparition. Some people had actually seen his possible suicide as part of a life-plan. Others thought he was just plain screwed up and smoking too much dope.

Maybe, it was often said, a woman might have saved him, if he'd been able to let a woman in. Or a man? Gay men liked to suggest that Nick – who, despite his elegance, his good looks and his profession, never seemed to have had a physical relationship – had been in the closet.

The most likely answer was that he was too well brought up in the careful, post-war Agatha Christie Fifties, too plain uptight middle English. *I can't really imagine Nick having sex with anyone* – a friend, quoted in the latest biography – *because he would have to take his clothes off and he was always far too shy.*

This in the Seventies, when Jimmy Hayter, close to the same age as Nick, and actually far more upper-class, had been *up to here with peace and lerve and ready to get steeped in the dirty stuff.*

Jimmy Hayter, who was Lord Stourport, who hadn't spoken to Lol again as Lol stood up, murmured 'thank you', nodded and walked away like he was walking on an open blade. Hayter's body never moving, only his stare coldly following him to the door.

'You'd have encountered people like him, right?' Lol said. 'I mean, you were just a little too late – especially with your background – to have been a real hippie.'

Lol picked up one of the plectrums, tortoiseshell, and then put it back, finding he'd rearranged them into a rough semicircle around the gravestone.

'You came in at the wrong end of the dream. When everybody was waking up into the cold daylight, trying to pull the covers over their heads and it was … all going rancid under there.'

Those sublime albums bombing, one after the other. No reason for it; they were massive these days, the songs ubiquitous.

Now he *had* risen and he *was* everywhere.

The last prophesy fulfilled. There was nothing left to say.

Lol stood up. He had no plectrum to leave. Hadn't used one in years, just his fingers and his nails on light strings.

As he walked away, a slow breeze passed through the brittling leaves on the oak tree, like a low sigh, and Lol turned and thought for a moment that a tall figure was shadowed under the tree. Slightly stooped. Raising a languid hand in a brief, shy salute.

Lol smiled and waved once and ran out of the churchyard, all the way back to where he'd left the Animal at the side of the road in a quiet lane with trees.

Only it wasn't there.

Using the landline, Merrily rang The Centurion in Roman Road.

A woman said, 'I'm sorry, Mr Gwilym's in a meeting. Who shall I say called?'

'When will the meeting be over?'

'I'm afraid I don't know. Can I take a—?'

'I'll call back,' Merrily said, the mobile starting to chime at her elbow.

'It's Adam Eastgate, Merrily. About that call I warned you to expect.'

'It hasn't happened yet.'

'Well, no. As it turns out, this is it.'

'Sorry?'

'I've been asked to make the call rather than somebody whose voice you wouldn't recognize. Bottom line, Merrily, I have to ask you if you ever do any work ... privately, like.'

'*Privately?*'

'You know what I'm saying.'

'Independently of the Diocese?'

'And on a confidential basis.'

'Like what?'

'Like the service in the Master House. Paul Gray says he'll go along with it, though perhaps I'm not the best person to make an approach to Mr Gwilym.'

'You want me to go ahead, despite the Bishop.'

'It's not seen as a confrontational thing. Just something we feel should take place, and if it's done quietly there won't be any of the problems Bernard was afraid of.'

'Who else would be there?'

'Me.'

'Anyone else?'

'It wouldn't be wise for there to be ... anyone else.'

'This is a tough one, Adam.'

'Aye. I can see that.'

'If I did it,' Merrily said, 'and it got out ... it could get me in a lot of trouble.'

Because there was a difference here. If she just went ahead with it on her own, it would be merely a small rebellion, out of conscience.

Where the royals are concerned – the royals and Canterbury – the smallest rumour can cause a seismic shift, and little folks like you can get dropped down the nearest crevice.

'It won't get out, Merrily. Nobody wants it to get out.'

'And the idea's been approved, has it, at the highest level?'

'I referred it up. The suggestion came back.'

'From?'

'Just from higher up.'

'When did they have in mind?'

'Soon as possible. Soon as you can get the people together. What's the earliest, do you think?'

'I suppose …' Merrily thought about it, counting days. 'I suppose the earliest might be the day after tomorrow. That would be … Friday?'

She looked at the calendar and her gaze caught the sermon pad, propped up now against the computer, open to the list of names: PIERRE MARKHAM … MICKEY SHARPE … SIGGI—?

'That would be Friday the twelfth?' Adam Eastgate said. 'I'm writing it down.'

MAT PHOBE?

'Or Saturday, I suppose,' Merrily said.

'The thirteenth.'

It was like one of those damn signposts being erected in the scullery, hammered into the floor in front of the desk.

MAT PHOBE?

Something about that name. Not a real name, obviously.

'Think about it and let me know early tomorrow,' Adam Eastgate said. 'OK?'

'OK. I will.' Her stare travelling up and down the names, alighting on—

SYCHARTH????

'Adam, tell me something.'

'If I can.'

'The threats received by the Duchy—'

'Oh, now—'

'It'll go no further, I promise. Come on. Someone's given you the green light to trust me.'

'Where did you get this?'

'From Jonathan Long.'

Which she had, in a way.

'Wales,' Merrily said. 'He was talking about Wales.'

'Aw, look, it was rubbish, Merrily. They decided it was all complete rubbish. A joke.'

'What sort of threats were they? Please. It's important.'

'I have to refer these things up, you know? They have to be looked into. Once we got them translated ... the grammar wasn't even right, apparently. I can't tell you any more.'

'OK. Thanks.'

'I'm sorry.'

'I'll be in touch,' Merrily said, going up the list from the bottom as she clicked off.

CROWLEY.

DE MOLAY

MAT PHOBE?

Printing that last one out again, separating the letters.

M A T   P H O B E

Then, in slight disbelief, she began to pick out individual letters, writing them down in a different order. Very lightly, so that it was almost a ghost of a word. As if she couldn't bear to give it more solidity ...

B A P H O M E T

42

Contex

Too early to panic.

It couldn't happen. Not on a mild autumnal Wednesday afternoon in Tanworth-in-Arden, in Middle England.

And he must have done this a couple of times before – distinctly remembering leaving his car in a particular place when it was actually somewhere else. It had definitely happened before.

If never with nearly four thousand pounds' worth of kit in the back, not including the Boswell guitar which was as close to priceless as anything he'd ever possessed.

Who was he trying to fool?

Lol stood in the road, in the empty space between two vividly green-gold beech trees. Standing exactly where he remembered parking the truck … and parking it not too confidently, because the Animal was so much longer than his old car.

But it had been a strange, unpredictable day. He needed to check and double-check before reporting it to the police. *Damn, damn, damn.*

The sky was clouding over, the sun hazed like a smear of butter on white bread, and he'd begun numbly retracing his steps to the church-yard, when his mobile played the riff from 'Heavy Medication Day'.

When he opened up the phone, a phone number he didn't recognize appeared in the screen.

A male voice he didn't recognize, either.

'Robinson.'

'Yes.'

'Try the pub car park.'

Lol said, 'Who's that?'

There was no answer.

Lol said, 'Listen ...'

There wasn't going to be an answer; this was the time of no reply. He began to breathe hard, that sense of dislocation again. He turned around, and the pub was directly opposite.

He didn't move, realizing he could actually see the truck from here, silver blue, centrally parked. A man in a suit, with a briefcase under one arm, came out of the pub and bleeped open a BMW. Nobody else was about.

Lol approached the Animal slowly, walking all around it from a distance, until he was sure there was nobody sitting in it. Clutching his keys, very much afraid that he wasn't going to need them. Not to open the driver's door, anyway.

Nor, as it turned out, the roll-top that Gomer and Danny Thomas had fitted onto the box, now bunched up at the end like an accordion.

There was a gap at the tailgate where the lock had been prised. When Lol pushed it, it jammed halfway, but that was enough for him to read the message.

YOU WON'T BE NEEDING THIS ANY MORE.
TRUST ME

The lettering was black and ragged. It had been wire-burned into the lightly polished face of the Boswell guitar which lay in its rigid velvet-lined case, like a child's body in an open coffin. The hinged top of the case had been bent back, snapped strings writhing in the air where the Boswell's neck had been broken.

On the square, the shadow of the medieval market hall had lengthened over the grey Lexus. In other circumstances, you could almost start to worry about what might have happened to the driver.

It was nearly four p.m., and Merrily realized she hadn't eaten today, at all – not good – but still wasn't hungry. In her mind, the candle was burning between the horns of the hermaphrodite goat and would not go out.

'This is the fourth time you been out yere, vicar.'

She spun round, and the candle flame seemed to waver.

'Some'ing on your mind, I reckon,' Gomer Parry said. 'Not that I been spying – just doing a bit o' tidying round the churchyard, collecting the ole windfalls, kind o' thing.'

'Sorry, Gomer, I'm ...'

'You en't bin around these past two days, vicar.'

'No. I meant to tell you ... it was all done in a bit of a rush.'

She'd thought perhaps he was slowing down, pottering around the village more, leaving the big digger jobs to Danny, but he looked bright enough, his bottle glasses full of light, his white hair projecting like the bristles on a yard brush, ciggy tin poking out of the top pocket of his old tweed jacket.

'No problem – I seen Janey and her explained. I'd come out a time or two, see if I could spot you. Thing is, vicar ... you got a minute?'

Gomer took her arm and nodded towards the market hall, and they moved between two oak pillars. Whatever it was, she didn't really have time for it, but this *was* Gomer Parry.

'Thing is, vicar, last time we was talking I wasn't exac'ly straight with you.'

That had to be a first; this man was embarrassingly straight.

'I'm sorry, been a bit preoccupied. What are we talking about here, Gomer?'

'You asked me about a partic'lar woman.'

'Oh.'

'And I was kinder talking all round the subject, if you recalls.'

'Well, I didn't really—'

'Which was wrong. Things between us, that en't how it's ever been.'

'No.'

'What I *should've* said, see, was there's stuff I could tell you – tell *you* – that shouldn't ever be repeated to nobody. On account of there's some things what, on the surface, is a bit ... your job, you'd most likely have to say *sinful.*'

'Not really one of my words, but never mind ...'

'But it en't. Not really. Not in the ... how can I put this ...? Not in the circumstances in which these things is being looked at, kind o' thing.'

'Not in the context of a particular situation?'

'*Context!* That's the word, vicar. In this yere contex, sin is ...'

'Relative?'

'Exac'ly.'

'And the context *is?*'

'Garway, vicar. Garway is its own contex. There's Hereford and there's Wales ... and there's Garway. And Garway's its own contex.'

'Gomer, I just want to say ... you don't *have* to tell me everything. I mean, I'm not—'

'I knows that, vicar.'

'However, as it happens, a situation has arisen where the more I know about the particular woman you were referring to, the more I might actually be able to help her.'

'That a fact?'

'So, frankly, any dirt you have on Mrs Morningwood, I'm up for it, basically.'

Gomer nodded, plucked the ciggy tin from his pocket.

'This qualify as a public place, vicar, under the law?'

'As there's no actual market on at the moment, I don't really know.' Merrily pulled out the Silk Cut and the lighter, an old rage pulsing through her at the attempted management of people's lives, the negation of God-given free will. 'But who gives a shit? Go on ...'

'This person. I think I tole you this person helps farmers, kind o' thing.'

'With tax problems and DEFRA forms.'

'DEFRA, that's a war, them bastards, vicar, but that en't really the issue in hand. And it en't only farmers. And it en't hexclusively Garway. Like, for instance, you met my ole friend Jumbo Humphries, Talgarth?'

Merrily recalled a man the size of a double pillar box who ran a garage and animal-feed operation up towards Brecon while doubling as a private inquiry agent.

'Now Jumbo, when his wife walked out – and this is confidential, vicar ...'

'Goes without saying.'

'Jumbo was lonely, you know what I'm sayin'? Not that he di'n't have no offers. But the kinder women *making* the offers, they had an eye to the business, which is worth a quid or two. What I mean is, not Jumbo. They wasn't looking at Jumbo, not even in the dark, and he knowed it.'

'It's sad, Gomer.' Merrily lit his roll-up, stepping back as a bus pulled in with a hiss of brakes. 'But it happens.'

'So this person … over at Garway … this person we been discussing … It was this person got Jumbo through a bad patch. Fixed him up. With his Michelle.'

'Oh. I see.' She looked at Gomer, his glasses opaque. She was thinking, Not a Thai-bride situation. '*Do* I see?'

'No,' Gomer said. 'Likely not.'

First Siân, then Robbie Williams.

Getting home half an hour earlier than usual, Jane was as unhappy and confused as when she'd left this morning. Life in flux, nobody you could count on.

Siân – it had been encouraging, in a way. All that about holding Mum in high esteem, treating Shirley's crap with the level of respect it deserved. It had *seemed* encouraging. But it could be a screen, couldn't it? You couldn't trust people in the Church because the Church was in flux, too, a time of rapid change, everybody grabbing what they could.

That was the trouble with the present. It was always in motion and, if you let yourself get dragged in, you could be pulled to pieces.

The past was different. You could get a feel for the past.

Jane looked around at the black and white village settling in for the dusk, the first lights kindling way back inside the Black Swan. The sense of an ancient heart. You could stand here, on these cobbles, at dawn and dusk particularly, and feel part of something at the deepest level.

This was most apparent when she was in Coleman's Meadow, on the prehistoric trackway to the top of Cole Hill. In the meadow where Gomer's JCB had – as if this was meant – uncovered the first stone. Eight to ten feet long. Awesome.

Finding the stones, fighting for the stones, had grounded her in a way she hadn't thought possible. But now she was expected to break it. The System said she must go away next year to college, develop around herself a new kind of life. With all the bureaucracy involved, it was even likely she wouldn't be here when – *if* – the old stones were raised again.

Ancient signposts to a mystical communion with the planet.

As above, so below.

She'd wanted to talk about this with Robbie Williams again. Discuss what she'd gathered from the internet as a result of his suggestion about the real identity of the Garway Green Man: *If that is Baphomet, is he guarding the altar? Or is he drawing attention away from it?*

History had been the last period before lunch, and she'd hung round as Robbie packed his notes into his briefcase, but he'd looked up with a faintly worried expression in his eyes.

'Ah … Jane. In a bit of a hurry today, unfortunately …'

'This is just a quick question, Mr Williams. It's basically about what happened to the Templar tradition after the Order was dissolved. I've been reading about Eliphas Levi and Baphomet, and he was French. What I was really interested in was what happened *here*.'

'Jane …' Robbie had come to his feet, buttoning his jacket over his beer gut. 'I need to make something clear. While one can only applaud your interest in the fringe issues of history, this is *not* part of the syllabus.'

'I never thought it was,' Jane said. 'It's *far* too interesting.'

'However, I get paid – and not as well as I'd like to be – to improve this school's reputation as an A-level factory. It's not about knowledge any more, Jane, it's about results and statistics.'

'That's a pretty cynical attitude, Mr Williams, if you don't mind me saying so.'

'Jane, if you were as close to blessed retirement as I am, having seen all that I've seen …'

'But, like, I thought you were *interested*. In Garway Church and everything. You seemed interested the other day.'

'Well, all I'm interested in at the moment,' Robbie said, 'is my lunch. And if you want to make the best use of your time here, I would suggest you pay more attention to the syllabus, because your essay on Charlemagne was skimpy, to say the least.' He swung his briefcase from the desk. 'Thank you, Jane.'

It made no sense. It was like he'd become a different person. She'd never ask him anything again. It was like there was suddenly nobody she could count on. Mum was working away, and Lol was out there making a career which, if it continued to build, would take him out of the village for months at a time. Lol and Mum, maybe their relationship had only worked when one of them was a loser.

And then there was Eirion … she'd chosen to end that before he did, because the writing was on the wall, anyway. One way or another, all the foundations were cracking, and Jane had spent the whole afternoon in a state of increasing isolation until, with the last period free, she couldn't stand it any more; she'd walked out of the school and caught a bus into Leominster, strolled around the town in a futile kind of way, shrouded in gloom, before grabbing the chance of a bus to Ledwardine.

She shouldered her airline bag and tramped wearily across the cobbles, and … oh.

The Volvo was parked in the vicarage drive.

The way her heart leapt – well, you despised yourself, really. *I missed you, Mummy*. God. Jane folded up her smile, buried it deep as she walked into the drive.

Inside the vicarage a dog barked when she fitted her key into the front door. Inside the hall, she recoiled at the sight of the woman in the kitchen doorway with her hand on the head of the wolfhound, like Britannia or something from an antique coin, only made more sinister by the dark glasses, the dark green fleece zipped all the way up, the crust of foundation cream and the ruin of a smile which, when you looked hard, wasn't a smile at all.

'You don't tell her where you got this, mind,' Gomer said. 'Her's gonner have a bit of an idea where it come from.'

Nodding at her sweatshirt, where it said:

GOMER PARRY

PLANT HIRE

'I think,' Merrily said, 'that I need to persuade *her* to tell me. May have to use you as a threat but … no way have we spoken. Gomer, this … I don't know what to say … this fills out so many gaps in my meagre knowledge. Just need to have a walk around for a while to think it all out, work out how to approach it.'

'Good luck, vicar.'

Gomer squeezed out the end of his roll-up, fanned the air. He hadn't asked about her own involvement with Mrs Morningwood; he'd know she'd have told him if she could.

They came out of the market hall from separate sides. In this village you could never be too careful. Merrily leaned against one of the pillars for a few moments, gazing out towards Ledwardine Fine Arts and the Eight Till Late.

Information overload. She didn't know where to start.

But, once again, circumstance decided, when Siân came out of the Eight till Late in her black belted coat with the collar up, an evening paper under her arm.

Merrily walked out.

'Siân,' she said. 'Something you forgot?'

43

Shadow

IN THE LOUNGE bar at the Black Swan, they ended up at the corner table where Merrily had sat with Lol the night she'd met Adam Eastgate. Seemed like weeks ago. Merrily made a point of buying the drinks. Coffees. And a cheese sandwich. Still not hungry, but this was no time to be light-headed.

'Unfinished business,' Siân said. 'Hate to leave loose ends. Luckily, she was out.'

'Who?'

'Shirley West. I expect Jane's told you.'

'I haven't spoken to Jane. She's at school. You've been to see … Shirley West?'

'We'll get to that. Have your sandwich, Merrily. You look as if you need it.'

'That's taken you all day?'

'Not *only* that. Although it did swallow several hours. Tell me, Merrily, are you on a fixed-term contract here?'

'Five years. Why?'

'What about deliverance?'

'No contract at all. I just do it.'

'I think you've been rather remiss there.'

'Well, I …' Merrily put down the sandwich, barely nibbled. 'You don't think about these things, do you?'

'*I* do. But then, I was a lawyer for over twenty years.'

Siân had unbuttoned her coat. Underneath, she was in civvies – navy skirt, pale blue sweater – looking almost uncomfortable in them, and Merrily realized how similar, apart from the wig, clerical clothing was to what a barrister wore in court.

'Someone wants to get me out?'

She looked steadily at Siân, who shrugged.

'Wherever you are, there's always *someone* who wants to get you out. But, since you ask, when your contract comes up for renewal, it's quite likely the terms will have altered.'

'Extra parishes?'

'That's the *most* likely. And if you don't play ball ...'

'The contract doesn't get renewed.'

'Doesn't happen often, but it happens. How much have you had to do with Mervyn Neale?'

'The Archdeacon? Not much at all. It's been mainly the Bishop. As you know.'

'Which might *partly* account for it.'

'I'm sorry?'

'Mervyn doesn't like you, Merrily.'

'He hardly knows me.'

'Perhaps ...' Siân sipped her coffee '... he simply dislikes what you represent.'

Which couldn't be womankind. Without the female clergy, this diocese would be in trouble. Merrily bit off another corner of her sandwich.

'Neale's a traditionalist,' Siân said. 'He doesn't, on the surface, object to the women's ministry, but he does expect us to keep a low profile.'

'What, like you have?'

'Well, yes, he *was* quite angry when it was suggested that I should shadow him for a month, with a view to possibly succeeding him when he retires.'

'That's on the cards, is it?'

'I hope so. I think it's something I could do.'

'Mmm, I think it probably is.'

'Because I'm a ruthless, ambitious bitch, presumably.'

Merrily leaned her head back against the oak panelling, shook her head, smiling faintly. *And you thought Gomer Parry was direct.*

'You don't like me, you don't trust me,' Siân said.

'Siân, it's not that I don't *like* you—' Merrily rolled her head against the panelling. 'Oh God.'

'You know what the problem is with Shirley West, don't you?'

'Sure, she thinks I'm some kind of chain-smoking punk priest who dabbles on the fringes of the occult.'

'Well, that, too. But what it really comes down to is her ex-husband being distantly related to the man often said to be Britain's most appalling serial murderer, ever.'

Merrily sat up, spilling her coffee.

'*Fred* West?'

'A sexual predator. And, of course, a Herefordshire man.'

'Shirley told you this? How—? You've only been here a couple of days.'

'Do calm down, Merrily, I'm not trying to take over your parish. I met Shirley West – Jane will tell you – I met her in the church last night. You'd hardly left before I had a phone call from Shirley asking to meet me. Jane – protecting your interests – eavesdropped on our meeting. Jane is … Well, how many teenage daughters would even spare the time? She's a good girl, Merrily.'

'I know.'

'Shirley … was desperately eager to tell me about the evil to which you were exposing your Sunday-evening meditation group. Among other things.'

'She made a bit of a scene on Sunday night. I didn't handle it very well. Wasn't feeling too good, actually.'

'No, you didn't look at all well when you left for Garway.'

'Still, I should've made time to talk to her.'

'If you made time for everybody, you wouldn't sleep. However, as I explained to Jane, I was rather concerned that Shirley might be causing mischief where you really didn't need it. So, when you … liberated me this morning, I decided to drop in on her, on that estate off New Barn Lane, not thinking she'd be at work. Her sister-in-law saw me and came out, and I identified myself and she invited me in for a cup of tea, and … I was there nearly three hours.'

'Her sister-in-law … Joanna? I think I've met her once.'

'Joanna Harvey. She doesn't come to church, and in her place I suspect I'd probably stay away as well, or attend another one miles away. Shirley moved here after her divorce, to be near her older brother, Colin. After just a few months of Shirley as a neighbour, Joanna's at the end of her tether. Desperately wants to move, just to get away from her, but Colin feels a certain family responsibility.'

'All the things I ought to know.'

'Shirley had been married seven years before discovering at a party that the late Frederick West had been some sort of distant cousin to her husband. Who hadn't bothered to tell her – doubtless suspecting the effect it might have. An effect evidently worsened by the way Shirley found out and the thoughtless jokes about what might be under the concrete patio that Colin had made. It preyed on her mind, becoming an obsession. She came to believe that her husband was tainted by evil. That evil hung over the family.'

For a shortish man, Fred West had thrown a long shadow.

Merrily said. 'His brother John was facing a rape charge when he hanged himself, exactly the way Fred had. Other members of the family have suffered emotional damage with predictable effects on their domestic situations. But … there are dozens of perfectly normal, well-balanced Wests …'

'It's clear that Shirley herself has psychiatric problems.'

'Though not immediately clear to me, apparently,' Merrily said.

'She moved into a separate bedroom from her husband, accusing him of unnatural sexual behaviour. He worked – still works, presumably – for a feed dealer, making deliveries to farms, and she accused him of having a relationship with two sisters who had a smallholding. Entirely unfounded, according to Joanna. There's more, but you get the idea.'

'Oh God.'

'She washes her clothes compulsively. She doesn't watch television and she doesn't read newspapers because of the filth they transmit. She began going to church for the first time since childhood about four years ago … obsessively. She joined Christian internet chat groups, particularly in America. Before moving here, she used to attend services at Leominster Priory, where she attached herself to a curate – Tom Dover?'

'I knew him slightly. He moved on.'

'And faster than he might have normally. Shirley would insist on doing his washing – washing his vestments, in particular. He's still a curate, near Swindon. I called him on my mobile about an hour ago. He said he felt guilty – ought to have told someone about Shirley.'

'But she's a professional woman. Branch manager at a bank.'

'Where, according to Joanna Harvey, she frequently offers unsought moral and spiritual advice to customers. Having kept her married name as a sort of penance. You really should be more careful, Merrily, especially after your problem some time ago with Jenny Driscoll. As I suggested to Jane, this is not an uncommon situation, particularly for women priests.'

'I realize that. What do you suggest?'

'She needs guidance. *Not* someone like our friend Nigel Saltash, but I do know a person – a psychiatric nurse and a churchgoer who I *would* have suggested as suitable for your deliverance team if I didn't think you'd be suspicious of anyone proposed by me.'

Merrily sighed. 'Siân—'

'And yes, after Saltash, I can accept that. One reason why I elected to be your locum – if I do become Archdeacon, I'd hate us to start on the wrong foot, due to … misconceptions. I accept we have theological differences, but I respect what you've achieved. Against the odds.'

'Siân, I …' Merrily found she'd finished both her cheese sandwich and her coffee. She felt like a real drink. 'I don't know what to say any more.'

'No need to say anything at all,' Siân said. 'Because I haven't finished yet.'

Siân had been the Archdeacon's shadow for a month. Learning the ropes. Learning many things.

'You know he's a Freemason.'

'No, I didn't.'

On the edge of a minefield here. It had often seemed to Merrily that paranoia about Masonic influence was exaggerated; she'd never had any problems, never really had cause to notice the Masons, although she was aware there *were* some in the Church. Besides, it was in decline, wasn't it? All the existing Masons getting on in years, very little new blood.

'Freemasons claim to be Christian,' Siân said. 'Although you would be hard-pressed to find, within Masonic dogma, any recognition of Christ. There's a very interesting book by a former vicar of New Radnor who'd become a Mason in – he maintains – all innocence and began to find it alarmingly incompatible. Have you read that?'

'No.'

'I'll send you a copy. Making my own position on this quite clear from the outset ... as a barrister I came up against it time and time again. I made a point of learning the Masonic signals so that I could spot them in court. You'd be surprised how often I saw them directed towards the bench, from the dock, and I still believe it's one of the best arguments we have for more women judges.'

'And women Archdeacons?'

Siân didn't smile.

'And women Bishops,' she said.

The bar noise meshed into white noise, the lights receding into a single point of light. Merrily pushed her plate to one side, her coffee cup to the other.

'What are you saying?'

Siân – *even Siân* – looked around at the handful of customers. Merrily spotted a couple of farmers she knew slightly and James Bull-Davies, former Army officer. OK, surely?

'The position of Bernard Dunmore is an ambivalent one,' Siân said. 'He was a Freemason, many years ago. Like a number of clergy, he apparently became aware of an incompatibility and hasn't had anything to do with the Craft in years.'

'But ...?'

'He's never actually renounced Masonry. And, as far as I can tell, I don't *think* he's ever formally left.'

'How do you know this?'

'I think you'll just have to accept that I do. Call it a nervous hangover from my years at the Bar.'

'And what does it mean?'

'I wasn't sure it meant anything. In his allocation of livings, the Bishop appears to have been fairness itself. Doesn't seem to have been unduly influenced by Mervyn Neale, although obviously reliant, to some extent, on his organizational recommendations.'

'And the Archdeacon?'

'Nothing I can prove, although perhaps I will one day. He doesn't like you. Doesn't like deliverance, as a ministry, and he doesn't like the way you handle it, the way you've widened the brief. I don't think— What have I said?'

'This morning, the Bishop told me I'd displayed a tendency to go *beyond the brief*. Like they're all saying the same things.'

'I do know he's had a number of meetings with the Archdeacon in the past few days – far more contact than in any of the weeks since I've been shadowing Neale.'

We unleashed you.

And now we're reining you in.

'You're fully aware of what I've been working on? In Garway.'

'I think so. And I think it might well be relevant. Your attitude on the phone this morning was rather extraordinary.'

'I was … in a state of shock.'

'Evidently. It made me wonder what on earth the Bishop had said to you.'

'He …'

It all began to tumble forward, the rape, the cover-up, the desperate need to tell somebody, just to stay sane. She held it back all the same.

'You don't *have* to tell me,' Siân said.

'He trotted out the usual stuff about the dangers of deliverance being connected with yet another murder. Which is valid enough. But then he said the Duchy of Cornwall also wanted me to forget it. I rang the Duchy. He'd lied. Why would he do that?'

'I don't know. He might simply have developed cold feet. Are you going to do what he says?'

'Erm …' Merrily sat back. 'Siân, this might be a naive question, but if you *were* to expose Mervyn Neale as having used Masonic influence in the course of his executive work in the Diocese, how would that affect your chances of getting his job?'

'That's a very interesting point.' Siân smiled, mouth only. 'I imagine I could say goodbye to the job. Even if the Church wanted to make a point of distancing itself from Freemasonry, appointing me, in the wake of a scandal – even if it were only an internal one – might be seen as a step too far. It's still a conservative organization.'

'But you'd still do it, if you had the evidence?'

'First and foremost, I'm a Christian,' Siân said. 'Of course I'd do it. *Are* you going along with what the Bishop wants?'

'No.'

'Then you'll need support,' Siân said. 'Or you could, very soon, find you've become a very small footnote in ecclesiastical history.'

'Huw Owen said much the same.'

'Interesting.' Siân looked at her watch, frowned and rose to her feet. 'You trust him, don't you?'

'I used to trust the Bishop.'

'It's a slippery slope, Merrily. Letting trust slip away.'

'You lose some, you … win some?'

'Yes. I suppose you do.' Siân picked up her bag, the kind of doctor's bag that exorcists were often assumed to carry. 'When we get outside, however. I'd really rather you *didn't* hug me.'

Merrily smiled.

'But get help,' Siân said. 'I implore you.'

44

The Morningwood Heritage

'I'VE BEEN TELLING Jane about my car accident,' Mrs Morningwood said, quite softly, looking at Merrily, 'And how you came to my rescue.'

'Mmm.' Merrily frowned. 'Sometimes people just happen to be in the right place at the right time.'

Jane and Mrs Morningwood were on the sofa, Roscoe stretched across both their knees, Ethel the cat watching warily from the edge of the hearth, where the fire glowed red and orange through a collapsing scaffold of coal and logs.

Merrily wondered how to get rid of Jane.

'And other stuff,' Jane said. 'You thought much about the significance of the number nine, Mum?'

'John Lennon always liked it. "Revolution Nine", "Number Nine Dream". Jane, I wonder if—'

'In the Garway context. The Nine Witches of Garway. Why *nine*?'

'It's three squared. The trinity?'

'And the sacred number of the Druids. But the point is, the number nine was also a sacred number of the Templars. When they first started out in Jerusalem, there were supposed to have been nine of them. Which, when you think about it, is ridiculous. Nine knights to protect all the pilgrims in the Holy Land?'

'Maybe it was just the nine senior knights, with a lot of armed underlings.'

'Nah, symbolic. Gotta be. Also – get this – nine Templars were required to form a commandery – like at Garway? Plus the order was in existence for 180 years, which, like ... one plus eight equals nine.'

'Sometimes, Jane, I think that without the internet the world would be a happier and less confusing place.'

'OK, I'll skip some of the other examples and cut to the chase. The burning of Jacques de Molay. He died on 18 March – one and eight? In the year 1314, one ... three ... one ... four. Do the math, as they say.'

'It's intriguing, Jane, however—'

'And how long did he take to die?'

'Nine minutes?'

'Hours, actually.'

'Ouch. And all this *means* ...?'

'It's to do with cosmic correspondences. As above, so below.'

'You don't actually know, do you?'

'Well, no, but if you put it all together, it's like the landscape and the community of Garway was being primed for some sacred purpose. The number and the symbols that keep recurring. The astrological pubs. You could probably go into the church and find the numbers nine – and three, of course – reflected in all kinds of architectural features. They were, like, building something into the landscape?'

'Like?'

'Just bear it in mind. Nine witches, nine original Templars ... maybe you're looking at the need for there always to be nine people in the know. Nine people preserving the tradition.'

Merrily said, 'Have either of you eaten?'

'We were waiting for you, Mum. Do you want me to make something?'

'I know we're trying to stop doing this, flower, but why don't you pop over to the chip shop?'

'It's peak time! There'll be a queue a mile long!'

'Chips,' Mrs Morningwood said. 'Yes, I think I should quite like some chips.'

It was fully dark now. The light came from the fire and just one reading lamp. Quiet light. Merrily sat down in the armchair opposite Mrs Morningwood, who'd removed her sunglasses.

'How do you feel now?'

'I'm sore. What would you expect?'

'I'm sorry.'

'But rested, thank you. I may go home tomorrow.'

'We can talk about that later. Erm … I've been finding out some background. My friend Lol … has been to see Lord Stourport.'

'Has he indeed?'

'Which means I can now tell you quite a bit about the days before the police raid on the Master House. Only it's … it's a bit of a one-way street at the moment, isn't it, Muriel?'

'Don't call me Muriel. Hate it. Sounds like a bloody librarian.'

'I've had some background on you, too,' Merrily said. 'Hard to avoid it really.'

Mrs Morningwood shook her head gently; even this was clearly painful.

'Just been talking to an old friend of mine,' Merrily said.

'In a community this centralized, Watkins, it would be surprising if you hadn't.'

'We didn't talk *much* about you. But we could have.'

'Who was this?' Mrs Morningwood's gaze was on the sweatshirt. 'As if I couldn't guess.'

'This friend … I think he knows a lot more about you than he felt able to tell me.'

'So go back and ask him.'

'You don't think he'd tell me?'

'You can try.'

'And, you know, I think I could probably persuade him.'

'To tell you what? You think there's some big secret? I'm the Pope's secret love-child?'

'The thing is,' Merrily said, 'I don't *want* him to have to tell me. I don't want him to feel he's betrayed you.'

'I don't know what you're talking about, and I don't think you do either.'

'Although I do think he *would* tell me. I'm just trying to convey to you that I'm …' Merrily held up a thumb and finger, minimally apart '… that close.'

'Watkins ... this is not about betraying *me*.'

'The first time we met, you took a phone call from a Mr ... Hinton?'

'I don't remember.'

'You were obtaining something for him. At first – putting this together from what I heard – I thought maybe you were fixing up Thai brides for lonely farmers. Doing the paperwork.'

Mrs Morningwood laughed.

'Then I heard about what your mother did, on the side. And there was something that Lord Stourport said to Lol. About country girls.'

'Country girls.' Mrs Morningwood sniffed. 'She was livid about that. Do you know how much they were paid? Well, I suppose it wouldn't sound very much in today's money, but *then* ... absolute fortune. Rural wages were a complete joke, even then. Farm labour one up from slave labour, and ordinary people would need two or three jobs to get by – many still do, of course, as you know. Ironically, it's largely the farmers themselves now. Tragic.'

'These were your mother's girls.'

'*Were*. It all rather fell apart after that. I had to laugh. She'd been ripping those girls off for years. And my grandmother before her.'

'The Morningwood heritage. How far does it go back?'

'That's it, really. Two generations. Before that, I imagine they *were* witches. Lived in a tiny little place over towards the White Rocks, I think it's a sheep shed now. But, you see, Watkins, it was part of the rural culture ... a *necessary* part of the culture.'

'We're talking about abortions?'

'And the rest. My grandmother, who never married, raised three daughters on the profits of what, basically, was prostitution.'

'She was doing it herself?'

Merrily trying for surprise, but once you knew, you knew.

'And then, as she got older, began pimping for youngsters trying to earn enough money to make something of their lives. It was like ...' Mrs Morningwood's mouth twisted at the thought, and her lip began to bleed again '... almost a *gap year* for some of them before they left the area, went to college, got themselves good jobs. Strong independent young women who'd learned how to ... handle men.'

'Can I get you something for that lip?'

'Won't die, Watkins. And when I say handle men, that was all it amounted to in most cases.'

'You make it sound like an essential social service. Which I suppose ...'

'Well, isn't it?'

'Still?'

Mrs Morningwood sighed. A shift in terminology for the new millennium. Sex therapist specializing in rural needs. As a teenager, she'd grown – despicably, she said – to despise her mother. She'd gone to London, to work as a secretary for a theatrical agent – loose term, *very* loose. Had ended up working on what she described as adult magazines. *Very* adult. All very enlightening and destined to alter her opinion of her mother and her grandmother. Got married, not for long. Had been single again when the letter from Mary Roberts had finally reached her.

'So was Mary ...?'

'Not up to the time I left. Eric Davies – that *was* a respectable job. But afterwards, perhaps inevitably, she made friends with the other girls.'

'How many girls were there at the time?'

'Three, I think. A very informal arrangement by then. My mother really was more of a herbalist, and the demand for herbs was increasing – from middle-class people by then, able to pay more, alternative health becoming quite an industry. She was still furious, though, when two of the girls took the Stourport shilling.'

'And Mary?'

'My mother always claimed she didn't know about that until it was too late.'

'I would have thought maybe she would've offered to get rid of Mary's baby?'

'Oh no.'

'She'd stopped doing that?'

'No, she was still doing it. She simply wouldn't tamper with a foetus conceived at the Master House. Call it superstition.'

'I'm not getting this.'

'It doesn't matter. It doesn't change anything.'

'But the tradition ... that didn't end.'

'It altered. My mother became ill. I nursed her over the final weeks –
all over very quickly, as it always used to be before the medical profession became part of the drug culture. During that time I fielded seven
phone calls from hesitant men. Two of whom I felt so sorry for that I ...
Well, what was I supposed to *do*?'

'A warm heart under that bluff exterior?'

'You can't embarrass me, Watkins. Rural needs are essentially
different to urban needs. No verge-crawling in the Land Rover. Extreme
discretion is crucial, and there's a certain mutual respect. Wasn't going
to dress up, mind. Take me as you find me.'

'Literally?'

'God, you're prurient. It was nothing where I couldn't pretend I was
milking a cow.'

'So Mr Hinton, the other day ...?'

'All sorted. Safely delivered. Delia, I think he's called her. It's not a
major enterprise or anything, I think I've supplied seven in two years. A
comfort, for mild-mannered chaps lacking in social skills. In one case,
because of the cost, one was shared between two brothers.'

'I see ... do I?'

'Delia – she and her sisters, the point about them is that they're not
impossibly beautiful. They don't *pout*. They're not *Hollywood*. The
fantasy in these parts, it's the girl in the T-shirt behind the counter at
Hay and Brecon Farmers. You know what I mean? Sometimes, the
outlet I deal with, I've actually provided them with photographs to
work from – from the local papers.'

Jumbo's Michelle, he really loves her, see, Gomer had said. *Wouldn't
swap her for a top o' the range quad bike. Had her reconditioned twice.
Jumbo weighs seventeen stone, mind ...*

'Mum?' Jane's head came round the door. 'You going to have them by
the fire or what?'

'No, I think we'll come into the kitchen, flower, if you want to get
some plates down.'

'OK.'

'Rubber dolls?' Merrily said. 'Inflatable girlfriends? That's why you won't go to the police?'

'How could I?' Mrs Morningwood easing Roscoe's head from her lap. 'Seriously, how could I? All right, it's mainly the inflatables now, nothing illegal there, but they'd start excavating.'

'I think you could handle it. The identity of rape victims—'

'Oh, don't be ridiculous, this is *Garway Hill*. Besides, even if they believed me after they discovered what they would very quickly discover … it isn't just me, is it?'

'You're worried about the clients.'

'It would be like a bomb under the hill. Don't get me wrong, Watkins, I don't fear personal exposure, but the handful of shy, vulnerable men throughout South Herefordshire, Monmouthshire, the Black Mountains, whose private lives would be taken apart, who'd would be subjected to the most degrading—'

'OK, I understand.'

And as they went through to the kitchen, she finally *did* understand. *She was asking for it, of course. Been asking for it for years, the old slag. Generations, even.*

'Besides,' Mrs Morningwood murmured in the hall, 'what he intended was to kill me. Don't you think?'

45

Past Rising

OBVIOUSLY, JANE KNEW there was something she wasn't party to. At one stage, washing the dishes, she looked at Mrs Morningwood and then tentatively grinned at Merrily.

'I hope Siân was still here when you got back.'

'Erm, no. She'd gone.'

'Pity. I was only explaining to her why it was so essential we should have a big vicarage. Like because of the, you know, damaged people you had to bring back sometimes?' Sheepish smile for Mrs Morningwood. 'Sorry.'

'Damaged,' Mrs Morningwood said tonelessly. 'And yet somehow still alive.'

And, perhaps sensing the need for a mother and daughter to talk in private, she went off – quite unsteadily, Merrily noticed, still worried – to the bathroom.

'Mum,' Jane said when she'd gone. 'There's something I have to tell you about, and it's not going to—'

'Shirley West?'

'Oh.'

'Siân told me.'

'As an example, presumably, of why your daughter would be unlikely to make it as a private eye.'

'That was the encouraging bit. I'm now going to tell you the rest. In absolute confidence. Just sit down for a minute.'

Even summarized, the story of Shirley's obsession made a sad sense. More than twelve years since Fred West had hanged himself while awaiting trial, a core of unexplained evil still hung in the air like an invisible planet. Shirley's story was not so ridiculous. Might not even be an illness.

'Well,' Jane said, 'I'm quite glad she's certifiably insane. I mean, it helps, doesn't it?'

'That's typically selfless of you, flower.'

'So, you know ... what will you do about her?'

'I think Siân's going to handle it herself. With some psychiatric support. Makes sense for me not to be involved. I think ... Siân was proving something to me. She didn't *need* to do that.'

'Yeah. She's not quite what I imagined.'

'From my comprehensive character assassination? She's made me feel a little wanting in the generosity-of-spirit department.'

'Maybe she's changed. Or maybe she's just seen another side of you.'

This kid was getting so smart she could scare you sometimes. Merrily sighed.

'She has principles. Moral fibre.' She tapped a teaspoon against an open palm. 'Perhaps it's time I got some.'

'Along with five more parishes?'

'Yeah, well ... who knows? Jane, look, go and hang around in the hall, will you, in case Mrs Morningwood needs any help?'

At the door, Jane looked over her shoulder.

'She wasn't in a car crash, was she?'

'I wasn't there.'

'Huh.'

'Look, I need to make a phone call, and it might take a while. You'll have to talk among yourselves. Numerology, Renaissance cosmology ...'

In the scullery, the sermon pad was still open to the word B A P H O M E T. She tore off the page and screwed it up very tight. Looked at the mobile and then – why fry your brains for these bastards? – picked up the big black bakelite receiver.

'I need some help,' she told Huw Owen. 'Badly.'

'Sycharth.' Mrs Morningwood smiled thinly. 'I ought to have known.'

'How would you?' Merrily said. 'He'd want to keep it very quiet that he'd been spending quality time at the old family home. Certainly wouldn't want the Grays to know … or would he?'

'Newtons. Still the Newtons, then.'

'Sorry, yes, the Newtons.'

The fire was burning low. Jane had taken Roscoe for a walk, with a clothes line doubled up through his collar and a home-made poop-scoop. Dogshit watch, smoking watch. Ledwardine, heart of the New Cotswolds, had them all now, and they never slept.

'Getting a foot inside the ancient portal.' Mrs Morningwood had a cigarette and a glass of neat brandy. 'That alone would make it worth-while to Sycharth. Other obvious attractions, of course. Nubile young things bathing naked in the Monnow. Would've taken a youth with more will-power than Suckarse to look the other way.'

'This would be the girlfriends, before they left?'

'Would've been the time when Sycharth's father, Gruffydd – keen as ever to shaft the Newtons – was apparently complaining to the parish council about Lord Stourport's habit of biking around the lanes stark bollock naked except for a pair of Doc Martens.'

'You ever meet Stourport?'

'I've told you, I wasn't there.'

'You knew Sycharth, though. When you and he were young.'

'He made a play for me once, at a barn dance. I was almost tempted to go out with him – he had an old Triumph Spitfire. Yellow. Passed his test on his seventeenth birthday. It used to roar sexily up and down the lanes. I always liked speed.'

A moist sadness came into Muriel Morningwood's bruised eyes. Days of innocence? Yeah, sure.

'Long time on the phone, Watkins.'

'I was consulting a colleague. Didn't want to miss anything out. Don't look at me like that, it's a priest. A proper priest. Nothing gets out.'

Mrs Morningwood drank some brandy.

'Tell me, what *were* they doing, apart from taking drugs and shag-ging? Do hate the way another generation has appropriated the word *shag* as if they invented it. Why can't they they come up with one of their own? Sorry, I'm rambling again. I don't think I want to know what they did to Mary Roberts. Not in this state.'

'Didn't you ask any of the other girls who were involved?'

'As far as I know there were only two. My mother wouldn't have anything to do with them again. I tried to talk to one about it – she just walked away. Too well paid. They've both left the area now. I don't think either of them was there at the end. You should get to Suckarse before he has time to fabricate a story.'

'You ever hear of a man calling himself Mat Phobe?'

'Never. Who's he?'

'It was all apparently stage-managed by this man. He seems to have decided there was some kind of Templar treasure hidden at the Master House.'

'Never heard of *that*.'

'Mat Phobe – it's an anagram of Baphomet – the sacred head? Also the name adopted by the occultist Aleister Crowley as leader of a Templar-based outfit experimenting with the magical power of sex.'

'That what the Knights Templar did, do you think?'

'They were more less accused of it, weren't they? Maybe riches led to decadence.'

'I can certainly see Sycharth in ceremonial robes.'

'They seem to have tried some kind of mediumistic thing, to put him in touch with his ancestors – the Welsh princes, he claimed, apparently.'

'His ancestors were sheep-shaggers.'

'People keep saying he doesn't speak Welsh,' Merrily said. 'Is he likely to know any Welsh at all?'

'Shouldn't think so. Wasn't compulsory at school when Sycharth was a boy, not in an Anglicized area like Monmouth. His son would have to learn it, I expect – Cynllaith.'

'How old's he?'

'Fifteen or sixteen.'

'Cynllaith? What's that mean?'

'Could be something to do with milk – *llaith*. Or – more sinister, according to my dictionary – *battle* or *slaughter*.'

'You're kidding.'

'Pretentions to warrior status. These sex rituals – was that just an excuse?'

'Was for Lord Stourport.'

'But in the course of it …' Mrs Morningwood's voice hardening '… one of them seems to have impregnated Mary Roberts.'

'That's how it looks.'

'And was, therefore, Fuchsia's father.'

'Yes.' Merrily heard the phone ringing, let it ring. 'I've thought of that.'

'Suppose it's Sycharth?'

'We're unlikely ever to know.'

'But does *he*? And if that child was born as a result of some degenerate ritual, Watkins, what might the effects of that be? I'm asking you as a priest.'

'As a priest, I don't really have an answer.' Merrily stared into the fire. 'Looking at it psychologically, I would think that would depend on whether she knew about it, wouldn't you?'

'If she knew, might she think of herself as inherently soiled and corrupt because of the circumstances of her conception?'

'It's possible.'

'And *did* she know, do you think?'

'It would explain some things, wouldn't it? But if she knew of her own connection with the Master House *before* Felix tendered for the job, why did she go along with it, *then* throw a wobbly? What was she like when you first met her?'

'Inquisitive. Lots of questions.'

'Not spooked at that stage?'

'No suggestion of it. This would've been their first visit, and they were both fired up with the idea of restoring the house in a sympathetic way. She wanted to know what I could remember about it – the atmosphere, the colours of the walls. Hard for me to recall what she asked in much detail because, of course, I knew at once who she must be and it had, as we used to say, rather blown my mind.'

'You *definitely* didn't say anything to her about that … or give any indication? I mean, if she saw you looking shocked …'

'I don't give anything away unless I want to.'

'Suppose Fuchsia really didn't know about Mary and the Master House until she actually came here. *Something* happened to make her go dashing into the church demanding a blessing and spiritual sanctuary from Teddy Murray.'

'Who would've recommended a five-mile walk in the fresh air,' Mrs Morningwood said sourly.

'If someone had already recognized the resemblance to Mary the way you did and made Fuchsia aware of it … then the idea of the place being haunted, something rising from under the dust sheets, might have been her own way of externalizing her feelings. Or is that psychobabble?'

'The past rising up to haunt her?'

'And she's a devotee of M. R. James, and perhaps she's learned that James went to Garway, where something happened to disturb him – and all *that* goes into the emotional mix. She's afraid she's carrying around something corrupt, tainted. She wants to be blessed, purified.'

What is this that is coming?

'Perhaps, for the first time, starting to question the fate of her mother,' Mrs Morningwood said. '*Did* Mary come back to Garway, after she wrote to me and I failed to respond? Was your friend able to find that out?'

'Mmm. I think so.'

'So they would have known about the baby. Sycharth and the other clowns.'

'I presume.'

Mrs Morningwood was silent. Merrily heard Jane coming in with Roscoe, big paws skidding on the flags in the kitchen.

'Sycharth would hardly have wanted a bastard child,' Mrs Morningwood said at last.

'Perhaps I'll get to talk to him tomorrow.'

'But first, I think you need to talk to the Grays.'

It was after midnight when Merrily switched off the lamp in the parlour. Mrs Morningwood had gone to her herbal bed, taking the dog up with her. Jane had gone over an hour ago to her apartment in the attic. Merrily went through to the kitchen for the last time, put some food down for Ethel, smoked half a cigarette and listened to the answering machine bleeping in the scullery. Eventually, she stubbed out her cigarette, went through and hit the button.

'*Coming over, lass. I've things to clear in the morning, so it'll be mid-afternoon.*'

Huw seemed about to hang up, then came back.

'*The bloke who cleared you for the Duchy. Nowt to worry about.*'

Another silence, questions drifting like steam in the scullery's sepia light. There was a soft tapping at the window; Merrily turned sharply.

'*But don't go near Dunmore yet,*' Huw said.

'You did say it didn't matter what time,' Lol said at the back door. 'I've been back an hour, but you were obviously busy.'

'Why didn't you just come *in?*'

They'd swapped keys months ago.

'I thought I'd walk around for a bit.'

Maybe it was the light or the lateness, but he looked washed-out, stripped down, drained, as sorrowful and weary as Jesus in *The Light of the World* that still hung in the hall.

'Do you want something to eat?'

'No, thanks. Not hungry.'

'You sure?'

'I'm fine. Really.'

'Come to bed, then,' Merrily said.

46

Call it Superstition

SHE WAS AT the farm by eight-forty-five. Not a problem; Roxanne reckoned she'd been up since five. A wiry woman, early thirties, in a dark blue fleece and a baseball cap over curly hair already greying at the front. Out by the gate with two sheepdogs when Merrily drove in; now in the kitchen, clinking mugs, scraping toast.

'You've just missed Paul, he's taken the kids to school, then he's got an appointment at the hospital, which always puts him in a bad mood. Very wary of the drugs, reckons your mate Mrs Morningwood does him more good. The doctors humour him on that score, and that makes him even madder.'

'What, reflexology?'

'Has it once a week now. Probably just as well he isn't here, actually – you talk to him about the Gwilyms, it takes him the rest of the day to calm down. And he isn't even family.'

The farmhouse was red brick and pebble-dash with bay windows downstairs. Built to function, two barns in front, no name displayed. The kitchen table was scrubbed pine, the coffee as bitter as Roxanne.

'You know they brought Foot and Mouth into the valley in 2001? You know that, do you? Way to get rid of all your stock, clean up on the compensation. Well, a lot of unscrupulous farmers did it, but rarely anything so blatant. He made no secret of it, he *wanted* it, he *embraced* Foot and Mouth.'

'You mean Sycharth Gwilym had his farm deliberately infected?'

'Yeah, but try to prove it. Well, we did, we told the press, but the press wouldn't use it. He's a big man now, Sycharth, the King of Hereford. Most of his money's in property and he wanted his stock gone, and he grabbed the opportunity and sod the rest of us. We had a lovely herd of Herefords, wiped out in an afternoon by the trigger-happy bastards from DEFRA. Paul cried. He stood out there and he cried. I wouldn't give them the satisfaction. I'm a Newton, I know what they are, the Gwilyms. Scum is what they are.'

Roxanne brought her coffee to the table, snatched off her baseball cap.

'Adam put us in the picture about what you're doing. I'll be there, never fear. Well, it *should* be me. I'm the Newton, no way Paul should be put through *that.*'

'It's not meant to be an ordeal.' Merrily spread some honey on a half-slice of toast. 'Most people say they feel much better afterwards. Some people even ...'

She didn't like to mention the sense of healing. An occasional side effect of a cleansing and not necessarily restricted to residents of the affected property. But ... too many false dawns in this household, you could tell.

'I'm sorry,' Roxanne said. 'I didn't mean you. Sycharth Gwilym. Always so considerate to Paul, opening doors, laying ramps. With a sneer on his face that he barely tries to conceal. Gives him a sick buzz. Or it did, when he thought we'd have to sell up and get out. So, yeah, I'll do it, you can count on me, I'll stand shoulder to shoulder with Adam Eastgate, and I'll look Sycharth in his shifty eyes and I'll pray to God for anything that remains of the Gwilyms to be eradicated from that house until the end of sodding time.'

'Knows all the history, that girl,' Mrs Morningwood had said when she came off the phone at seven-thirty a.m., 'but you'll need to keep her on track. All she really wants is to pour venom on the Gwilyms.'

Was the venom deserved? Rage could be inherited, the reasons for it long forgotten. Sins-of-the-fathers.

'You know what this is about,' Merrily said to Roxanne. 'Some people refusing to work in the house.'

'Poor bloke. I showed him round, the first time he came. He was all right, I thought.'

'But did that make any sense to you? Why people were scared.'

'Just the one person, I think?'

'Maybe one more.' *The darkness of the inglenook, the crackle of bird bones, the face.* She took a hit of the coffee. 'Possibly.'

'Well, I never lived there, obviously.' Roxanne crunched toast. 'My parents'd been over here for some years when I was born, so this is the only home I've ever known. But I know my mother was glad to move out of the place.'

'You know why?'

'Not really. When I was a kid, the times it was empty – between tenants – I always wanted to get inside, it looked so mysterious, like an old castle or something. But it was always kept locked up, and my mum told us it was dangerous. I mean falling slates and stuff. Then it would be let again, to some family – people with horses once – but they never stayed long. I remember one couple, the Rogersons, banging on the door one morning and the woman yelling, "You should've told us! Should've told us about it, we'd never have taken it."'

'You ever find out what had happened to them?'

'Nope.' Roxanne shook her head. 'Wasn't talked about in front of us kids. Any more than I'd talk about it in front of mine.'

'They didn't want to sell it?'

'No, they didn't. I suppose the farm was doing well, and it was an asset. Also, the Master House is in the centre of the land, and they didn't want to sell any land. So there'd be access to organize, a road to put in, rights of way ... and the Gwilyms were always hovering. They'd bought another farm – the one Sycharth has now – and the Master House was between us and them, and even if we'd sold it to someone else, what was to stop them selling it on to the Gwilyms?'

'What's to stop the Duchy doing the same?'

'I don't think they would. He doesn't give up on things, the Prince, what I've heard.'

'I wouldn't really know. Was much said about what happened when it was leased to a commune?'

'That was before my time, but I've heard there was a lot of drugs and wild parties. Oh ... and I also remember, when I was little, some chap with a big beard coming to the house, saying he was researching a history of … I think it must've been the Templars, and could he have a look around the Master House? And my dad was quite rude. He said, "No, bugger off, we've had enough of all that."'

'So you heard that they were into the Templars. The commune.'

'Must have.'

'Did you ever hear any stories about treasure?'

'What?'

'Treasure being hidden at the Master House?'

'Treasure?' Roxanne laughed, pushing fingers through her curls. 'If there was any suggestion of treasure at the Master House, you don't think we'd've ripped the place apart to try and find it? The only thing they ever found, my dad used to say, was a priest's hole, when he was a boy – there was a lot of persecution of Catholics around Garway. But that was completely empty, so they blocked it up again.'

'What about the history generally ? You know much about that?'

'Only that it used to be very important, apparently, when the Newtons first came. We have an old … hang on, I'll show you. Won't be a minute.'

Roxanne put down her toast and got up, brushing crumbs from her fleece, vanishing through a door. Merrily looked out of the bay window. It had been dark when she left, and the early sun was still muffled. She couldn't see any landmark that she recognized, not the church, nor the top of the hill with its radio mast. Certainly not the Master House.

It was as if the Newtons had sought out a spot without any prominent landscape features, somewhere with no visible history.

When Roxanne returned, she was carried a wedge of dark wood a couple of feet long and a paperback book. She put the book on the table and held the piece of wood up for Merrily. It was a plaque, gilt-edged. It said:

HONOUR THE MASTER
CARE FOR THE CUSTOMS

Roxanne leaned the plaque against the table.

'My family, when they moved in, there was a maiden aunt who

threw herself into researching the history. We've still got a box of her papers – we keep being told we ought to have it all published as a book, but it would take a lot of work. But this aunt – Aunt Fliss – said it was important for the family to realize that we hadn't just bought a farm, we'd taken on a very powerful piece of history that one day would come into its own.'

'What did she mean by that?'

'Don't think she ever worked it out fully, but it was obviously about the Grand Master of the Templars. People think it's called the Master House because it was the main farm, but it's because the Grand Master stayed here when he came to Garway. Aunt Fliss had had *this* thing made to put up over the fireplace, so future generations wouldn't forget. My mum and dad brought it with them when they moved out. We still have it hung in the hall. Sentimental value, I suppose.'

'But is there any actual evidence that de Molay came to Garway?'

'It's here.' Roxanne put the book in front of Merrily. *Knights Templar and Hospitaller in Herefordshire* by Audrey Tapper. 'You read this one?'

'Not had time to read anything much, to be honest. This has all happened very quickly.'

'Well, there you are.' Roxanne opened out the book and flattened its spine. 'This is the bit. This is when Edward II started imprisoning English Templars after they were closed down in France, accused of all this heresy and stuff. One of them was called John Stoke, who'd only been a Templar for about a year and he came to Garway, and he made this confession about what they made him do.'

The account of it, Merrily read, had come from the St John Historical Society, presumably linked to the Hospitallers who had taken over Garway from the Templars.

He was in Garway during the visit there by Grand Master Jacques de Molay. Stoke's deposition when the Templars were arrested was that he had been called to the Grand Master's bedchamber at Garway and in front of two other foreign knights he was asked to make proof of his obedience and to seat himself on a small stool at the foot of the Grand Master's bed.

'So de Molay's bedchamber ... was that definitely at the Master House?'

'That's what we were told,' Roxanne said. 'He was a bit of a boy, wasn't he, old Jacques?'

De Molay then sent to the Church for a crucifix and then two other Templars placed themselves at either side of the door with their swords drawn. Stoke said that he was asked to deny 'Him whom the image represents' but he replied 'Far be it for me to deny my Saviour.' The Grand Master ordered him to do so, otherwise he would be put in a sack and carried to a place 'by no means agreeable'. Through fear of death he denied Christ, 'but with his tongue and not his heart.'

'Makes you think, doesn't it?' Roxanne said. 'I like that bit where the poor guy's threatened with being put in a sack if he didn't renounce Jesus Christ. Toss him in the Monnow, you reckon, or just the nearest slurry pit. So, I mean, were the Templars Christians, or were they into something a bit off-colour? It's interesting, really. Wish I had time to go into it.'

'Or the confession could be fabricated. After the suppression of the Templars, it was easier to slag off Jacques de Molay than go into some dungeon.'

'That's what Aunt Fliss used to say, apparently. She said he was a good man. But then, who wants to think they're living in the house where some psycho was holding court?'

'Roxanne, can I ask you ...? I mean, you probably won't have an answer to this under the circumstances ... But how do the Gwilyms tie in? I mean, they're supposed to have been in that house since the Middle Ages, is that right?'

'So they *say.*'

'So are they claiming to be descended from the Templars or what?'

'I don't know. I mean, yeah, it was their house and they were pretty pissed off about losing it to us. But I thought it was just about money and land. But then I've never had anything to do with them – I was being told not to from a very early age. And then I learned the sort of things they did and what a shit Sycharth was. I mean, there's got to be something, hasn't there, but he's clever. When he learned about Paul, he was like, "Look, I know the fix you're in and why don't I take it off your hands?" Oh yeah, like I *want* my dad and my grandad turning in their graves.'

'You weren't ever tempted?'

'No ... and he blew it anyway, didn't he? I mean, yeah, the Master House was falling into ruins and nobody in their right mind was going to want to rent it now. So the only option *was* to get rid of it. And, like, when we had another approach, six or seven months later, from a chap in Abergavenny, we did start negotiations ... until we found out he was a proxy bidder for Sycharth.'

'Devious.'

'No more than you'd expect. Then Paul was reading about Harewood Park and all the property the Duchy of Cornwall was buying in Herefordshire and we thought, what's to lose? So we took a lot of photos and printed up stuff on the history and posted it off. Couldn't really believe it when they went for it, but ... well, good things happen some-times. And it meant the Gwilyms were stuffed. So maybe old Jacques *was* on our side.'

'Getting de Molay on your side.' Merrily nodded at the plaque. 'That's what this is about? I mean, the caring for customs bit ... you – the Newtons – clearly went out of your way to observe local traditions. The Watch Night?'

'Not in my time.' Roxanne put on a shudder. 'Thank God. But there was always a feeling – and I do feel that way myself sometimes – that either a place is working for you or it's working against you. It's very much a thing you get with farms.'

'And the Master?'

'I wouldn't go that far, but then we're not in the house. That's Prince Charles's problem now. Did ... did Mrs Morningwood tell you about Naomi Newton?'

'I don't think so.'

'Thought not. That's the one she doesn't tell. The lovely Naomi ... she was the youngest sister of my great-grandmother – and of Aunt

Fliss. All daughters of John Newton, who bought the farm off Mrs Gwilym. Naomi ... she was the beauty. Well, this was during World War One, and there weren't many men around – all off getting killed in France. Except for Madog Gwilym – can't remember how *he* avoided it. Running the farm or a club-foot ... something.'

'They all had very distinguished-sounding Welsh names, didn't they?'

'Pretentious gits. Anyway, Madog Gwilym didn't go to war and he fancied his chances with Naomi. This was before the feud set in – all the anger was on the Gwilym side until this happened. Maybe Madog suggested Naomi owed him one for the way the Newtons got the farm, I don't know. But he had a go and she wasn't having any, and she actually called him a coward. In public. In church, actually.'

'Garway Church?'

'Before a congregation of mainly women praying for the boys at the front. Naomi Newton publicly telling Madog Gwilym he wasn't a man. Imagine.'

'What did he say?'

'He's supposed to've walked out of the church in this absolute dead silence. Following day, Naomi's out collecting the eggs and he's waiting for her, and he's like *I'll show you whether I'm a man or not*. Drags her into the trees and forces himself on her.'

'She was raped?'

'He denied it, of course, he said she was up for it, well, don't they always— Well, no— Let me get this right, neither of them said anything at the time. Naomi didn't tell anybody at first. Her brothers were at the war, the only man around was her father, John, well over sixty by then and working day and night to hold the farm together, and she knew what he'd do if he found out and she was afraid for his health. But then the worst happens. Finds out she's pregnant ... and she goes along, on the quiet, to ... the local woman who deals with eventualities like this.'

'Would that have been ... Mrs Morningwood?'

'Oh, you know. That's all right, then. Her gran, this would be. She goes to Mrs Morningwood's grandmother for an abortion. Mrs Morningwood obliges ... but it all went horribly wrong. I don't know what happened, but she got home and there was nobody in at the time, and she began to, you know, haemorrhage?'

'Oh God. It wasn't like you could pick up a phone and call for an ambulance.'

'No. Whether she tried to ... you know ... sort it herself, nobody quite knows, but when my great-grandmother came in with Fliss, they found Naomi on the floor in the big room, in a big pool of blood, her life just ... ebbing away. They hadn't even known she was pregnant. They're desperately trying to stop the bleeding and make her comfort-able ... got a big fire going, and somebody sent for Mrs Morningwood but, of course, it was too late. Mrs Morningwood was stricken with remorse, and my grandmother and Fliss, well ...'

'Must've been shattered and ... furious.'

'They say Mrs Morningwood could never show her face at the Master House again.'

Something clicked.

'Aunt Fliss,' Merrily said. 'Felicity Newton?'

'That's right.'

First time I'd seen a dead 'un ... Face like the skin on a cold egg-custard.

'She was ninety-eight when she died,' Roxanne said. 'Whole village came to pay tribute. They say she was a lovely old girl. They laid her out where Naomi had died, in front of the inglenook, and everybody came.'

'Even the Morningwoods.'

'I'd guess. Likely the first time any of them'd been through that door since Naomi died. Wasn't her fault, mind, she only tried to help. But they say my great-grandmother and Aunt Fliss could never sit in that room again without seeing Naomi trying to raise herself up on an elbow ... you really want to know this? Gives me the creeps even now.'

'Well, I probably don't,' Merrily said. 'But on the other hand ...'

She simply wouldn't tamper with a foetus conceived at the Master House. Call it superstition.

Something else explained.

Roxanne leaned on the shoulders of a dining chair.

'Yeah, I know what you're saying. Something else to remember, when you go in there with your Bible and your holy water. I was eighteen before my mother told me about it. Wish she hadn't bothered, some-times.'

Roxanne sat down and poured herself some more of the powerful coffee from the pot and told it quickly.

'Seems Naomi sits up in the blankets, blood all over her legs and the fire roaring behind her, and she curses Madog Gwilym – curses him in the name of the Grand Master, Jacques de Molay. Kind of … you know, last breath, before she lies down and dies.'

'Oh.'

'Yeah.'

Ironically, the sun slid out in the south-east and filled the bay.

Merrily said, 'Madog?'

'Didn't last the year out,' Roxanne said. 'Came out of one of the pubs one night – The Sun or The Globe, one or the other – saying he didn't feel too well, and collapsed, stone dead at the side of the lane.' Roxanne drank some coffee, winced. 'What a place this is.'

47

A Rough Saw

A WHOLE SUMMER had come and gone since Merrily had seen him last. His hair was still long and rough but more yellow-white, now, like old bone, his dog collar faded to the colour of parchment.

He likes the effect he has, she thought, one hand on the kettle, one hand on the tap. This combination of old hippie and Victorian scholar. He's very much aware of his image.

She hadn't been back from Garway more than a few minutes before he'd trudged in with his case, a hand raised to Merrily, a nod to Mrs Morningwood, before pulling out a chair and spreading papers and books over the refectory table like dealing hands of cards.

'I thought you weren't coming till this afternoon.'

'Got someone to see at two. Might be a bit knackered after that, Merrily. Up far too late last night, thanks to you.'

'Sorry.'

'No consideration, this lass. Leave that for now. Sit down here. Read this.'

'This is Huw Owen. Mrs Morningwood, Huw.'

'Oh aye?'

Huw looked up over his reading glasses. Mrs Morningwood was wearing black jeans and another Army sweater with shoulder patches. Her injuries looked like war wounds and, if anything, worse than last night. One eye was half-closed and weeping; she wiped it with a tissue and put on her sunglasses.

'I've got a sore shoulder,' Huw said. 'Reckon you can do owt?'

'Massage, Mr Owen?'

'I were thinking summat in a pot.'

'That can be arranged.'

'Ta.'

Outside, it had started to rain out of a half-blue sky. Merrily accepted the pages of text Huw was waving at her, glimpsing a Maltese cross before he grabbed them back.

'Save you some time and bullshit.' He turned over a couple of the sheets, tapped a paragraph. 'Start there.'

'What is it?'

'It's about how to become a Knight Templar,' Huw said.

'Now or then?'

'For you, never. It's a lads' thing.'

Who comes here? Merrily read.

Answer: *A pilgrim on his travels, hearing of a Knights Templar encampment, has come with a hope of being admitted.*

'This somebody's primary school project, Huw?'

'Save the sarcasm. Over the page and read the bit I've marked.'

Merrily sat down. Under the heading **Obligation**, she read about the pilgrim having his staff and cross taken away in exchange for a sword, placed in his hand by the Grand Commander.

After which, he swore that he would never knowingly take the blood of a brother Templar, but espouse the brother Templar's cause, knowing it to be just. And if he failed …

'Oh dear.'

… May my skull be sawn asunder with a rough saw, my brains taken out and put in a charger to be consumed by the scorching sun and my skull in another charger, in commemoration of St John of Jerusalem, that first faithful soldier and martyr of our Lord and Saviour. If ever I wilfully deviate from this my solemn obligation, may my light be put out from among men, as that of Judas Iscariot was for betraying his Lord and Master.

Merrily sighed, put down the papers.

'Masons.'

'Masonic Order of Knights Templar,' Huw said. 'But fear not. Only Christians are admitted.'

'That's good to know.'

'It's in the rules, lass.'

'If you're going to have your skull sawn open and your brains fried, best to have it done by a good Christian, that's what I always say.' Merrily propped her elbows on the table, chin falling into cupped hands. 'Huw, I'm feeling tired already. This is a big subject, I'm a little woman. I know nothing about Freemasonry.'

'Why I've come over, lass. I'm a man, and I know a fair bit.'

'What?' She looked up. 'Does that mean ...?'

'No. Not that I haven't been approached, mind. Twice, in fact.'

'Since being ordained?'

'*Only* since I were ordained. Despite all the disapproving noises and a number of critical reports, there's still scores of clergy in the Masons. Most of 'em at ground level. Not so many in the Templars, unless they've got a private income. Can't pick up your surcoat and sword in Asda.'

'They actually ... dress up like Templars?'

'Oh aye. Full bit. Costs an arm and a leg for a full Templar kit, but they get it back. One way or t' other.'

'So I've heard. Huw ...'

Huw looked at her, thin smile.

'Why do I need to know this? Are you telling me the Bishop of Hereford ...?'

'That'd be nice, wouldn't it? But, sadly, Brother Dunmore, according to my information, never progressed beyond basic Craft Masonry and hasn't been to a Lodge meeting for a number of years. Although the bugger's never formally resigned.'

'Why would a man like Bernie get into it in the first place?'

'Happen his dad were in it. That's how it usually happens. Fathers, brothers. Family tradition.'

'What do they get out of it? Apart from contacts and favours. Allegedly.'

'Get out what you put in. Most of 'em, it's a social club. Relaxed night out. Well, relaxed after you've gone through the bit where they hold you at knifepoint. For others, it's a spiritual journey. Sounds like a joke, but for some it becomes just part of your life – it *is* your life. Endless passageways, lass.'

'Leading to?'

'The light. Masonic light. You're travelling towards enlightenment. Through knowledge.'

'Gnosticism.'

'A prominent Mason, Canon Richard Tydeman, said – famously – that trying to describe the joys of Masonry to an outsider was like trying to describe the joys of motherhood to a spinster.'

'How would he know?'

'Suffice to say it brings a sense of order and direction and personal satisfaction to men who were just meandering along. Gives their lives a very clear focus. Whether this—' Huw shook the papers '—mirrors any actual Templar rituals we'll never know because the Templars never wrote owt down, but it's become one of the most popular and sought-after degrees in Masonry. Read the next bit.'

The sword is taken from the candidate and a skull placed in his hand

Furthermore, may the soul that once inhabited this skull, as the representative of John the Baptist, appear against me in the day of judgement ...

'What's that say to you, lass?'

'Baphomet,' Mrs Morningwood said, and Huw smiled at her and stretched his legs under the table, hands behind his head.

'One major theory is that Baphomet translates as *baptism* – the official start of a spiritual life. The head, in this context, is therefore the head of John the Baptist, and some scholars are convinced that's what the Templars venerated.'

'And that's the Christian bit, is it?' Merrily said.

'Or the Christian veneer. Borrow a Biblical figure, make him your own. Regular, ground-floor Masonry you only have to accept a supreme ruler of the universe. Whose name, for the record, is Jahbulon, which they're not supposed to say outside the temple. And which opponents of Masonry say is a weird combination of Christian and Satanic – principally, Jah, for Jehovah, and Baal, the opponent or Devil. The Methodists

brought out a report in 1985 that reckoned the name "Jahbulon" consti-
tuted the single biggest barrier to a true Christian being a Mason.'

'Personally, I'd've thought that threatening to saw open somebody's
skull ...'

'That's just the Masonic Templars. Your bog-standard Craft Mason
merely accepts that if he gives owt away his tongue will be ripped out by
the root and buried in the sand of the sea at low-water mark.'

'Oh well, that's OK, then.'

Merrily thought of the Templar who claimed he'd been brought
before Jacques de Molay at Garway and ordered to *deny Him whom the
image represents* or get himself put in a sack and dumped somewhere
less than congenial.

Huw was looking at her over his glasses.

'The skull bit – it's quite likely the original Templars swore a similar
oath. Fighting-men in brutal times. The idea of Jahbulon is a total
composite god. Three syllables, note, a trinity. Again, in line with what
many scholars accept as Templar belief, which was a cobbling together
of Christianity, paganism, Judaism and Islam. I believe some of the
Templars *were* Gnostics. I think it's likely that some *did* support the
bloodline-of-Christ theory. And I think some of them were devoted to
undermining Christianity from within.'

Mrs Morningwood got out her cigarettes.

'Mind if I ...?'

'Aye, please yourself,' Huw said.

'Mr Owen ... how many of these Knights Templar Masons are there?'

'Thousands in this country. A proportion of them higher clergy.'

'And they're here? In Herefordshire?'

'You could say that.'

'OK.' Merrily sat up. 'Where's this leading, Huw?'

'All roads lead to the cathedral. But you knew that. You had it from
Callaghan-Clarke.'

'She said the Archdeacon was a Mason.'

'Mervyn Neale is Grand Commander, I'm told.'

'Of the Templar Masons?'

'On an Archdeacon's screw, you can afford the kit,' Huw said.

48

Oddball

THINK ABOUT IT, Huw said. The oldest cult in the West.

He talked. He was persuasive. Clouds had closed the sky's one sunny opening, like a cut healed over, and the kitchen had gone grey. Merrily left the lamp off.

Occult: it meant hidden. Freemasonry was occult in every sense, Huw said. A template for all the nineteenth and early twentieth century magical orders – notably the Golden Dawn, where Crowley started, and W.B. Yeats. The symbols, the ceremonial, all there.

'But how much of basic Masonry,' Merrily asked him, 'is actually based on the Templars?'

'Some Masonic scholars would say the lot. The Temple of Solomon, all the architectural jargon? God with a set square and protractors?'

'Where did you find all this out?'

'General knowledge, lass.'

'I mean about Mervyn Neale.'

Huw said that was fairly widely known, too. Not as secretive as they used to be, the Masons. Not in much of a position to be, now they'd been outed in popular books and most of the rituals were online. Taken Huw all of twenty minutes to find and download the Templar initiation ritual, with the sword and the skull and the threat of sunburned brains.

'The Archdeacon,' Merrily recalled, 'was with the Bishop at the Duchy reception in Hereford, where Adam Eastgate first mentioned the problem with the Master House.'

'Merv's ears pricking up. Always been fascinated by Garway, the Masons. Funny you've not run into the bugger up there.' Huw looked at Mrs Morningwood. 'Where do you come into this, lass?'

'*Lass.*' Mrs Morningwood smiled wistfully. 'How kind.'

'This Sycharth Gwilym on the square, you reckon?'

'Ticks all the right boxes, I should've thought, Mr Owen. His particular business, in a city like Hereford …'

'Still a lout of clout in Hereford, the Masons,' Huw said. 'So I'm told. Cathedral. Tory council. You going to see Gwilym today, Merrily?'

'I'll call The Centurion again. Go this afternoon, if he's free.'

'We'll have a quick chat before you go. Just go over them family names again – Sycharth … Gruffydd … Fychan …?'

'Madog.'

'Aye, that's a good one.'

'And …' Merrily glanced at Mrs Morningwood. 'Cynllaith?'

'*Cynllaith,*' Huw said. 'Lovely. People round there really don't know where all these names come from, Mrs M?'

'We're inclined to suspect Wales,' Mrs Morningwood said, and Huw smiled.

'I'll do a last check. Use your computer, lass?'

He stumped off into the scullery, shutting the door, and Merrily turned to Mrs Morningwood.

'People certainly seem to know about Jacques de Molay. Or they did.'

'Naomi Newton.' Mrs Morningwood took off her sunglasses and applied a tissue to an eye. 'I suppose Roxanne related that episode in all its gory detail.'

'Well, *you* certainly didn't.'

'Better you heard it from them. Not my family's finest hour. Haunted my poor grandmother to her own dying day.'

'Anything else you're keeping to yourself that might be relevant?'

'Darling, I have over half a century's worth of knowledge. Who knows what's relevant?'

Huw was back within a few minutes, nodding, satisfied.

'If you were worrying about the Duchy of Cornwall, no need. You're looking at the first generation of male Royals *not* tied up with Masonry. Duke of Edinburgh, he were one – lasped now, mind. Queen's not eligible, of course, but her old man, George VI, he was *well* in. And so it goes.'

'If Charles broke the chain,' Merrily said, 'how does the Masonic hierarchy feel about that?'

'Aye, well, you might've put your finger on summat there, lass.'

'Erm …' Merrily shook out a Silk Cut. 'In your message on the machine last night, you talked about …'

'The feller who advised the Duchy of Cornwall that you wouldn't blab.'

'I think I've managed to contain my curiosity quite well.'

Huw looked at Mrs Morningwood, who gathered up her cigarettes and matches.

'I need to go and bathe my eyes.' She stood up, Roscoe stretching at her feet. 'Perhaps apply something foul-smelling to other abused areas.'

'Nice dog,' Huw said.

'Interesting woman,' he said when she'd gone. 'Always been attracted to strong ladies. When you get past a certain age, mind, almost all womankind develops a strange and sorrowful allure.'

Merrily sat back, arms folded, gazing at the ceiling.

'All right,' Huw said. 'Sorry for the anticlimax. You were right first time. Well, I couldn't say owt on the phone, could I?'

'You bloody *denied* it!'

'No big deal, anyroad. I'm not an official consultant or owt like that, just acknowledged as not linked to any of the factions in the Church. Safe pair of ears, in other words.'

'You've met him?'

'No. Never. No need. Best not to, really. Basically, this is summat I inherited from Dobbs. No offence to you, but he could never trust a woman. And you weren't around then, anyroad. Essentially, there's a handful of us – Jeavons is another.'

'Ah.'

Canon Llewellyn Jeavons, once tipped as the first black Archbishop of Canterbury – until his wife died and he went strange, becoming an expert on healing and deliverance with an email address book containing Somali witch doctors and Aboriginal songline-hoppers. It figured.

'It was decided that certain people close to the throne needed a bit of looking out for. With regard to spiritual aspects of their lives and work. This lad, his heart's in the right place, but he will keep putting his foot in it.'

'BMA chauvinism and architectural carbuncles?'

'Tip of the iceberg, lass. He gets frustrated and fires off letters to Government ministers. Well, fair enough, I say. An independent mind. If a man thinks he can see the civilized world going down the pan and he wants to use whatever influence he's got to try and stop it, I'm all for it. But *they* don't like it. Far as the Government's concerned, the Family ought to know its place. Which is on the sideboard.'

'Strictly ornamental.'

'Exactly. You heard from that chippy little copper?'

'Bliss? Yesterday.'

'Got a feller on his back, you said.'

'Jonathan Long.'

'Aye. Slime like him, see, times've changed. Used to be the spooks automatically supported royalty as an institution. Now they're Government animals. Servants of spin. And if the Government of the day should contain a number of people of, shall we say, republican instincts, in key positions ... You know what I'm getting at?'

'Go on.'

'For instance, Governments, national and European, don't like alternative medicine, they like straight doctors, drugs and drug companies. They like GM foods and meat imports and they don't really give a shit for animal welfare. Or farmers, for that matter.'

Huw stopped and looked at Merrily. Merrily shrugged.

'Plus, unless you're Islamic and they can't decide whether to bang you up or kiss your arse, this is now a secular country. Merlin the Wizard, he could be heading for the sideboard, too, and he knows it. And yet, despite what anybody says, there's a great spiritual yearning out there.'

'Just that the way some of it's expressed doesn't please some of our more traditional colleagues,' Merrily said.

'And if some of these oddball spiritual pathways appear to have been trodden by the heir to the throne – well, not good news for the Church, but not necessarily bad news for the republicans. Use it to shaft him again – eccentric's one thing, bonkers summat else. There's quite a body of opinion thinks this could turn out to be a good time to lose 'em.'

'Dump the monarchy?'

'Or stand well back and allow it to dump itself. A lot of cynicism about the Family right now. What's your view?'

'Expensive, undemocratic. And some, on the fringes, have been free-loading airheads. But, at the end of the day, I suppose I feel happier that they're there. They represent something I feel kind of reassured to have around. Plus, can you think of a contemporary politician you could stand to see as President?'

'Happen you'd've got on with Dobbs better than either of you thought possible.'

'I'm guessing Dobbs was closer to all this than you. He knew Laurens van der Post, for a start.'

'Aye, he did. Knew him way back, and renewed the contact not long before his death. See, there's a lot of superstition around the monarchy, and Charleses haven't been too lucky. Charles I, executed – very public human sacrifice. Charles II had to hide in an oak tree, thus becoming the Green Man. You heard that one?'

'Don't think so.'

'The head of Charles II peering through the foliage ... the green man to the life.'

'I suppose it is. What's the significance?'

'A title which, for different reasons of his own choosing, could easily be applied to the future King Charles III. But because Charles is seen as an *unhappy* name for a king, the word is he'll adopt one of his other names and become King George VII. Which doesn't change things *much*, as your green man in churches has also been associated with *Saint* George. But that's by the by.'

'Huw, aren't we getting just a bit ...'

'I'm giving you the folklore. The mythology. The superstition. Dobbs was a mystic. He believed the monarchy – good or bad, strong or weak – was preserving something fundamentally essential to the spiritual welfare of Britain … part of the soul of the nation, if you like. That if Church and State were still in bed together, nowt much would go wrong in the great scheme of things.'

'So Charles suddenly announcing he wants to be defender of faiths plural …?'

'Weakens it. At the wrong time, Dobbs thought. That's where he and van der Post fell out. All that about all religions being the same dog washed, that came from van der Post.'

'I don't knock it,' Merrily said. 'If we can coexist …'

'Aye, in theory. In practice, it gets politicized, and Islam wants to run the show. And that's where the Templars came in – the first fusion. Picking up Islam from the Saracens, Jewish mysticism, Egyptian mysteries, happen some Celtic paganism and goddess-worship via the Cistercians. They were accused of undermining Christianity from within and happen there's some truth in it. A multifaith multinational, building up massive wealth, very, very quickly. Undermining kings and popes.'

'And *did* they practise some kind of ritual magic?'

'It were said they used their knowledge of the so-called dark arts in warfare. Change the weather? Bring down mist, create storms? We're never really going to know what they were about.'

'And you see van der Post in the Templar tradition?'

'In some ways. Mate of Carl Jung, who was an admirer of the Gnostics … and can you find a better Jungian archetype than the green man or the Baphomet? Ah, you can go on like this for ever.' Huw started gathering up papers. 'Folk might well be asking why the Duchy's suddenly buying Templar properties in Herefordshire.'

'Just the one, surely?'

'No. Let's not forget the big project – Harewood Park. Large estate, with an old chapel in the middle, granted to the Knights Templar in 1215 by King John.'

Upstairs, Roscoe started barking.

'Why don't *I* know these things?' Merrily said.

'And a satellite of Garway, as it happens. Could be pure coincidence, but some folks might see a significance. The Masons, for instance. They don't like no longer having a foot under the throne. If he appears to be into Templarism, they're happen wondering if he might not be ripe for a new approach.' Huw looked up. 'How do, lad.'

Lol had let himself in, having slipped off home in the early hours. Merrily thought he still didn't look too happy.

For some reason, he was insisting that when she went to see Sycharth Gwilym, she shouldn't go alone.

49

Let Her Squirm

THE WORD ACROSS Hereford was that The Centurion was already a gold mine. Converted out of a single-storey derelict factory off Roman Road, to the north of the city. Good access, sweeping views, plenty of parking.

And now that Roman Road had become the outlet for the network of new roads serving Hereford's secret bypass ... why, you'd almost think Sycharth Gwilym had learned something in advance.

Merrily had been thinking about this and what it might imply but now, suddenly, she wasn't.

'He did *what*?'

Sitting up hard, the seat belt straining.

'Didn't seem a good time to tell you last night,' Lol said.

'For God's *sake*!'

'I'm not saying Gwilym operates on the same level, but maybe it's as well to know the kind of people you just might be dealing with.'

'This ...' Merrily shutting her eyes '... is all my fault.'

Broken into the truck, hot-wired it, driven it away and forced the box. Then used another kind of hot wire on the Boswell. She stared at Lol, an acid sensation in her chest. Knowing he hadn't gone to the police because that would have meant explanations. Same with the insurance.

'It's *not* ... your fault. Can't say Prof didn't warn me about the kind of people he employed.'

'It was your most precious ...'

'It was just a guitar.'

'Four grand's worth. More than that, a huge sentimental ...'

'Maybe,' Lol admitted.

'I'm going to call Al Boswell, see how much it would cost for him to replace it.'

'Merrily, we don't even *tell* Al Boswell. He'd take it very personally, and he isn't getting any younger and all his guitars are like children. And neither of us has four grand to spare, and even if we *did* ...'

'*Bastard.*' Tears stinging her eyes. 'Plus, he's giving you a clear warning that he's going to try and destroy your career.'

'What could he do? Independent producer, independent label ...'

'... Reliant on major distribution networks and chain stores. Sorry if this sounds like I'm getting drunk on conspiracy theory.'

'But you ...' Lol glanced sideways. 'You're OK, though?'

'Mrs Morningwood's offered to give me more reflexology tonight.' Merrily leaned back, trying to kill the tightness. 'I'm fine. Much better. So *this* is why you were insisting on coming with me.'

'I'll stay in the truck when you go in, but I'll be just outside. Call you on the mobile after an hour?'

'How could they know the importance of the Boswell?'

'Look ...' He sighed. 'Let's leave it for now.'

'But how?'

'It was in *Mojo*. Someone showed me a copy at the gig. Concert review, picture of me and what – unmistakably to any musician – is a Boswell.'

'How did you manage at the gig?'

'Still had the Takamine, which they hadn't damaged. You said do it for Nick, so I did. He was sitting at the back. He didn't walk out.'

'*Lol?*'

'Kidding. I think.'

'But it went well?'

'Strangely, it did. I felt very tired afterwards. Slept for half an hour in the car park with the top of the box held down with bailer twine. Look, be careful in there. None of this smells good. Stourport, Gwilym, Mat Phobe.'

She'd told him about the anagram.

'Of course, we only have Hayter's word that Mat's actually dead,' Lol said. 'This the entrance?'

Merrily looked up at an archway of sandstone.

'Think it's supposed to look like a Roman villa?'

'Chapel of Rest, circa 1963.'

'Maybe '65,' Merrily said.

This time, when she'd called, the receptionist had said that Mr Gwilym would be happy to talk to her at two-thirty. When she walked in five minutes early – best black woollen coat – he was already waiting, on the edge of a mosaic tile circle, standing between two small fountains burbling into bidet-type projections. Bending to her, handshake smooth and soft, like suede.

'Mrs Watkins.'

'Good of you to spare the time.'

'How could I not? All so intriguing. My office is just here. Can I order you a drink? Coffee ... wine?'

'Just had lunch, thank you, Mr Gwilym.'

'Here?'

'A sandwich. At home.'

'Most remiss of me not to have offered you a proper lunch. My apologies.' He shouldered open a matt-white door in a recess. 'Business, of late, has been utterly frenetic.'

His voice was public-school English but – whatever anybody said – there was posh South Wales down there, something slow and rhythmic like an evening tide washing against a jetty.

'I wouldn't have had time,' Merrily said. 'But thank you, anyway.'

For some reason, she'd been expecting barrel chest, spider veins, flashing eyes, belligerent – someone it would be easy to goad into saying too much. But Sycharth Gwilym was a loose, big-boned man with a jutting chin and grey-brown hair which rose and fell, like the plume on a knight's helmet, and his manner was relaxed, his eyes pale and tranquil. And when you looked into them you didn't see anything of Fuchsia Mary Linden.

Merrily's confidence waned. This was going to take time and maybe skills that she didn't have.

Mr Gwilym waited for Merrily to sit before moving behind his desk.

The office had a picture window with a view over the car park, over the city, towards the cathedral and the river. White walls and a glass-topped, white-painted desk with the wood grain showing through. Twin swivel chairs in grey leather. A small conference table.

'So ...' He sat down, leaning back, composed. 'You wanted to ask me about the Master House.'

Behind his head was a large framed print: an engraving of a robed man with a forked beard, sitting in a Gothic canopied throne, holding a sceptre.

No prizes.

'You do realize,' Sycharth Gwilym said, 'that the house hasn't been in my family for over a century?'

'I do know that. But it does seem to have been occupied by Gwilyms for several centuries before that.'

'I'm not entirely sure about Gwilyms, as *such*, but various of my ancestors, yes.'

Start off with the routine stuff. Merrily brought out a pad and a pencil.

'Do you know exactly how long the family was there?'

'I do not know when the family was *not* there. Although records – such as they are – go back no further than the fifteenth century.'

'That would be the time of the Owain Glyndwr rebellion.'

'Indeed. Mrs Watkins, may I ... inquire the purpose of this? The stories I hear about the nature of your mission to Garway are probably far more lurid than the truth.'

Merrily told him why the late Felix Barlow had refused to work in the Master House, what had happened to Felix and Fuchsia, and he lifted his jaw.

'Oh. *Not* more lurid then.'

He didn't smile. There was always a point, during every inquiry of this kind, where you felt fairly foolish, where you thought, *What am I doing here?*

'Mr Gwilym, look, I'm well aware that we live in a secular age and most people consider me some kind of anachronism and the basis of my job barely rational, but ...'

He didn't say anything. Why should he? Let her squirm.

'… All I can say is that sometimes I've been able to help people feel more comfortable about their situations or a particular place.'

Sycharth Gwilym crossed his legs.

'And who would you be helping in this particular instance, Mrs Watkins? The Prince of Wales?'

'Well, I don't imagine anyone knows, at this stage, who'll eventually be occupying the Master House. We'd just like them not to be bothered by whatever remains of whoever was there before them. Or whatever they did.'

'Ghosts?'

'If you like.'

'By which you mean the spirits of the dead?'

'Or aspects of memory. Lingering guilt.'

Sycharth Gwilym nodded patiently.

'I appreciate, Mrs Watkins, that you are doing your best to tread carefully, and I shall try to assist you however I can.'

'Thank you.'

He extended a hand, offering her the floor.

It seemed a wide and exposed area.

50

Sycharth

SHE SAT IN the grey swivel chair, trying not to think of cigarettes.

'Do you remember the last time you were in the Master House, Mr Gwilym?'

He didn't hesitate, nodding in a resigned way.

'Yes, I am rather afraid that I do.'

'When would that have been?'

'Oh ... more than thirty years ago, certainly. I was a young man. I'd been invited, along with other local youngsters, to a party – the kind of party I would *not* attend today, but I expect that in your own, clearly more recent, youth, you also ...?'

Gwilym said that the Master House had been leased by the Newtons to a group of people who had money to spare, took drugs and behaved with ... a certain lack of inhibition. He supposed that, as country kids, they'd been fascinated and flattered to be invited to join in, half-expecting celebrities to be there.

Merrily said, 'So that would've been you and ...?'

'Mainly young women – perhaps another reason I was keen to go.'

'Do you remember their names, by any chance?'

Do you remember the black girl?

A minimal shake of the head. Pointless asking that at this stage.

'And what happened at the party?'

'I was offered cannabis, which I felt obliged to take. And which must have had an effect because I recall very little of what happened afterwards.'

'That's a shame.'

'Although I do remember, towards midnight, someone suggesting

364

that – given the age of the house and its atmosphere by candlelight – we should hold a sort of seance. With the intention of making contact with the dead.'

'For what purpose?'

'I doubt whether there's a logical answer to that.'

'A *sort* of seance?'

'I do remember some of the people there being excited to discover that many generations of my family had lived in the house. Someone suggested that it would be interesting for me to be put in touch with my ancestors.'

'How did you feel about that?'

'Hardly in a position – or, I would guess, in any state – to say no.'

'And how did they go about it?'

'All a blur, I'm afraid, Mrs Watkins.'

'Ouija board?'

'You mean letters and an upturned glass? Not that I *recall*.'

'Do you remember which of your ancestors they were trying to reach?'

'I imagine any one of them would have been more than welcome. Why? Do you think we might somehow have conjured up something that is still, ah, walking the place?'

'It's just that … your first name, the names of several of your fore-bears and your son seem to correspond to a particular pattern. One called Owain. Then there was Gruffydd. And Fychan?'

'My father. And my great-grandfather.'

Merrily looked up at the engraving of the fork-bearded man with the sceptre.

'The last man to try to bring about an independent Wales by force, in the fifteenth century – having himself declared Prince of Wales – was Owain ap Gruffydd Fychan.'

Was that an actual movement in Sycharth's sleepy eyes?

'Widely known as Owain Glyndwr. And *his* father's name …' Merrily consulted the pad '… was, I believe, Gruffydd Fychan ap *Madog*.'

'You have a better knowledge of Welsh history than most of your countrymen, Mrs Watkins.'

'Welsh friends. Now. Owain's father, I think, was baron of somewhere called … *Cynllaith Owain*?'

No reaction.

'And Glyndwr's own mansion in north-east Wales was, of course, called … *Sycharth*.'

'Well done indeed, Mrs Watkins.'

'So the Gwilyms have a family tradition of male children being given names connected with Owain Glyndwr. Who is said to have stayed at the Master House while on the run from the English, after his campaign collapsed.'

'I believe that is the story, yes.'

'One your family is evidently very proud of.'

'Yes,' he said. 'I suppose we are. Especially now, in a time when Owain's vision is becoming reality. How gratified he would be to see the formation of the Welsh Assembly … as a start. Not yet enough, but a start.'

'And all done without anyone being killed,' Merrily said. 'Or a single castle being burned to the ground.'

'Yes, quite a number of castles in this area were destroyed. And people killed. Still, many landowning families in the vicinity of Garway supported his campaign. The whole area – even as far as Hereford itself – had been part of the old Wales, and allegiances remain to this day.'

'And here he is on your wall, here in England. The *Mab Darogan* – Son of Prophecy? Who, according to legend, never died, just faded into the landscape of his beloved Wales, until such time as Wales has need of him again.'

'I am a fan,' Mr Gwilym said.

'But if his daughter was at Kentchurch Court, just down the valley, why would he need to spend time at the Master House?'

'To his enemies, Kentchurch would have been a rather obvious place to go. Not that he didn't, but …'

'Maybe there were other attractions at the Master House?'

'I'm sorry?'

'I was wondering …' Merrily was gazing up at Owain, the sceptre rising meaningfully from between his legs '… if perhaps there was … I don't know, a Gwilym daughter? Who, when Owain was in hiding and understandably a bit depressed about the way things had turned out, devoted herself to … kind of cheering him up a bit.'

'You are suggesting that we might be descended directly from Owain Glyndwr.'

Merrily shrugged.

'All right,' he said. 'Some of my family have believed that. There was a woman called Elinor Gwilym, born around the turn of the fifteenth century, who became quite a matriarch in my family. Some of my ancestors bore quite a resemblance to …' He glanced up. 'It has even been said that I … Anyway, which of my countrymen would *not* wish to be related to the greatest Welshman in history, the last real Prince of Wales?'

'Quite.'

Merrily was remembering the way Adam Eastgate had looked at her when she'd reminded him, rather tactlessly, that Edward II was only the first *English* Prince of Wales.

'However,' Gwilym said, 'I doubt that the great man would have deigned to appear to a bunch of stoned kids.'

'Of course, Owain wasn't the only great historical figure to have stayed at the Master House. Would your ancestors have been there while the Templars were in Garway?'

'It was a Templar farm.'

'Perhaps hosting Jacques de Molay in 1294?'

'So it is said.'

'And whatever he brought with him?'

'I don't understand.'

'I'm not sure I do either, but people keep mentioning the possibility of Templar treasure winding up in Garway.'

Sycharth Gwilym laughed.

'Your family never looked for it? Although, when you think about it, I expect the Gwilyms had already lost the house when all this speculation started about the Templars and their wealth and the secrets they guarded.'

No response.

'Be a good reason to want the house back,' Merrily said. 'Especially if you had all the family records.'

'What are you suggesting?'

'Just passing on gossip.'

'Ridiculous.'

'Yes. I expect it is. It's just that a friend of mine – a Welsh friend – was pointing out that Glyndwr's campaign was fired by the unjust treatment of the Welsh by the English marcher lords. And, more specifically, a personal injustice, when some of his own land in North Wales, near the English border, was seized by his neighbour, the Lord of Rhuthun.'

'That's recorded history.'

'Owain then sought justice from the English parliament and was turned away. Lord Rhuthun kept the land. Another version of the story suggests that Lord Rhuthun was close to the king of England, Henry IV, and blackened Owain's name at court. Either way, it started a devastating war.'

'And?'

'Lord Rhuthun's name was Reginald Grey. That's an interesting coincidence, isn't it?'

Sycharth Gwilym raised an eyebrow.

'I mean the way the Master House fell, quite recently, by marriage, into the hands of the *Grays*. Unlikely to be any relation, but I suppose it has a certain … poetic resonance.'

Gwilym shaking his head dismissively, but Merrily wasn't abandoning the punchline.

'And *then* … just when you thought you were going to be able to buy it back, and can well afford to – this house, the house that puts you at the centre of so much crucial history, handed by the Grays to … well, not to the Crown exactly, but, even worse, to—'

Merrily's phone chimed in her bag. Not now, Lol, please …

She saw Sycharth Gwilym wetting his lips and shut her bag on the phone.

'… To the latest *English* Prince of …'

'I think you had better answer your call,' he said. 'Go outside, if you like.'

'Thank you … I'm sorry.'

When she stood up and was taking the phone to the door, Merrily saw Sycharth Gwilym standing up too, following her out. When she was holding the phone to her ear, he'd closed the office door behind them.

'Lol,' she said, 'look—'

'Do yourself a favour, lass,' Huw said. 'Get over to the cathedral. Now.'

'Huw, if you can give me just a few minutes, I'll call you back.'

'I wouldn't hang around, I were you.'

'Most pleasant talking to you, Mrs Watkins,' Gwilym said as she folded the phone. 'You are a most intelligent and charming woman. But I'm afraid I have a meeting at three-thirty.'

'Mr Gwilym …' Dropping the phone in her bag, feeling a fizzing of panic in her stomach. 'Before you go … the main reason I came was to ask if you'd be interested in joining me and one of the Grays and a representative of the Duchy of Cornwall at a short Requiem service at the Master House.'

'I think I shall probably discover a prior appointment on that occasion,' Gwilym said. 'As it is not our house any more.'

The two fountains trickled. Merrily felt spray on her face.

'I was thinking that, as the house no longer belongs to either of you, this might be a good time to draw a line under the years of bad feeling between the two families. For instance, I was hearing only this morning about your great-grandfather. Madog? The way he died?'

'I beg your pardon?'

'Outside the pub.'

'That's a lot of nonsense. Madog seems to have had a heart condition.'

'Anyway, I was just thinking we might … heal some history.'

'The idea,' Gwilym said, 'that history can – or should – be healed is, to some of us, anathema.'

Merrily looked over at the woman receptionist who wore a pale dress secured with a brooch at the shoulder, Roman-style. She was on the phone.

'The people leasing the house – Lord Stourport …'

'Mrs Watkins, I don't remember his name, but I'm sure he wasn't a lord.'

'And another man who called himself Mat Phobe ... do you remember him?'

'No.'

'Do you remember a black girl called Mary?'

'*No*. I'm sorry, you'll have to excuse me.'

'Do you know what happened to—?'

She watched him slip away under an archway. The phone rang, and this time it *was* Lol.

'Merrily, if Gwilym's there don't react, but I've just seen Jimmy Hayter going into the main bar.'

51

The Deal

WHEN JANE GOT in from school, the Volvo was parked in the vicarage drive, but there was no sign of Mum, just Mrs Morningwood and Roscoe. Mrs Morningwood was unwinding her scarf.

'I've been across to the shop, Jane. He was getting tired of cat food. My God, I felt like the Phantom of the bloody Opera in there, the way people stared.'

'You should've asked me to go,' Jane said. 'As I understand it, nobody's supposed to know you're here.'

'Felt liked a caged tiger today, darling, I can tell you.'

'Where's Mum?'

'In Hereford. Talking to Suckarse. Wish I was a bloody fly on *that* wall.'

'Mrs Morningwood, while we're on our own ...' Jane shed her bag and her parka in a pile on the flags, pulled out a chair at the kitchen table. 'You got beaten up, didn't you?'

'What's wrong with a car crash?'

'What's wrong with it is I'm seventeen. As distinct from, like, nine?'

'Poor Jane.' Mrs Morningwood sat down. 'Balancing on the cusp.'

'What's that mean?' Jane looked at the ruins of what she guessed had once been a seriously cool woman. 'Who did this to you? Why can't you just spit it out?'

'I well remember being your age. The fear of making a commitment to the wrong future.'

'The future. Right. I hate the sodding future.'

'Yes, that's how things *have* changed, isn't it? When I was your age we couldn't wait to plunge into it, like a deep blue swimming pool. Now the pool seems have gone and you're looking down into hard, cracked mud.'

'Yeah.' Jane decided she wasn't going to get anywhere on the phoney car crash. 'You believe in clairvoyance, Mrs Morningwood?'

'Depends how you're spelling it.' Mrs Morningwood broke into a fresh packet of cigarettes. 'I accept, to an extent, the phenomenon of clairvoy*ance*. While remaining generally sceptical about clairvoy*ants* – people who profess to prophecy.'

'A woman once did a tarot reading for me,' Jane said. 'She said – for instance – that I'd have more than one serious lover before I was twenty?'

'Not the most ambitious prediction, darling.'

'I went out with this guy for, like, ages? Well over a year.'

'A serious commitment.'

'We were good friends.'

'Quite rare.'

'And I'm thinking, you're *seventeen*. And you're in danger of becoming, like, *half of a couple*?'

'Too cosy?'

'I mean we'd nearly broken up a couple of times, but it never lasted. Then he went to university – last month. And I just stopped answering his calls.'

Mrs Morningwood sat and thought about this.

'You mean you were angst-ridden because your love life was lacking in angst? No one else on the horizon?'

'There was this guy I *quite* fancied. Not realizing that he was married. At one stage I was kind of thinking that could be, you know, quite … quite an experience. Being the other woman. But then I thought …'

'Breaking up someone's marriage?'

'Then I thought of my dad betraying Mum. He had another woman. He was a lawyer, and she worked in his office and they got killed together in a car crash when I was little.'

'Oh dear.' Mrs Morningwood sounding less than sympathetic. 'I … did that once, you know. Broke up a marriage.'

'What happened?'

'*I* married him, and it was a disaster. After the decree nisi, I ran into his first wife, and she was into a new relationship and very happy. She said she was … grateful to me. Quite.'

'And what about you?'

'Pretty pissed off, darling, but that's life, isn't it?'

'Nobody else, since?'

'Oh, quite a few. But none of them ever became friends.'

'And that's the moral, is it?' Jane said. 'If he's also a friend, hold on to him.'

'Oh, I *never* talk about morals, of any kind. Nor do I give advice. What else did your tarot reader tell you?'

'Well, that's the problem. She knew what Mum did, and she had an agenda. So I can't really trust the rest.'

'But you trusted what she said about your love life.'

'I don't know.'

'Have you had sex with the married man?'

'Actually, erm, no. But I think I could make it happen.'

'Well, of *course* you could—'

'Actually, it's already been kind of good for me. In a life-changing way, really. What's he …?

Roscoe was on his feet about half a second before the front doorbell rang.

'I'll get it.' Jane stood up. 'You'd better pop into the scullery in case it's Bliss or somebody who asks questions.'

In the hall, she opened the door to a guy in a green hiking jacket. Clergy shirt and a dog collar underneath. Familiar-looking baggage at his feet.

'Hullo.' Dome head, big friendly smile through his white beard. 'Would you be Jane, by any chance?'

'Um, yeah. I'm afraid Mum's out, though.'

'Oh, well, look, I'm Teddy Murray. Odd-job man at Garway. Your mother was staying with us for a couple of nights and had to leave in a hurry. Said she'd come back for her stuff, but I know how busy she is and I happened to be passing through, en route to Hereford, so …'

He picked up the bags and beamed.

'Oh, right,' Jane said. 'Great.'

'Must say, this is a lovely village, Jane. You're both very lucky.'

'Yeah. I suppose we are.'

'Well, I'll just … leave them here, shall I?'

Teddy Murray dropped the overnight bags over the threshold, into the path of Roscoe who'd come trotting through from the kitchen.

And Roscoe just went totally crazy.

Snarling. Like *all*-snarl, huge jagged teeth exposed, like the ripper teeth on a circular saw. This Teddy Murray backing away into the drive.

'*Roscoe!*' Jane down behind the dog, desperately hauling on his collar through the hackles. She could be in trouble here. 'Oh, God, sorry … sorry …'

Getting dragged through the doorway, Roscoe's jaws opening and shutting like a gin trap on a spring.

'Guard dog, eh?' Teddy Murray trying to smile from a few metres back. 'I suppose two girls on their own in a big house …'

'Back to the …' Jane's knees grazed on the mat '… obedience classes.'

'Tell your mum I'll talk to her again,' Teddy Murray said.

Jane got the door shut, the dog inside, the snarl reduced to a low rumble. Blowing out a lot of air in a whoosh, she went back into the kitchen where Mrs Morningwood was standing in the middle of the floor, face like hardening plaster.

'My fault, darling.' Her voice clearly on autopilot, somewhere different from her thoughts. 'Should have shut him … somewhere.'

'He hasn't done it before, has he?' Jane said. 'I mean, like … tried to savage somebody?'

'Oh.' Mrs Morningwood was expressionless. 'No. No, he hasn't.'

Huw was in the North Transept with his old mate Tommy Canty, lighting a candle.

'Dunmore's here.'

'Where?'

Merrily looked around. Six candles were burning on a tiered stand in front of the renovated shrine of St Thomas Cantilupe. Back in the

Middle Ages, there'd been long queues – scores of pilgrims, sick people and relatives of the sick. Tommy Canty had been Beckett-class in his day.

There was a container of candles you could buy to light and ask for the saint's help. Huw fitted his candle into one of the holders.

'Bishop's in one of the chantries. Trying to reach an arrangement with his Governor.'

'That's why you've got me here? To face up to the Bishop?'

She was feeling very much on edge. Lol had driven her down to Broad Street, dropped her on the corner by the Cathedral Green and then, against all her pleas, driven off back towards Westgate and Roman Road to find the man who'd destroyed the most beautiful guitar in the world.

'Dunmore wants to talk to you,' Huw said.

'About what?'

'About what he's just trying to clear with his God.'

'Bernie's who you came to see? He was your appointment?'

'And every bit as knackering as I'd figured. You forget how shit-scared they are. Bowed under the gross weight of centuries of solemn, dark ceremonial.'

'Not as many centuries as the Church has. Not by a long way.'

'Only the Church doesn't threaten to rip your tongue out by the roots if you finger a brother or shout out *Jahbulon* on the bus.'

'Fair enough. What's he going to tell me?'

'I'd say whatever you want to ask. So have a think about it before you go in.'

'Seriously?'

'Unless he chickens out.'

'What did you say to him?'

'Mr Gwilym helpful, was he?'

'Didn't intend to be, but I rather think he was. What did you say to the Bishop?'

'I'd better be off, lass.'

'You're going?'

'Nowt else I can do here.' He looked over the candles to the shrine. 'See you, then, Tommy.'

Nodding to the tomb in which there hadn't, for many years, been anything of Tommy.

'Huw, I think I'd rather you stayed.'

'Lass …' Huw bent to her. 'It's *part of the deal.* Just you and him.'

'Oh.'

'I won't pray for you.' He put a hand on her shoulder. 'Already done that bit.'

He pointed to the seventh candle.

'What did you say to him, Huw?'

'Didn't need to say much. Callaghan-Clarke'd already been in.'

'Oh.'

'Just get on with it, eh?'

Looking slightly irritable, Huw left Merrily in the cold light of the North Transept, the handful of candles a small and lonely glow.

52

Male Thing

LOL WAS STANDING next to Jimmy Hayter's champagne Jaguar, the
formula fantasy flashing past: he hot-wires the Jag, takes it away, calls
Hayter on his mobile with directions.

And then what?

As he didn't know Hayter's mobile number or how to hot-wire a car,
there wasn't much point in taking it further. He just stood there, leaning
against the front of the Jag, in full view of the picture window identified
by Merrily as the window of Sycharth Gwilym's office.

The sky had gloomed over again and it began to rain. Lol didn't
move. The mobile in his pocket was switched on. Until he had a call
from the cathedral, there was nowhere to go.

After twenty minutes, his grey *Alien* sweatshirt dark with rain, he still
hadn't moved.

He was very cold.

After twenty-five minutes, it stopped raining and Lord Stourport
came out.

The walls and ceiling of the fifteenth-century Chantry Chapel of Bishop
John Stanbury were of richly foliate stone. It was like being under a
copse of low, weeping trees in winter.

'I'm going to retire, Merrily,' the Bishop said.

It wasn't warm in here but he'd taken off his jacket. There was a small
green stain on a shoulder of his purple shirt.

'You always say that,' Merrily said.

She was sitting next to him, facing the golden-haloed Virgin and Child
in the triptych, Gothic-spired, over an altar the size of a boxed radiator.

Bernie Dunmore had lost some weight in the past year and his tonsure had expanded.

'It is possible, you know,' he said, 'to be a Freemason and a priest, without compromise.'

'But hard, I'd've thought.'

'Hard, yes. My father and two uncles were Masons. When I joined, I was barely out of theological college. For a while it seemed almost compatible. The lodge included two canons and the Dean. Several bishops were still active Masons, then. Not now, of course.'

'You could've left.'

'Yes, of course you *can* leave. But they consider that the vows, once made, cannot be revoked.'

'But you never actually did.'

'Haven't been to a lodge meeting or a social event for well over twenty years. But it always seemed to me that to publicly renounce the Craft would've caused more fuss than it was worth. I've never courted controversy, as you know.'

'Why did you stop going, in the end?'

'They ... they tell you it can't be incompatible because it isn't a religion. And then you find yourself asking, but is it an *anti*-religion?'

'Anti-faith, anyway.' Merrily kept her eyes on the Virgin. 'Gnostic. The search for some kind of God within yourself.'

'Yes. In a way.'

'And *is* it?'

'Anti-religion? I still can't decide. We even have Masonic services, as you know, at the cathedral. All I know is that at some stage, I prayed for help. The answer was: get out.'

'But you didn't.'

'It wasn't a *problem*, Merrily. Not until ...'

'Last week?'

Dunmore was silent for what must have been close to half a minute. It had become darker in the chantry, the stained glass in the window dulled. Merrily sensed that it was raining outside.

'You were approached,' she said.

'Nothing so formal. I was advised that well-intentioned, well-regarded men might be damaged by ... your inquiries.'

'Well-intentioned, well-regarded Masons.'

'The word was never used.'

'But the person who gave you the advice ...'

'Was someone who had given me good advice on many occasions, let's not forget that.'

'Archdeacon Neale.'

'It was felt that you were going too far into areas that weren't essential to what you were being asked to do.'

'What, you mean God's work?'

'It ...' Dunmore gritted his teeth. 'You always go *too bloody deep*, Merrily. Anybody else, it would be in and out, a quick blessing, a Requiem. You had to ask questions, even getting Jane to ...'

'What?'

'Ask questions. At school.'

'How would you ...?' Merrily thought about it. 'The history teacher? Robbie Williams?'

'Richard Williams.'

'On the square?'

Bernie sighed.

'Knight Templar, perhaps?'

'He's a medieval historian, Merrily.'

'Bloody hell, Bernie, this is worse than CCTV. Do you know Sycharth Gwilym?'

'Not personally. I know he's become a prime mover in this city, fingers in pies.'

'But Mervyn Neale knows him, presumably.'

'Yes.'

'Knight Templar?'

'*Yes, yes, yes.*'

'Have you come across Lord Stourport?'

'No. Lapsed. I believe. Look, Merrily, it doesn't mean they're all corrupt. It's done a lot of good. Straightened out men whose whole lives might have been selfish and pointless.'

'Well, not for me to judge. But, just to put you in the picture, Bernie, over thirty years ago Stourport and Gwilym were both involved in pseudo-Templar rites at the Master House in which women were abused. One of them has never been seen again. She was the mother of Fuchsia Mary Linden, found dead on the railway after her friend was murdered. Oh, and it seems likely that Stourport or Gwilym was the father.'

'God ...'

'Or possibly a third man who called himself Mat Phobe, who Stourport says is dead. I've just been to talk to Sycharth Gwilym, who I'd say is suffering from a severe case of censored-memory syndrome.'

'What would you expect?'

'There's also been ... another incident. Someone very nearly killed.'

'Who?'

'You wouldn't know her. And if one of them knew another had committed a murder, would he keep quiet?'

'I ...'

'Bernie ...' Merrily looked at Bernie Dunmore hard, through the dense, sacred dimness of the chantry. 'I can't believe this – you're sweating.'

'Don't ... don't ask me to explain, because I can't. I cannot rationally explain it. I'm going to retire next year, and I shall leave Herefordshire.' He had his hands clasped on his knees; he stared down at them. 'The call I made to you yesterday morning. Forget it. It never happened. Do what you have to.'

'I don't know what I'm going to do. I couldn't prove anything – I don't know the half of it. Not yet, anyway.'

'If it's a matter for the police, go to the police.'

'Can't. Not yet. Bernie, how important – say to the Masonic Knights Templar – would it be to uncover some long-hidden secret at Garway, connected to the original Templars? Big kudos there?'

'That's not a question I can answer. Probably be up to the individual.'

'I'm told some Masons have got quite obsessed over the years about Garway.'

'Some men, it rather takes them over, yes.'

'Especially now? The day after tomorrow being the seven hundredth anniversary of the suppression of the Templars. Saturday the thirteenth.'

'Friday.'

'It *was* Friday, when it happened. Friday the thirteenth, which—'

'I meant at Garway. The service at Garway's tomorrow.'

'Is it?'

'Been ... quite a problem for us, Merrily. For me. The C of E is obviously in two minds about the Templars. We have their churches, but we weren't the ones who persecuted them.'

'We probably would've done, though, if we'd existed at the time.'

'You know the Vatican's being asked to apologize?'

'For the suppression? No, I didn't.'

'Some of the modern Knights Templar societies are calling for it. Doesn't affect us, one way or another, but holding memorial services is a bit iffy, politically. Churches, as you know, have two different roles. Places of worship and historic buildings open for tourism.'

'So we show the tourists the Templar coffin lids and the remains of the circular nave ... but as for including the Templars – Baphomet and all – in a religious service ...'

'Dicey. *Very* dicey. And, officially, I should have said no.'

'Teddy Murray doesn't seem too enthusiastic either.'

The Bishop smiled through the dull sheen of sweat.

'You really *don't* know the half of it, do you?'

Mrs Morningwood was feeling her throat through the silk scarf. Her throat where the marks were.

Jane said, 'You look like Mum looked ... when she came out of that house.'

Roscoe looked up at Mrs Morningwood, whimpering. She clasped his head to her lower thigh.

'I'm going to make some tea,' Jane said. 'Or can I get you a brandy?'

'What house?'

'Well, the Master House.' Jane filled the kettle. 'You remember ... No, you don't, you'd gone, you'd left us to it. You said Roscoe wouldn't go in. You said you always trusted the dog.'

'I do.'

Mrs Morningwood looked down at Roscoe; he was panting. It was like they were tuned to the same wavelength, the woman and the dog, picking up messages that nobody else could hear.

'Jane, will you tell me about this?'

'I'm sorry, I thought Mum must've told you. Maybe I should keep quiet.'

'Up to you, Jane.'

Jane walked to the window, looking out at the orchard, at the last red apples near the tops of the highest trees.

'She looked like death. Like she'd just seen ... I dunno, Lol in a porno video or something.' Jane turned to face Mrs Morningwood. 'She always insists she's not psychic, maybe because she doesn't like to believe anyone else is.'

'Did she tell you what happened?'

'Oh yeah. It was when she found the green man. Which is actually Baphomet. But it's the same thing – Baphomet, Pan, the green man ... the male thing in nature.'

'This is in the church?'

'No, no ... . in the house.'

'That's what I thought you meant.'

'It's in the fireplace. Behind the inglenook. Someone's put a green man, or Baphomet, on the wall inside the inglenook where nobody would normally see it. You didn't know about it?'

'Is it old?'

'Probably not. Could be something to do with whatever stuff was going on there back in the 1970s. But then it might be old – might be original Templar. Might've been brought from somewhere else at some stage. Dunno, really.'

'And your mother found it disturbing.'

'You ask her now, she'll probably deny it. Are you all right, Mrs Morningwood?'

'No.' Mrs Morningwood sat down. 'No, I don't think I am.'

'You want me to call the doc or something?'

'Don't be silly.' She looked up. 'Do you think Merrily would mind if I borrowed her car? I'd bring it back tonight.'

'I'd have to ask. You might not be insured.'

'In that case … you can drive, can't you Jane?'

'Sure.'

'You see, I came in your mother's car. Mine's at home. Your mother's gone with …'

'Lol. In his truck.'

'Would it be possible to take me home? Just for a few minutes, so I can collect some medication.'

'Herbs?'

'Won't take me long, darling, I know what I'm looking for. I suppose I could phone for a taxi …'

Herbs? No way.

'No,' Jane said. 'No, it's OK. I'll get the keys.'

'Good. I can pick up my Jeep.'

'Oh.'

This would mean she'd have to drive back on her own, on her provisional licence.

'OK,' Jane said.

She'd need to get the L-plates off before Mrs Morningwood spotted them.

Because, whatever this was about, it was not about herbs.

53

Damage

'TEN COVER IT?' Jimmy Hayter said.

Lol stared at him. It had started to rain again. Big spots on Hayter's buttermilk Armani.

'I could go to twelve, Robinson. Cash, by tonight. Leave it in an envelope for you, at the desk in there.'

'Twelve what?'

'Twelve K.'

'Perhaps you could explain what you're talking about, Jimmy.'

'I heard you had a guitar irreparably damaged.'

'Wow,' Lol said. 'It's amazing how quickly word gets out.'

'I've always liked to help underprivileged musicians.'

'So I've noticed.'

'Twelve, and you and your priest leave me alone. And you *don't* lean on my fucking Jag.'

Lol didn't move.

'Jimmy, you are … I think what our friends over the ocean would call *a piece of work.*'

'All right,' Hayter said. 'You tell me what you want.'

'I'll be reasonable about it. Four grand in an envelope and a bit of honesty.'

'I could …' Hayter's face might have darkened, or it could have been the sky. 'I don't think I need to spell out what damage I could do to your … what you laughably call a career.'

'Well …' Lol shook his head, sighing. 'I mean that's just the point, isn't it? I *don't* call it a career, and you already *have* spelled it out. Or your … employee, with whatever destructive implement he carries around with him. And the thing is—'

'Whoever did that … might have gone further than instructed,' Hayter said.

'—Thing is, I'm really not anywhere near significant enough to be damaged by somebody with your level of connections. I mean, what are you going to do … like, sabotage the renewal of my six-album contract with the Sony Corporation?'

'Maybe he concentrated on the wrong guitar.'

Hayter turned away, shoulders hunched against the rain which had drained the colour out of the city below them, making the Cathedral spectral. Then he turned back.

'We haven't done anything wrong.'

'Who?'

'Me and …' Hayter jerked a thumb over his shoulder towards The Centurion '… him.'

'Mr Gwilym. Who you haven't seen in thirty years.'

'Actually, I hadn't,' Hayter said. 'Not until today.'

'So what … I mean, why the reunion? Can't be the anniversary of the ritual abuse of Mary Roberts, surely?'

Lol, the wet soaking through to his chest, suddenly felt this kind of transcendent exhilaration. Somehow, he had the bastard.

'It wasn't like that,' Hayter said.

'So tell me what it *was* like.'

'You want to come inside?'

'Jimmy, do I *look* stupid?'

'I'm getting wet.'

'Rain's healthy. Start with Mat Phobe. Move the letters around and it becomes Baphomet. That's this head thing the Templars are supposed to have worshipped. And also what Crowley called himself, when he was doing sex magic with the OTO.'

'Yeah, we did our share of that. Mat had this obscure book, with the rituals of the OTO. You needed women. Or men would do, in some cases, but we never went there, like I said. Unlike some of the Templars, apparently.'

'What happened to Mary?'

'I've told you.'

'No, you haven't.'

'I told you I went to London to meet my old man.' Hayter's eyes were half-screened by his heavy hair. 'And Gwilym went home to *his* old man's farm. And when we got back, she'd gone.'

'Gone where?'

'I don't know.'

'So when you and Gwilym had left the premises, who was left?' Mickey what's-his-name and ... Mat Phobe?'

'No.' Hayter wiped the air with both hands. 'That's absolutely as far as I go, Robinson.'

'You haven't even explained why you're here yet.'

'Fuck off.'

'What about the four grand? I could after all ...' Lol started to laugh, hair dripping, leaning back over the bonnet of Hayter's Jag '... seriously damage you.'

'It'll be on the desk by tonight.'

'Hey, I'm not going in *there*. Especially at night.'

Hayter started to walk away, then turned.

'HSBC. The bank?'

'Centre of town?'

'With your name on it. One hour. You'll need some ID.'

Hayter walked back to The Centurion, quickly, through the rain.

54

The Confines of the Triangle

MERRILY SPOTTED THE Animal, a serious presence in the Broad Street traffic, and ran out across the cathedral green as Lol pulled in on the yellow lines. Holding on to his left arm as she climbed in from the running board.

'God, you're soaked!'

'Where's Huw?'

'Left ages ago.' Merrily hauled the passenger door shut. 'You OK?' Checking him out, peering into his face as he waited for a gap in the traffic. 'You saw him?'

'Hayter? Yes.'

'And?'

'I'm not sure.'

'He admits it was him?'

'Not exactly, but ... Where're we going?'

'Somewhere we can talk,' Merrily said. 'I'm trying to come to terms with something that ... I don't quite know what it means, but it's disturbing.'

'Hayter's worried. He's floundering.'

'So he bloody should be.'

'He offered me ten thousand for the damage to the Boswell.'

'What, just now?'

'He implied that the guy who did it overreacted. It must've happened very quickly. He was still thinking I was trying to blackmail him, told his guy to follow me. Guy rings him from Tanworth after I've left the truck to go into the churchyard. Hayter – some kind of knee-jerk thing – tells him what to do to show me what I'm taking on.'

'How did he find out you're on the level?'

'I'm thinking two possibilities.' Lol turned left into Bridge Street, traffic congealing around them. 'Maybe he called Prof back, in a rage, and Prof explained the situation. Or he talked to Gwilym on the phone and Gwilym did some checks.'

'What did you do ... about the money?'

'Told him to make it four grand and give me some honest answers. We reached the same point, where Mary disappears, then he clammed up. He says the money will be at HSBC in an hour. Unless he already has some arrangement with them, I don't know how he's going to do that, so maybe he was just lying, to get rid of me.'

'But he and Gwilym are together?'

'For the first time, he insists, since Garway. What does that suggest?'

'I may *just* be able to tell you in a few minutes.'

Lol drove down to the car park near the swimming pool. By the time he'd found a space big enough for the Animal, Merrily had the mobile out, was consulting its index of numbers.

'I just want to try something, see what reaction I get.'

She put the call through. The rain had stopped again but the sky was smoky over the hills.

'Good afternoon,' Beverley Murray said professionally. 'This is The Ridge.'

'Beverley, it's Merrily Watkins. Sorry to bother you. Don't suppose Teddy's around?'

'Oh. Merrily ... haven't you seen him? He was supposed to be calling at your place with the bags you left behind.'

'Oh, well, actually I'm not at home. Perhaps he's left them some-where.' Unlikely that Mrs Morningwood would have answered the door, especially to someone from Garway. 'It was very kind of him, but there was really no need, I'll be back there, probably tomorrow. In fact ...'

She told Beverley she'd only just found out that the special service for the Templar anniversary was tomorrow, the twelfth, rather than Saturday, the thirteenth.

'Oh ... yes, that's ... There *has* been a change of plan, I think.'

'Only, I know Teddy was feeling a bit apprehensive about it, and I was thinking there was nothing I could do because I've got this wedding on Saturday … but, of course, Friday's not a problem.'

'Oh … Well, I think …'

'And obviously I've learned a lot about the Templars in the past few days. So, you know, I'd be happy to take it off his hands …'

'Merrily, I—'

'So, do you know what time it is? That's all I wanted to know, really. I'll come up and meet him an hour or so before and we'll work it out.'

A silence. Merrily watched rain clouds tangling in the rust-coloured sky over Dinedor Hill.

Beverley said, 'Can I call you back about this, Merrily?'

'Sure.'

Merrily clicked off, sank down in the seat.

'I wasn't getting the right messages. From Beverley.'

'This is the wife of the guy who's standing in as vicar at Garway.'

'Mmm, they're waiting for a new team minister. Beverley was telling me how stressed out Teddy was and how it would be bad for him to get involved in any exorcism, and that he didn't really want to do a service to commemorate the seven hundredth anniversary of the suppression of the Templars. Which, of course, led to all kinds of torture and burnings at the stake, for which the Roman Catholic Church is now being asked to issue a formal apology.'

'By whom?'

'Some neo-Templar groups. The Vatican won't authorize an apology, of course, because the Templars are still very iffy. The accusations may, at least in part, be true. No religious organization is totally clean.'

'Certainly not one consisting largely of trained killers.'

'There is that.'

'You really want to do this service?'

'No way. I was just seeing what reaction I got. The situation is that the C of E didn't want to be involved, but Teddy said a lot of people had been pushing for something at Garway. What he didn't say is that this was going to be a *Masonic* service.'

'Oh …'

'Reluctantly approved, possibly under pressure, by Bernie and conducted – something else Teddy didn't say – by a Mason.'

Merrily watched a trans-Euro container lorry coming off Greyfriars Bridge inside a grey haze, thinking maybe she knew this city no better than its driver.

'Teddy Murray, it seems, has been on the square for many, many years. Which opens up so many scary possibilities that I don't know where to start.'

'Suggests a special relatonship with Gwilym.'

'Mmm. And it means he's been extremely parsimonious with the truth in his various conversations with me. The guy's always so vague and far-back. Butter wouldn't melt. She said he'd actually been to the vicarage this afternoon.'

'Your vicarage?'

'Ostensibly to bring my bags back. Unlikely. It suggests he wants to talk about something. I'll see if …'

Merrily rang home. No answer. Jane must be back by now, so she left a message saying she could be late, was reachable on the mobile, if Jane could see her way to calling.

'What do we do now?' Lol said.

'Pick up the money for the Boswell?'

'It's not going to be there, Merrily.'

'Be interesting to see. Stourport clearly very much wants you off his back.'

They parked at Tesco, walked round the corner by All Saints Church and Lol went into the bank on his own.

Came back with a thick yellow envelope.

'Let's not get too excited, it might be a letter bomb. Or something.'

Insisting on her getting into the truck while he opened it on his own in the car park, up against a perimeter wall.

He slid back into the truck.

'I've never had a fifty-pound note before. Let alone eighty of them.'

'Well, well …'

'And there's also this.'

He laid a plastic CD case on the dash. Merrily grimaced.

'I do hope it's not death metal.'

'I seriously don't like to put it on.' Lol took out the CD, held it up to the light. 'Doesn't *look* like it's been tampered with.'

'Oh, for heaven's sake ...'

'Now?'

Lol switched on the engine, loaded the CD, turned up the volume.

A background hum was relayed through six speakers. A lot of rustling, movement of objects. A female voice.

'*Is this what you wanted?*'

'*Yeah, yeah ... over there.*' Male voice. '*Near the mirror. And don't talk again, all right? Just keep quiet. Whatever happens, you keep quiet. This is important.*'

After about a minute of near-silence, the girl said:

'*Ooh, kinky.*'

And the man hissed:

'*'King shut it!*'

'That *could* be Hayter,' Lol said, 'but ...'

Merrily said, 'The girl ... did that sound like a Brummie accent to you?'

'Maybe.'

'Christ.'

The atmosphere – a suggestion of burning, a hissing – was issuing like steam from speakers on either side, filling the cab. After some minutes, another male voice came in, up-and-down, liturgical.

'*I conjure thee by the name under which thou knowest thy God and by the name of the prince and king who rules over thee. I conjure thee to come at once and to fulfil my desires, by the powerful name of Him who is obeyed by all, by the name Tetragrammaton, Jehovah, the names which overcome everything, whether of this world or any other ... Come, speak to me clearly, without duplicity. Come in the name of Adonai Sabaoth, come, linger not. Adonai Shadai, the king of all kings, commands thee!*'

Background noise, with swishing movements. An exclamation of distaste. '*Sulphur! Jeez!*' A nervous giggle.

After a while, another voice.

'*Told you it was boll— Sorry.*'

Then the whole incantation repeated. Twice.

Near-silence this time. A thump, as if the tape had been unsubtly edited. Then two voices, one going, '*Oh my—!*'

Cut off by the second, louder, triumphant.

'*Welcome. Thou wert invoked in the name of him who has created heaven and earth and hell. I hereby bind thee so that thou shalt remain here, within the confines of the triangle, while I still require thee and leave not without the licence to depart, and then not without answering the questions I shall put to thee.*

'*That which was brought here on the instructions of the Grand Master and Grand Preceptor of all England, Jacques de Molay, to be hidden from those who would purloin it ... if it be still here, I command you to inform me of its true location and if it be not here I command that you so inform me.*'

More invocation of the secret names of God. The question repeated. No clues as to what hidden item they were hoping to locate. It went on for another ten minutes, with edit bumps, until whatever had been welcomed was formally dismissed and the recording ended.

'The problem with ceremonial magic,' Merrily said, 'is that it can be incredibly tedious. The language they use ... stilted, pompous. Mock liturgy.'

'Very defined, though,' Lol said. 'Very exact, focused on what they want and closing up all other avenues. I don't know what to make of it. All smoke and mirrors, or what?'

'Actually, it involves both smoke *and* mirrors. This ex-Catholic priest Eliphas Levi – huge admirer of the Templars – once claimed to have conjured up a spirit for a friend of Bulwer-Lytton, the writer. Admitting that he couldn't really be sure what he'd got, but claiming to see the figure of a man. And he asks it the designated questions and gets the answers in his head.'

'No big, sonorous voice echoing around the temple?'

'Inside your head,' Merrily said, 'is usually as good as it gets. Apparently.'

'So who were they trying to invoke here?'

'Dunno. You go through the Key of Solomon and all these magical texts, you get a selection of spirits – funny names, Biblical-sounding roots – which perform certain functions to order. Finding hidden treasure – that's a big favourite.'

'It's been quite heavily edited.'

'Because this stuff takes for ever,' Merrily said. 'But, yeah, it also covers up essential facts. Like, we don't find out exactly what they're after or who they're trying to talk to. Or what they get out of it ... if anything. It's just rich kids messing around, trying to scare themselves. Like, hey, we've done all the drugs, had all the weird sex, let's do Other Spheres of Existence? Point is, why did Hayter want us to hear it?'

'Sign of good faith? He said that if he found any of the tapes he'd let me know. I thought that was just to get my phone number. Which, of course, he put to good use a short time later.'

'But why is he telling us *anything*? Went to a lot of trouble here. He must've either shot straight round to the bank with it, or he'd taken it earlier, making provision for collection by someone else. He didn't have to offer you any money – there was no way you could pin the Boswell on him.'

Lol ejected the CD, slid it back into the plastic case.

'Well, he doesn't want us to drop it, does he? He's just trying to steer us away from *him*. More or less editing himself out. Like, "something did happen, but it wasn't down to me." The girl ... could that be Mary?'

'Perhaps I'll play it to Mrs Morningwood. And of course, Sycharth's not in there at all. Where's his big Welsh-language scene?'

'Yet Hayter told me about Gwilym. Without mentioning his name.'

'But that, presumably, was before he spoke to him again,' Merrily said. 'Now it's like they're on the same side, both pointing at the guy who conducted the ritual.'

'Saying this is the bad guy, Mat Phobe, and he's dead? End of story?'

Merrily's mobile chimed.

'I don't know. It might be somebody they can't— Hello?'

'I think I should like to talk to you, Merrily,' Beverley Murray said.

55

Monty and Jane

'So WHERE DID it happen?' Jane asked.

The Volvo roared and surged because she'd put it back into second gear instead of up into fourth. *Shit.*

'Was it at your home?' Jane said. 'Is that what this is all about?'

Mrs Morningwood glanced at her.

'It wasn't far from home. It's an established fact that most car accidents take place on roads that are well known to the victim. Familiarity breeding carelessness.'

'Yes,' Jane said. 'Very good.'

She wasn't *totally* stupid. She was driving slowly but trying not to make it *suspiciously* slowly. She'd left a message on the table for Mum telling her the truth, that she was driving Mrs Morningwood home to collect some stuff, but not the entire truth, that she'd be driving back, almost certainly in the dark, unaccompanied by a qualified driver.

She could do this. Country roads all the way, a wide arc around Hereford.

'So what was it like growing up in Garway, under the shadow of the Templars?'

'Good question,' Mrs Morningwood said.

Obviously any question unrelated to her having been viciously assaulted was going to be a good one.

'Like, the first time I went up there,' Jane said, 'I was noticing things. But maybe if you grow up in a place you take it all for granted.'

'In this case, Jane, I think not. Even people who profess no interest at all in the Templars are, I think, affected in some way. It's one of those areas that seems to … I don't know … condition the way people think and behave. It somehow imposes its own rules and strictures. You noticed yourself the names of the pubs. I've never worked out how far they go back, but I don't think it matters. They might simply be echoes from memory. The people are the memory cells of the hill.'

'Cool.'

'My mother, for instance. I don't think she once mentioned the Templars to me as a child, but she knew about the Nine Witches. I can name them, she used to say. Every one.'

'So who were the other eight?'

'I never asked, she never told me. Of course, when I was a child, a witch meant an old woman in a pointed hat, stirring a cauldron. They were probably all around me and not all of them women.'

'Are there nine now?'

'Probably. It's not a coven or anything, Jane. It simply suggests that there are always going to be nine people who, whether they know it or not, have been entrusted with the guardianship of the hill and its ways. Whenever an issue arises which might damage us, certain people will project … a certain point of view. I can't explain it any better than that.'

'People with Garway in their blood?'

'Nothing so prosaic as blood, Jane. It's in their very being. I really do believe that. It conditions how one does what one does.'

'Like your herbalism? Healing?'

'Or dowsing. Water-divining. Or painting, sculpture, gardening, furniture-making. Everything somehow relating to the place and its relationship with the heavens and infused with … a special energy. Sometimes.'

'As above, so below. Paracelsus?'

'I'm not aware that Paracelsus was ever in Garway, or even if someone so loud and demonstrative would have been welcome here. We're very low-key. Which is why I've always felt that Owain Glyndwr, as depicted by Shakespeare, would have been unlikely to have fitted in either.'

'Archetypal Welsh windbag?' Jane figured she had a good working knowledge of Shakespeare, the big ones, anyway. '*I can call spirits from the vasty deep.*'

'Anyone who goes around telling people he can call spirits is usually bugger-all use at it,' Mrs Morningwood said. 'Do you mind if I smoke, or are you like most kids, indoctrinated by the fascists in Westminster?'

'Are you kidding? In our house?'

'Thank you. I'll open the window. You see, that's why I suspect Glyndwr was not such a windbag. Although the wind does appear to have been important to him in other ways.'

'Huh?'

'Vast amount of mystery and superstition attached to the man – the wizard, who could manipulate the elements, alter the weather, leaving opposing armies drowning in Welsh mist. A very Templar thing to do. I can't believe that, coming here a mere century or so after the dissolution, he wasn't exposed to the full blast of residual Templarism. Some of them would still have been here, undercover now, sitting on their secrets.'

'But he only came here towards the end of his life, didn't he?'

'Who says that was the first time? I think not. Besides, the Templars may have favoured Welsh independence, just as they supported the Scots at Bannockburn. I've even heard it said that they included among their number Llewelyn ap Gruffudd, the last official Prince of Wales, in the thirteenth century. His dates certainly fit.'

'Really?'

'The Templars seemed to like governments being fragmented, Jane. Made it easier to sustain their own international power-base.'

'Right.'

Jane slowed at the single-lane Brobury Bridge over the Wye, waiting for every possible oncoming car to come across before chancing her arm. Dorstone Hill, narrow, winding and wooded, wasn't going to be easy. When she and Eirion had come last summer he'd had to keep reversing to find somewhere to pull in to let other cars get past. And she was ... well, crap at reversing.

She'd stopped talking, to concentrate, but Mrs Morningwood seemed to want to talk, as if she was afraid of where her own thoughts might lead her.

'OK,' Jane said. 'So, like, is Garway the way it is because of the

Templars? Or did the Templars only come here because Garway was already, you know, this really charged-up landscape? Maybe back into Celtic times?'

'Mixture of the two. Whatever was here, they certainly enhanced it. It's an unstable area, too. Has a major geological fault line. Climatic anomalies are often noted. We used to talk about gusts of wind from The White Rocks, which are supposed to be a Celtic burial ground. And then, of course, there's M. R. James.'

'*We must ...*' Jane's hands tightened on the wheel. ' *... have offended someone or something at Garway ...*'

'My God, Jane, for a child you're remarkably well informed.'

'Thanks.'

'Anyone under forty's a child to me now. It's the wind again, you see. Why did James have this chap discover a whistle that could arouse the wind on the site of a Templar preceptory? It's never explained in the story.'

'But you think the Templars ... and Owain Glyndwr ...?'

'And farmers in this area, at one time. John Aubrey refers to *the winnowers of Herefordshire* who believed they could arouse a wind to blow the chaff from the wheat, by whistling. Whistling up the wind. That's undoubtedly where Monty James got the idea from.'

'You reckon?'

'It's the only possible connection.'

'But M. R. James didn't even come here until years after he'd written that story. He didn't come until this Gwen McBryde came to live here with her daughter. Erm ... Jane.'

'Well we don't know for certain that he hadn't been here before that. But, as an antiquarian, it's most unlikely that he hadn't heard of Garway.'

'I keep thinking of Jane MacBryde,' Jane said. 'How old would she have been?'

'When they came to Garway? About thirteen. You know her father was the artist who illustrated some of the early stories?'

'And Jane also ... drew things.'

'Jane had a macabre imagination. Clawlike hands emerging from tombs.'

'Do you know what she looked like?'

'I'm afraid I don't. Nobody ever described her to me.'

At the turning to Dorstone Hill, Jane snatched a quick look sideways. Mrs Morningwood had her old Barbour on and the sunglasses, her cigarette arm on the open window, a small smile on her still-swollen lips. Roscoe's head next to hers, his grey fur flattened in the slipstream.

'Do you want to know the story?'

Jane McBryde had known in advance about the visit to Garway Church. Although it wasn't more than a few miles from their home and she'd probably been before, visiting somewhere with Uncle Monty was always a joy. He was kind and he was funny and full of good stories – well, everybody knew that now, and Jane McBryde had read them all.

Uncle Monty, of course, could spend all day poking around old churches and Garway Church, with all its Templar relics, was a special treat. One of his most famous stories – Jane found it deliciously terrifying – had been about a Templar preceptory and what a solitary sort of professor had found there … and came to wish he hadn't, or at least had left it well alone.

Monty didn't really notice – he was probably safely in the tower or the vestry or somewhere, bent over something, his glasses on his nose – when Jane slipped out of the church and started looking round the outside walls, feeling along them with her hands.

'What *you* after?'

The girl was a few years younger than Jane, maybe eight or nine. She had blonde hair and a wild look. The year was 1917.

Jane McBryde said, quite open about it, 'I'm looking for a hole in the wall. I want to play a trick on my uncle.'

'How do you know all this?' Jane said. 'I mean, you're not making it up or anything?'

'I am telling it,' Mrs Morningwood said, 'just as my mother told it to me.'

'So the blonde girl …'

'Norah. My mother was quite a forward child. Not many of the local kids would dare approach a stranger. My mother, knowing every stone in the tower below her own height, was able to show her one quite close to the ground – perhaps in the area where the circular nave would be excavated just a few years later – which could, with the aid of a stick or a small knife, be eased out of the wall.'

Mrs Morningwood began to smile for real, shaking her head.

'Imagine the scene an hour or so later when Monty and his ward are strolling around the tower, perhaps planning to take in the famous dovecote, and Jane says, "Why's that stone sticking out, Uncle Monty?" and Monty gets down on his hands and knees, the stone pops out and so does … a very old and grimy whistle.'

'Oh … cool.'

'Nothing engraved on it, of course, but you can imagine the look on Monty's face. Perhaps, after the initial shock, he has an inkling that he's been set up, but he's very fond of Jane, realizes all the trouble the girl's taken over this, and goes along with it.'

'Did he blow it?'

'My mother, watching from behind a gravestone, reported it as follows: *Better not blow it*, Monty says. *Who knows what might happen?* And young Jane's hopping up and down. *Oh do blow it, Uncle Monty! Do!* But Monty pockets the whistle, saying, *Perhaps I'll blow it later. Let's continue with our exploration.*'

'And did he?'

'Well my mother, despite having no idea what any of this was about, never having read the story, was fascinated to find out. And so she followed them, through the churchyard, along the footpaths, and all the time Jane McBryde's pulling Monty's arm and saying, *When are you going to blow it? Please blow it now!*'

'My mother remembers Monty stopping at the top of a rise which is very well known to me, and he takes out the whistle. *Should I?* Gives it a good wipe with his handkerchief, puts it in his mouth, puffs out his cheeks … nothing happens. Takes it out of his mouth, bangs it on a stone to get the dried mud out of the hole at the end. Back in the mouth, young Jane jumping up and down, nothing happens at first and then … *peeeeep!*'

'You're like … not making this up, are you?' Jane said, changing smoothly down through the gears.

'I'm telling it to you exactly as it was told to me by my late mother. Monty blows the whistle once, pops it back in his pocket. Couple of minutes later a gust of wind comes in – probably from the White Rocks – and down comes the rain.'

'You're kidding …'

'My personal theory is that Monty knew there was a good chance of a change in the weather and wanted to wait until it was imminent to blow the whistle – to turn the tables on Jane. However, it rains harder and harder, and they run to some trees. But, with the wind, the trees are offering precious little in the way of shelter, and Jane's dress is getting soaked and Monty's rather concerned now that she'll catch cold. Her poor father, of course, having died very young. Possibly the last of his drawings being, in fact, the "Whistle" ghost with its *intensely horrible face of crumpled linen.*'

Jane stayed in second gear for the descent, the road like a tunnel through the trees. It wasn't raining, but it was dark enough to put on the headlights, dipped.

'Monty's perhaps very concerned now that his own joke is going to backfire and Jane will catch pneumonia – usually fatal, remember, in those days, before antibiotics. And then, through the trees, he spots a house … grabs Jane by the hand and they go dashing down. Monty's banging on the front door, shouting, "Hullo! Hullo!" but no answer. My mother follows them to the edge of the yard. She sees Monty turn the handle … and the door opens. My mother's hand goes to her mouth because … well, because she knows what's in there.'

'What?'

'The force of the wind … *slams* the door wide, exposing a dim room, with the curtains drawn across the small, high window. Monty calls out, the rain thrashing down behind them. No answer. A small lamp is burning. He sees a long trestle table with a sheet covering something, just as a sudden gust of wind from outside blows the sheet away. And there, awaiting its coffin, lies the corpse of Naomi Newton, above which the white sheet is dancing in the wind before collapsing to the floor in a twitching sort of heap.'

'Oh my God,' Jane said. '*Newton*. The Master House?'

So caught up in the story that she'd driven up one side of the treacherous Dorstone Hill and down the other, round a seriously nasty left-hand band and into the broad sweep of the Golden Valley, where the oddly graceful fibreglass steeple of Peterchurch church was embossed on the low cloud mass like some downmarket Salisbury Cathedral.

'A year later,' Mrs Morningwood was saying, 'M. R. James returned alone to Garway and got into conversation with my grandmother, who had her own reasons to be fearful of the Master House. He was a touch embarrassed. *As if my own imagination was punishing me*, he said. *Perhaps I'm haunted by my own ghastly creations.*'

'Right. Wow.'

Jane drove on, in silence, still not sure whether or not Mrs Morningwood had made the whole thing up.

But remembering something.

Before they'd left, taking the spare car keys from the rack in the key cupboard at the end of the hall, she'd noticed something missing. The outsize key to the Master House had been hung on the rack by Mum, who was probably fed up with the weight of it and the memories it evoked every time she opened the bag.

The fact that the key was no longer there could mean one of two things – that Mum had put it back into her bag in case she had to go there at short notice. Or ...

56

Bevvie

WHAT WAS MOST unexpected was the aggression.

'Oh, let's not waste time,' Beverley said. 'All that false bonhomie. All this, "Let's help old Teddy out of his fix." You're not a bonhomie sort of person, are you, Merrily?'

Under the halogen lights in the stainless steel kitchen. Beverley's hair down around her shoulders. A Chardonnay bottle half full on the chopping board, with two glasses, Beverley rapidly draining one, a different woman.

One who wanted to talk. Had maybe wanted to talk for a long time, to somebody. Building up to this, flushed and brimming now.

Oh God, how you could miss the signs …

'As if you didn't know, Merrily, *exactly* why you couldn't do that service.'

The dusk was dropping like a roller blind. Merrily had gone into The Ridge on her own, leaving Lol in the truck with her phone, in case Jane or somebody rang.

'Well, I think,' she said, 'that he could've told me about it.'

'Told you about it? He doesn't even tell *me* about it. Lodge nights, out comes the black case. *Off to the Boys' Club, Bevvie, don't wait up.* Like an old-time gangster with a violin case. Never yet seen the inside of that little black case.'

'That seems to be the way it goes,' Merrily said. 'Except on Ladies' Evenings, of course.'

'Never been to one. I'm going to sit there with a bunch of old biddies dripping jewellery, smiling fondly at my husband and listening to endless self-congratulatory speeches? All rise for the provincial grand almighty … whatever.'

'Yes, that could be very trying.'

'My first husband played golf. A golf bore. Golf Club social events. Merrily, is it something *about* me? Safe, practical, reliable … and, above all, blatantly incurious.'

Merrily said nothing. Beverley poured more wine. Merrily left hers alone, wondering how best to play this, remembering something.

'These guests – the ones coming tomorrow.'

'Germans. Have you ever *met* German Masons? Last year it was Americans. Sold to me as a hiking group, but they never seem to hike further than the church, with their video cameras and their calculators and their … set squares.'

'Why was it changed from Saturday?'

'I think they were afraid that, on the actual day, it might be too crowded with, you know, *normal* visitors. That ordinary people might actually want to go to the service. Whereas Friday, as a working day, they'll be left to get on with it … especially at the time it's being held.'

'When?'

'Straddling midnight. So that, come the dawn on Saturday …'

'The time of the original raids in France in 1307.'

'The church draped with Templar banners. They're all rolled up in the tower. It's going to be the highlight of his … his life, probably.'

'Sad?'

'No, it's not sad. Quite frightening, actually. Do you want to sit down?'

'Where is Teddy now?'

'Hereford. Little Boys' Club. Won't be back much this side of midnight. Don't you like this stuff? Shall I open a bottle of red or something?'

'I'd rather you made it coffee,' Merrily said.

Lol had never used this phone before, and the first time the call came in, he accidentally killed it. He was fiddling around for some way of recovering it, when the church-bell noise it made started up again.

'Merrily?'

'She's not around at the moment,' Lol said. 'Can I take a—?'

'Lol Robinson?'

Lol froze. For a second he thought it was Hayter's man again.

'Frannie Bliss, Laurence. Where is she?'

'Talking to somebody. Not far away. There a problem?'

'Yeh, there is. I expected to have heard from her by now. When last we spoke, she seemed ... I don't like it when she's quiet.'

'I'll get her to call you.'

'Why's she quiet, Laurence?'

'Maybe she likes to think things out.' Lol looked down from the parking area across to the darkening hills of east Wales. No lights anywhere. 'I thought it was a wrap from your point of view. All sorted.'

'Somebody saying it isn't?'

'You know I don't mix in those circles, Francis.'

'Well it isn't. You tell Merrily it isn't. Tell her ... You're norra blabber, are you, Laurence?'

'No.'

'And still a vested interest in keeping her intact.'

'More vested all the time,' Lol said.

'We've had PM results on Barlow and Fuchsia. I'm not going into details, but the extent of Barlow's injuries, the level of force, the level of trauma, that doesn't look like a woman. Not often a woman's method, either.'

'What ... blunt instrument?'

'A bluntie, you see, generally speaking, they don't. Requires a level of controlled rage. And *sustained* rage. And where's the motive here? Where, at the end of the day, is the damn motive?'

'So why did she kill herself?' Lol said.

'Yeh, well, *did* she? See, another thing, the effects of a railway engine running over a head are *highly* effective at concealing whether there might have been an earlier injury rendering the victim incapable enough, or dead enough, to be taken there and laid on the line.'

'Carried there?'

'Already dead, most likely. There's a lorra shite talked about the accuracy of time-of-death assessment, largely as a result of TV pathologists who say, "Oh, the victim passed away between ten fifteen and ten forty-five." In real life, they can just about tell you what day it was.'

'You're saying there could still be somebody out there ...?'

'I'm planting the thought. You can add it to the list of reasons why she needs to call me. On the mobile, naturally.'

Lol sat there, looking out over unlit Wales, wondering how many other crucial calls Merrily might have missed.

'When we first came here, I thought we might walk the hills together. Walk to the pub, gentle strolls home by moonlight. Maybe get a dog. He didn't want a dog. He didn't do that kind of walking. His kind of walking, you're out at dawn, proper hiking boots, and you aren't back till dark and the worse the weather is the better. Him and the landscape. Walking his way into it. *Throwing* himself into it. As if he didn't have much time to learn all there was to learn.'

'God's own weekend retreat,' Merrily said.

They were sitting at the window table in the former dairy. Beverley tossed back her head.

'The vacant vicar. The silly vicar. *More tea, vicar*? He plays that role so well. *God's own weekend bloody retreat.*'

'Balm for the soul.'

'All the clichés.' Beverley breathed out slowly. 'Jesus, Merrily, I haven't really talked to anybody like this in years. It's like a big stone being rolled off your chest. Does it bother you that I don't believe in God?'

'Evangelism's never been my thing. People come to it in their own way. Or not.'

On impulse, Merrily had left off the dog collar this morning. Pectoral cross over a black sweater. Some people were put off. This one, definitely.

You often heard clergy wives talking like this, their scepticism deepened by living day-to-day with a so-called Man of God, all his doubts, all his weaknesses and failings.

'Teddy know you don't believe in God?'

'We've never talked about it. He doesn't care one way or the other. I was a good source of money when he needed some. Big house to sell. Silly me. When I think back, I thought *I* was playing *him*, like a fish on a hook.' Beverley drank some coffee. '*He* was playing *me*. I didn't see it. He can be so charming. And needy, in this selfless, stoical, *noble* way. I bet you saw through it right away. I bet you've been mauled by the best.'

'No,' Merrily said. 'Actually … no.'

'He didn't make a move on you?'

Merrily looked into Mrs Murray's flushed face. Maybe this was paranoia, after all.

'Silly of me. Of course, he wouldn't with you. He wants you out of here, done and dusted, quick as possible. When you left the other morning, he laughed. Women in deliverance, he said, that was never going to work.'

'He said that?'

'I watch, you know. I've been watching for some time. Thinking why are we here on this bleak bloody hillside? Why do we stay here? We have no real friends, no roots. At least, *I* don't.'

'*He* has?'

'He's found something. It's like he owns the place, now. Comes in from his walk, it's like he's had sex. Actually …' Short, bleak laugh '… I'm sure he has, sometimes.'

'Beverley …?'

'Sometimes we get lone women staying here. Of a certain age – divorced, bereaved – here to come to terms with something. And he'll take them out for a walk. Talk to them in his vicarly fashion. Balm for the soul. They'll go out for walks together. Balm for the soul, balm for the body. He *ministers* to them.'

'You *really* think that? Where would he take them?'

'In the grass, in the woods. I don't know where he takes them. It's therapy, isn't it?'

'So when … when you talked about going with him if he ever went to get treatment from Mrs Morningwood—'

'Very sexy woman, isn't she, for her age? Not like me.'

'Beverley, you're—'

'Goes through periods when he hardly looks at me. Hardly seems to know I'm there. We even have separate bedrooms when there are no guests. *Oh certainly, if it helps you get a better night's sleep, Bevvie …*'

Beverley looked away, out of the window. Almost dark now.

'Other times – phases – he becomes almost frighteningly demanding. Rough. Animal. Well, I was quite flattered at first. This gentle, diffident clergyman. As if it was *me* bringing something out. I've never been very … you know. Men found me passably attractive, but not …'

A wind was rising, leaves blown against the glass.

'And then, you see … at some point …' Beverley swallowed too much coffee, choked, slapped her chest hard. 'Don't know how it took me so long to notice. Me with my genteel, suburban … At some point, after we'd been here a while, it became obvious that at … at *those* times … it wasn't anything to do with me. Wasn't me at all. Sometimes, I'd see his eyes above me in the moonlight. His wild, enchanting blue eyes. Wide open. And somewhere else.'

Merrily looked into Beverley's eyes and saw loneliness.

Thinking back to Beverley begging her not to involve Teddy in whatever she was planning for the Master House. Not taking it in as well as she might have, self-pity taking over instead.

She'd been ill that night, and desperately tired. Missing the whole point. It wasn't *Teddy* who was overstressed, vulnerable …

His workload was becoming ridiculous, poor man. Four large parishes in Gloucestershire, and the phone never seemed to stop ringing.

Didn't tally with the man she'd first met in the shadow of Garway Church who'd said he'd *never been a particularly pastoral sort of chap.* You could get away with a lot in the Church, ignore things. Especially if you were a man. Men were seldom doormats.

'Beverley … when you said he was playing you like a fish …'

'Seems all too clear to me now. Although I don't want to believe it. The implications of it are more disturbing than I can bear to think about for long. I lie in my bedroom and I stare at the ceiling, and I think, you're wrong … you have to be wrong. It's all too … elaborate. Machiavellian.'

The final straw … a wave of absolutely awful vandalism … desecration. Gravestones pushed over, defaced, strange symbols chiselled into them. And one night someone broke in and actually defecated in the church, which was horrible, horrible, horrible …

Merrily had begun warming her hands on her coffee cup, the implications forming like a numbness on her skin.

57

The Turning

HALF A MILE or so out of Garway village, Jane slowed right down: roadside cottage lights up ahead, a row of them curtained by a tingly kind of mist. This place was called The Turning, Mrs Morningwood said. She was winding down her window, annoyed.

'Rather thought it would still be fully light when we arrived, but you're a more careful driver than I expected, Jane.'

'A lot of people have accidents in their first year on the road.' Jane held the Volvo on the footbrake at The Turning, flattening the clutch. 'You still want me to go down here, or what?'

'Don't think I said anything about going down here, did I?'

'Well, seeing you nicked the key to the Master House from the rack at home, I just thought ...' Jane turned to her. 'Like, was it something I said? About the green man or the Baphomet behind the inglenook? You have an idea what that's about?'

'I would have liked to see it,' Mrs Morningwood admitted. 'I'm not too sure about going now, though.'

'Would you go if I wasn't with you?'

'Possibly. However ... Look, Jane, don't hang around, there's a vehicle behind you. Keep going.'

'Right. OK.'

Jane thought, *Sod it*, turned left into the downhill lane that led to the church, Mrs Morningwood sighing down her nose and mumbling something about thanking God she'd never had a child.

'You want me to pull in by the church, so we can can follow the footpaths, like we did on—?'

'No, that *would* take for ever. There's a track a few hundred yards further on that leads to within a stone's throw of the place. Broken white gateposts. Bit rough, but you should be all right, if you go carefully. You have a torch anywhere?'

'It's behind the seat at the back. Ah!'

'*Jane, for—!*'

A rabbit had appeared up ahead in the dipped headlights, Jane slamming the brakes on, Roscoe falling into the well between the seats, and there was a tortured scream. Not Roscoe, not the rabbit … this was somebody's brakes right behind them.

The Volvo stalled.

Oh no. It had to happen, didn't it? This was where the guy in whatever vehicle had nearly rear-ended them would come leaping down, total road-rage situation, bawling her out.

'It's all right.' Mrs Morningwood looking over a shoulder. 'He hasn't hit us. And he isn't getting out. Just carry on.'

Jane turned the key and the engine coughed and …

'*Oh sh—*'

… Died.

'Try again.'

Mrs Morningwood still looking over her shoulder and her voice was lower and toneless, like with tension, like she was controlling something.

'What's wrong?'

No sound from the vehicle behind. Looked like a Land Rover. No blasts on the horn, just its headlights on full beam so you couldn't look in the rear-view mirror and keep your sight.

'*Try again.*'

The engine fired. Jane went carefully into first gear, let out the clutch, crawled away, looking for the entrance to the track.

'Keep driving, Jane.'

'I thought you said—'

'*Go!* Keep on. I'll direct you.'

'But the track—'

'Forget the bloody track.'

'OK … whatever.'

Jane speeded up, put the headlights on full beam, the hedge springing up all white like a mesh of tangled bones.

'OK, what's the matter?'

'Carry on to the bottom,' Mrs Morningwood said. 'Then go right.'

'Is there something wrong?'

When they reached the bottom of the road there were no headlights in the mirror.

'Was that somebody you know?'

'We'll go to my house,' Mrs Morningwood said.

It was like there was a ritual maze all around Garway Hill, marked out in lanes worn into the landscape over centuries. The rule was: high hedges low ground, low hedges or barbed wire meant that you were climbing. But it was impossible to tell one way or the other at nightfall in the mist. How many years did you have to live here before you knew where the hell you were?

'Left,' Mrs Morningwood said.

'Here?'

'This, Jane, is where I live.'

'We just did a complete circuit? I thought we'd be halfway to Monmouth by now.'

'Stop here. Anywhere.'

The mist had thinned quite a bit. Jane saw a row of low houses without lights. They looked unnatural, all the windows black.

When they got out of the Volvo, Mrs Morningwood put up a hand and laughed.

'Wind from the White Rocks.'

'How can you tell?'

'Blown a tunnel through the mist.'

That made sense?

Mrs Morningwood went to the front door but didn't open it, just shook the handle.

'Now we'll go round the back.'

They followed Roscoe along the path at the side of the house. You could see the hulks of chicken sheds to the side, and a fence.

'Where do you grow the herbs, Mrs Morningwood?'

'Garden at the back, where the chickens can't get in. Pick quite a lot from the wild. Keep your voice down.'

They came to a glassed-in porch, and Mrs Morningwood squeezed past Jane and went inside, picking up a torch. The beam showed that the back door inside the porch was already open, Roscoe surging through the gap as Jane said something stupid.

'Do you, like, usually keep it open?'

'He's been in.'

'The door's been forced?'

'Spare key in one of the chicken houses,' Mrs Morningwood said. 'Nobody would know that, unless they'd been watching me for quite some time. He's telling me he could come back any time. Whenever he likes.'

She went in briskly, but breathing hard, flicking switches, rooms springing out at Jane as the lights came on. She looked at Mrs Morningwood, her cracked Barbour and her cracked face, and knew that, for her, this wasn't like coming home any more.

'This is where you were attacked, isn't it? This is where it happened. That's why Mum brought you—'

'Yes, Jane.'

'Was it someone you know?'

'Didn't then.'

Jane looked down at Roscoe who was prowling, sniffing in corners, his tail well down.

'And he's been back,' Mrs Morningwood said. 'Bastard's been back. Wants me to know.'

They were in the kitchen. There were some jars on a dresser. They had screw tops. The tops had been taken off and laid next to the jars. Mrs Morningwood stood and looked at the jars but didn't touch them. Jane felt a stirring of fear.

'He's not—?'

'He's not here now. Dog would know. Besides ...'

'I thought you had people looking after the house.'

'Dawn and dusk. See to the chickens.'

'What ... what are you going to do?'

'Going to get all the rest of the herbs in the house, all the preparations, put them all in a bag, take them away and get rid of them, bottles, everything.'

'You think they've been tampered with?'

Mrs Morningwood turned, took Jane by both arms, looked into her eyes.

'Go home, Jane.'

'Now?'

'Shouldn't've done this. Big mistake. Get in your car, go home. Give your mother my apologies. Drive carefully.'

'What about you?'

'Got my Jeep.'

'But I can't—'

'*Go.*'

'Mrs Morningwood, what's going on here?'

'Be careful at the entrance to the track. Visibility's not good at the best of times.'

'You're coming back, though? To Ledwardine?'

Mrs Morningwood didn't reply, following Jane along the path to the Volvo, wet mist shivering in the lights from the house, and Jane knew she ought to ask her to give back the key to the Master House.

'Tell you what?' Mrs Morningwood said. 'Take the dog.'

She opened one of the rear side doors, pointing. Roscoe looked at her and growled.

'In,' Mrs Morningwood said. 'You too, Jane.'

Jane got in and started the engine, watching Mrs Morningwood walk back to the house, not turning around, stumbling once. Jane thought that Roscoe had whimpered, realizing a moment later that the small noise of distress had been in her own throat. She took in a deep breath, started the car, drove to the entrance of the track, just out of sight of the house and stopped, keeping the engine running.

Up ahead, the mist had closed in again, pale and shiny in the headlights like the doors of a big fridge.

Jane got out the mobile to call Mum, because there really was no alternative now to a confession. But there was no signal.

58

Excellent in Fields

BEVERLEY WENT TO answer the door, and Merrily stared into the dregs in the coffee cup, and there was no question of disbelief. For a proportion of priests, being a good and altruistic person was always going to be the price you had to pay to maintain the buzz.

Merrily remembering, as usual, the first time she'd felt it: period of personal crisis, stumbling into a tiny, unexpected Celtic church, watching the light on the walls, the blue and the gold and the lamplit path. A safety in stone, but also transcendence. The path opening up from there.

But there were different paths and different kinds of light.

Staring into the brown dregs, thinking about the Roman Catholic priest, Alphonse Louis Constant, who had made friends with a teenage girl and become Eliphas Levi, conjurer of spirits, fan of Baphomet … while still, if she was remembering this correctly, stressing the importance of God in magic and the magic in God.

And the spark of it that some of them fed and nurtured within themselves. Gnostic fire. The growing of the god inside.

She felt Teddy Murray at her shoulder under the gaze of Garway Church. *I suppose, seen from above, it does look rather as though its neck has been broken. Like a chicken's.*

When Beverley came back into the dairy, Lol was with her, looking worried, saying to Beverley, whom he'd never met before, 'The Turning? What would she mean by The Turning?'

'*Where?*' Merrily said, spinning. '*Where is she now?*'

Looking wildly in different directions from the rim of the parking area, where the tarmac crumbled into dirt and weeds and signs indicated two separate footpaths.

'She doesn't know exactly,' Lol said. 'Don't panic. She had to drive up the hill to find a signal. Down by the church, mobiles don't work. None of them, apparently.'

Merrily remembered putting 999 into the screen, entering Mrs Morningwood's house after the attack. It wouldn't have worked. They might both have been dead.

'But she thinks she can find her way back to The Turning,' Lol said. 'On her own.'

'Apart from the dog, apparently. We'll wait for her there.'

Lol bleeped open the truck, Merrily jumped in.

That *bloody* woman.

They parked in the church entrance, the truck taking up most of it, and walked to the top of the lane where it met the slightly wider country lane which served as Garway's main highway. Merrily had suggested that maybe Lol could drive up and down, looking for Jane, but he wouldn't leave her. He told her what Bliss had said about Felix's killer.

No great shock. Not really.

'What's Bliss doing about this?'

'Probably nothing,' Lol said. 'They have a result ... likely to stand up at an inquest ... the cops are overstretched ...'

'Clean-up rate.'

'Target figures. What counts. There's no evidence, anyway. No more than a feeling backed up by Bliss's professional experience of what kind of murders women do and don't do.'

'Why did he call, then?'

'He wants you to be aware of it. Just in case you ...'

'Stir something up in my fumbling way.' Merrily stepped into the roadway. 'Where the hell *is* she, Lol?'

'Driving very, very slowly. Just have to hope the traffic cops are too overstretched to be patrolling Garway.'

'Please God.'

Merrily stood there in the middle of the road, the mist torn into rags by a wet breeze, the tarmac shining.

Work it out.

Freemasonry. Sycharth. And Stourport – who couldn't finger a fellow Mason but said *this is his voice.*

Wished she'd heard him in church. Praying and preaching, mens' voices changed. Actors. *The Church is a faded but still fabulous costume drama.* Mick Hunter had said that, her first ambitious, duplicitous, womanizing bishop.

Teddy Murray wasn't like Hunter, not a flamboyant stage presence. Teddy was an actor in a long-running drama, playing a man who liked a quiet life. *The countryside calms and strengthens. One of the functions of a parish priest is to remain centred and ... essentially placid.*

Which Beverley had translated as *passive.*

Wrong, wrong, wrong.

'What did you learn in there?' Lol said.

'I'm just trying to put it all together. Just ... give me a minute, and I'll tell you.'

Fuchsia.

He had, of course, met Fuchsia, when she came running into his church after whatever happened to her in the Master House. Fuchsia looking so like her mother. Disturbingly like her mother. Disturbing for some.

Strong guy. Strong enough to carry a body across a field in the dark, to the railway? Oh yeah, he could do that. He was good in fields. He was *excellent* in fields.

'There you go,' Lol said.

He drew Merrily back, out of the road, as headlights streaked a cottage wall.

With an expulsion of relief, she slumped against him, watching the Volvo crawling round the corner and pulling in at The Turning, a dog barking inside.

Almost like a real family, all the angst, all the tension. Merrily drove, Lol beside her, Jane in the back, arms around the dog, voice swollen-up.

'Mum, there was nothing I could—'

'Recriminations later.' Merrily swung into the track that led to Ty Gwyn and all the empty holiday homes. 'How long since you left Mrs Morningwood?'

'I don't know. Twenty minutes, half an hour? When did I get through to you, Lol?'

'At least half an hour.'

Merrily pulled up in front of Ty Gwyn and they got out, all of them.

No lights in the house. The chicken houses shut down. Took a couple of minutes to find the house was all locked up, including the back door.

Lol shone the torch at the carport. No Jeep.

Roscoe sniffed around the porch, showing no great desire to go in. Merrily stepped back.

'She's not here. Jane, I'm not getting this … *what* did she say she was going to do?'

'Throw out the herbs and mixtures and stuff. Like they'd been contaminated? That doesn't sound convincing, does it?'

'Well, you can see that it might be, from her point of view. But no need for urgency, was there?'

Merrily looked back towards the Volvo.

'Look,' Jane said, 'if I had to take a guess …'

'Go on.'

'The Master House. I'd told her … I told her what happened to you. In the inglenook?'

'When?'

'Before we left. I'm sorry, I thought you'd probably told her yourself.'

'And how did she react?'

'She was interested in the inglenook. The Baphomet. It was like it had helped her put something together. But she was in a bit of a state, anyway. This was after that guy you stayed with called in with your bags, and Roscoe—'

'You *saw* him? You saw Teddy Murray?'

'Well, he came to the door, didn't he? He said you'd left the bags behind and he was just passing, so he … It was kind of embarrassing, because Roscoe just like … went for him?'

'Went for him how?'

'Shot through the doorway, snarling, teeth bared? Mum, I'm just thinking, if she's gone to the Master House, she wouldn't take the Jeep, she'd walk.'

'No. I don't think she would. Tell me about Roscoe. What happened?'

'Me trying to drag him back. Didn't actually get to him. I don't think the guy wanted to hang around after that, though.'

'What did he say?'

'He was like, "Oh, I see you've got a guard dog." Two women on their own, that kind of thing. Trying to make light of it, but I think he was shaken, as you would be. He's not exactly a Jack Russell, Roscoe, is he?'

'Did he see Mrs Morningwood?'

'Didn't leave the kitchen.'

'Right.' Merrily turned away from the house. 'We should go. We need to find her, don't we?'

Teddy: how much circumstantial evidence did you need?

'OK,' Lol said. 'This Murray, the feeling I'm getting—'

'This is all my fault, isn't it?' Jane said. 'You think I shouldn't've brought her. Only, the way she—'

Merrily said, 'Jane, there are no circumstances I can, at this moment, imagine under which it would've been OK to bring Muriel Morningwood back to Garway. Let's leave it at that, for now.'

Lol backed off into the darkness, shaking his head.

Jane said, 'I'm sorry. Am I … I mean, when am I going to be allowed to know what happened to her?'

'Yeah, well, that was my mistake, flower. I should've told you. Mrs Morningwood was raped. And she's deeply traumatized. Either more than she knows or more than her pride will let anyone else know. And that … is the main reason we have to find her.'

It was too dark to see Jane's face.

You should look for two white gateposts, one broken in half.

Straight in this time, no oblique approach.

There was still a lot of track, well overgrown, the Volvo whingeing and grinding in second gear. Feeling a wheel slip, Merrily pulled the car

417

back from the rim of a ditch, as the central chimney stack of the Master House rose up palely in the headlights.

The wind rising now, the last flurries of mist passing like the slipstreams of barn owls.

She dipped the lights, stopping the car against a wedge of impacted red mud, about fifty yards short of the hollow where the farmhouse lay, looking big and whole and intact and solid by night. Like it might have looked a century ago, in transit between Gwilym and Newton.

Merrily switched off the engine, put out all the lights, and the house vanished.

Except for a mustardy glow behind a window.

'Oh God,' Jane said. 'I told you.'

Lol said, 'I don't see the Jeep.'

A landscape full of trees and hollows, ground mist, no moon; Merrily told him there could be half a dozen cars parked here and you wouldn't see them.

She'd worked out that the light was upstairs, probably the bedroom over the room with the inglenook.

'And obviously, we can't all go in.'

'I think we can,' Lol said evenly.

'Not if we want to learn anything. She's already told Jane to go home, and she doesn't yet know what a sensitive and discreet person you are, Lol, so …'

'Yes?'

'I'll go.'

'No.'

'Look, you're just out here – what – twenty yards from the house? You can … watch my back.'

'Yeah, I can give you covering fire. Merrily, this is—'

'The best and most direct way to expedite a difficult situation.'

'You don't know it's her.'

'Who else could it be?'

Lol turned his head towards Jane and back at Merrily.

'He's in Hereford,' Merrily said. 'At a lodge meeting. The service tomorrow night … seems to need planning.'

'It's not as if we can have phone contact down here.'

'You checked?'

'Yes.' Lol snapped the phone shut. 'Nothing.'

'If you can bear to keep the windows down, you'll be able to hear everything for miles.'

'Not the way the wind's getting up.'

'You can always hear a scream,' Merrily said. 'Trust me. I can do a scream you'll hear.'

59

Joy You

AT THE FRONT door, under the overhanging skull-shaped broken lamp, Merrily waited and looked back and questioned the sense of what she was doing.

Inevitably, what kept coming back was the last time she'd sat in that car in a rising wind, having planned to go and check out the Master House, thinking of how she'd been shafted and then *Sod this, I'm going home.*

No guarantee that, if she'd come here then, it would in any way have altered her opinion that Fuchsia had made the whole thing up.

But it might have.

And in any case that didn't matter. What mattered was giving in to the resentment, after Bliss told her about the Special Branch. Stomping out into the rain to walk it off and then going home anyway to moan on the phone to Sophie.

Lessons learned. She pushed at the door and it yielded enough to be shouldered open, the damp-earth smell wafting out at her as if she was going outside, not in.

It was colder too, a kind of airless, stagnant cold. The floor felt hard and ridged where the decayed linoleum had been ground into it.

Time slowed.

She saw a thin light falling on the cage of the iron fire-basket in the inglenook. A light, somehow, from up the chimney and, as she watched, it went away.

Merrily stood for a moment, listening to her own breathing, her own heart and the footsteps on the stone spiral steps, and there was no time for a prayer before he was standing at the foot of the stairs, the wire of a hurricane lamp hanging from his fingers, its low, sallow flame bringing up the red stains on his surplice.

'Great minds, eh?' Teddy said.

He put the hurricane lamp on the floor, its wick turned down low.

'God!' Merrily laid a palm flat on her chest, feeling the ridge of the pectoral cross. 'Bloody hell, Teddy, scared the life out of me.'

He didn't say anything, just stood there, with the lamp at his feet fanning pale fronds of light over the scarred and lumpy walls. He looked ... avuncular, with his easy, white-bearded smile, his large teeth, bright eyes, forehead like the top of a brown egg. Walking boots.

'Just been up to the ...' Merrily put on a rueful smile. 'Called at The Ridge, to pick up my stuff.'

'Oh, *Merrily* ... I dropped off the bags at your home a few hours ago.'

'Yeah, I know. Sod's Law, Teddy.'

'Didn't your daughter tell you?'

'No, Beverley told me. I mean, just now. Haven't seen Jane since breakfast – I've been in Hereford. Damn. Thank you. But I mean, you shouldn't've bothered, anyway.'

'Not a problem, I was going past. More or less.'

'Anyway ... Now, since I was here, I thought we ought to have a word, clear up a few things, but Beverley said she didn't know where you'd gone, so I thought I'd just ...'

'Thought you'd drop in here instead, and get things ready for your Requiem?'

'Well ... yes. Always helps, doesn't it? Always things on the day that you'd wished you'd thought of earlier, like ... an altar? It's amazing how often you turn up to do a Eucharist and there's nothing to use as an altar, so I've got this folding—'

Talking too fast.

'Anyway, you know all that stuff.'

'Yes,' Teddy said. 'And I think it's terribly brave of you to come to somewhere like this, on your own, after dark. It's just that I thought you – or rather the Bishop – had called it all off.'

Bugger.

'Well ...' Merrily stared into the lamp. 'I thought it was time to stand up for what I believed, for a change, instead of bowing to politics, so I went to see him today, persuaded him to let me go ahead. I thought it was important, I mean, to do something. Get rid of all the years of bad feeling and rumour, let this place go into a new era, clean.'

'Good for you, Merrily!' Teddy said.

'Of course, I thought I'd have a bit more time to make the arrangements because it wasn't going to be until Saturday, but then Beverley said your memorial service was being held tomorrow, and I obviously wanted to tie in with that, that whole Templar thing, so ...'

'Well, you know, I didn't want it to become a circus, Merrily.'

'No. I can understand that.'

'All these odd people who seem to turn up at anything to do with Templars.'

'Yes ... in fact, I did want to—'

'It's why I'm here,' Teddy said.

'Sorry?'

'Someone in the village was telling me that some people had been seen around the church and the Master House with metal detectors. Treasure hunters, you know? We get them all the time, and they've been known to cause quite a lot of damage, but ... well, nothing on this scale before.'

'In ... in here?'

'If you come upstairs, I can show you. Hell of a mess.'

'Oh.'

'Why I'm wearing this.' Teddy plucked at the surplice. 'It's an old one I keep in the Land Rover to use as a kind of overall. Cover up my clothes.'

'Oh ... yeah. I was wondering about that.'

What Merrily *could* see now was that the red marks on the surplice were not blood but stone dust. Surprising how many clergy did that, recycled old vestments.

He beamed at her and gestured at the stairs with one hand.

'Interesting, really. There's a ... Well, I'd heard about it, of course, but it was blocked up over fifty years ago by the Newtons. It was apparently pretty inaccessible, not much use as a storage area, reduced the floor space upstairs, and so they bricked it up. Priest's hole, Merrily.'

'Oh.'

'Quite a lot of Papists here after the Reformation. An independence of spirit remaining from the time when the Templars owed no money or allegiance to anyone but the Pope himself. Quite a bit of persecution.'

'Yes. Actually, I was going to—'

'Anyway, what happened, I saw these two guys coming up from here towards the church, just before dark, shouted to them ... and, of course, they took off. Came down here to investigate, door was hanging open, dust everywhere. They'd ripped up the floorboards upstairs, prised away the bricks, exposed the cavity.'

'It's in the wall?'

'Back of the fireplace. Come and look.'

Teddy stood back from the stairs.

A test.

Merrily remembered the room upstairs, the smell of decay, probably dead mice and rats. The skeletal remains of two beds.

How she'd thought of M. R. James and the room at the Globe Inn.

And if she didn't go up with him now, she'd be revealing fear. Fear of a colleague in the clergy. If she did go up ... what?

Problem was, it rang true, this story. More than hers did, anyway. The light falling into the inglenook had been an indication of something being knocked through, perhaps the wrong stones being taken out.

She said, 'Why would they ... I mean, what did they expect to find?'

What had *Teddy* expected to find?

Or was he going to put something in? Brick it up again.

'I don't know,' he said. 'I've not been able to see. If you were to hold the lamp for me, perhaps we might ...'

'Well, maybe not now, Teddy, if you don't mind. Best clothes?'

'Oh, it's not too bad, now the dust has settled. They must've left in quite a hurry. Left this behind.'

He bent down, came up holding a crowbar, a long one, heavy-duty. Held it in both hands.

'Well ... well-prepared, then,' Merrily said. 'Templar treasure – that what they were looking for, do you think?'

'Templar treasure.' He looked at her, head on one side, lamplight glazing his eyes. 'What a joke.'

'Is it?'

'If there *was* treasure, it wasn't *their* kind of treasure – gold and jewels.'

'No?'

'Perhaps something much more ... abstract than that. The essence of an ethos.'

She was starting to feel very cold. Cold and scared enough to shiver. Mrs Morningwood. Where was she? *Had* she been in here tonight? And if she had ...

It was crazy. No rape victim would deliberately expose herself again to the ...

... Rapist.

But how could you think that of easygoing Teddy, *placid* Teddy? How could anyone?

'I keep hearing stuff about Jacques de Molay being here,' Merrily said. 'Some ex-Templar's confession. Jacques de Molay forcing him to deny Jesus Christ or be ... put into a sack or something.'

There was a sack in the inglenook, an animal-feed sack of thick plastic. Maybe two.

'Ah,' Teddy said. 'That old tale.'

'You don't believe it?'

'Confessions could be extracted without too much difficulty in those days.'

'Not so easy now.'

'No?'

'To get someone to confess,' Merrily said. 'Not so easy.'

Wondering how quickly she could get out of here, if necessary. How fast she could run. Wearing a skirt.

But then all she had to do was open the door and scream for Lol, and he'd be down here in seconds, ready to face Teddy.

And his crowbar.

And Jane ... Merrily flinched at an image of Jane's soft face raked across by the sharp end of a crowbar wielded like a weapon of war. Like a Templar's ...

She straightened up. Patted some red dust off her best dark blue woollen jacket.

'You know what, Teddy?' she said. '*I* think you've been misleading us all.'

'This is so weird.'

Jane and Lol had got out of the car. The night wind was blowing Jane's hair back. She faced into it.

'I can't believe she did that, Lol. Can't believe how much she's changed ... even this past year Or you, come to that. Never used to notice people changing.'

'No.'

'Scary, really.'

'Yes.'

She didn't think he'd taken his eyes off the front of that farmhouse once since Mum had gone in. He was like Roscoe, sitting upright on the grass between them, Jane resting a hand on the dog's neck, feeling a quiver there.

'When we came here – I mean to Ledwardine – I had no respect for Mum. I *despised* her. For being a priest. For making me watch her ... pray and stuff. How *could* she, you know? How could she put me through that?'

'That's normal,' Lol said. 'Oh God, Jane, I forgot. Eirion rang.'

'Irene?'

It was out before she could stop it.

'He, um ... he said you hadn't been returning his calls.'

'Did he?'

She looked at Lol's shape in the darkness, tense. He used to look very boyish, in a wispy kind of way. Even just a couple of years ago. There was grey in his hair now and he had an air of faint regret. Maybe the wasted years. And there was still anxiety. Not so much about his career as a fear of losing Mum. And how to handle a priest.

'He said he must've rung about twenty times,' Lol said. 'He sounded pretty upset. He thinks, um ... he thinks you're having an affair with a married man.'

'Coops.'

'That would be the guy, yes.'

'It's over,' Jane said.

'What?'

'He's given me what I need.'

Lol took his stare off the house for nearly a second.

'The best places to apply for courses in archaeology.'

'Jane …?'

'I was thinking, well, if I hate the idea of the future so much, like the way the world's going, why not just like … immerse myself in the way it used to be.'

'You told your mum about this?'

'No.'

'Why not?'

'Because I wasn't certain. Coops took me on a field walk. You just, like, walk a line through a … field. And pick things up … bits of stone, bits of pottery, and it's like you're peeling away the layers. It was amazing. Unexpectedly amazing. The feeling of … I dunno … *contact*.'

'That's … fantastic, Jane. You've found it? At last?'

'Yeah. Maybe. I'd have to get accepted somewhere first. How did he sound?'

'Who?'

'Eirion.'

'Seriously pissed-off.'

'Oh God. Sometimes I can't believe what a total bitch I am.' Jane looked down at the long stone house. 'What do you think they're talking about in there?'

'I don't know. I don't like the feel of this, Jane.'

'You think Mrs Morningwood is … I mean, we know nothing about her, really. What are we going to do? About Mum.'

'I don't know. I'm not her … boss.'

'Yeah, but you love her. Trouble is,' Jane said, 'she thinks the boss does, too.'

'Which …? Oh.'

'She's inclined to trust the bugger too much, if you ask me. Faith doesn't always win through. Look at all the good people He … Good people who get shafted. Destroyed. Happens all the time.'

She had to stay with this. Nobody else was going to find out. She sank her hands into her jacket pockets for warmth.

Misleading everybody. Not really. Teddy could have been standing up in various pulpits for thirty years and preaching from the Gnostic gospels and nobody would notice. Faith was flaccid. People no longer heard. Congregations didn't *listen*.

'I meant the Templars, that's all.' Merrily keeping her voice light. 'You like to pretend you have only a cursory knowledge, but the first time we met you said you were a historian by inclination, and it's just not *possible* for a historian to live in a place like this without getting …'

'Obsessed?'

'Totally immersed, I was going to say. I bet you were so excited when you found The Ridge. Like your … like your whole life had been moving towards Garway.'

Teddy looked up, first in surprise. And then, maybe, in suspicion, his eyes sullen in the lamplight.

'Yes. I suppose so. I applied several times for this parish. Always went to someone else. I suppose the time wasn't right. And, as a team minister, with the other parishes, I wouldn't have had the space I have now. This has been a happy coincidence. A time to be seized.'

'You knew a lot about them before you came? The Templars?'

'Yes, I suppose I studied quite a bit. A good bit.'

'Before theological college.'

'Yes. Theology was … an interesting tangent. I grew up at a time when you could follow your …'

'Stars.' Merrily found a smile. 'As it were.'

'I was born in Hertfordshire. There's always been a lot of Templar activity around Hertford itself.'

'Hertfordshire to Herefordshire?'

'Interesting. One letter and almost the whole width of a country away. In Hertford itself, there've always been rumours of tunnels under the town, connected to the Knights Templar, the Holy Grail. There's still an organization there. An Order.'

'Of Templars?'

'It didn't go away.'

'Secret?'

'To an extent. But enough on the surface for them to call on the Vatican to apologize for the inquisition of 1307.'

'You think the Vatican *should* apologize, Teddy?'

'It would just be a token gesture. The Templars never needed tokenism. They dug out their own heritage. Literally.'

'From the site of Solomon's Temple. Or is that a metaphor?'

'It's both. Like Garway. This place is as important as Solomon's Temple now. More important.'

'Because it hasn't altered? Apart from the odd radio mast, much the same now as it was in the thirteenth century.'

'And even the mast is symbolic. Like the hill itself, it communicates information that not everyone can receive.'

'As above, so below.'

He shrugged.

'You get periods of great activity and illumination,' he said. 'Periods of urgency.'

'And this is one?'

'The only one we'll know in our lifetime. We have to … do the right thing. Exactly the right thing. Just to survive.'

'We?'

'The Templars.'

'That's a state of mind, is it?'

'It's a state of being. Seven centuries ago, they were the greatest combination of spiritual and physical power the Western world has ever known. It's probably hard for a woman to understand.'

'Probably, yes.'

'A mocking tone, Merrily?'

'Hell, no. I believe it. I believe if you immerse yourself in something, it creates within you enough of an illusion of power to … to *be* power. It's likely to be a destructive power, of course, but that's what the Templars did, isn't it? They destroyed. Violent guys. Killed the infidel.'

'And were sanctioned to do so by St Bernard of Clairvaux. As a result of whose influence they were also granted independence of all other ecclesiastical powers, except the Pope himself. *The Templar is a fearless knight,* St Bernard said, *who, as the body is covered with iron, so the soul is the defence of the faith, Without doubt, fortified by both arms, he fears neither man nor demon.'*

Teddy folded his arms over his reddened surplice, smiling.

'Defence of the faith,' Merrily said.

'To defend faith the Templar needed knowledge. Only knowledge cancels doubt.'

'And who's the demon? Baphomet?'

'He's just a symbol, you know that. An aspect of the green man. Ubiquitous. The life-force in nature.'

Also, Merrily thought, the *sex*-force in nature.

Thinking of the night before the rape, at dinner at The Ridge: nut roast and gossip. Had it occurred to Teddy then, over that meal, that if Mrs Morningwood was the victim of a sex crime the list of possible suspects from her client book would direct police attention, from the start, far away from the Master House? He *must* have known about her. All his walks, his coffee stops at farms along the way.

Or had he simply fallen in lust with the idea? Just like old times. Watching Muriel from the hill, fantasizing about how he'd do it? Mild, cheerful Teddy Murray lacing his hiking books, pocketing his condoms. Already out there, probably, when Merrily was taking that dispiriting early call from the Bishop. Circling Ty Gwyn like a hawk, in complete command of his landscape.

Baphomet. Mat Phobe.

And now, at last, in the unsteady glow, she could see him with long hair, reddish, tangled around his face, an eager, mid-twenties face, bum-fluff on the jawline. Enthusiastic. Full of a raging fire, blown up by the bellows of testosterone and whatever other chemicals Jimmy Hayter had obtained that week.

'So who's the infidel now, Teddy?'

'Today, Merrily, I'm very much afraid that term would have to include most people.'

She didn't know if there were any anti-Islamic implications here, didn't want to. He came further into the room, pushing the lantern with the toe of a walking boot, propping the crowbar against the side of the inglenook.

'Are you getting what you wanted? To make your historic connections?'

'More or less.'

'I admire you, Merrily. You've taken on something that is, transparently, not for women, and you're sticking in there. That's really rather courageous.'

'Thanks.'

'Look, if you want to get off, I'll carry on here for a while. Clear up some more of the mess.' He dug into a trouser pocket, pulled out something white, balled-up, snapping it apart. 'Got to take precautions, all these dead rodents. Sure you don't want to see the priest's hole? In fact ...'

Surgical gloves.

Putting them on as he stepped into the inglenook, dragged a yellow feed sack, thick plastic, out into the room, and then a second one.

'Can't say they didn't come prepared. Obviously collecting some of the rubble in these, to clear it out of the way, give themselves more space. If you step under here. Merrily, and look up the chimney, you can actually see into the priest's ... oh.'

Teddy glanced back, in mild annoyance, to where one of the feed sacks had fallen on to its side and some of the contents spilled out over the edge of the hearth. The contents included what looked like a clavicle, part of a ribcage. Finally, the top half of a skull, no lower jaw, with rubbery fragments of skin and black hair, rolling gently, with a *clink*, into the lamp.

Merrily screaming the scream as Teddy Murray casually stepped out. Choked off with heart-in-mouth shock, the scream wasn't much of a scream at all, in the end.

And by then Teddy had her by the hair with one hand, the other half-clawed in her face, twisting. His mouth up close, whispering some words, but the only ones she heard, as he was forcing her to her knees in the dirt, were '... *joy you.*'

60

Crumpled Linen

THE IMAGE HAD formed in a hollow of powdery yellow light, while Lol was fighting for consciousness.

with consciousness had come this unendurable pain and his let go for a moment, storing the one frozen tableau: a man into a sack.

have passed out a third time, if only momentarily, because, ing, the yellow scene had gone and so had all the light.

t move, working out where he was, what had happened, the solving at one stage into the velvety coffin of the broken guitar.

Confusion. Panic. Need to get up. He planted a hand on the floor. His shoulder screamed, his head pulsed, his memory rewound.

One blow was all he could remember, and the whistling of the air before it came.

Below the shoulder he'd already damaged getting in. The oak door had jammed and he'd thought someone had locked it from inside and he'd taken a wild run at it, gone crashing through to meet the steel bar swinging out of near-darkness, sending him spinning around, his head ramming the door.

Ah. Old oak: the hardest.

Lol cried out into the darkess in his head.

Hands cool on his face now, the soft voice from the meditation in the candlelit church. Black jeans and sweatshirt, hair tied back.

'Can you speak? Oh, God, please …'

The night air made it real.

Up on the rise, the wolfhound was going crazy in the Volvo, as if someone had gone past, someone he wanted to kill. And Jane, hearing him, was going, 'Where's Mrs Morningwood?' and wouldn't stop until they'd all gone back into the earth-smelling house, where Lol couldn't do the stairs.

Jane had kept asking him if his shoulder was broken and he didn't know – how were you supposed to tell? He waited at the bottom of the half-spiral, tense and sweating, almost sick with the headache and the pain in his upper arm, until they came back, the mother and the daughter, having found nothing up there, nobody.

At some stage, he realized that Jane was doing all the talking.

When they were outside again, he got close to Merrily, was able to say, 'He touch you?'

'Kind of,' she said. 'Once. After I screamed. It's all right.'

'Didn't hear it,' Lol said, horrified. 'I didn't hear the scream.'

'Walls are two feet thick. We never thought.'

It came back to him how they couldn't stand it any longer, he and Jane, not either of them. Making a joint decision that Lol should go in.

'Look,' he said to Merrily. 'Never … never *do* that …'

'Again. No.'

'You knew it might be him, didn't you?'

'Never again,' she said and clung to his good arm all the slow way back to the car. 'Hospital,' she said. 'Where's the nearest? Abergavenny?'

'Call Bliss. Drive till we find a signal and call Bliss.'

'Ambulance first. Please, Lol.'

'Can't let him get away. Have to find the bones.'

Moving sluggishly through the rutted field, Merrily at the wheel, Lol recalled his dreamlike memory of the bones and the yellow sack, the scene for ever vivid with shock. Bones? Sack?

'Two sacks,' Merrily said. 'A whole body. A skeleton. In pieces. He took it away. In the sacks. Must have got out the back way. Jane and me – upstairs, just now – we saw the priest's hole. It must have been in there, all these years.'

'Where anybody could have found it?' Lol said.

'No. Somebody, I think it was Roxanne Gray, told me about the priest's hole, which the family had blocked up many years before. Fifty years? Maybe the commune people had rediscovered it and blocked it up again. With something inside. Someone.'

'Mary,' Lol said.

'Mary Roberts. Mary Linden.'

'Need to get Bliss.'

'Don't move,' Merrily said. 'Please don't move more than ...'

'Need to find him. Before the bastard dumps the bones in the river or something. Or he'll walk away from it.'

He saw Merrily clench the wheel.

'*Enjoy you,*' she said. '*Going to enjoy you.* That was what he said.'

She looked at him and he felt the scream that was going on inside her.

Jane said, 'He's got to be insane. Not just psychotic.'

'I don't think he's insane at all,' Merrily said. 'That's the trouble. Just driven towards something we can't really understand. The only hope we have is that if they find that body maybe they can match the DNA against Fuchsia.'

'He *is* insane,' Jane said, leaning over from the back seat. 'Because if he thought he could ...' putting her arms around Merrily from behind, and her arms were quivering '... if he thought he could just kill you and leave you ...'

'He was wearing surgical gloves.' Merrily turned to Jane. 'And he wouldn't have just left me. When we were upstairs, just now, and we looked down into the priest's hole? Struck me then that it was vacant. It had a vacancy.'

As they reached the top road at The Turning, she started to laugh, dangerously close to hysteria, and then she said, not even sounding surprised, 'He's there.'

Lol saw a flash. Out in the road, lit up in headlights, the surplice billowing.

Lit up in headlights, but not from the Volvo.

Merrily braked hard and the Volvo stalled, as was its habit. An engine roar and he flew up like a swan, this great, white flapping thing.

*

Merrily was out of the car before Teddy Murray hit the tarmac. She saw a wheel of the Jeep rolling easily over his head and she heard – one of those sounds you knew you were never going to forget for the rest of your life – the crunching of his shiny skull like an egg in the road.

Long minutes, then, of people continuously fading in and out of cottages and unseen farms, like a video rewinding. Atmosphere of near-mute horror. Merrily trying several times to talk to Mrs Morningwood and failing. Only getting close when the emergency services arrived and Mrs Morningwood was leaning against a wall, head in her hands, rocking backwards and forwards like a child on a fairground ride, blood and tears oozing between her fingers.

The back of the ambulance yawning and the most senior paramedic telling Mrs Morningwood that she had to come with them and getting reminded that while it might be a police state it wasn't yet an *NHS* state.

'Look at you,' the woman paramedic said calmly. 'Look at your face ... your neck ... look at your eyes. Please, my dear, these are serious injuries. At least let us check you out in the—'

'It's what I *do*. It's what I *do*, you idiot!'

'What's she talking about?' the paramedic said. 'Does anybody know?'

'She's a herbalist,' Merrily said.

'Oh, well, that's a big help, then, isn't it, if she's got a fractured skull. That *is* blood in her hair, you know.'

'I do think you'd better go with them,' one of the police said. 'We can take your statement later.'

'You can take my statement now.'

Mrs Morningwood peeling herself from the wall. Merrily saw a cop carrying ROAD CLOSED signs from a blue van. The wind was dying and the mist was coming back, swirling down from the hill. Mrs Morningwood limped into the road towards the Jeep, and a police-woman held her back, and she started to weep again.

'Can't you get him *out*?'

'Don't look, madam, that's my advice.'

'Do you think I'm some sort of *innocent*? You think I don't know what I've done? I've killed the poor fucking vicar!'

A policeman said to Merrily, 'Is that your car, madam, the Volvo?' and she nodded and the copper said, 'Did you see what happened?' and Lol came over, and Merrily thought this was going to be the best time to get him into the ambulance.

'I saw it,' Lol said quietly. 'You couldn't miss him, all in white. He just ran out into the road. Wasn't even walking, he was running. I don't think there's anything she could've done.'

Merrily stared at him. He looked past her.

'We'll need to take a proper statement, sir,' the policeman said. 'What happened to your arm?'

Lol explained that his friend had had to brake hard to avoid running into the Jeep and he mustn't have had his seat belt on properly. Went into the windscreen with his head. The arm … he wasn't sure.

'Right, if you give your name to my colleague and then let's get you into the ambulance.'

'It'll be OK. Honestly.'

'I'm sorry, sir, but *all* injuries at the scene of an accident …'

'No problem.' Lol tried to put both hands up, managed one. 'Anything I can do.' He looked over at Mrs Morningwood. 'She's going to be traumatized for life. He just … just came out.'

'It's true,' Jane said from behind Merrily. 'There's no way she could've avoided him.'

Merrily glanced back at Jane; it sent a pain into her neck, from when Teddy's hand had slammed into her face, twisting her head round. Different person. Like the Templars, sometimes pastoral, peacefully monastic, then the sword out, red to the hilt. Merrily stared at Jane and Jane stared back, defiant.

'She didn't have a chance,' Jane said.

Another cop was asking Mrs Morningwood where she'd been going at the time of the accident and Mrs Morningwood was saying, 'I was looking for my dog. My dog's escaped. You haven't *seen* a dog anywhere, have you?'

Merrily looked at Teddy's body, no need to cover it because the surplice was up over his face, moulded to it by the blood and tissue and brain matter. Crumpled linen.

Cleansing

MERRILY'S ALB, AN appeal for purity and simplicity, now had dirt-stains on both arms and across one shoulder, as if emblematic of the kind of soiled priest who concealed rape, murder …

Or was just a doormat.

Pray for doormat.

On the back door, she drew a cross in holy water and asked that, by the holy and cleansing power of God, this entrance might be blessed.

Muriel Morningwood took off her dark glasses. Her eyes were black and red and still glaring with tears. A lot of tears these past two days.

'How's his wife taken it?'

'I wouldn't like to say.' Merrily looked around. 'I think we need to do every room.'

Her alb had a cord at the waist, like the Templars used to wear, under the cross.

'You've seen her, though, I assume.'

'Her son was coming over today to pick her up. Unsurprisingly, she'll be putting the place on the market.'

Beverley Murray, face of scrubbed stone, looking at Merrily as if convinced she, or God, or both, were in some way behind this. Merrily had told her nothing. Beverley had said she'd have left Teddy, eventually, but Merrily didn't think she would have. They tended not to, clergy wives. Or not for a long time.

'You think he beat her?' Mrs Morningwood asked.

'I think he was oblivious of her, much of the time. Focused on his own perceived role in some kind of … alternative history. And she just got on with it. One roof, two lives.'

In the washhouse or utility room or whatever – well, there were still pegs on the wall, where coats would have hung – Merrily put down the flask of holy water, a sense of everything moving past her, out of control. A sense of *blur,* all the rushing spirits, waves of panic. *Please, God, calm.* She straightened up.

'At some stage, you might stop looking at me like that,' Mrs Morningwood said.

'Maybe.'

Or not. Despair soaked in again. Merrily picked up the flask of holy water, hugged it to her bosom. You never knew anybody quite well enough. Never sure who to trust, and yet you did have to trust. *It's a slippery slope, Merrily,* Siân Callaghan-Clarke had said. *Letting trust slip away.*

And support. Support for the insupportable.

'What have we done, Muriel?'

'We?' Mrs Morningwood put her glasses back on. 'You've done nothing at all, darling. Except, perhaps, step over the edge of other people's madness.'

Even though she knew he wouldn't be back, Muriel would have new locks put on the doors. Life, she said, was a series of knee-jerks, stable doors banging in the night. She'd refused to come back to Ledwardine, had gone alone to the house at the end of the holiday cottages to sleep downstairs on the chaise longue with the dog.

Well … to lie there. No herbs would have produced restful sleep that night. Or the next. It had all finally come down on Mrs Morningwood. She'd brought it down, one big knee-jerk, connecting a foot with an accelerator pedal.

Eccentric, deranged, Beverley Murray had said. *The way she drives around in that big Jeep, taking corners too fast.*

'Who is Muriel Morningwood?' Frannie Bliss had asked yesterday, having looked at the report from Traffic. A heavily-loaded question, and Merrily had given him the Need to Know. Waiting for him to mention the discovery of bones, but he never had. It would come.

This morning, with arrangements for the Requiem finalized, she'd driven over to Ty Gwyn, finding it clean as a pharmacy. Sterile, something sucked out. Unexpectedly, Mrs Morningwood had asked her to bless the house. And the greenhouse and the garden, where herbs were grown and chickens pecked around.

'Jane said he'd been inside again.'

'Meddling with the herbs. Unscrewing jars. Sniffing, I expect.'

'Why?'

'Don't know. They've all gone, now.'

'But you'll get more …'

'I expect so. I need the money. That wasn't all. He'd been through the drawers. Found Mary's letter. Took that. And some photos.'

'Would he have known you had that letter?'

'No way he could. Unless Fuchsia …'

'You showed it to Fuchsia?'

Mrs Morningwood had nodded.

'I don't know about this, do I?' Merrily said. 'I don't know the half of it.'

With the afternoon seeping damply away, Lord Stourport stood at the edge of a copse, wet leaves around his shoes.

'They weren't even there, then, these trees, I'm pretty sure. And I'm good at land. It's like looking back at a different lifetime.'

Meaning, *We were different people.* But that was the easy way out, Lol thought.

Hayter said, 'What's she doing in there, your woman?'

'Trying to make the place feel a bit calmer. Before the Requiem.'

'And that draws a line under it, does it, the Requiem?'

'Just starts the process, I think.'

'I do not like this,' Jimmy Hayter said. 'I shouldn't be here.'

He'd arrived over an hour early, while Merrily was still setting out the folding altar in front of the inglenook. Mrs Morningwood had walked over to join her, and Jane had taken Roscoe for a walk. It was an hour or so from sunset, Lol's head still aching if he moved too fast or turned his back to the wind.

'You could still go to the cops,' Hayter said. 'And I don't yet believe you won't.'

It was why he'd come and why Gwilym would come, too. Nervous, and with every reason. Not out of the woods yet, maybe never would be.

'No cops so far,' Lol said, 'apart from traffic cops. Apparently, there's, um … In Garway, there's a long tradition of independence.'

They walked up to the top of the rise, and now you could see the skewed, sandy tower of Garway Church.

'OK,' Jimmy Hayter said. 'I'll tell you. We *did* know him before.'

'Murray?'

'We were at Cambridge together. There was a magic society, like you got at a lot of universities. Recreated the rituals of the Golden Dawn, then the heavier stuff. I was in it for a while, so was Pierre. Most of us, a bit of fun. Murray … it took over his life to the extent he shuffled off with a disappointing second – me saying I'd've thought he'd be able to magic up a better fucking degree than that. He didn't care. *This* was his life's path.'

'So he wasn't doing … theology, or …'

'Nah. He was doing women. And drugs. All kinds. All this Carlos Castaneda stuff was fashionable then – mescaline, jimson weed, the Way of the Warrior. My guess is that's what got him into the Templars – European spiritual warriors, monks in armour.'

'The Templars did drugs?'

'Maybe. He thought so. Apparently, they introduced a lot of herbs into Europe from North Africa. He'd try anything for a new experience. And women, like I say, he was good at women. Urbane, diffident most of the time. Then he'd just turn it on. Focus, you know? Like a laser. He'd focus on a woman and he'd make it happen, and then, when she was crazy for him, he'd lose interest, go cold on her. The making it happen was all.'

'How did he wind up here with you, then?'

'We had money, he didn't. Scholarship boy, from a family of modest means. Unlike my merchant-banker friend, Pierre, who was into the back-to-nature bit – funny that, isn't it? One bad experience of nature, red in tooth and fucking claw, and Pierre's been in the City ever since.'

'So who actually found this place?'

'Teddy. Or Mat, as we were instructed to call him. Mat Phobe – we never worked that out, you know. Doing drugs, it can take you months to master word games. Like Woodstock. F … U … C … K – what's that spell? Fuck knows.'

Hayter cackled and stood on a green mound, looking down at the Master House.

'He was well into the Templar stuff by then, and we knew nothing. Very excited when he found out that the place we were actually living in had *connections*. He had us doing excavations, digging up the floors, taking stones out of the walls. We kept moving furniture around to cover up the current hole in case the owners came in. Like the PoWs at Colditz. He always thought there was a tunnel to the church.'

'Find anything?'

'Nah. Mat also had this idea that when Jacques de Molay came, he brought something with him to hide at Garway because it was so remote. He was thinking the Mappa Mundi, or a prototype – nobody really knows where that came from or how it wound up in Hereford, but it was evidently made around the end of the thirteenth century, which fits. He kept going into Hereford to look at it in the cathedral. Dragging us along, or one of the girls. Never seemed much to me. Not exactly great art, not much of a map.'

'So, what—?'

'It's a very Templar creation. Shows Jerusalem as the centre of the world. No, I've got it wrong, actually … he didn't think there was a *prototype* of the Mappa Mundi at Garway, he thought the Mappa Mundi *was* the prototype. All those symbols and strange creatures around it, but they're quite roughly drawn. He was convinced there was a finished version hidden somewhere, a perfect magical map, connecting the world to the universe. A total concept. He thought they'd created it as a kind of magical control thing. And that … that was gonna be Teddy Murray's Holy Grail.'

'And he thought it was still hidden at Garway?'

Lol looked around and saw an intimate, enclosed landscape, small mellow fields, encrusted with autumn woodland, dipping to the sandstone church. Warmth, shelter. Despite last night, he liked it here.

'Maybe a cave under the hill … or even under the Master House,' Hayter said. 'He was ingesting a lot of stuff, and it got crazy. He thought he'd find out by asking spirits and demons. Walking the hill, tripping out. We'd do these invocations, and he'd get messages. *We* wouldn't. Just him. And Gwilym, once.'

'The Glyndwr link.'

'Mat said Glyndwr was a magician, a Templar and a prince and he would have learned the whereabouts of this secret … chamber … temple … whatever. A magical link had to be made between Gwilym and his ancestor. This took weeks, making the poor bastard fast and bathe daily in the Monnow and wash his balls or whatever in the holy well. All kinds of mystical shit.'

'And that about Gwilym speaking Welsh, did that actually happen?'

'Couldn't tell you, cocker, none of us could understand a bleeding word. It's a mug's game. You don't get anything you can see or touch or put in the bank. Nothing except the feeling of something out there playing with you. End of the day you just come out with your health ruined, your humanity eroded and fuck-all else.'

'And yet he wanted to come back?'

'Well, I *say* fuck all. I think he did find something. Something he didn't want to share.'

'How do you know about it, then?'

Lol sat down under a hawthorn tree, resting his left arm on his knee. At Nevill Hall Hospital, outside Abergavenny, they'd found a very deep bruise but no fracture. Still hurt quite a bit, though, right across the shoulder, and it was scary because he couldn't hold a guitar and something hurt when he formed chords. His best guitar smashed, his chord arm … was he being told something?

'This was in the last days,' Hayter said. 'He wanted us out of the way. He wanted to be alone there. I told you how I had to go to London, see my old man?'

'Seemed very convenient,' Lol said. 'Also he wasn't *quite* alone, was he?'

'The girl.'

'Mary.'

'Yeah. This Mary turns up again and says she's had a baby and she wants it to grow up with a father.'

'Which of you would that be?'

'Dunno. Dunno to this day. Anyway, she didn't mean she wanted a father, she meant she wanted money. A packet. For starters. Well, I'd spent up on the lease on this place and a surfeit of substances to abuse, and my old man wasn't exactly flush. And Gwilym, he had a Triumph

Spitfire to support and a dad with no need of a spare granddaughter. That was when Mat said, take a weekend away, I'll deal with it.'

'Just like that.'

'Look … it was cowardly and irresponsible, but … we were cowards and we were irresponsible. And we were young. And we came back, Mary was gone, and a day or so later we were raided by the police, and that was an end of it and I was very glad to get away. Only I didn't, and neither did Gwilym. He'd got us where he wanted us.'

'You didn't even have proof she *had* a baby.'

'She had photos. We kept staring at them, see which one of us she looked like. Kid looked like all of us, with darker skin. Mary said she was living in this place where there were a lot of hard guys who'd come and get heavy with us. End of the day, it was blackmail. Extortion.'

'And blackmailers get what they deserve?'

'Robinson, look, we didn't think he'd *killed* her.'

'What did you *think* he'd done? He had no money.'

'I don't …' gritted teeth '… know. We weren't there, we didn't care.'

Lol said nothing, thinking of the magical, chemical hell of the girl's last days. Hayter leaned against the tree-trunk.

'Few years later, when I'm getting into some good money through music-promo, he's back in touch. Somewhat reluctantly, we have a meeting, him and me and Sycharth, on neutral ground – in Evesham, I think it was. He looks different. Short hair, suit. He tells us that Mary died in the course of "a ritual".'

'I can't believe this, Jimmy.'

'Yeah, well, if you'd been there, you would have. Mat tells us he's been to theological college and he's a curate now – that was the bit *we* couldn't believe. Reckons it's going to be a breeze. Not great money, but a free house. Couple of days a week mouthing simplistic platitudes at old people and the rest of the time you can do what you like, and you never get fired.'

Lol thought of Merrily, shook his head slowly. She'd told him what Murray may have done to his last church, in Gloucestershire, to build a case for stress, early retirement.

'He says it's therefore in his interests that elements of his past should never be revealed,' Hayter said, 'and he's sure it's the same for us, too.

Well, it was certainly the same for Sycharth. Me, less so, but the thought of being implicated in a bad death, that whole Michael Barrymore scene, only worse … because the body was *still there* …'

'Nightmare?'

'Yeah. He said it was quite safe, unlikely to be found.'

'He thought *that*? Did you even know where he'd put it?'

'Wouldn't tell us that. If he was the only one that knew, we'd go on needing him. He said one day he was going back there. Like it was his destiny. Great things to be discovered. Maybe he was still talking about the map, maybe something else, I don't know. But he knew Gwilym wanted the place back in his family because of the Glyndwr thing, and when it happened, he said, he'd dispose of the body.'

'There's incentive,' Lol said.

'Meanwhile we needed to stick together. Mat had a proposition that he said would *formally* bind us together, in secrecy.'

'Oh …' Lol almost smiled '… like brothers?'

'For the record, I had no particular wish to become a Freemason. Standing there, stripped to the waist, some old fart prodding you with a sword, you feel like a dick.'

'You have to be invited to join, don't you?'

'Yeah, well, he fixed all that. He was already in. He'd wanted to get in for the Masonic secrets, wherein great *Templar* secrets were preserved. I didn't get it then and I don't get it now, but some guys, this search for secret knowledge, they'll do anything. And Masonry, it frees you up in other areas of your life. Find you don't have to worry about money. Or support.'

'So you did it.'

'Yeah, I did it. And they were pleased to have me, a young businessman with a title in the pipeline. 'Course, it's heavier than you think it's gonna be, and, no, you *don't* go back on the oath, trust me.'

'Not even if you know a brother's done a murder?'

Hayter ignored that.

'The extraordinary thing … Mat said, *Next time we meet, you'll both be on the pathway to a material success you'd never dreamt of.* And that was true.'

'*Are* there Masonic contacts,' Lol asked him, 'in the music business?'

THE FABRIC OF SIN

'Not many, but I *have* been successful, in unexpected ways. Saved the old homestead, the way the old man never managed. And Sycharth, he's gone more Masonic than I ever did, and he's into big contacts and *big* money. You look at the prime new developments around Hereford, you'll keep coming across the name Gwilym in the small print. Struggling farmer to Master of the fucking Universe.'

'*He* wasn't hugely successful, though, was he – Mat?'

'Got what he wanted. Made it back into Garway, to pursue his dream of inheriting the great Templar legacy. De Molay, Glyndwr ... Murray. When a suitable property came available he got the signal from Sycharth and Sycharth greased the wheels. Mat buys The Ridge, having found a woman with the readies. He could always find a woman, whatever kind he needed at any particular time. This case, one with money to spare, poor bitch.'

'So he's camped up here, walking the hills and waiting for Gwilym to buy back the house?'

'Gwilym told me Murray said the time was coming. It would happen around the anniversary of the 1307 inquisition. He'd seen the signs, all this shit. Points out the significance of people by the name of Gray ... you know about that? OK, well, then this guy Gray develops MS.'

'He wasn't claiming ...?'

Hayter shrugged.

'Bad prayers, Robinson. The power of bad prayers.'

'This gets sicker, Jimmy.'

In the bedroom next to the chimney, the light was the purple of bruises, the smell of decay was worse and the two bed-frames looked, Merrily thought, like medieval appliances for obtaining confessions.

The holy water glittered mauve.

Merrily said, 'Heavenly Father who never sleeps. Bless this room and guard with your continued watchfulness all who take rest within ... within these walls.'

Muriel Morningwood picked a cobweb from Merrily's alb. With hindsight, the alb had not been a good idea.

In a corner of the room, the floorboards had been removed, stones and cement hacked out, revealing the priest's hole. From an oblique angle, you could see down into the hearth, where Murray had removed more stones so that the bones could be tipped directly down into the waiting sacks.

Merrily lowered herself into the space. It seized her like a trap. Rubble, dirt, a stench. She didn't want to breathe. Her throat felt raw and constricted, and she remembered the lesions on Muriel's neck.

It wouldn't have taken much.

You wouldnt know me Muriel. Theres nothing of me no more I am so thin and my head feels like a rotten egg sometimes and what can you do with a rotten egg ...

'Oh God, bless this space where Mary lay ...'

Croaking out the words, sprinkling out the water.

Hadn't lain here at all. Had probably been arranged squatting, strangled, stripped of any residual dignity.

'...may her spirit rest in peace and may the light of Christ rest upon her and in this place.'

When she finished, Mrs Morningwood had turned away.

'Never said she was a saint. Probably trying to get money out of them. Needed to make a life for the child, didn't want to be in a tepee for ever.'

'Which I suppose brings us to Fuchsia,' Merrily said. 'Where all this began – for both of us, I suspect.'

Glasses in her hand, Mrs Morningwood stood at the top of the half-spiral, lit by a diagonal shaft from a cracked skylight. Merrily three steps below, on the curve.

'I haven't ... been one hundred per cent truthful about Fuchsia.'

'No kidding.'

'When she first came to see me, with Barlow ...'

'And you recognized her ...'

'... I obviously had to see her again, on her own. Whispered it to her as they were leaving, and she was back the same afternoon. Sat her down on the chaise longue and made some herbal tea, for relaxation of the mind.'

Mrs Morningwood backed away along the landing, agitated.

'I asked her how she'd got her name, Fuchsia, and she said she didn't know. She said people had told her that Fuchsia was a character from Mervyn Peake and she'd read *Titus*, and said how much she liked that kind of book. And then I asked her if she liked M. R. James because he'd been here, and it turned out she'd read a few of his stories. And I told her the story I'd told Jane, that I'd got from my mother.'

'Why?'

'Told her several local stories. She loved them. She was eager for more. Me, I was simply putting off the moment. Wanting her to trust me. Eventually, we went for a walk on the hill, where Mary and I had walked all those years ago. That was when I told her.'

Mrs Morningwood shook her head in some sadness. She was wearing a cream cotton dress and a grey woollen cardigan and looked almost demure.

Merrily said, 'And?'

'And everything changed … I thought she was putting me on … thought it was joke, you know? But I can see her now, backing away into the sun. Arms out, warding me off. Didn't want to know. Didn't want to *know* about her mother. Had her own amorphous fantasy. Princess rather than prostitute.'

There's this kind of tribal mysticism in Tepee City, Felix had said, *and she had a period of building fires in a clearing in the wood and looking for Mary in the smoke.*

'What did you tell her had happened to Mary?'

'Disappeared. Tried to downplay the seedy side, but the damage was done. Didn't want to hear any more *at all.* Next thing, Barlow the builder comes banging on the door asking me what sort of rubbish I've been feeding her because Fuchsia can't work in that house any more.'

'So she passed on to Felix what you'd told her? Because if he knew that when I saw him, he certainly wasn't letting on.'

'No, she came out with the M. R. James story, the dustsheets, the face of linen. She'd read that story.'

And she'd played it well, hadn't she, in the church of St Cosmas and St Damien. '*Who is this who is coming?*' And still Merrily's feeling was that the desire for a blessing had been real. That Fuchsia *had* felt menaced by the house. By her mother's ghost, then … just as Mary had felt an estrangement – not exactly unknown in the annals of mother/daughter psychology – from the infant Fuchsia.

The baby cries whenever shes <u>WITH ME</u>. Thats not how it should be !

And because of Felix's feelings for Mary, she'd wanted him out of there, too. As if she thought Mary would come between them.

'The coincidence of him bringing Fuchsia here, that terrified her,' Muriel Morningwood said. 'Maybe she thought he'd been here, too ... that he *was* her father.'

'And you wondered that, as well.'

'Although, now I think Mary simply used him – soon as she'd learned Felix had some money in the background, pulling that stunt with the cord. Saying he must've been chosen by the baby as its god-father or guardian or what you will. Making provision for the child.'

'Ah.' A light coming on. 'And you thought Fuchsia might've killed him because of what *you'd* told her. So not only had you failed to save the mother, you'd—'

'Driven the daughter over the edge.'

'You could have told me this the other night, Muriel.'

'Told you enough, that night. Was feeling pretty shell-shocked generally.'

Merrily stared at the wall. *Had* there been some kind of psychic expe-rience, perhaps while actually working in a room concealing the skeleton of her mother? If ever there was a situation crying out for the paranormal ...

'Anything else you're not telling me, Muriel?'

'Not intentionally, no. Well ...' Muriel raised her eyes towards the skylight. 'Sycharth. Until you told me, I didn't know for certain he'd been here in the Seventies, but ... I suppose I *wanted* him to have been involved. I said he'd made a play for me. Truth is, I'd made a play for *him* a year or so earlier. No taste at that age and he did have a Triumph Spitfire. Bastard had me, then sneered. Called me a whore.'

'Oh.' That certainly explained the hostility. 'Well ... he's a worried man now, Muriel.'

Merrily went back to the stairwell, brushing red stone-dust from the alb.

'Look ... before we go down to *that* room, I'd like to try and get the sequence right. Did Fuchsia go rushing into the church, finding Teddy there, *before* she first came to see you?'

'My feeling now is she saw him at least twice. If he was as shocked as me the first time—'

'He'd surely be a bloody sight *more* shocked. He might've been looking at his daughter. And more than that—'

'Looking into the face of someone he'd murdered.'

Murray had said, *When the girl turned up here asking for protection ... sanctuary ... I confess I was completely thrown.*

'Yes,' Merrily said. 'He'd have to know, wouldn't he? He'd want to see her again. What about last Saturday? She almost certainly came back here last Saturday, on her own, because I spoke to Felix on the phone and he was very uptight, convinced she'd been back. Taken the van, key to the Master House missing ...'

'Why would she do that, though?'

'Maybe deciding she'd have to deal with it or it was going to torment her for ever. I don't know. We're unlikely ever to know, but is it possible she saw Teddy Murray then? And is it possible she told Teddy Murray what *you*'d told her about mother?'

'And perhaps he followed her home,' Mrs Morningwood said. 'Just as he followed Jane and me yesterday.'

'*What?*'

'Back here, from your vicarage. He obviously recognized the dog. He would've waited on the square in his Land Rover. He had patience, that man.'

'Yes.'

And then, if he'd followed Fuchsia home, returned to Monkland the following evening. The lonely caravan, a blunt instrument – like a crowbar – and an element of surprise. There was no way of knowing which of them he'd killed first or how he'd gone about it. Whether Felix had been a target, or collateral damage. Or, as Fuchsia's body had been loaded into the Land Rover, part of a murder–suicide scenario.

Had he enjoyed it, all of it, the way the Knights Templar had evidently delighted in killing for their cause? The two sides of the Templars, pastoral and monastic and then the gleeful savagery. The ecstasy of blood.

*

A Mercedes 4x4 drew up in front of the Master House.

Nobody got out.

'Sycharth,' Jimmy Hayter said. 'He'll wait till the last minute before he goes in. This is gonna be hard for him. Especially with Gray here.'

Lol said, 'Your meeting with him yesterday ...'

'Robinson, watch my lips.'

Hayter's lips were a flat line.

'Murray wanted you both back for his service, though,' Lol said. 'Didn't he?'

The memorial service which would have been held yesterday and wasn't. Several men in suits, whom word hadn't reached in time, had arrived to find a black-edged card on the door, informing would-be worshippers that, owing to the tragic and sudden death of the Rev. Edward Murray, all services should be considered cancelled until further notice. Some consternation, apparently.

'Maybe the original plan was to do something here,' Lol said. 'Continue some process Murray had started thirty-odd years ago.'

'Yeah. Maybe. He'd been studying all that time, been through degrees of Masonry I didn't know existed.'

'But then, despite Gray's illness, Gwilym didn't manage to get the house back and it was sold, very symbolically, to the Duchy of Cornwall, so you had to arrange it at the church.'

'No, it was always going to be the church.' Hayter said. 'The church is all-Templar. He was going to bring something to the church that would reconnect the wires, as he put it.'

'What?'

'We weren't privileged to know.'

'You're lying again, Jimmy.'

'Robinson, you ...' Hayter dug his fingers into the grooves of the hawthorn. 'Gwilym and me, we met to decide what to do about him. We'd had enough.'

'What, like you broke the Boswell?'

'That's how *I* wanted to play it, yes. Frankly. And knew the right people.'

'Like he claimed to have made Mr Gray ill? Think how *that* backfired, Jimmy.'

'Look … Robinson … we didn't do anything. Gwilym said, let me talk to him. And he did. And the agreement was, after the seven hundredth anniversary, that would be it. Murray's side of it was to remove the body. If it turned up during restoration, we'd be well in the shit. Not Murray, because nobody ever suspects the vicar, do they, unless it's choirboys or kiddie-porn?'

'And what was your side of the deal?'

Hayter's mouth flat-lined.

'You know he took the bones away, don't you?' Lol said.

'What?'

'He took them away in a couple of plastic feed-sacks.'

'How do you know that?'

'Only they've disappeared. They could be anywhere now.'

Hayter sprang off the tree, and you could almost see the sweat rising like sap.

Before they stepped inside the inglenook, Merrily did St Patrick's Breastplate, Mrs Morningwood repeating every line. Whether she believed any of this was anybody's guess, but she went along with it.

In the torchlight: Baphomet.

Mrs Morningwood felt around the coarse, sardonic sandstone contours of his ageless face.

'You know, it's actually quite old. I'd thought it would be some sort of replica, the kind of thing you get from garden centres.'

'Why did you think that?'

'Because, when Jane told me about it, I assumed it had been put here by Stourport's rabble. I thought that was what you were picking up in here – I do accept these things. I may be cynical but that doesn't make me a sceptic.'

'Yeah, well, I'm supposed to be sceptical and analytical about this stuff, but I was affected and I can't explain it. And I still don't know why it made you encourage a learner driver to bring you over here.'

'Oh lord, I didn't know *that*, darling. Apologies. The reason I wanted to see it – and as things turned out it was damned prescient – was that Jane pointed out, quite rightly, that it was inside the inglenook and facing the back wall. Facing the priest's hole, in fact, which I'd heard about – years ago, from Roxanne's mother, as it happens.'

'You wanted to come here and look if the hole had, at some stage, been unblocked.'

'It made sense. I did think Mary was dead, I did think they'd killed her. And having the face of Baphomet gazing at the tomb – that seemed to me the disgusting kind of conceit that they'd have gone in for. I was half right ... and half wrong. This is old. Could be as old as the one in the church. And yet ...'

'It's not quite like the one in the church, as I remember it,' Merrily said.

'It *has* been removed, though, darling, look ... that's modern cement, isn't it? Some of it's already been chipped away. This is part of what Murray came for. You have a chisel?'

'Crowbar be OK?'

'Splendid.'

He'd left it in the hearth. If this wasn't the instrument of Felix's death, it could have been. Fuchsia, too. Whatever, it had been held by the same hands. Merrily held it across both of hers. Didn't move, faced Mrs Morningwood over the iron firebasket.

'*Did* you kill him deliberately, Muriel?'

Muriel turned slowly from the stone, lifted her head, exposing her throat – the bloodied dents of thumbnails around the windpipe.

'Yes,' Merrily said. 'I know.'

'He'd learned from Fuchsia that I knew whose child she was. He knew that after Fuchsia's death I wasn't going to leave it alone. He knew – obviously from Sycharth – about my family history. He knew that I was talking to you because ... you told him?'

'No reason not to. Or so I thought.'

'And he knew that people in my line of work sometimes get raped and murdered. And he enjoyed it. Without remorse. He was never a Christian.'

'Did you intend to kill him, Muriel? I need to know. Had you been waiting? Being patient and watchful, the way he was?'

'You don't want to be an accessory, darling. Or your lovely boyfriend. Or your extraordinary daughter. So don't ask me stupid questions.

Because I've gone through a kind of purgatory, and I'd go through it again. Now give me the bloody crowbar … Thank you.' Mrs Morningwood prised away a lump of cement. 'As I thought …'

'What happened to the bones?' Merrily said.

'Back off, or you'll get dust in your eyes.'

'Is it conceivable you saw where Murray put the bones?'

'How would that be possible?'

'Let me take you through it. There's a narrow public footpath just along from The Turning. Goes between two cottages down to the church, then links to the path leading here. If somebody happened to be parked nearby, watching Teddy Murray dragging two sacks up the field, this person might notice where he'd put them. Temporarily. Before using that footpath to make his way back to the road and The Turning. Giving the watcher time to get back to his or her car, switch on the engine and wait for him to appear on the road with – metaphor-ically-speaking – a big red cross in the centre of his surplice.'

'I suppose a vivid imagination is sometimes quite useful in your job.'

'We looked everywhere, Lol and Jane and me. Most of the morning. He wasn't carrying them when he walked – sorry, *ran* – into the road. We thought he must have hidden them somewhere, but evidently they'd been picked up by then.'

'You're wasting your time and mine.'

'Not that you'd be the first person anyone would suspect. What with all the injuries you received in the accident – the eyes, the lip, the neck, the head? Don't think the terrible poetry of all this has been entirely lost on me.'

'Shine the torch up here, would you?'

'Why did you get me to bless your garden this morning, Muriel?'

'Do you want to know what's here, or not?'

'They could connect Mary's DNA with Fuchsia. Find out the truth.'

'Truth …' Both hands inside the stone, Muriel began to ease some-thing slowly towards what passed for light under here. 'Truth is not what's settled in courts or reported in the papers. Truth simply … exists.'

'Muriel, this makes no sense.'

'Darling, it makes *Garway* sense. Hold out your hands.'

Requiem

THE FIRST OF them to come in was Adam Eastgate. Hooded eyes, military scrutiny. Looking around at the drabness and the pitted plaster, the floor that was half-flags and half-linoleum, shrivelled and long-embedded like mummified skin, and he sighed.

'We don't often make mistakes.'

Maybe it was one of his sayings.

'Well,' Merrily said, 'if you're thinking of selling it on, I'd urge you to vet any potential purchaser extremely carefully. But I expect you do that anyway.'

'I don't recall mentioning selling it,' Eastgate said. 'That would be a bit defeatist.'

'Adam ... sorry, this is Mrs Morningwood.'

'Aye, I know,' he said.

Which was unexpected.

She'd been thinking that, if Muriel hadn't been here, now might have been the best time to ask Adam Eastgate again about those threatening communications the Duchy had received. The ones possibly containing Welsh phrases, perhaps suggesting that the Prince of Wales's purchase of Templar properties on the Welsh Border had been ... noted. Probably with disfavour.

Letters which, if you were looking for an author, might point towards a Welshman fanatically proud of his family's links with the greatest national hero of all time. Or, less obviously, but more likely in Merrily's view, to someone who had no cause to love this Welshman ... and a personal need, which could no longer be suppressed, to let light into dark places.

Some of us do know our Welsh pronunciations but can't resist taking the piss.

'Merrily,' Eastgate said, 'you look, if you don't mind me saying so, like you've been doing a spot of cleaning.'

'Yes, well …' She pushed hair back from her face. 'Women in the clergy … not afraid to get our hands dirty. And, erm, everything else.'

He smiled; he still looked less than comfortable.

'So this'll be for Felix, will it? And the woman?'

'Going to be a bit non-specific, Adam. Straightforward Eucharist, quite short, relating to a number of people who had connections with this place. And, if I could just say this, what happened to Felix … that may not be quite what you think. It's quite important we don't blame Fuchsia. I'm telling everyone this.'

She watched Mrs Morningwood approaching Eastgate, gripping his arm.

'Ah … *I* know who you are, now. Recognise the Geordie accent. You're the chap who left a message on my machine the other day. Been away, you see.'

'Just a query, Mrs Mornington.'

'Wood.'

'Aye. Sorry. I was just given your number. Only, I gather you're quite well known as a herbalist and a healer, kind of thing, and not the only one in this area.'

'Quite a few in the general area, involved in different disciplines. Eight … nine, perhaps.'

Merrily shot her a look.

Eastgate said, 'So if this place – and I'm talking off the record and in a very tentative way – were to become – assuming it could be done without damaging the character – a centre for alternative health … do you think that would have local support?'

Mrs Morningwood wrinkled her nose.

'There's a good possibility.'

Bloody hell. Merrily remembered Jane raising the idea, not entirely seriously.

'This is a bit sudden, Adam.'

'Not really.'

'It would've come down from …?'

454

'The place things come down from,' Eastgate said, as Jane herself came in, holding the door open for Roxanne Gray, pushing Paul in his wheelchair to within a few feet of the relic that Mrs Morningwood had found in the inglenook.

John 20.

A text often used during funeral services, with or without the Requiem Eucharist. She read it to the gathering.

'On the first day of the week, Mary Magdalene came to the tomb early …'

Except for Paul Gray in his wheelchair, the congregration was standing. Adam Eastgate at one end, Sycharth Gwilym at the other, tight-faced, uneasy, no sense of a man who'd come home. In the middle, Roxanne and Mrs Morningwood. Lord Stourport on his own by the door, hands in pockets, breathing down his nose. Next to him, Lol and Jane and, at their feet, lying down, nose between his front paws, the dog that Mrs Morningwood had said would refuse to come in here.

It was the biggest congregation you'd get in Garway this particular weekend.

It added up to nine people.

'Peter then came out with the other disciple and they went toward the tomb. They both ran, but the other disciple outran Peter and reached the tomb first and, stooping to look in, he saw the linen cloths lying there …'

On the portable altar, a simple white cloth, wine and actual bread to celebrate the Eucharist.

A Requiem, then, for some people she could name, one she couldn't. And one she was she was still agonizing about and would do, right up to the moment.

In front of the altar, on a trestle they'd found in the barn, where a coffin might be at a funeral, was the sandstone urn, size of a small chalice, recovered from a recess half the size of a bread-oven behind the face of the Baphomet.

They'd managed to remove the top, she and Mrs Morningwood. Some powder in the bottom … had to be ashes.

Lol had told her what Stourport had said about Teddy Murray's intention to bring something into the church for his gnostic, Masonic service. She'd asked his advice, and Lol had said, do it. If *anybody* needed it …

Merrily let the ritual unwind at its own pace, still unsure.

Listening.

There was no name on the sandstone urn, no words at all. For all she knew, there could be dozens of these all over Europe; there would've been a lot of ashes. No clues when it had been walled up or who had first brought it here. But it made sense.

Merrily took a breath, picked up the urn, kept her voice fairly low. She commended to God the souls of Fuchsia Mary Linden and Felix Barlow and, in her head, in a second of silence, Mary Roberts Linden, sleeping in the herb garden.

She cleared her throat. The marks on her alb were like smuts on a spectator backing away from the flames into the shadow of the Cathedral of Notre Dame.

Or maybe the smears on a doormat.

Do this.

'We also commend to God's keeping the soul of Jacques de Molay.'

She looked up briefly and saw Jane's eyes widening, didn't look at other eyes.

'… knowing he died in pain and persecution. We pray to God to … forgive him and bring him eternal light and peace. May the peace of God which passes all understanding be with him now and in this place.'

At some point, the door blew open, the dog stirred and whimpered and the wind came in from the White Rocks.

CLOSING CREDITS

THE MYSTERIES OF Garway and Garway Hill are many. Not all of them made it into this book, and of the ones that did, not quite all, as you may have noticed, were solved. Which is the way of things. I couldn't find anyone who could even suggest why the dovecote has 666 chambers ... although *there has to be a reason.* And it *is* on private land, by the way, so you need permission to visit it. The church and its enigmas, however, are fully accessible.

M. R. James's line about causing offence at Garway is accurate. Many thanks to Rosemary Pardoe, editor of the indispensable *Ghosts and Scholars* website devoted to Jamesian matters, for being patient with Jane ... and me.

Sue Rice, local historian, and her mum, Doreen Ruck, natural dowser, introduced us to the magic of Garway, and Sue's advice and help throughout has been invaluable. John and Sue Hughes showed us the tower and Church House which, although it served as the Templar commandery and has a priest's hole in the region of the inglenook, is *not* the Master House. Thanks also to Elaine Goddard, Vicar of Garway and neighbouring parishes (see, I *did* leave the church alone) and Audrey Tapper, author of the definitive guide to Garway mysteries, *Knights Templar and Hospitaller in Herefordshire* (Logaston Press). Listening to John Ward, dowser and Egyptologist, in Garway Church was enlightening on possibilities relating to the Mappa Mundi, the Masons and hidden things. I gather he's working on a book – look out for it.

Owain Glyndwr: Everything about him in this book could well be true. Thanks to Alex Gibbon, author of the fascinating *The Mystery of Jack of Kent and the Fate of Owain Glyndwr*, and John Scudamore, of Kentchurch Court.

The Duchy of Cornwall: like Merrily, I've never met the Man, but his land steward, David Curtis, was hugely helpful. Thanks also to Amanda Foster, of the Buckingham Palace press office and Mike Whitefield, Duchy-approved conservation builder, who described some of the problems facing Felix Barlow.

Exorcism: Peter Brooks provided crucial eleventh-hour assistance to

Merrily as well as background information on *other aspects* of the investigation. Liz Jump, now curing souls in M. R. James's birthplace, also described first-hand experience.

Hay-on-Wye bookseller and esotericist Tracy Thursfield came up with some crucial ideas and was always ready to talk them through, between customers, whenever I staggered disconsolately into Addyman Annex, and she and Ian Jardin lent me a couple of significant books.

From the ever-obliging British Society of Dowsers, thanks again to Richard Bartholomew, Ced Jackson, Helen Lamb and John Moss.

Watching the ingenious Gruff Rhys setting up his *Candylion* gig (the most wondrously whimsical album of 2007, by the way) showed me exactly what Lol was up against touring solo. This surely can't go on.

Thanks also to Prof. Bernard Knight (forensic pathology), Jodie Lewis (archaeology), Simon Small (spirituality), Mari Roberts (film awards), Mark Owen and Terry Smith (Templars), journalists Nicola Goodwin and Dave Howard (background and crucial contacts) and Mark Worthing (teeth).

Oh … and not forgetting the Rennoldsons of Geordieland.

Bibliography also includes: *The Knights Templar* by Helen Nicholson (Sutton), *The Knights Templar Revealed* by Butler and Dafoe, *The Dragon and the Green Man* by Paul Broadhurst (Mythos), *M. R. James, an informal portrait* by Michael Cox (Oxford), *Herefordshire, the Welsh Connection*, by Colin Lewis (Carreg Gwalch), *National Redeemer: Owain Glyndwr in Welsh Tradition* by Elissa R Henken (Cornell), *The Holy Blood and the Holy Grail* by Baigent, Leigh and Lincoln (Cape), *Beyond the Brotherhood* by Martin Short (Grafton), *Historic Harewood* by Heather Hurley (Ross-on-Wye civic society) and *Darker than the Deepest Sea – the Search for Nick Drake* by Trevor Dann (Portrait).

Thanks, as ever, to Carol 'I don't buy this bit' Rickman for intensive editing, inspiration in the darkest hours and making me get it right even at the expense of several eighteen-hour days, my agent Andrew Hewson, the almost paranormally laid-back Nic Cheetham for extending the deadline well beyond injury time, virtually feeding it page by page to ace copy-editor Nick Austin. And Krys and Geoff Boswell and Jack for maintaining the website www.philrickman.co.uk against all odds.